All the

HAPPILY EVER AFTERS

WILLOW WINTERS

DON'T LET GO

THE COLLECTION

Seductive. Addictive. Captivating.

The irresistible heroes in these stories have those three features in common.

Some stories are second chance; others are fated love. But every single one of them, you'll crave to the last page.

This is a collection of tales published by Willow Winters but no longer available. These stories touched my heart, but were exclusive at the time so if you didn't snag them then, they were lost to you forever.

I wanted to make sure you could read all of my work and now you can.

Happy reading, xx

The stories available in this collection are:

Infatuation, the first novella in the *USA Today* best-selling bundle, Drawn to Him.

Desires in the Night and **Keeping Secrets**, both shorts published in exclusive bundles with best-selling author Adriana Locke.

Bad Boy Next Door, a novella I wrote years ago that I still often think about. The damaged hero and second chance love in this romance is one I wish I could go back to often. It's the final tale included in this collection for a total of 4 stories not available anywhere else!

INFATUATION

PROLOGUE

Lila

THE AIR IS FRIGID AND THE LAND BARREN AS I STARE STRAIGHT ahead at the quaint Alaskan island. More than that though, it's hauntingly beautiful. I wrap my hands around the cold metal railing of the boat as it bobs in the water, bringing us closer to the shore.

It's not as cold as I imagined it would be, although the breeze and the cool spray of ocean water send a trail of goosebumps down my arms.

It's hard not to go to the very edge and lean forward, since I want to see everything, but the waves are harsh and unforgiving. And I don't trust my own grip. Chills run along my spine as I step away and sit back on the bench, farther away from the edge of the boat.

I've never been to a place so gorgeous before, and I'd never planned to come here either. I'm only here to interview a man I've never met.

I watch the fog billowing up the trees. The colors are shades of soft blues and grays. The thin clouds let only the faintest bit of light through as the night drifts in. Picture perfect fails to describe the sight right before my eyes.

I have to remind myself that I'll only be here for one week. I need to get this job done and leave this place, but my God, Ketchikan is beautiful.

It's an old town, founded on the beliefs of ancient clans.

Everyone knows everyone on this island.

I spent the entire flight to Seattle looking up details of this place once the internet proved useless in discovering anything at all about Alec Kulls, the man my employer was so eager to interview.

All I know is that his family has a rich history, and wealth that keeps the island independent. There's not much known about the town otherwise, simply because they don't rely on anything but the land itself.

As the fog dips lower, revealing more of the pine trees that seem to sit on the far edge of the ocean, I think I see a man. I blink as my lungs still, depriving me of breath. And just like that, he's gone.

There's no way anyone could be out on the edge of the forest, so close to the ocean. I couldn't have seen what I think I saw.

My eyes search the thick trees over and over, but there's nothing to be found but the dense forest.

It was far off in the distance, but I know I saw him. Out of instinct, I grab the arm of a stranger to urge whoever it is to look with me.

An old man in a thick winter coat gives me a scowl that makes his wrinkles seem even more pronounced.

The wind whips across us and I let go of him, feeling embarrassed and alone. I swallow thickly, turning away and muttering a small apology. That's how I've felt since I landed in Seattle and drove straight to the dock. Alone.

I lick my lips, wrapping my arms around my chest and shaking off this odd feeling spreading through every inch of my body. It's slow, like the very waves that rock the ship.

My eyes flicker to the trees on the mountain. He's vanished.

I can still see him in my memory; I swear he was looking at me, too. Even from so far away, looking so small in the dense brush. I can practically feel his gaze on me even now.

My heart flips in my chest in an odd way. It feels like I should run. It thumps hard at the thought, as if confirming my instincts. But just then the small crew moves about me, preparing to dock.

There's only one way to the island, and it's by boat. *This boat.*

Once I step off this ship, there's no going back.

A tingle travels along my skin and pricks the back of my neck. I stare into the trees as the boat rocks and pushes my body forward and the men hustle to tie the thick ropes to the ship. I can't explain why I know without a doubt that the man really was there, and that he was waiting for me.

CHAPTER 1

EVERY WORRY IS LEFT BEHIND AS I STEP INTO THE PLEASANT warmth of the bed and breakfast's entrance. All this tension and anxiety must be from lack of sleep. I brush the water from my jacket and wipe off my rubber rain boots on the worn welcome mat. The cabin looks like a quintessential grandmother's home. It's just like the pictures I saw online.

The smell of apples and cinnamon hits me the moment I stop in the foyer. I inhale the comforting scents deeply and listen to the crackling of the fire on the far right. The dim lights and warm glow make every touch in the place feel homey.

I roll my suitcase to the sofa and stop, spotting a crockpot on the entry table and white ceramic mugs next to it.

Hot cider. I know it in an instant. I'm quick to shrug off my jacket, looking behind me as I hang it over my suitcase, searching for the owner. I almost put the jacket on the old sofa; it's a dated floral print, but the throw neatly folded over the back of it looks plush and inviting. My jacket is coated with a thin layer of mist from the light rain outside, so I wouldn't dare put it there.

I look around the corner and see a small dining room with a wooden table and chairs. In the center of the table is a stack of pale blue cloth napkins and a set of white salt and pepper shakers that look like owls. But not a soul is there either.

It's quiet, but welcoming.

The cabin itself is small, and someone must've heard me come in.

I shake off the cold from the outdoors, feeling the soothing heat from the fire and go to the crockpot before searching out anyone. I need something to warm me up. Just a moment to myself while my nerves settle. I've been on edge every minute of this trip. I know part of it is my fear of flying. It's a stupid fear. I've heard every statistic, and I've been told over and over that flying is safe. But I'll be damned if I could breathe for even a second of that six-hour flight.

The heavy smell of cinnamon greets me as I lay the glass lid down on the table and pick up the ladle, pouring a serving and then another into one of the mugs.

I'd give anything to shake this overwhelming apprehension that seems to be clinging to me.

I close my eyes, letting the heat of the cider travel through my chest and the taste of apples and cinnamon tickle my tongue. I smile into the mug, taking another sip before slowly sinking into the sofa and letting the flames of the fire warm me.

I roll my head to the side wanting to ease the tension, but it only makes me that much more tired. Already I'm exhausted from this trip, and it's only just begun.

I wish I could have stayed longer in Seattle. It's absolutely gorgeous, although opposite in beauty to this island. Where Seattle has intricately designed buildings that tower over you and the old streets lined with planted trees and cobblestones, here the nature is untouched. It's not arranged to complement the city structures; the mountains and forests are the sights here. The few houses I saw earlier were tucked back into the thicket and seem to blend in.

That could be due to the hour though. We arrived in the evening as the fog was settling in. Funny how the fog in Seattle seems to dim the city's beauty, but here it only adds to the island's atmosphere.

I take another sip of the cider, watching the flames lick along the logs. My nails click as they tap rhythmically against the mug. Of the two places I've been today, I prefer the island. It has a sense of ancient tradition, the land feeling mostly unsullied.

I grew up in Philadelphia, and seeing the beautiful city of Seattle blew me away. But this remote island is like no other place I've ever been. It calls to me in a way I can't explain.

"Miss Travers?" a small voice calls out from behind me, pulling me from my thoughts. I stand so quickly I nearly spill the cider, feeling embarrassed once again that I've made myself at home and didn't bother seeking anyone out.

"Yes, here," I answer, setting the mug down on the coffee table and turning to face an elderly woman. She pushes a pair of thin-framed glasses up the bridge of her nose as she walks around the back of the sofa to greet me. "Mrs. Joslin?"

"Call me Ada, please," she answers me.

At first I smile and tug my sweater down, ready to get to my room and pass out from the long day, but something in her expression catches me off guard.

There's a smile on her face, but it doesn't reach her eyes and the way she wrings her fingers nervously makes me question the pleasant tone of her voice. "Are you checking in?" she asks.

I find it odd. Obviously I am. What else would I be doing here? I hesitate, trying to remember if today is the first day I booked. I turn halfway, still facing her and trying not to be rude as I lean down to dig inside of my purse for the papers. I fucking hope I didn't screw this up. I don't need to start this trip off by being kicked out of the one bed and breakfast for miles and miles.

"I believe it's today," I say although it comes out sounding like a question.

"Yes, of course," Ada says with confidence and an upbeat lilt that wasn't there before. I peek up at her, the papers in my hands crinkling as I unfold them. They confirm I've booked the entire week; today's date is the first day of my stay.

She tucks her hands into the pockets on the sides of her pale pink flannel pajama shirt and nods. "Do you need help with your bags?" she asks me warmly, but there's a chill to her expression.

"Is everything alright?" I ask her as I shove the papers back into the pocket on the inside of my purse.

"Yes, yes. I just wasn't sure if you'd had a chance to see Mr. Kulls yet?"

"The interview is tomorrow," I reply and she nods slowly. I called before booking and spoke to someone here, possibly Ada, although I don't remember. I wanted to make sure the bed and breakfast was close to the estate. It turns out that it's the only bed and breakfast, so I didn't have much of a choice.

"Am I all set to stay?" I ask her warily.

"Of course, dear, of course," she answers with much more pep in her tone. "Right this way!" she says as she grabs the handle of my suitcase before I can and starts walking off. I look behind me at the mug of cider and then grab my jacket before it falls off my luggage.

For a woman so short she walks quickly, and I have to hastily increase my stride to catch up to her.

"Breakfast will be ready when you are," she says as we pass the small dining room and head down a narrow hallway. The walls are speckled with photographs tucked in a variety of colored and shaped frames. She turns her head to look at me, and my eyes are ripped away from the photo of a young boy and to her gaze instead. "Simply call the number on the phone in your room or come to the front, and I'll have breakfast served for you."

She stops at the last door on the very end and takes out a key, unlocking the door and then handing the key to me. It's an actual key, long and heavy. I think it's made of cast iron, and it catches me by surprise. "If you need anything at all, please don't hesitate to ask," she says and her voice is soft and comforting and the small smile on her face is genuine. Her pale blue eyes are sincere, and I almost second-guess her hesitation in the foyer.

"Thank you, Mrs.—Ada," I say and then peer into the room, taking the handle of my suitcase.

"I'll be right down the hall," she says and then turns to walk off. I watch her for a moment and then let out a heavy sigh. Traveling is meant to be stressful. And that's what I'll chalk this up to.

The sound of the wheels rolling is muted as I drag the suitcase onto the plush cream carpet and close the door with a soft click. I lock it out of habit and then drag the heavy bag to the bed. My purse falls off my shoulder and onto the crook of my arm as I struggle with the damn thing. I stare at the bed and then to the suitcase. There's no way I'm getting it up there.

I don't have the energy for anything other than to slip into my PJ bottoms and a baggy t-shirt. My makeup can just wait till the morning, and brushing my teeth can wait, too.

As I crawl into bed I nearly moan at the thought of sleeping peacefully.

I'm finally on land and in a beautiful cabin tucked away on this gorgeous island. I close my eyes and the moment I do, I remember the man from earlier.

My heart stills and my eyes pop open as I pull the comforter up tighter around me and try to forget. I need to sleep, and that's just what I do. But the vision of the man comes back over and over as I drift to sleep. I can't keep him away although I can't quite see his face or any identifying features at all. Each time there's something different about him or the mountain that makes me question whether or not he was real.

But I dream of him. Of climbing through the forest and standing at the edge.

In my dreams, he was waiting for me. And instead of fear, I only feel… wanted.

CHAPTER 2

Lila

THE MORNING AIR IN PHILADELPHIA CAN BE AT TIMES, STALE. Suffocating, even. The sounds of other people are constant, along with car horns and yelling for cabbies. My street, in particular, is busy as it's just beyond the more crowded shopping districts.

This is nothing like that.

I inhale deeply, taking a moment to sway back and forth on the porch swing. Time seems slower here. The toe of my boot drags back and forth as I stare forward, waiting for the car that's coming to pick me up. It's not a cab; they don't have those here. Ada's cousin is happy to see me to the Kulls' estate though. Last night the captain of the ship, Drew, drove me here last night.

I chew the inside of my cheek, wondering if I should tip him. Obviously I should. I didn't tip Drew though, he seemed offended I offered. I shake off the memory of the way he looked at me and take a look around.

I'm definitely not in Philadelphia anymore.

The sound of a critter rustling in the dry leaves behind me makes me pop up and off the swing in an instant. I turn around just in time to watch something run off, my hand on my chest and the chill of the morning breeze traveling through the gap in my jacket. A deer, maybe? I'm not sure. But I let out a small huff of a laugh at how absurd I am. Of course there are animals here. Online it said the population of black bears here is higher than the number of humans.

Just as I turn back to face the gravel dirt road that leads to the cabin,

Ada steps out onto the porch. At the same time, an old Chevy pickup truck pulls into the driveway. I watch Ada's face as she cocks a brow in surprise and purses her lips.

The truck comes to a stop, and the sputtering sounds of the engine are silenced. Her cousin, I think she said his name was Brant, opens the faded red door as she walks out to meet him.

I clear my throat, feeling the tension between them as she asks him, "You couldn't bring the car?" in a voice that makes damn sure to display her irritation.

I bend down to pick up my purse; it's heavy as hell, and the thin straps dig into my shoulder. It feels like I've stuffed it with bricks, but it's only my laptop that has it feeling so damn heavy.

I walk slowly down the steps, moving closer to the truck with a smile plastered on my face. I couldn't care less what car we drive in so long as I get to my appointment on time.

The two of them turn to me, stopping mid-conversation which only makes me self-conscious. *Maybe I should have stayed on the porch.*

"It's so pretty out today." I barely get the words out, the strength in my voice diminished by them staring at me. I clear my throat as I feel my smile falter.

Brant looks up and nods his head, patting his keys on his jeans. The plaid coat he's wearing appears rumpled as he shoots me a smile. "Not so bad today. It's gray a lot here, so you got lucky I suppose," he answers in a deep voice.

"You've got everything you want to take?" Ada asks me, but the same look in her eyes from last night is back. All morning things were smooth and easygoing. I thought last night must've been my mistake. That maybe it hadn't been as awkward as I thought it was. But right now, clear as day with a full cup of coffee in me, I can feel something's off.

"I've got everything," I say and nod once, feeling my body tense and my expression change. She must see it too, because the other version of her comes back.

"Have a good trip," she says cheerily and starts to walk back to the porch. "Oh, and interview," she adds with a nod, although her voice is lower and more subdued.

I watch her over my shoulder, shuffling the straps of my bag slightly until Brant slaps his hand down on his truck and asks, "You ready?"

It's awkward. We're sitting in silence. Well, the radio is playing softly, but ever since I got in the cramped back seat of the truck, no small talk has been made. The front seat has no seatbelt, so I'm tucked away in the back, safe and sound. I suppose I could comment on the weather… again.

My purse is next to me, leaning against a toolbox that's definitely seen better days. My boots kick a pair of cleats sitting in the back of the truck as we drive over a hole in the road.

"How long do you think it'll be?" I raise my voice to ask Brant, and his eyes find mine in the rearview.

"Another half hour or so," he answers me. He turns down the radio and glances at me in the rearview again. "What's the interview about?"

"The island mostly," I reply. Sharon Hartfield, my boss and the editor of The Morning Reads, was adamant I interview Mr. Kulls. But the typical synopsis and agenda were missing. Sharon didn't give me anything to go on other than, "Whatever you can get from him." It makes me nervous. She's been giving me more and more responsibility, but this interview is different from the usual protocol.

"The island," Brant repeats easily, nodding his head and looking over to the left as we come to a red light.

"The views here are amazing," I speak without thinking as my breath is taken away. The small town is old and not quite updated yet, but it doesn't feel as though it's needed. There's an undeniable charm to the aged buildings and traditional touches. What's striking is how it's intermingled with nature, which is also untouched.

I watch a small stream of water flow down the foreboding mountain on my left. Utterly gorgeous. "What about the island?" Brant breaks me from my thoughts as the truck moves forward, bringing us back to the interview. To work.

I clear my throat and pull at my seatbelt. "Well, the island is mostly self-sustaining and I've heard it's due to traditions and in a good part because of the Kulls?" I say although it's really a question. More of a hunch I've gathered.

Brant nods his head slowly, but doesn't speak. Just as my hope of gaining a little intel dies, he says, "The brothers brought back more jobs, a better economy I suppose."

"What do you mean?" I ask.

His hands twist on the wheel as if debating on telling me something. I almost have to press, but after a moment he sighs and says, "His father was different is all."

"Have the Kulls always…" I don't know how to end my question, but I don't have to.

"Everyone here descends from ancient clans. Mostly two. And we followed those traditions, but Alec's father did not. It was more about money than anything else." He huffs in obvious disapproval, but continues. "They already had it all. They're the wealthiest and determine most of what goes on around here."

I reach into my purse as I ask, "What traditions did their father stray from exactly?"

Brant's eyes find mine in the mirror as he answers, "All of them."

My pen clicks in the quiet air as I get out my small notebook. It's leather-bound and filled with scribbled notes. I turn to a clean page and ask, "So the new generation of Kulls, they're bringing back the old traditions?"

When he doesn't answer me, I look up to see Brant smirking as he says, "Not quite."

He doesn't continue, and the look on his face is as though he knows something I don't.

"Could you elaborate?" I ask him.

I watch as his jaw clenches and the truck makes a wide turn onto a cobblestone road. It looks new and clean; unlike the others I've seen so far.

"Some traditions died a long time ago, and their father wanted them all to go. He wanted industry here, and that caused a lot of tension."

"Political tension?' I ask.

Brant clucks his tongue and says, "You could say that."

"I don't see much industry here," I point out. It's true. Everything looks like small mom and pop stores.

"There's some, but not much. In the last couple of decades, the town's focus has been on sustainability and self-reliance."

"Since the sons took over?" I ask him to clarify.

Again he shrugs and says, "It was happening regardless of the Kulls. They have the wealth, but their father's disregard of our ways shook their foothold in the law." I jot down all of these gems of history. Brant continues telling me about their water supplies and electrical systems, although most of that info I saw online. The history of the Kulls that's not exposed yet is more of what I want.

"What happened to his father?" I ask.

He shrugs and the truck turns down a path that's shaded by trees, obviously a driveway. "He grew old," he finally answers, but the sight of the estate takes my immediate attention.

It's grand and intimidating. Old money would best describe it. The once copper roof now has a rich patina in a beautiful shade of pale green. It's the perfect accent for the cream stone and manicured dark green ivy along the side of the house, as if they knew all those years ago when it was built that it would look stunning at this very moment. Besides the ivy, there's no shrubbery in sight, only the pine trees on either side.

"Oh," I manage to get out only that single word as the truck stops in front of the estate. The loud rumbling of the engine seems so out of place here. I glance down at myself, smoothing out my cream silk blouse and taking a steadying breath as I reach for my purse. The second my back is turned, my door opens.

A gasp slips from my lips as my grip tightens on my purse straps. The man staring back at me is as breathtaking as the scenery. His eyes are a pale blue and at complete odds with his dark brown hair. It's so dark, it's nearly black.

"Miss Travers," the man says with a deep voice that echoes through my body and heats my blood. For a moment, I'm stunned from the intensity of his gaze but also from the way he said my name. Like he already knew me. *Like he owns me.*

It's only when he takes a step back that I regain my composure and slowly slip out of the truck. It's high up off the ground and when I look down, the man offers me his hand.

I slip my small palm against his and his fingers wrap around my hand as I take the large step down. The heat between us travels through me instantly. Embarrassingly so.

I quickly retrieve my hand and hold the straps of my purse with both hands, taking a step back, my ass bumping against the truck.

In the confines of the truck, I thought maybe this man was staff or a butler, I'm not sure who, but I didn't expect Alec to be the one opening the truck door for me.

Standing on the edge of the long driveway, staring straight at him, I'm sure it's him. His high cheekbones and the rough stubble along his jaw are just as they were in the photographs online. Alec Kulls. The pictures didn't do him justice in the least.

"Mr. Kulls," I finally get a grip and offer my hand out for a handshake. He takes a moment to look at it, leaving my hand dangling in the cold air before accepting it. And again, the instant he touches me, electricity rips through my body, making my thighs clench and my nipples pebble.

"Nice to meet you," he says, and his low voice makes my heart stutter.

I don't know what's come over me. I rip my hand away again, trying to ignore the tingling prickle at the back of my neck. It's not until Mr. Kulls shakes Brant's hand and the two share a glance that I snap out of it.

"Her bags?" he asks Brant, and the trace of a smile on Alec's lips falls when Brant shakes his head.

Mr. Kulls' eyes narrow and Brant merely shrugs his shoulders, but there's a smirk on Brant's lips that makes me think there's something else between them.

"Thank you so much for having me and agreeing to this interview," I say to Alec with more strength than I realized I had left. As my senses slip back into place, I turn to Brant. "Oh, and thank you so much for the ride," I start to say while I dig for my wallet.

"Don't you dare," Alec says and the tone of his voice makes my blood chill. I hear the slap of two hands meeting and look up to see Brant palming folded up cash.

"My pleasure, Miss Travers." The way Brant says my name seems to be in a mocking tone. But not to me, its focus is on Alec.

"Thank you," I mutter in a small voice, feeling as if there's a joke I'm not aware of, yet somehow a part of.

I watch Brant walk around to the other side of the truck before taking a glance at Alec. "Thank you, I could have paid-"

"Not a problem at all," he cuts me off and when his eyes reach mine again, the corners of his lips seem to tug up slightly.

"Why don't you come in?" The way the words fall from Alec's lips is tempting and seductive in a way I hadn't expected. It's not that he's flirtatious in the least… it's something else.

I take a few steps, following him, my eyes taking in the details of his tailored and clearly expensive suit until he peeks over his shoulder. I feel the heat of a blush rise up my cheeks as he smirks at me, clearly catching me in the act. I part my lips to utter an apology or explanation, but all sense of professionalism seems to have left me. Luckily I'm saved by Mr. Kulls as he opens his door and says, "Let's get this interview started."

CHAPTER 3

"I TRUST YOU HAD A SOUND FLIGHT AND TRAVELS?" MR. KULLS asks me as he closes the tall front door. Like the rest of the house, it has history; the dark rich walnut was obviously carved by hand.

"I did," I answer politely. "Thank you for asking." I try to remain professional as I take in the the estate. The high ceilings and intricate architecture are magnificent. "And again, thank you for the interview, Mr. Kulls."

"Alec, please," he says, reaching his hand out, and it takes me a moment to realize he's asking for my coat. I'm quick to respond, moving my purse to the floor so I can shrug off the jacket. The cool draft stays with me for a moment, but the home itself is warm and instantly replaces the cold.

"Thank you… Alec," I add his first name, feeling the shy blush creep back onto my cheeks. This is quickly becoming unlike any interview I've done before. And I'm well aware it's because I'm attracted to Alec. I have to remind myself that I'm working. That this is a job and I'm a professional, for fuck's sake.

He gives me a small smile that slowly widens as he hangs my coat on an iron rack to the left of the grand foyer. As if he can't contain his mirth, maybe because he senses the attraction, or maybe because I'm obviously flustered. I'm not sure which.

"This way," he says and starts walking, the sound of his oxford shoes smacking against the granite echoing off the walls.

The inside of the estate is just as stunning as the outside with rich red walls and marble stone floors.

I hurry my steps to catch up to him. "This is your family's estate?" I ask to get my mind back on track. The little pieces of Kulls history Brant gave me were interesting. I could whip up something interesting about companies that have been passed down through generations and stay within families, easily tying this story to a relevant family company back in Philadelphia.

I nod my head and sneak a look to my left at him. That could be a good spin. Related, yet interesting to compare. Although I'm much shorter than Alec, my strides are in time with his as I follow him down a long corridor past several closed doors and into an office.

Or maybe a library. My Lord. Alec stops behind a large oak desk covered with stacks of papers, devoid of a computer or any technology at all. Behind him are a set of three large windows, the towering mountains and pine trees making it seem as though they're paintings and not a vista of the outdoors. The telling sign that it's the actual view is the snow that's started falling and sweeping across the sky in the breeze.

My purse slowly slips from my shoulder and lands with a thud on the intricate, darkly colored, handwoven rug. The walls to my left and right are lined with bookshelves and what must be thousands of books.

My lips part, my mouth hanging open, but I don't even know where to begin.

"You're out of your element, Miss Travers?" Alec's voice caresses my consciousness, and I dare to look him in the eyes.

"I am," I tell him honestly. I've worked for Sharon for three years now, assigned an interview every other week or so. I've been blown away a few times, but nothing like this.

His lips twitch again, although he keeps the smile at bay. "Please, have a seat. Unless you'd like to explore first?" He cocks a brow, waiting for my response and gesturing to the shelves of books.

I shake my head with a tight smile and pull my blouse down so that it covers the tight black leggings to nearly my knees.

"Tea first?" Alec offers as I settle into the leather seat, my hands gripping the carved armrests. "No, thank you," I reply as he pours a cup on the other side of the desk. I watch as the steam rises, and the soft sound of the tea spilling into the cup is soothing. The clink of the porcelain cup hitting the saucer almost makes me wish I'd said yes.

My brown boots come up mid-thigh and brush against one another as

I cross my legs. "May I have a look around once the interview is over? I'm curious to see the estate."

Alec nods once and walks around the desk to take the seat next to me, surprising me. I clear my throat and angle the chair to face him just as he does.

"Of course," he says, leaning back with his right ankle on his left knee and his hands clasped in his lap. "Whenever you'd like."

"Thank you," I tell him as I bend down and pick up my notebook and pen. "I really appreciate it."

"No recorder?" he asks and I shake my head. I flip through the pages and find where I left off with Brant, making a clean line and writing Alec's initials where the break starts. "I prefer this way," I explain.

"Alright then… Lila." He says my name as if it's a way to tease me. I raise my eyes to him, the pen still on the notepad. "What would you like to know?"

With his father in mind, I ask a question I hope will put him at ease and allow me to uncover new details about the Kulls. "Your business is family-run from what I've read?"

He nods his head once, running his thumb along the tips of his fingers. "Myself and my two brothers, Marcus and Elliot."

I scribble their names down and ask, "And before you three, did your father run it with his siblings or was he an only child?"

"My father did everything on his own. He was an only child and alone most of his life."

I lift my head to look into his eyes as I say, "Alone?" Alec only nods in response.

My back settles against the leather as I give him a small smile and ask, "Could I take you up on that offer for tea, Mr. Kulls?" My voice is soft and sweet.

He smirks at me, rising from his seat, but not answering me. As he pours the tea I watch the snow falling behind him, covering the already white ground.

"You don't have to coax me, Lila," Alec says, placing the cup on the saucer and bringing it to me. "I'm happy to address whatever it is that's on your mind."

Goosebumps flow down my arms. *Caught in the act.* "Was I that obvious?" I ask him, not willing to hide the fact that yes, I was playing into his ego to get him in a favorable mood.

"What do you really want to know?" he asks, passing me the tea.

I swallow thickly, taking the hot cup and watching as he retakes his seat. The steam drifts up and begs me to take a sip. I lift the cup to my lips, but I don't drink just yet. "Brant, the driver," I start to explain, not sure if he knows who I'm talking about.

"I know who Brant is. Just spit it out," he says with his fingers steepled and the tips tapping against one another.

Although I appreciate his no-nonsense attitude, I'm intimidated, but I won't shy away. "Brant mentioned that your father broke tradition?" I say as I glance back down to my notes. Alec gives me a look of confusion at first and then lets out a heavy sigh as his eyes flash with a knowing look.

"That's not very fair of Brant. It wasn't just my father." Alec looks over his shoulder and out of the window and then back at me. "You want to hear the history of the town?" He gestures behind him to the shelves and shelves of books as I nod. "I've got plenty of books that will tell you the ins and outs of the economy and where our money comes from. The names of those who took office and how the laws changed over time. There are even books on heritage and marriages."

I purse my lips, nearly ready to tell him that I want to hear about only *his* father and their family's history, but he continues.

"You'll find the Kulls have been influential since as far back as we can date. The history of the island starts with my family, and we've maintained our position throughout generations."

"What position is that? You don't hold offices."

"There's a small sheriff here and elected officials, but they hold positions to fill in seats and make sure things run smoothly. The Kulls maintain wealth, not only monetary, but also land and the decisions to invest in certain industries have been critical to our island's economy."

"So, you provide the jobs?"

Alec shakes his head. "Not exactly. More like we make sure there are jobs available, because we make sure the resources are already here before they're needed. As a result, the money on the island doesn't have to go overseas. The estate holds a huge stake in the natural resources here. If anything runs low, we acquire and disperse it as needed."

I can feel my eyes narrowing, but before I can ask anything further, he adds, "In the last two decades, we've ensured that the island can sustain the three-hundred-person population on its own. With modern technology, access to anything a person can desire is available through the shipping ports. This town likes to keep its traditions, to stay independent and maintain a relatively hidden and quiet lifestyle. We make certain it's possible."

I take a moment to write the information down, but it's not what I wanted to discuss. This is simply business jargon. It'd make for an interesting piece maybe, but one question pops out at me. "What's in it for you?"

"This is simply what the Kulls do, and of course the income and notoriety are a bonus," he says as he taps his pointer finger to his lip. "That's not quite what you were after, is it?" he asks me after a moment.

"It's not," I tell him honestly.

"What then?" he asks, leaning forward with his elbows on his knees.

"What *traditions* were left behind?" I ask Alec, and he shakes his head as he sits back in his chair.

His eyes search my face for something, but I'm not sure what though. Finally, he answers, "The island descends from ancient clans who took pride in nature and made every decision based on customs and folklore." He licks his lips, and my eyes are drawn to them. "Even marriages were determined by old traditions, up until my grandfather's generation." I nod, and he continues.

"Although the island fell out of the old ways with the industrial revolution, some beliefs still carry on to this day."

"Which ones?"

A huff of a laugh leaves him as he says, "Ones my father refused to teach us, I'm afraid."

"Why's that?"

He noticeably swallows and for the first time he seems uncomfortable, but before I can take it back, he speaks. He looks past me at the books behind me as he talks. "He married my mother according to what he was supposed to do, and she passed away giving birth to my youngest brother, Elliot. They were only together for twelve short years."

"I'm so sorry," I say and he waves off my apology, continuing.

"He wasn't supposed to remarry. The elders wouldn't bless a second marriage. They're all gone now with no one left to replace them, because my father made sure of that. Back then, everyone took their word as law. They said my mother was the only one meant for him, and that if he remarried it would be an atrocity and place shame on our family."

Alec gives me a sad smile as he continues. "He demanded the ritual regardless. It involves a tincture for those who haven't found their partner. The tales say that once you've had a taste of it, within a day's end you'll have found the one you're meant to be with."

"A tincture?" I ask, cocking a brow and shifting my legs to get more comfortable. The tea cup rattles in my lap as Alec nods his head and continues. It's almost a fairytale-like story. Or maybe something darker, but this is what I want to hear. Even if the article ends up being paragraphs about business, shipping docks and sustainability, I'd rather spend hours listening to tales like this.

"My father said the elders lied, and that he'd found his new wife the very next day after drinking the concoction. When she died only a few months into their marriage, it hit my father hard."

"How old were you?" I ask him cautiously.

"I was only seven. Elliot was six, and my brother Marcus was twelve."

"And then the three of you took over the company years later. Because he'd passed away?"

Alec nods. "For ten years, things took a turn for the worse, for both our family and the island, but we recovered. A decade and a half later, and all has been salvaged."

"Do you believe your father?" I ask him.

He grins at me, a devilish look that makes me question my naivety. "My brothers and I didn't get this company back on top with tradition and folklore."

My eyes fall and I feel foolish until he adds, "Three months ago, I went with my brother Marcus, and we bought the mix from the old women on the far side of the mountain. They live by the land there and still carry on the old traditions."

"Why did you go there?"

Alec taps his fingers against his knee as he answers, "Marcus is older than me, and all three of us have lived relatively solitary lives." His gaze wavers for a moment, a sadness coating his voice as he adds, "Marcus wanted a wife. He wanted someone to love. So we went there for the tincture, the very same one my father claimed worked for him."

"You drank the tincture?" I ask to clarify.

"I did." He nods as he answers me.

"And?" I can't help but ask, "Did you meet your soul mate?" I try to add a note of humor to my voice, realizing how foolish the notion is, but the romantic heart in me is beating slowly, waiting for an answer with bated breath.

"My brother went out searching for his. He's desperate for someone in his life. I only drank it to prove a point to him." The coldness in his voice catches me off guard, and something in his tone makes my heart clench with nearly unbearable pain. "I stayed in this room for the next day and a half." He holds my gaze as he adds, "I didn't see a soul."

My blood turns to ice and I look down at my notepad trying to take a few steps back, but I feel lost and emotional. His story made me feel hopeful, alive. Like how I used to get when I was a child reading Disney books.

"All I did was read," he says in a tone that sounds sympathetic and comforting; like he senses this upsets me and wishes it didn't.

I clear my throat and stare past him as he says, "The time has gotten away from me." He stands, and I finally notice the snow hasn't stopped falling. There's not a spot remaining which isn't blanketed beneath a thick layer of snow.

"You can stay here tonight," Alec says with no room for negotiation in his tone. "The mountain isn't safe for traveling."

CHAPTER 1

Lila

"I REALLY DON'T WANT TO PUT YOU OUT." I STARE OUT OF THE window in the kitchen. The ground is still carpeted with several feet of snow, but it's practically raining now. "I think-"

"Brant's not going to be able to make it up the mountain safely with the hail," Alec says confidently, cutting off any excuse that I have. I open my mouth to protest, but he turns to me with his brows raised.

"Don't worry, Lila," he says with a small smile. "It happens from time to time here." His eyes flicker to me and then back to the chicken on the cutting board.

I don't know how an interview turned into having a sexy stranger cooking for me. It feels like a date in every possible way.

"It doesn't where I'm from," I say uneasily, looking outside. The bay window has a small seat attached. It's so out of place in the updated and masculine kitchen.

The seat itself looks it should be littered with pillows and have a small shelf of books next to it. It's a tempting reading nook, just outside of the kitchen and a few feet from the dining room table. I could see myself sitting there and writing.

"Would you like a seat?" Alec asks as he catches me staring at the window seat.

"Oh, no, I'm fine here," I say. Tucking a stray lock of hair behind my ear, I try to shake off this awkward feeling, but it won't go away.

"Relax," Alec says, setting down the knife and walking to the sink. He washes his hands as he talks over the sound of the faucet running. "As you can imagine, snow-ins aren't so uncommon here," he tells me.

I watch his broad shoulders move as he dries his hands off and checks the thermometer of the oven. As he does, the beep goes off letting him know it's up to temperature.

"I'm sorry," I tell him. It's so obvious I'm uncomfortable, and I don't want him to think I'm ungrateful.

He picks up a cherry tomato from the small pile on the counter and tosses it into his mouth, turning to face me and leaning against the island.

"I understand this is different and I have to confess, I'm partially to blame."

My eyes whip up to his, and I'm not sure how to respond.

"To blame?" I echo. My blood heats with the way he looks at me.

"I may have requested that you be the one to come here," he says and then reaches over and takes another cherry tomato between his fingers. He holds my gaze as he pops it into his mouth. The action is sensual in a way, but threatening as well.

I take a breath, trying to keep it even. Trying not to let what he's just admitted affect me.

As if reading my mind, Alec smiles, chewing and swallowing the tomato slowly with his hands raised in the air. When he's finished with it he lets out a small laugh that lightens the mood. "Maybe I shouldn't have told you that." His eyes sparkle with something they haven't before, an easiness and humor that make him seem less dominating and intimidating. "I just wanted you to know that I hadn't planned on this," he gestures to the window. "But I did want to meet you," he adds as he cocks a brow at me and then turns to the counter, moving the chicken to a tray and slipping it into the oven.

"I read a few of your articles. You're a talented writer, and you're attractive. You can't blame me for wanting you to be the one to conduct the interview," he says, closing the oven door. He turns to me and adds, "Maybe I could even take you on a date?" He raises his hands again, palms out and says, "No pressure. I just thought you may enjoy seeing the town and taking a tour."

"We're snowed in," I answer him with the obvious response, not sure how to react to this man.

My body is on fire at the thought of him wanting me. Just the fact he's interested in me is driving adrenaline through my blood. At the same time, I'm easy prey for him. Someone for him to use up and spit out. I'm practically trapped in his home. I take in a heavy breath, hating how the last thought somehow makes me even hotter.

"Not tonight, but perhaps tomorrow if the weather lets up?" He takes a few steps closer to me.

"I would enjoy that," I answer politely and then grip the back of the island chair and pull it out so I can take a seat.

"You just need to relax, Lila," Alec says as he walks over to a carved cherry liquor cabinet, pulling out two bottles of wine, one red and the other white. "Usually I would have white, considering the meat," he says, reading the labels of each bottle before peeking up at me. "But which would you prefer?"

"Whichever you'd like," I answer, not really caring which one he'll choose. The tables have turned, and as my fingers twine around one another I have to remind myself that I'm leaving in a few days. That this isn't really a date. Although it damn sure feels like it, and he's said he's interested in me.

It would be a mistake. I watch as he grabs a bottle opener. *A beautiful mistake.*

He opens the bottle of white easily, pouring one glass and then another. They clink together as he picks them up in one hand and takes the seat next to me.

He places the glasses down on the counter and passes mine to me, simply sliding it across the counter as if it's an offering. I can't help but let out a small laugh. He smiles in response, a handsome smile that makes my fingers itch to touch the stubble along his jaw.

"You're very handsome, Mr. Kulls." I finally give in to a bit of my desire, and pick up the glass of wine, holding on to it for support in this decision.

His grin widens and he leans forward just slightly to say, "Alec, Lila. My name is Alec to you." He pauses for a moment, then flashes me a smirk and adds, "Unless of course you'd like to scream 'Mr. Kulls' in bed?"

My face heats instantly as he rises from his seat to attend to the beeping oven and he's quick to say, "I do believe Alec may be easier."

The sweet wine touches my lips and the taste is delicious, but I can't think of anything other than this man on top of me, making me scream as he thrusts inside of me repeatedly.

"I think you've maybe thought a little too far ahead, Mr.—Alec," I'm quick to correct myself. I watch as he works in the oven, turning the chicken breasts and then setting the tongs back down on the counter before coming back to his seat.

"Mmm, that could be," he says picking up his glass, but not sitting. I cross my ankles and turn in my seat to face him.

"This isn't very professional," I tell him with a serious look, or at least the most serious I can manage. He shrugs his shoulders and then takes a sip from his glass.

"Do you want it to be?" he asks and then adds, "That's fine if you do. I understand the attraction may only be on my end."

My heart thumps hard in my chest. I don't think this man knows how to be subtle. He's honest and to the point. But I admire that.

"It's definitely not just one-sided," I admit, and then bite my tongue. I'm thinking I should add that this is dangerous for me. I could lose my job. More than that though, this man could crush me. I've never had a one-night stand because I know I don't really do casual. I've been wined and dined and then thrown away before. It hurts too much.

I don't recover easily, and I prefer to avoid relationships. But it's been so long since I've been touched.

Alec's deep voice rumbles, "That's good to know." I don't think a man has ever looked at me with the same level of desire. It's tempting and frightening all the same.

"So, tomorrow?" he asks me, and my brow furrows with confusion.

"Tomorrow?" I repeat.

He smiles at me, and the smell of his cologne, or maybe his natural scent hits me with a powerful force that makes me lean in closer to him.

"Would you like to go out with me tomorrow?" he asks.

His gray eyes swirl with a mixture of desire and something else—a desperate need. I nod my head slowly and say, "I'd love to."

CHAPTER 5

Lila

MY EYES POP OPEN AS I HEAR ALEC IN THE KITCHEN. MY BARE feet pad on the wooden stairs and I clutch his white dress shirt I'm wearing tighter. *His.* I'm fucking mortified.

I hardly slept, even with a stomach full of hot food and delicious wine. I was *this* close to sleeping with Alec, to kissing him and making a fool of myself last night. I don't know what came over me.

Nothing has been normal about the last two days.

And I don't know what to expect today. Or where to find my clothes. We didn't have sex; I know that much. I'm fairly sure I asked for a dress shirt to sleep in. *Specifically, a dress shirt, because that's an obvious choice to sleep in.*

I roll my eyes and try not to groan at the thought. This is worse than a walk of shame. I didn't even get to have sex.

As I turn the corner headed toward the kitchen, I spot my suitcase in an instant. The faded blue and bulky casing stands out like a sore thumb on the window seat.

I cast a furtive glance at Alec, hoping I can sneak in and grab it, but it's no use. He looks up at me from his laptop and says easily, "Good morning."

My grip on the dress shirt tightens as I try to swallow.

"Morning," I mutter and glance at my suitcase, desperate to change and try to collect myself.

"Drew brought it over this morning." Alec closes the laptop and leans back in his seat, his eyes assessing me. "I thought about bringing it up to you, but I didn't want to wake you."

My throat's tight as I answer, "Thank you."

"How did you sleep?" he asks. I wonder if this is normal for him, to have random women in his clothes parading through his house half-naked on the weekends.

The thought makes me angry and fuels me to walk toward my suitcase. *Last night was a mistake.*

"Fine, thank you," I answer him brusquely although I can't look him in the eyes. I stop when he asks me, "Is something wrong?"

"Just feeling out of sorts." I hope he'll just accept it and let me go about my way. I'm a fool for getting drunk last night.

"Do you need help with that?" he offers and rises from his seat.

I shake my head so fast that my hair swishes against my shoulders.

"Are you being shy?" he asks me, walking around the counter to a coffee maker. The sight is instantly accompanied by the smell of coffee, and that alone is enough to tempt me to stay just a bit longer.

Shy? Not quite the right word. I clear my throat. "Just a bit embarrassed about last night," I admit, feeling anxiety creep through me.

"Nothing to be embarrassed about," Alec says as he takes a mug out and pours a cup of black coffee. I note that he doesn't add either creamer or sugar as he takes a sip.

He stares at the coffee and then across the room to look at me as he says, "I enjoyed last night."

The way he says it makes me question if we did have sex. We didn't though. I distinctly remember coming on to him and being denied.

I hesitate to come up with a response, and he smiles at my frustration. "It was fun having someone to talk to. I really enjoy your company, Lila," he says with his voice full of sincerity.

I nod my head once. "It was… fun," I finally say.

A deep rough chuckle fills the room. "Is that why you seem to be in a hurry to leave?" he asks, and it makes me feel like shit. I don't want to be obvious, but really, what did he expect? Maybe it would have been different had I woken up in his bed in the morning, but then again, it probably would have made me feel even more like shit.

"I just don't do this," I say and gesture between us.

"I don't either," he's quick to reply and then takes another sip of his coffee. He gives me a tight smile as he says, "You're the first person to stay here since my brother's left."

His admission catches me off guard. I'm not that naïve. I narrow my eyes at him, but he only shakes his head. "I wouldn't lie, Lila." He reaches into the cabinet, turning away from me and picking up a mug. The ceramic clinks against another cup before he sets it down on the counter.

"Would you like a cup? Maybe some coffee and a hot shower will have you feeling better?" he offers.

The thought of both a hot shower and fresh cup of coffee makes me relax almost instantly.

Yes, that's just what I need. "Please," I answer and walk toward the island. I'm acutely aware I'm only in Alec's dress shirt and my underwear, but he doesn't seem to mind in the least. His reaction is surprising, in the best of ways. "When I came down here, I wasn't sure what to expect," I tell him and watch for his response.

"And?" he asks me.

"And what?"

"Are you happy I hadn't run off?" he asks with a smile and then brings the cup to me. "Sugar?" he asks. I stare at him from across the counter.

"You don't have to do this," I tell him simply. "You don't need to cater to me and do all of this-"

"Do you think I don't want to?" he cuts me off, not bothering to wait for me to answer that yes, I do like sugar and creamer. Instead he goes about fetching both, setting them on the counter opposite me. "I'm not doing anything I don't want to, Lila." His brow creases as he looks back at me. "Like I said, I enjoy your company and there's certainly nothing wrong with me being accommodating for a guest."

"Thank you," I whisper, giving in and trying to show my gratitude.

"You're skeptical, and it's because I'm attracted to you," he tells me as I spoon out a large heap of raw sugar and dump it into the steaming mug. I nod my head once, my eyebrows rising.

"Yes," I say and look him in the eyes. "You just want to get into my pants?" It was meant to be a statement, but it turned into a question.

He smirks at me. "If that was the case, we'd still be in bed, Miss Travers."

I glance down at a dark gray swirl in the granite countertop and then back up to him, picking up the small porcelain pitcher of creamer and watching it lighten the dark coffee. "Why is it that we aren't?" I ask him slowly and carefully, dreading the answer.

When I look up at him, I find him looking at me with pure unadulterated pleasure. As if I'm the most amusing thing he's ever seen.

"What's so funny?" I ask, feeling a small smile pulling my lips up simply in response to him.

"You're cute," he says and that smile gets bigger. I shake my head and take a sip of the coffee. It smells rich, tastes delicious and the warmth is desperately needed. It's heaven.

"You make me nervous," I tell him as I put the mug down.

"You're less nervous when you're drunk," he tells me and then lays his forearms on the counter, leaning closer to me. "But I didn't want to take you to bed and have you not remember it."

I nod and feel my cheeks flame, casting my eyes down.

"You did promise me a date last night," Alec says as he pushes away from the counter and out of my reach, the movement catching my attention.

"Did you really bring me out here…" I start to ask and then have to trail off as my head pounds with a morning headache from caffeine withdrawal or maybe a hangover. I grip the mug with both hands. "Did you bring me out here simply because you wanted to sleep with me?" I can't help but ask him the annoying thought that's been bugging me.

Alec scratches the back of his head, looking away from me for a moment. "I shouldn't have said that last night," he starts, and I have to cut him off.

"Are you saying you should have lied?" I ask. I don't know why I'm feeling so defensive, or so much like I want to run.

"I'm saying, your editor contacted me and I requested you. I looked into the others, but I admired your writing and found you attractive," he says easily, the tension in the air dissipating. "It doesn't hurt that I've been alone for a long time and the thought of taking you on a date after the interview… well, I couldn't say no to that."

"Our interview isn't over," I say, trying to remember if I even started a write-up last night. I'm confused with which direction to take the article. Do I go with something that will sell but still be business-oriented that my editor will find appropriate? Or should I stick to what I really want to write?

"First dates are interviews, Lila. And ours went great last night," Alec says with his eyes on me as he raises the mug of coffee to his lips. There's a challenge in his gaze, and I play along.

"Last night was *not* a date." The strength in my voice is gone, and I have to bite down on my lip to keep from smiling.

He doesn't hold back his own as he sets down the mug and swallows. My eyes are drawn to his neck and then up to his lips as he licks them.

"If that's the way you want to play this, that's fine. I'd love to have another *non-date* with you tonight, Miss Travers. But first, an interview over coffee and brunch in town."

"Just an interview?" I ask him, feeling disappointed although I've brought this on myself.

He closes the space between us with his large strides. He gets near enough to where I can touch him if I want, near enough to where he could lean down and put his lips on mine. But neither of those things happens. Instead he leans against the counter and merely stares down at me. The heat crackling between us begs me to initiate something. I refuse it though, gripping my coffee mug and pretending the sexual tension doesn't exist.

"It was never just an interview," he says just above a murmur and the way he says it makes me more than certain those words are the absolute truth. He leans forward, his lips close to my ear, his hot breath trailing down my shoulder and he whispers, "Shower first, and then our date."

CHAPTER 6

I suppose it's only natural that Alec takes me to a quaint diner. It's a small town, and it makes sense we'd have an early brunch in a corner booth on the far end of a mom and pop shop.

And maybe it makes sense that everyone keeps giving us odd glances, too. I'm new, and unfamiliar. But constantly feeling their gazes makes me uneasy. I keep glancing between the dark blue paisley window covers and the small crowd on the other side of the diner. Each time there's someone staring back. It's almost like a game at this point.

"Are they bothering you?" Alec asks me, bringing me out of my thoughts.

I shake my head, both hands wrapped around the white ceramic mug in my hands. Tea this time, not coffee. I limit myself to two cups a day for the sake of my teeth. Coffee's worse than smoking for your teeth, or so I've heard. "I'm just not used to…" I pause and take a moment, trying to come up with the right word. "Attention."

I can still taste the sugary icing from the honey bun I practically devoured. I have a sweet tooth that this diner could certainly satisfy, and I keep eyeing the bit of icing left on the plate sitting on the edge of the table.

Alec nods his head, looking down at the cup of black coffee he hasn't touched since the waitress set it down. "It may have been a mistake to come here," Alec murmurs as he looks past me for a moment.

"Oh?" I chew the inside of my lip, letting my nerves get the best of me. I feel like I'm walking on the edge with this man, teeter-tottering between falling for him and keeping myself guarded. I'm not sure which way I'll fall, but either way, I know I'm going to land hard on my ass.

Alec leans forward, resting his forearms against the pale blue tablecloth and says in a hushed voice, "They're watching us to see who you are to me." His piercing gaze holds me steady as his words register. The small chatter and clinking of utensils turns to white noise.

"Who I am?" I ask him as my heart seems to slow, each beat hurting just slightly. Just enough to notice it.

I look down at my cup and lift the tea bag up with my spoon and then lower it back down, letting the dark tea mix with the hot water. "Who would that be?" I ask him although another question rests right on the tip of my tongue.

"A good girl who deserves more than a man like me," he says without missing a beat.

I search his eyes, wondering why he said that. "Are you a bad man?" The words slip out without my consent. The moment they leave my lips, I want to snatch them back to keep Alec from hearing, but they're already gone.

He doesn't flinch like I thought he would. He doesn't seem shocked at all by my question. And maybe that's more alarming than anything else.

"My father was," Alec says, not breaking my gaze. "And recently there was an incident with my brother."

His expression reflects pain at the mention of his brother. His light eyes smolder, and his lips turn down.

"Did you hurt him?" I ask. I hardly know Alec, but I can sense a darkness in him. More out of pain than anything else. But it's there, just beneath the surface. It's in the way he carries himself. Even the way he speaks.

Alec shakes his head and says, "Never." He taps his fingers against the mug, and I look up past him at a woman in the very back. She's staring at us shamelessly, and I hate it.

"My brother's a good man. He's nothing like my father." His voice holds conviction, and I find myself confused.

"What then?"

"Do you remember how I told you about the tincture? How I drank it to prove to my brother that it was pointless?" he asks me, and the reminder makes my heart flicker with pain. As if it splinters.

I simply nod and pick up the tea cup, holding it closer, but not drinking.

"He found someone that day, and their relationship is questionable," he says.

Immediately my defenses rise as I blurt out, "It's no one else's business." Anger brims just beneath the surface. "No one has a right to judge a relationship-"

Alec cuts me off by saying, "Even I question it, Lila." I'm silenced and stunned by his admission. "I'm not sure she wants to…" He trails off and runs his hand through his hair, the air turning uncomfortable. "I'm not sure she's interested in being with him as much as he is her," Alec explains, and that definitely changes things.

My eyes catch a glimpse of a man turning to look over his shoulder at us. He's quick to look away, but it's then that everything makes sense. Small towns and gossip go hand in hand.

"Did your brother hurt her?" I ask softly, chancing a glance at him.

His expression hardens, but he hesitates to answer. "She said no and he did as well, but…" He pauses and clears his throat, readjusting in his seat. "It doesn't look good from the outside," he finally says.

"What does it look like from the outside?" I ask.

His expression hardens and he mutters, "Like she's going to leave him." He blows on his coffee and takes a drink before adding, "It'll destroy him if she…" Alec doesn't finish, shrugging his shoulders and setting the coffee mug down.

My fingers trail down the hot ceramic and then I lift it to my lips as Alec tells me, "I haven't talked to anyone about it."

"About your brother?" I ask.

He nods. "It's been difficult to handle because I don't know how to help," he admits, and my instinct is to reach my hand out to him. He huffs a sad laugh, putting his large hand over mine and squeezing it lightly.

"This is too much, isn't it?" he asks me with that sadness reflected in his eyes. "I haven't even known you for twenty-four hours, yet I've told you more personal things than I've told anyone else really." He lets go of my hand to take a sip of his coffee.

"Why me?" I feel compelled to ask.

"I don't know," he says after a long moment. "Maybe it's just the situation." He pulls his hand away, nestling his back against the booth and I miss the warmth of his hand instantly. "I feel helpless about my brother.

I'm alone for the first time in a very long time, and I'm only just now realizing how empty my life has been." His confession makes my face crumple.

He gives me that sad smile again. "Being quiet and holding it in hasn't worked well for me. When I saw you," he says and his eyes burn into me, "I felt like you would understand somehow. Or at least that you would keep my secrets."

"Maybe you feel safe with me because I'm leaving," I offer and when I do, his expression changes. He straightens his shoulders, and it's obvious he doesn't like what I've said. "I mean that I'm not a threat to you in any way." I try to lighten the weight of my words as he recoils right in front of me.

"You have no idea how much you threaten me. You make me feel weak, Lila."

Every inch of my skin tingles with awareness. I lick my lips as his eyes heat.

I can't breathe; I can't even react. Just two weeks ago I was on the other side of the country, completely oblivious to this man's existence.

He runs his hands through his hair again and turns to his left, looking out of his window. "I'm sorry," he says before turning to look me in the eyes and adding, "I know it must sound crazy."

"Someone asked me once if I believed in love at first sight," I say without thinking, just speaking what's on my mind. "I told them no, but I was lying."

Alec huffs a small laugh, and it makes me smile. "Not that I'm saying it's love, because it could be lust," I say.

"There's definitely lust," Alec says in a low tone that vibrates through my body. My chest and cheeks warm and I take a sip of the lukewarm tea, feeling a mix of emotions. I keep thinking back to the tincture. How Alec drank it, how he stayed in a room all day and refused to see anyone. Maybe he delayed it? It's naïve and childish to think of potions and magic, or rituals and séances. Those things don't exist in real life.

I shake off the feeling and my eyes catch sight of a young girl staring at us. Her mother's hand is on her shoulder and everyone else turns away when my gaze reaches them, but not the young girl.

I smile back at her and lift my hand to wave. With the motion, Alec looks behind him, and as the girl waves back he hesitates, but waves as well.

"You're cute," I tell him as I reach into my purse for my wallet.

"First, that's my line. Second, don't you even think about paying." He reaches into his back pocket and pulls out his wallet before I can reach mine at the bottom of my bag.

"Well, thank you; it was going to be a business expense though."

"I think business is over, Lila," Alec says with a look in his eyes that strums my desire to life. "We should get out of here."

CHAPTER 7

"**I** SHOULD GO BACK TO THE CABIN," I TELL ALEC, BUT I DON'T MEAN it. Every bit of me, down to my very soul, feels for him. In such a short period, he's opened up to me, confided in me. He needs someone so desperately.

We drive in comfortable silence. Maybe he's thinking the same as me. *Where is this going? What are we doing? How will this end?*

The moment we stepped into his warm foyer and out of the cold, the questions seemed to fall silent, replaced by a desire I can't contain.

I slip off my coat slowly, not looking at him, but watching in my periphery as he locks the front door.

"You should…" Alec starts to say as he tosses the keys onto the front entry table. "You definitely shouldn't come upstairs with me," he concludes as he takes two steps closer to me. He stops a foot away, but the proximity is suffocating.

"That would be bad, wouldn't it?" I ask him, although it's not really a question. It's definitely a bad idea to give in to him. To set myself up knowing I'm going to fall hard for him.

My heart begs me to question him. To ask him what he'll think of me after, and try to plan how this could possibly work.

But the moment my lips part, his large hands grip my thighs and pull me up into his arms. I slam into his chest, our lips crashing together and he steals the words from my lips with a hurried kiss. As if letting one more second pass would have killed him.

My chest rises and falls as my fingers spear through his hair while he carries me up the stairs.

As soon as I break the kiss, Alec's lips move to my neck, his hands squeezing my ass as he kicks open a door.

I should say no, but I have no intention of depriving myself of this man. I want him. It's that easy.

A gasp leaves me as he tosses me onto a large bed. The room is dark with the thick curtains shut, but it's warm and the bed is soft and welcoming.

My eyes are transfixed on Alec as he quickly pulls his shirt over his head, leaving it to fall into a puddle of fabric at his feet. My lips part, and my breathing quickens. My pussy is hot as my thighs clench of their own accord.

I lick my lips as his muscles ripple in the dim light, accenting each hard line. My fingers dig into the comforter, gripping the fabric with the need to keep me right here. His light gray eyes, filled with nothing but desire, hold my own as he unbuttons his pants, shoving them down in a swift push and unleashing his hard as steel cock.

Fuck.

I'm fully clothed, and the man in front of me is naked and gloriously so as he crawls across the bed to get closer to me.

I don't have enough time to admire him, or to think even. My mind is a mess of thoughts, but the overriding one is to give in to every urge and let this man have me however he wants.

"I need," I clear my throat, suddenly feeling shy as he settles between my thighs and unbuttons my jeans.

"What?" he asks me, leaning forward and sneaking in a kiss. I lean into it, but he pulls away and then reaches down, gripping my shirt in his hands and pulling it over my head.

"I'm… I need," I stammer and then just close my eyes to spit it out. "Birth control."

He laughs, his hot breath sending goosebumps over my body as he buries his head in the crook of my neck. "I'll send for some in the morning. The morning after pill?" he asks, finally leaning away so he can look me in the eye with his brows raised.

I push him playfully on his shoulder. "This is so embarrassing," I huff in a whisper.

Alec doesn't seem to hear me, or if he does, he doesn't care. I fall to the bed and reach behind me, unclasping my bra, preparing to show myself to him.

He doesn't hesitate to pull the straps down and rip the lingerie away, tossing it carelessly to the floor.

I don't have a second to let my self-consciousness show; he immediately leans forward and moans as he sucks my pebbled nipple. His teeth scrape along the sensitive nub, and I beg him to fuck me.

"Please, Alec," I whimper and it's only then that he lets my breast go with a pop of his mouth. He picks my body up in his arms as though it's easy, kicking the covers down and laying me higher up.

It hits me then that this is really happening.

His fingers slide up my thighs slowly and tug my jeans and panties off easily. The rough denim sliding down my skin only makes the pleasure more intense.

Alec pushes my clothes to the side of the bed, and moves his hand to my pussy. His fingertips slide along my slick sex, and my head lolls back with the faintest touch of pleasure. My clit's already swollen with need and begging for the same attention.

"Fuck," he says with his eyes wide and staring right at me. "You're so fucking wet and ready for me." I can't breathe, and my body's still as he sucks my arousal from his fingertips before moving them back down and pushing two thick fingers into me without hesitation.

My back bows and my body begs me to turn and move away as he finger fucks me, stroking along my front wall. His other hand grabs my throat and pins me down.

My hands instinctively fly to his wrist and fingers around my neck. His grip's not tight or threatening, but the way he plays my body is too intense.

It's like he owns me. Like he could do whatever he wants to me.

And in this moment, he could.

He repositions his hand so his palm smacks against my clit over and over, and the sounds plus the look in his eyes push me over the edge nearly immediately.

A strangled moan and my nails scraping along his wrist and forearm are the only signs he needs that I've come undone. I struggle to catch my breath as he pushes my thighs wider and lines his dick up.

Fuck, he's too big. I squirm beneath him as the head of his cock slips between my lips and pushes into my hot entrance.

A strangled cry pours from my mouth. My eyes squeeze shut tight.

"Shh," Alec hushes me, leaving gentle kisses on my jaw. "I'll go slow at first," he says in a comforting voice as he pushes in deeper, rocking his thick cock in and out of me, each time sliding in more. His girth stretches my walls with a sting that amplifies the pleasure still very much on the surface and pulsing through me.

In one swift move, Alec slams himself in me to the hilt and my head arches back, digging into the mattress as a silent scream leaves me. My walls tighten around him, spasming from the shock as he kisses my neck and grips onto my hips to keep me in place. He gives me a moment, but only a small one and my hands reach down to his, holding on with my nails digging into his skin.

"Alec," I murmur with the insecurity I feel. I don't know if I can take this. *It's too much.*

My head thrashes as he moves out slightly and then forces himself back in. He does it again and then once more, and I can already feel myself on the brink again. So close to being overwhelmed with another release.

Alec's hot breath travels down my skin like the lick of a flame as he groans, "Yes… Cum for me again. Let me feel you cum on my dick."

His dirty words are the last straw and for a second time, I come undone under him. But Alec doesn't wait for me. He doesn't let up. He continues to fuck me as the sensation washes through me and paralyzes me with unadulterated pleasure.

He pistons his hips, thrusting his thick length into me over and over again mercilessly. I scream out, "Alec!"

My heels dig into his ass, urging him on even though it's too much. Waves of intense heat roll through my body, burning every inch in slow creeping waves. Each one more threatening, more consuming than the last.

"Alec," I moan as I feel the impending fall of my release coming. I know it's close; I can feel it slowly making my fingers and toes curl. My head thrashes and I hold my breath, but Alec never stops.

He's ruthless and unforgiving as he continues to pound into me. The sound of me crying out his name and his low moans mix in the hot air.

I struggle to breathe when he rides through my orgasm and forces more from me.

His hard body lies on top of mine, pinning me down and keeping me still while he pushes my release higher.

I almost cry out for him to stop, almost try to push him away. But the final wave of pleasure is too intense for me to do anything other than cry out and lie victim to its intensity.

Alec groans deep and low in the crook of my neck as his fingers dig harder into my hips with a bruising force as he erupts inside of me. I feel his thick cock pulse as hot streams leave him, filling me completely. He pumps his hips in short and shallow thrusts until we're both spent.

Leaving me on the highest high I've ever had, my body shaking and the cold air slipping between us as he rises between my trembling thighs.

I breathe heavily as my body lies limp on the bed, exhausted and sated and deliciously used. I'm vaguely aware that Alec's climbed off the bed, but the dipping and creaking of the mattress is a telltale sign. I listen to the faint patter of his bare feet as he slips into the en suite.

The warmth between my thighs leaks out slightly, and the realization wakes me enough to reach down and prevent it from slipping between my legs and onto the comforter. Before I have to shuffle awkwardly off the bed, Alec towers over me, pushing a hand against my chest. I fall easily for him and spread my legs.

He wipes my thighs and between my legs with a warm wet cloth, kissing the inside of my left knee and then pulling the blanket up over my naked body.

"No need for a dress shirt tonight," he whispers and kisses me quickly on the lips before disappearing again.

Although I smile and hum a small thanks of gratitude, inwardly I wish I'd just fallen asleep.

This situation is a nightmare because there's only one way for it to end.

With me shattered. I can already feel it happening.

Alec Kulls will ruin me.

CHAPTER 8

Lila

Tap, tap, tap. The only sounds in the room are of my fingers on the keys.

I should be in the cabin; I should be writing my article. I should be getting ready to leave more than anything.

Instead, I'm making myself comfortable in the library. *Alec's library.*

I lift my eyes as the door creaks open and Alec walks in, a bundle of small logs under his arm. My fingers stop moving for the first time in what must be hours.

"Why didn't you tell me it'd gone out?" he asks as he kneels in front of the fireplace. The smell of burnt wood drifts toward me as he picks up the cast iron poker.

"I thought you were busy," I tell him honestly. "That, and I'm…" I hesitate to say the truth, but I put the laptop down on the ottoman and shrug a bit as I confess, "I'm afraid of outstaying this welcome."

He huffs and doesn't answer me, putting in another log and stirring the hot embers, exposing bright oranges and reds.

"I don't mind," he says as he looks over his shoulder. He gives me a coy smile, letting his eyes drift over my body in a way that leaves no doubt he likes what he sees.

I pull my knees into my chest, and hide my face from him. I'm in his pajama pants and a white undershirt… also his.

We basically match, and I have no intention of getting out of these clothes.

At least I'm wearing clothes now. I passed out in Alec's arms and woke up to him hard and ready to fuck me again. And again. As I shift on the chair, I feel a dull ache between my thighs, and it only makes me want more of him.

I like to pretend that I'm trapped here in this massive estate with him, but I know I'm not. I have no excuse for practically shacking up with him over the course of this *business trip*.

This is bad. So, so bad.

But it feels *so good*. It's like the real world doesn't exist here. Everything is fresh and new, and Alec wants me.

I've never been with a man who's so honest. A man who doesn't mind catering to me, and acts like this is all completely natural. I can't help but think it's because it's temporary. Because I'm leaving.

The thought is unsettling and I shift in my seat, tearing my eyes from him.

"Hey," Alec gets my attention and makes his way over to me. He brushes his hands off on his pants but keeps his eyes on my face. "What's that look for?"

"What look?" I play dumb. I don't want to be the clingy hookup that got emotional before leaving. But that's exactly what I am.

This isn't me. I've never done a one-night stand before, simply because I don't know how to handle it. Let alone a few one-night-stands-on-vacation. If that's even a thing.

"Stop it, Lila." Alec admonishes me in a deep voice that sends shivers over my skin and hardens my nipples. "Don't overthink it."

He bends down, taking my chin between his thumb and forefinger and tilting my head up so I'm forced to look him in the eyes.

I pull away from him, hating that I'm getting emotional over whatever it is we have.

"It's easy for you to say," I tell him and instantly regret it. He lets out a heavy sigh and takes a seat on the ottoman, pulling my legs into his lap.

"I hate that you think that," he says and I watch his expression for any indication he's lying, but he's not. Maybe this connection is real. But if that's true, it makes it all the harder to leave.

"Don't think about tomorrow," he says as he leans forward and braces his hands on the sofa on either side of my head. He towers over me, staring into my eyes. "We have right now, so let's hold on to right now."

I close my eyes as he leans forward, pressing his lips against mine for a sweet kiss. He deepens it and I react, moaning into his mouth and parting my lips for him. My hands reach up, gripping his shirt and pulling him closer to me.

I don't want this to end. I'm too afraid to say it out loud though. Too afraid to admit that I'm falling too soon, and too hard.

This was never supposed to happen.

Even as Alec moves his hand to my waist and pushes my legs apart with his hips, I know I can't stop myself.

I never had a chance with him.

CHAPTER 9

Lila

"**I** WANT A TRINKET," I SAY LIGHTHEARTEDLY, ALTHOUGH MY heart is heavy. It's my last day here, and our time together is quickly coming to an end.

I spent most of yesterday in Alec's bed listening to the tales he remembers from when he was a child, or writing.

The words flow easily here. But I've only written poetry and short stories. Not anything related to the interview. That can wait till I get back home. I won't let it interrupt what this place is making me feel. The inspiration and muse are strong here. And I love it.

"A trinket?" Alec asks as he picks up a piece of pottery. It's handmade of clay with filigree work, painted deep green and coated with a gloss. It's beautiful and would be perfect for a candle holder. I take it from his hand, adding it to the small collection in the wicker basket that was at the front of the shop.

"*Trinkets*," I correct myself with a smile. This is the fourth shop we've been in, and every one is full of the most beautiful things. Handwoven blankets, old books with that aged smell I love, artisanal decor. And the food—I practically moan just thinking about it.

"Is the entire island like this?" I ask Alec as I raise a candle to my nose. I inhale the lavender scent deeply and close my eyes.

I love everything about this place. I can't help but think I'm being shortsighted, or maybe it's a case of the grass is greener on the other side. But I want to stay.

I don't want to go back to a small, cramped apartment where I don't know a soul and probably never will. I don't want to go back to an office that's constantly moving at a pace that's tiresome to keep up with.

I just want to go back to the cabin, or truthfully, home with Alec, and write.

I place the candle back down onto the shelf and frown as I shake off the uneasiness flowing through me. I don't know what's come over me, but this pining and longing for something I can't have needs to end.

I look up as Alec stiffens as the sight of someone walking across the street catches his eyes. I follow his gaze and watch a small woman walk beside a man who looks so much like Alec. Maybe a bit older, since there are faint streaks of gray on his temples and he's not dressed in a suit, plus his hair is lighter. But they're definitely related. I sneak a glance at Alec, not letting him realize that I see, that I notice something is going on.

The woman seems so out of place. It's almost like she's scared, and I notice how the other people around them are watching, too. They have looks of sympathy on their faces.

"She's had a difficult pregnancy," the older woman behind the counter says in a soft voice. A voice meant for me alone, but Alec hears, too. He sucks in a breath and stares at the woman for a moment, but she meets his gaze evenly.

"Who are they?" I ask Alec.

He swallows before admitting, "My brother and his…" He doesn't finish, and I can tell why. There's something odd between them, something tense and uncertain. Something that scares them both. "Belle."

I take a look over my shoulder to see Alec's brother gentle a hand on the woman's waist. He pulls her closer to him and she lets him, seeming to melt into him. It's a gesture that makes my heart ache. There's a love there, but it's hurt and sad.

"Do you want to say hello?" I peek up at Alec after I ask him, but he simply shakes his head.

"Another time, perhaps," he says and turns his back to them, facing the woman and gesturing to the baubles in my arm.

"But I'm leaving," I protest without thinking. As if I have any say in who I meet from his family. I'm embarrassed for a moment, but only for the briefest of seconds, because he smiles down at me, brushing his fingers against my cheek.

"Why don't you stay?" Alec suggests. He lets out a heavy breath and shoves his hands into his suit pant pockets. "You could work from here, couldn't you?"

My heart flutters, loving that he wants me to stay. Maybe it's the romantic in me, the folklore, the beautiful surroundings, or maybe it's the way he looks at me.

I could. So easily.

I have to turn my head to hide my smile. It's foolish though. I clear my throat, shaking my head. "I can't stay," I tell him and even as I say the words, my heart hurts. This fling or whatever it is between us wasn't smart. How can I be so attached to someone so quickly? "I'm sorry," I tell him sincerely, the smile slipping and my true disappointment coming through. I feign another smile, expecting him to shrug it off, but he doesn't. His pale blue eyes stare deeply into mine, pinning me in place.

The air tenses between us, heating my blood and stealing my breath. It's not the reaction I imagined.

After a moment he nods once, and he doesn't play it off like he's unaffected. He takes a breath and then looks like he's going to say something, but instead he swallows thickly and looks away.

I'd love to stay here. The setting is an author's dream and the untold stories of Ketchikan are enough to tempt me, even if Alec wasn't into me like this. I truly want to stay here. I'm genuinely drawn to the land and the culture. There's a reason those who visit the island stay.

"I really can't," I whisper, both to myself and to Alec.

"One more night then?" he asks me in a low voice as he trails his finger over my shoulder, brushing my hair out of the way and planting a small kiss on my collarbone. I look up and into his eyes, so full of vulnerability and desire, a mixture of both that tempts me in the worst way.

I nod, not trusting myself to speak and close my eyes as he presses his lips against mine.

One more night, and then I have to leave.

He deepens the kiss, and it feels like so much more. Like he's giving me everything he has.

I'm almost afraid of staying with him. Afraid I'll never want to leave. But I know tomorrow I'll be gone. And I won't let fear keep me from having just one more night with him.

CHAPTER 10

Lila

THE ENGINE CLICKS AND CLACKS AND SNARLS. LIKE IT'S SPITTING, rather than rumbling. I stand on the deck, gripping the handle of my suitcase and watching the waves crash against the shore. They aren't harsh or threatening like they seemed to be the last time I was here. It's simply the way it is. It's never going to end; the waves will always batter away at the shore.

"I'm really sorry, Miss Travers," Drew says as he walks out of the cabin of the ship and to the very back of the boat, closest to where I'm standing on the wooden deck.

"What's wrong?" I ask him as the salty breeze whips my hair in front of my face. It's chilly today, colder than it has been and being near the ocean is only making it worse.

Drew's face crumples as he says, "It's going to be a few hours, maybe more before I fix her." He motions behind him with his thumb.

I glance to my right where three more boats are tied to the dock. "Surely there's another boat?" My heart beats faster as I think about having to stay here on this island, so close to Alec, for a while longer.

"It's been a while since they've been up and running and on this water," he says and runs his hand over the hair at the back of his head, looking over to the boats and then back to the cabin. "I'm sorry, Lila," he says with sympathy, climbing off the boat and onto the dock.

Fuck.

My thoughts immediately stray to Alec.

It doesn't matter that I want him. Or that he wants me, too.

That can't be enough, but as I question myself, I can't think of a damn thing else that matters.

Maybe it's fate, a little voice whispers in the back of my head, so full of hope.

"How long do you think?" I ask Drew as he takes off his gloves and taps them against his palm.

"No longer than a night I'd think," he answers and then waits for my response.

Just one more night. I tell myself it'll only be one more night, but I already know I'm lying to myself. I was able to walk away once. I don't know if I'll be able to again.

I clear my throat and look over my shoulder, but before I can ask Drew, he answers the unasked question.

"You need a ride?"

Knock. Knock. Knock.

The bitter cold makes my knuckles hurt as I look between Drew, sitting in his car with the engine still purring in front of the Kulls' estate, and the closed door. My nerves are getting the best of me, and anxiety is racing through my blood.

"Don't turn me away," I whisper to the door and raise my fist again to knock harder, just as it swings open. Warmth flows from inside the house, and it makes the outdoors feel that much colder. My arm slowly falls to my side as Alec stands in the doorway, wearing nothing but a pair of slacks on that are hung low on his waist. His broad shoulders fill the span of the door as he takes a step closer to me.

"Alec," I speak his name just above a murmur. His pale blue eyes peer into mine, filled with questions and then the sound of Drew driving away takes his eyes from mine. It's only then that I feel I can breathe.

Shit, I think as I turn around and watch Drew pull away... with my suitcase in his car. He'll be back in a few hours either way, at least that's what he told me. But he could've waited, damn it. I swallow thickly, knowing I have nowhere to go. I'm stuck here and if Alec turns me away, I'll be all alone. I'll be leaving this beautiful place exactly how I came here. Alone.

"Lila, I thought you were leaving?" he asks and then a chill sweeps through me. Before I can answer he moves aside and pulls me into the house, wrapping his arm around my waist as if his hands belong on me.

He releases me long enough to shut the door, and I instantly miss his touch. I stare at his muscular back as he closes and locks the door, the click filling the silence. He turns slowly, spearing his fingers through his hair. "I thought you would have been gone already."

I clear my throat and answer. "I was supposed to," I confess. "But the boat is…" I falter over my words. "It's not working," I spit out.

"Oh," Alec's gaze falls to the floor for a moment, and his forehead creases. "So, you're only here for… how long?" His voice is filled with disappointment and it cuts me deep, making my heart pain.

"A few hours, maybe another day," I tell him. Why does it hurt so much to tell him that? It's only been days. It shouldn't be this painful.

He nods his head and looks down the hall before forcing a smile to his face. "Well, let me feed you at least."

"I'm sorry, Alec," I whisper as he reaches for my coat and helps me slip it off.

He doesn't respond, merely hanging my coat up before turning back to face me. "Lila," he says and then licks his lips. "You know I don't want you to go."

I nod my head, my fingers intertwining with one another but they stop as he takes a step closer to me, filling the space between us. The heat from his body warms mine and draws me closer to him.

"I want you," he whispers, his lips trailing along the shell of my ear as he moves his body in front of mine, his fingers caressing down to the curve of my waist. And like a moth to a flame, my hands rest against his chest and I lean into his touch, wanting more of him.

He kisses my neck, an open-mouth kiss that makes my head lean to the right so I can expose more of myself to him.

"There's something real here," he says as he grips my ass and pulls me closer to him. The sudden movement makes me gasp.

"I don't think I can promise I'll take it slow, but I can promise to try," he says, staring into my eyes. The way he looks at me has me mesmerized. Trapped, even.

"If you just stay, I'll do whatever I can to keep you." He tells me words that make me want so much more. Words I've only dreamed a man like him would say to me.

I know it's not logical, and it's not safe on my part. Not for my career, or for my heart. It's reckless and naïve. But he's so right that there's something between us. *Something more.*

"I'm afraid," I tell him, and my words seem to float between us. They're riddled with the anxiety I feel. Knowing if I stay, it's all for him. I'd be committing so much to and trusting a man I barely know. But a man who makes me feel alive and cherished. A man I want more from. *More with.*

"I want you, Lila, and I'm afraid to let you go again," he says in a whisper. His weakness, his confession is what does me in.

I nod my head although there was never a question asked.

Nonetheless, it makes his expression change. "Stay with me?" he asks.

I nod again and say, "We can take it slow?"

He chuckles and breaks his gaze for a moment. "I'm not sure how slow, but I'll do my best." He lowers his forehead to mine and whispers, "I don't want to scare you off again."

"You didn't," I tell him honestly, gripping his arms and looking deep into his eyes. "It wasn't you. It's just this…"

"It's intense," he says the words I'm thinking. It is. *It's overwhelming. It's too much.*

"It's perfect," he whispers against my lips and then gives me a quick kiss. He breaks it before I'm ready and I find myself nearly falling as he pulls away. A rough chuckle spills from his lips as I touch my fingers to my mouth.

"We're really doing this?" I ask him.

He takes my hand in his. "I want to," he answers. "I want you."

I could tell him so much more in this moment, but I'll save it for a later date. "I want you, too," I tell him.

He brings my hand to his lips and kisses my knuckles.

"We have plenty of time, Lila. Let's start with something to eat."

CHAPTER 11

Alec

One week later

THE TRUTH AND PERCEPTION ARE TWO DIFFERENT THINGS. "You know the town will talk," Drew says to my left as I look out over the ocean. We're deep in the forest on the very edge of the property. My grandfather used to take me here. He said this was the best position on the island, the most powerful. Because it's where the people come and go.

"They're already talking," he adds.

"I'm aware," I answer, not bothering to take my eyes away from the crashing waves. A heavy sigh leaves me, knowing my love is going to have questions and there's still a road ahead of us with twists and turns. But if they tell her anything that makes her question me, I'll simply answer her honestly. I finally look at him, shoving my hands in my pockets as I say, "She knows I'm head over heels for her, and soon she'll have a more important reason to stay." I turn on my heels without waiting for him and walk back to the family lodge.

Lila will be back soon.

The sticks break under Drew's weight as he hustles to catch up to me. "Are you sure it was wise?" he asks and I cock a brow at him, not knowing which part of this entire ordeal he's talking about.

"Was what wise?"

"The fake birth control?" he asks and I don't let my stride break. I don't let him see that I'm affected in the least. I don't know if the tradition had anything to do with what's between Lila and me, but I'm too chickenshit to go against it. And according to legend, the bond must be sealed with conception before the next full moon.

Losing Lila wasn't worth the risk. It's one of a few lies. I may have deceived her, but it's for us. She'll forgive me because what we have is real. It's so fucking obvious. I'll never let her go.

I shrug as we come up to the back porch of the lodge and I climb the three stairs, gripping the wooden railing to keep me grounded. I'm not sure how she'll react when she finds out I've lied.

But she knows the kind of man I am.

The kind who goes after what he wants. *Who* he wants.

That day I took the tincture I was so sure I'd prove to my brother how foolish he was being. It only took one article to prove how wrong I was. Lila's face stared back at me, and all I could do was read her articles. Everything she'd ever written, everything I could find online. I was infatuated the moment I saw her.

And I'll keep her with everything I have.

"I'm not sure she'll ever find that one out," I say, looking at him from the corner of my eyes and making sure the threat is clearly evident.

He raises his hands in surrender but says, "The pregnancy may give it away." His voice is low, careful to make sure no one can hear.

I stop just outside of the sliding glass doors. "I know it's not right to start it off like this," I start to tell him, thinking about every deal I planned and manipulated, every lie and deceitful action. It's not right, but this situation isn't normal.

"She'll forgive me if she ever finds out," I tell him with confidence. "My intentions are pure." I only want to love her. To keep her and have her. I'll spoil her with everything she could ever want or need. The lies were necessary. If she knew the truth, surely she would have run far and fast.

He nods at my admission, but his eyes flicker to the floor.

"What?" I ask him.

"So were your brother's," he answers me. My body tenses at the thought of Annabelle.

I clear my throat and ball my hands into fists as I say, "She's nothing like that." I take a step forward, closing the space between us as the anger builds. "*This* is nothing like that."

I love my brother Marcus. I've always looked up to him, thought well of him. But what he's done, *what he's doing*, it's not right. I just don't understand why. There must be a reason.

Either way, my Lila is nothing like Belle and our situations aren't comparable.

"I'm not saying that," Drew answers me with strength in his voice although he cowers slightly. I calm my breathing, the adrenaline pumping hard in my blood.

"I'm not saying that at all," he repeats and takes a step back. "I'm just saying that maybe," he takes a breath and looks behind me, straightening his stance and looking casual. I peek over my shoulder to see Lila walking toward us. The pea coat she's wearing is a teal color that pops amongst the tree line, making her stand out even more.

The sight of her reddened cheeks and windblown hair makes my body crave to touch her, to hold her. To keep her safe.

She's mine.

"I'm just saying," Drew says in a low voice, gaining my attention again. He swallows and lick his lips. "Be careful with her," he adds and his eyes search mine, a hint of worry evident.

I nod once and take a step backward. She's not his concern, but I'll put him at ease.

"If she wants to leave me," I start to answer him with the promise I know he needs, but I can't give it to him. "Then I'll convince her otherwise." I tell him the truth, and his gaze drops.

"I love her, Drew." My words make his eyes drift back up. I offer him something that I know will put him at ease, but unexpectedly, also puts me at ease. "I'll bring her to the shops often. She's curious and loves the town."

"Alec!" I hear her call out from behind me with happiness in her voice.

I quickly add, "If she ever looks anything but in love and happy in every way, tell me." I hold his gaze as I hear her call out again, the sounds of her coming closer to the porch getting louder and more evident.

As soon as I hear her boots hit the wooden deck, Drew nods his head. "I'll tell you," he says.

"And I'll listen," I reply and then quickly turn around to face my love with a welcoming smile. My heart clenches thinking that one day, Drew may come to me and tell me she's unhappy. I won't let it happen.

A gorgeous smile widens across her face as she comes closer, and I walk to meet her halfway. "Good morning," I tell her and then press my lips against hers, wrapping my arms around her waist and pulling her into me, muffling her greeting. She moans softly as her lips mold to mine and I only break the kiss because I know Drew's behind us.

The blush creeps up to her cheeks as she bites her bottom lip and tucks her hair behind her ear shyly.

It only makes me want her more.

"Hi Drew," Lila says sweetly although it only makes her cheeks redder, and she can't look him in the eyes. She's so innocent and pure, so easy for me to take for myself.

A soft wind blows and I tuck a loose strand of hair back behind her ear and kiss her one last time before moving to the doors.

"Let's go in," I tell her and then glance at Drew. His expression is one of contentment at least as he nods and says hello in return. "This house is filled with stories."

And I'll tell her every one of them.

One day she'll understand.

Until then, I know she has feelings for me. And what I feel for her is real.

Everything else be damned.

A Note from the Author:

I am determined to, one day, return to this world. I have a feeling that day will come sooner rather than later, and when it does, Lila and Alec will have more to their story and each of the Kull brothers will have their own stories as well. Until then, I hope you enjoyed *Infatuation*.

DESIRES IN THE NIGHT

CHAPTER 1

Valarie

THE RAIN HAS STOPPED AND THE ABSENCE OF THE BATTERING against the car roof makes the hushed sounds of the radio I'd turned down sound louder. My tired eyes flicker to the radio station on the dash; I don't recognize it and a few scans through the next dozen stations prove to find me nothing of interest. With a flick of my wrist it's silenced and only the hum of the car engine and the warm night air ride with me.

The lights go bye quickly, illuminating and then darkening the old country roads. They're asphalt, but the back ways of getting around. The mountains on the right side of the road are covered in thick trees that hide the light of the moon. But the stars on the left side are bright and give enough of a soft glow that it's comfortably dark.

The gentle light and sweet smells of late spring make me feel as if maybe this was the right decision. Maybe it is the right choice.

I'm close. I know I am.

A soft sigh leaves me as I loosen my grip on the wheel and try to readjust in my seat.

I'm so close to my destination. How long I'll stay; I'm not sure. But every second I get closer, is another second the anxiety stirs into desire in the pit of my stomach.

I read the large green signs as I drive by. Looking for a name that's familiar. A few of them resonate in me. Sending a chill down my spine and a heated desire straight to my core. *I'm so close.*

These back roads may not be familiar to me. But they hold memories.

Memories I've dreamed about in the last few months and images that have haunted me.

They play in my mind as I drive down the windy roads.

There's no one here, not a soul out this late at night.

I remember how he pushed me down into the dirt. How my knees scratched on the pavement. I can still remember the sound of the officer's zipper being pulled down and the tug of my hair at the base of my head.

He tasted sweet. I only wanted to lick him at first. Just to tease him like he was doing to me that night.

Just the drop of precum that sat in the slit of his dick. It glistened in the evening light with the silence surrounding us only interrupted by my heavy breathing.

My thighs clench as I remember him punishing me. Shoving himself deep down the back of my throat. As far as he could until I gagged.

But I was eager for more. I didn't care if it was too much for me to take.

My knees were dirty, my hands trembled as my parked car hid us from view.

It was quick and over before I was ready.

That was the first time, years ago when I was only in my early twenties. Young and stupid. Wanting a thrill and more than that, wanting to be fucked the way I'd always dreamed of. There are some desires that are best for the night.

According to the GPS, I'm now driving on that very road. Searching out the same desire as if I might stumble upon it before I get to a place I've never wanted to be.

The last time I was here, I couldn't wait to leave. A small Podunk town wasn't the place where my dreams would be made… or so I thought.

My gaze flickers to the clock on the GPS. Estimated time of arrival is only seventeen minutes. It's odd how my heart sinks and a sense of loss flows through me as I turn onto the main road.

But the loss is quickly forgotten on the deserted road.

Only because it's not quite deserted.

My fingers just barely tip the turn signal down, my grip tightening on the wheel as I spot him.

The parked cop car immediately follows behind me.

My heart beats harder and I can't stop myself from staring into the rear view mirror, searching for his face.

For his hard jaw, just barely speckled in rough stubble. His short hair, buzzed on the sides and longer on top. And his eyes. The way his dark green eyes pierced through me, shredding me of anything that could save me.

And the second I see it's him, I lose myself in the memories and desires that have been devouring my every waking moment.

I'll remember the power and hunger in his eyes that first night on the side of the road forever.

Thud, thud, thud, my heart hammers as the seconds pass.

The tension cuts off my breathing and I can't stand it.

My nerves get the best of me before he can even turn his lights on, forcing me to pull over on the right, right next to a patch of tall oak trees.

Or maybe it's not nerves, it's desperation. It must be, because I can't breathe until he's pulled right behind me and parked.

Closing my eyes, I try to swallow, I try to steady my breathing.

My imagination runs wild for only a moment. Hearing my small feet crash through the fallen branches and leaves on the bed of the small forest, as I run from him. How he'd topple over me, catching up to me quickly.

My lips kick up into a smirk as I turn my keys and click the ignition off. He'd only let me get as far as he wanted.

And then he'd take me. In the dark of the night.

My eyes raise at that thought and to the sound of his police car door shutting behind me. Only a deserted street lies ahead. No one to see what I truly want.

He didn't even have to turn his lights on, let alone the siren.

I stare at his broad shoulders as he stalks towards me. The dark blue uniform is stretched taught over his muscular chest. There's something about that dip just beneath his throat too. The lights from his car shine behind him and cast shadows over his high cheek bones.

I close my eyes listening to the sound of his boots approaching.

I know exactly what I'm going to do. And what I'm going to let him do to me.

But this is my guilty pleasure. It's everything I've been dreaming about for months.

CHAPTER 2

Alex

MY DICK IS ALREADY HARD. I'VE BEEN WAITING FAR TOO LONG for her to come back.

She doesn't know that I knew she was coming tonight.

Maybe she thought she could sneak into town without telling me. Maybe she thought she'd make it all the way to the Inn without having run into me.

She should know better than that.

A deep rough groan is stifled in the back of my throat as my dick strains against the zipper of my slacks. I've been waiting for an hour in that exact spot. This is the perfect location. No one comes out to this part of town this late at night. She knows that too. She had to know.

My heart flickers as I get closer and see her head resting back, her eyes closed. Her chest rises slowly in the thin cotton shirt. Her skin is flushed, the pale blush rising up to her cheeks.

My boots scuffle the small broken pieces of asphalt beneath my feet and her long lashes flutter as she turns her head to face me.

A moment passes as I take her in. From the stray locks of dark brown hair to the small freckles on her cheeks that trickle down to her shoulder. Even with the faint light and tired eyes from driving for hours, she's fucking gorgeous.

"Officer?" her sweet voice is shaky. Her entire body is trembling just slightly. Even as she grips the seatbelt laying across her lap. I know her name without needing her license.

But she called me "Officer" and if she wants to go back to playing like we used to, who am I to say no?

"License and registration." Every slight movement makes the tension hotter. Her soft locks of hair fall down her back as she reaches over to the glove compartment. She lets her ass stick out and takes a second too long after she's found what she's looking for and a satisfied groan leaves me.

I don't have the patience to wait any longer. But for her and her forbidden fantasies… fuck, I'd do anything to have her.

The darkness in her doe eyes swirls with recognition as I lean forward, setting my forearm onto the roof and lowering my face to the window.

"I'm going to need more than this Miss."

"Mrs." She's quick to correct me, her previously soft and sultry voice ringing out clear in the night air. My eyes search hers for a long time. Besides her ragged breathing and my heart pounding in my chest, all I can hear are the sharp chirps of the crickets in the thicket of the forest to our right.

"Mrs. then. I'm going to need a little more from you," I tell her.

"What would you like?" she asks as her eyes flicker from mine to the lock on the door. She bites down on her lower lip and rings the seatbelt in her hands.

My words escape me for a moment. Only a moment as I remember crashing my lips against hers and biting down on that lip myself. So sweet and innocent. The night I met her, that's all I thought she was. I don't like to admit it, but sometimes I can be wrong.

"You're going to need to get out of the vehicle," I tell her as I slip my hand in through her window and pull the handle myself.

I can't help how my lip twitches into a smile at her faint gasp.

With her eyes cast down and her lips parted, Valarie slowly slips from the car and I nearly groan out loud from the sight of her. Her pale yellow skirt sways around her thighs and her heels click on the pavement.

The car door clicks shut softly as I watch her chest raise and fall with each heavy breath she's taking. So innocent. She did this on purpose to tempt me. This woman standing in front of me isn't at all the sweet little thing she appears to be.

"Follow me," I give her the command as she clasps her hands, so eager to touch me. I know exactly what she needs, what dirty thoughts are playing through her head.

The second I splay my hand on her lower back, it's like a bolt of electricity that shoots through me. My body recognizing hers, *needing* hers.

My pace quickens as I practically push her to my car. Her thigh bumps into the hood and makes her gasp, but grabbing her wrist, I pull her around to the side opposite the street so we're out of view. She stumbles and nearly falls, making her wavy hair cascade in front of her face.

"Officer, what's the meaning of this!" she protests and I'd laugh if I didn't feel like I needed her lips wrapped around my cock, more than I needed the air I breathe.

"I don't have time for games, Mrs…" I don't finish the thought as I unbuckle my belt, "on your knees."

"Officer," she breathes in protest even as she licks her lips and falls onto her knees on the hard ground instantly. Again she holds her hands, ringing her fingers around one another as I take my time, unbuckle my belt and the slowly sliding the zipper down.

The sight of her like this is everything I've wanted since the last time we did this.

"I know you know what to do," I tell her under my breath as the dark night seems that much darker. My fingers spear in her hair and I make a fist, bringing her forward, but my dirty little slut is already sucking me down. Her fingernails digging into my thighs with eagerness for more. Shielding her teeth with her lips she takes in as much of my dick as she can, into her hot greedy mouth.

My head falls back with nothing but pleasure as the intense sensation sings in my blood. The need to fuck her mouth like it's her cunt rides me hard, but I hold back just slightly. Just enough to let her have some fun.

Her cheeks hollow and she tries to swallow my dick. The sensation feels too fucking good. My toes curl as I grunt and shove myself deeper down her throat. Again and again until I have to stop. I pull away, making my dick pop out of her mouth before she can make me cum.

"I want you," she barely gets the words out as she tries to catch her breath.

She wipes her mouth with the back of her hand. Still on her knees, she stares up at me like I can command her. And so I do.

"Beg for it," I tell her knowing all the things she's told me she wants.

Shame heats her cheeks, making them flushed and that much more gorgeous.

"Show me how much you've missed me."

CHAPTER 3

Valerie

"Y OU WANT THIS SO BAD DON'T YOU?" HE ASKS ME AS IF HE doesn't know how much I've wanted to relive this night. "You're dying for it. Your cunt needs me."

"Please, fuck me." I have no shame this time. I want him. I'm throbbing against him with desire and I have no intention of being denied. I place my splayed hand against his chest and push against him. With little resistance, he leans back against his car, slowly dropping to the ground until he's seated on the dirt with me, his hooded eyes finding mine.

I lean into him and place my lips at his ear. "I want you. And you better not fucking deny me."

"Fuck me then," he groans and takes my head in his hands. His lips crash hard against mine. His strong tongue runs along the seam of my lips and I part for him. My pussy heats with anticipation as he nips at my bottom lip, making me moan. I can feel him stroking himself and that knowledge makes my skin heat even more. I need him inside of me. Filling me and stretching me with his cock.

I position myself so that the head of his dick is at my entrance. I'm already needy, and wet and I didn't even bother wearing panties. I'm that desperate. He stares into my eyes with his lips parted as I gently glide down his massive cock.

"Oh my God," I moan at the heavenly feel; it's so fucking good. I can barely breathe as his cock sinks into me. Fuck!

There's a hint of pain and I'm sore instantly. It's been way too long. I can feel my face scrunch as his fingertips dig into my hips and he shoves himself roughly inside of me. Although it hurts for a moment, the fullness makes my body sing with pleasure.

Even with the intensity of what we're doing, the second my eyes meet his, none of it matters. His heated gaze stops me, every part of me. He holds me in a trance of relentless need and desire. It's all I can see, all I can feel and I can't move until he grips my waist and let's out a deep groan of need. Even still, his gaze doesn't leave mine.

I move a few inches up and down and then sink all the way down his length, whimpering as the mixed sensation of pleasure and pain causes my limbs to tremble. I still as his dick hits my wall, pushing against it, and let my tight pussy relax around him. My head falls onto his shoulder as the hot sensation overwhelms me. I can barely move, barely do anything at all.

He takes my head in his hand and kisses me sweetly. His lips are soft and I quickly deepen it. Wanting more of him and of this. I want this night to be burned into my memory just as that night was years ago. He pulls back first, breathing heavily and staring back at me with wild eyes.

"I thought you wanted to fuck?" he says in a calm and rough tone that doesn't match any of this. All it does is make me simper, the desire and need to fuck what's mine comes back to me full force.

I lick against his lips and he gives me his tongue to suck. I moan into his mouth as I pick my body up and then glide down his length, my arousal makes the movement effortless, although his girth is still stretching me. I lean back and pick up my speed while my hands rest on his muscular pecks. Riding him at my own pace. The chill in the air sends goosebumps down my flesh. Hardening my nipples and heightening the sensation that much more.

His hands stay at my hips, but he doesn't control the movements. His head leans forward and he takes my nipple into his mouth, through the thin fabric of my blouse and sheer bra; he bites down and pulls back. Fuck yes! The simple movement makes my pussy ache. I arch my back at the spike of pleasure and wanton heat in my core. But just as soon as he gives me the delicate mix of pleasure and pain, he takes it away.

He relaxes against the car watching my pussy move over his dick with a hungered look in his green eyes. His heated gaze of adoration sends yet another surge of arousal through me.

"I want you so fucking bad," I whimper, my words laced with the loneliness I've felt for too long.

"I'm right here," he tells me and his words draw my eyes to his lips, and then to his throat as I watch him swallow thickly. He's mine. I have him again.

He rocks his hips in a sharp motion and it forces me to cry out as he tears through me quickly. Fuck!

My clit hits against his pelvis every downward stroke and the moisture that's gathered there makes my pleasure all the more intense.

I stop my movements and stare at him. He's letting me ride him. He's given me control. But it's false control. I find myself wanting him to fight for it. I want him to *take* me. It takes a moment for him to look up at me. He bucks his hips against me, causing me to moan as his eyes find mine. As we both catch our breath he asks, "What's wrong?"

I pause for a moment before admitting the truth, "I want you to fight me."

Before I can blink, he's spun us around in the dirt, forcing us both to our feet as he stands and then crushed my body against the car with his.

I can barely breathe as my back presses against the cold window of the car and I stand on shaky legs. His forearm presses against my shoulders and pushing against him proves useless. He's a hard wall of brick and he has me right where he wants me. I can't move or fight him in the least.

His lips crash hard against mine, stealing what little air I have in my lungs before he spins my body around, pinning me against the car. My legs are on either side of his with his hard dick nestled between the slick folds of my pussy. Both my wrists are captured in one of his hands and held above my head. My breasts are pressed against the car with his heavy chest pushing against my back. I gasp in shock. *Holy fuck!* My heart races in my chest. His speed and strength are terrifying and invigorating at the same time. It wasn't like this before. But then again, we're both in need and the time for playing is over.

His other hand slips between the car and my body, and he circles my clit with heavy, unrelenting pressure. "Oh, my God," I moan against the window. The feeling is so intense I try to move away, but I'm trapped. I can hardly move any part of my body.

He whispers into my ear, "you questioning my dominance, sweetheart?"

My pussy clenches at his words, feeling empty without him inside me. I shake my head slightly the best I can.

He slams his dick inside of me to the hilt and I scream out his name while my orgasm rips through my body. He groans into my neck. "You feel so fucking good."

His words bring me that much closer to yet another release as he starts rutting me from behind. Each thrust harder and faster than the last.

I love every bit of what he's doing to me. I can hardly take it, but at the same time I want more. I want all of him. I need all of him. My heart clenches in agony. I find myself wanting to beg, but I don't know what for. His lips kiss over the skin of my shoulder and neck hungrily.

He nips my ear and sucks on my neck, quickening his pace.

The sound of his hips slamming into me fuels my need to cum. I try to push against the car, to move away as the feeling becomes too much. The metal is so cold against my skin. Everything is so cold except for him. I need to be closer to him but the sensation is too much. I can't. I can't.

I try everything to escape, but I'm pinned. I can't get away from the intensity of need running through my body, heating and numbing every inch of me.

"No no, sweetheart. You wanted me to fuck you like this, remember?" The danger in his voice is intoxicating. I was a fool to think I could fight him. But I love it so much. The taste of forbidden and the excitement of what he can do to me. Fuck, I've missed it. I've missed him.

"Take it sweetheart." His growl makes my pussy clamp down and just as I'm about to cum all over his dick again, he roughly pinches my clit making me scream his name. My strangled moan carries through the empty night as my lungs stop and my entire body tenses. The heat travels through me in waves. Hard and fast and crashing through my shaking body.

I've never cum so hard in my life. I pulse on his dick as my body trembles uncontrollably. I feel him release at the same time. His dick throbs inside of me, heightening my own pleasure.

Even with the fog of desire clouding every thought, I smile against the car, sagging my body and feeling the cold against my bare skin. This was everything I've needed.

He's what I need. A truer statement doesn't exist.

"Fuck." He breathes into my neck. "I've missed you so fucking much."

He breathes heavily and his words come out with desperation. "I'm not letting you go again."

As the high from what we've done starts to fade into the dark night, my ragged breath comes back to me.

And as it does, a pair of lights shines down the road signifying a car driving towards us.

"Shit, shit, shit."

CHAPTER 4

"Fuck," I mutter beneath my breath, still stumbling with my belt as I hear the car roll up. Dammit Jimmy. He was a cock block in high school and I suppose some things never change.

I round my car and head towards the parked cop car as the passenger window rolls down.

"Everything OK here, Alex?"

I can hear Valerie's heavy breathing as I walk out onto the asphalt.

"Yeah Jimmy everything is fine." I turned around looking over my shoulder to see Valerie. Her skin is still flush from what we've just done but she's smoothing out her skirt as she steps to the side of the car and comes into view.

"Actually I have somebody I'd like you to meet," I tell him with a proud smile on my face as I wrap my arm around her shoulder. Valerie's soft body molds to mine and her arm squeezes around my hip. "Jimmy, this is my wife, Valerie. I've been dying for you to meet her."

"Well I'll be," Jimmy says leaning across the dashboard and sticking his hand out the window for Valerie take it.

When we met all those years ago, she scooped me up within weeks and took me back to her hometown. I've always wanted to be a police officer and it just made sense to leave with her.

She met me as a kid playing pretend. It was just a Halloween party and just a costume of the man I wanted to be. A night of flirting turned into so much more when I followed her home. Halloween is for pretend and recklessness. And so I thought my sweet angel would only be with me for a night. But Valerie's proved me wrong since the day I met her.

"All Alex has been doing since he's been here, is talk about you." Jimmy's comment gets a chuckle from Valerie.

Her sweet smile and soft voice is everything to me. I've missed her so damn much since I've come back here. "We can't thank you enough for sending him down here during this hard time."

Valerie takes a step towards Jimmy's car, both of her hands resting on the open window as she answers him with sincerity. "I'm so sorry to hear about the fire."

"It's mostly all fixed up now," Jimmy says confidently, although his gaze shifts behind us and into the dark forest. He's an emotional man and the loss has been hardest on him. "But I can't tell you how wonderful it's been to have Alex back here."

"He's always talked about coming back," Valerie says, looking over her shoulder. Her hair falls down to her lower back.

My grip on her tightens as I say the words, "it's always been home to me." Valerie's eyes go and soften as she nods just slightly. Just for me.

When I left years ago, I was young and in love. And I'd still do anything for her. She knows this place calls to me though.

As I look at her and then back at Jimmy, he seems to understand exactly what we've been doing here. I can practically see the light bulb turn on in his head. He swallows thickly and all the warm welcome and good wishes seem to leave him.

The leather of his seat groans as he leans back in his seat and gives us a wave. "I'll be seeing you two tomorrow night at the barbecue?" he asks and we answer in unison, "we'll be there."

"I'm really looking forward to meeting everybody," Valerie says. There's an eagerness in her voice but also hesitation. I know she never wanted to stay here and I'd never keep her here if she didn't want to stay.

I can't help that this place will always be home to me though and will always be the place where we first met. Where I first fell in love.

"Well, all right; till tomorrow night then," Jimmy says and drives off before Valerie can get another word out. She's left with her hand still in the air as the red of his rear lights become smaller in the distance.

I wrap my arm tight around her waist and pull her closer to me, even though her eyes are watching the cop car.

"Come here," I pull her in close and up against me, her small breasts press against my chest. Her warmth makes the hot summer night feel cold around us. I can't get enough of her. The tip of my nose brushes her before I lean down for a long slow kiss. The kind that I've missed every day since I've been here.

It's been months since the fire broke out. It cost our town some of my childhood heroes. My best friend's fathers and mothers. There's nothing like a tragedy to bring family back together. I left as soon as I could, transferring out here, but my heart stay behind until she could come with me. And now that summers out and schools over. She only has a few months to be with me. Unless she's thought about what I asked. A wish. I can only hope she knows how much it means to me.

"I missed you so much," she tells me, as she leans against me, her fingers gripping onto me like I'll float away if she lets me go. Her cheek presses against my chest and I breathe her in.

I've missed you too," I tell her as my heart twists with the pain of being away from her for so long.

"I don't want to leave you again for so long," she whispers, letting her words linger in the hot night air.

"Stay with me then." I tell her and my heart pings. It's been easy for me, but she'll be giving up her job and starting over. I know there are positions available here, but I don't know if she's ready to move.

Her voice cracks and she has to swallow before looking me right in the eyes, "I can do that," she tells me and I can feel how much she means it. "I'm here to stay."

"You mean it?" I ask her although I don't know why. I can hear it in her voice.

"Always, Alex. I love you."

I crush my lips to hers, pulling her closer and then letting my hands roam down her curves. I've missed her more than a man should miss his wife. It takes everything in me to break the kiss, knowing we have to drive in separate cars before we get to the Inn, my family's place. But we'll be there soon and then I'll have her all to myself.

"I love you too." I whisper against her lips, slowly prying myself away from her. "Always."

KEEPING SECRETS

Fair warning before you start reading. I write gritty with twists that hold a darker edge. This short story turned into something I wasn't expecting and may be different from what you're expecting as well. Either way, I hope you enjoy it and love their tale like I do.

CHAPTER 1

Ella

It's all white. Everything in the bridal suite is white.

I suppose that's the way weddings should be. Not that I would know. It's not my wedding.

The sound of zippers being zipped up and hairspray being sprayed mixes with the chatter spilling from smiling, red lips.

"The red is perfect," Sara says, but the bride doesn't hear. "It matches everything." *That* catches the bride's attention.

"Nothing is done." Her eyes are wide and nearly spilling tears. "There's not a thing set up upstairs."

The bridal suite is on the first floor and the wedding will be on the second floor of this reclaimed farmhouse.

I down the champagne still in my flute that I've been sipping to calm my nerves. Aiden's going to be here, standing only a few feet from me. With pictures being taken every minute, videographers and photographers too, there's no way I'll be able to deny what I feel for him when the pictures are printed. Aiden's always said he can read the truth in my eyes.

What's the saying? Wearing your emotions on your sleeve? I absolutely do that, and even if this dress doesn't have sleeves, my emotions will be there, ready to show every one of the guests at the wedding exactly how I feel for a long-lost ex. They know he was my everything and they think him going to war is what broke us apart.

But they don't know the truth.

"I'm sure they're getting everything set up. There are still five hours before the guests come, and they can set everything in half that amount of time," I quickly say to Viv, the bride, and my best friend. Her pale blue eyes whip to mine, pleading with me to tell her that's the absolute truth.

"Seriously, it doesn't take long and everything will be perfect."

"I don't think the cake is here yet," one of the other bridesmaids says as she walks into the suite. The phone in her hand has her attention as the door clicks shut and everyone stays silent, waiting for the bride to go off at one more setback, that's not at all a setback.

"I need to call her, right now." Viv storms off and away from me, her silk white robe clutched at her chest. So, I settle back in the corner, nestle in my chair, and pretend not to think of Aiden, the counterpart to me, and a groomsman in the wedding.

He came back a different man, but the man I love was still there. I've been desperate for the love we once had, but we can't show love for one another with our kinds of secrets.

"Hey." I hear Lauren before I see her, and then hear the champagne as she pours it into my empty flute. "You okay?"

Her makeup is flawless, a perfectly plucked brow raised as she waits for me to answer her, pulling a chair closer to me.

I have to clear my throat and take a sip of the sweet bubbly before I can look her in the eye.

"Just nerves," I answer her with a faint shrug and forced smile. "I swear I'm more nervous than Viv is," I joke.

Lauren's gaze wanders across my face, judging me for honesty, and I'm sure I fail her test. Her words are softly spoken, "You haven't been the same since the party last week."

A thump and a flutter compete in my heart and my throat closes as she asks, "Is it because of Aiden? I know you guys have been together on and off, right?"

She's pushing for answers; answers I won't give. I'm not ready to, not today of all days.

I won't do or say anything at all to make a scene at Viv's wedding. I would feel fucking awful if I did. She and Jason have been together since high school and this day is far overdue.

Lauren's right, though. I haven't been the same since the party. The joint bachelor and bachelorette party.

That night changed everything. I knew it would never be the same when I walked into the crowded room, but I only felt the presence of one man. Aiden's eyes were on me before I'd even slipped my pea coat off. As the thin wool slipped down my bare shoulders, I watched his gaze turn into that of a predator, sizing me up as his prey.

The music was loud, the laughter louder, but I swear I could hear how his breathing hitched. His crisp dress shirt pulled tighter across his broad shoulders and with his shirt sleeves rolled up, I could see how the muscles in his forearms tightened as he gripped the armrest when I walked past him to go to Lauren and Viv, in the far corner of the room.

They were focused on their martinis. I was focused on how Aiden's gray eyes pierced through me and how his tight grip turned his knuckles white.

I have to remind myself where I am and who I'm with before I let my thoughts get away from me. Slipping my hand to the dip in my throat and then lower, I let my fingers trace what's hanging on the end of my necklace, tucked just beneath the thin silk of the robe.

"I'm fine," I tell her shaking out my hands and plastering a wide smile onto my face. "Her being tense and anxious is just working me up."

"Okay, keep your secrets. I have a bet with Amy that you're fucking him, just so you know."

"She thinks you two fucked that night," Lauren's gaze stays glued to my face, waiting for a confirmation.

Although my heart races, I play along with Lauren's goading.

No one knows what happened the night of the party. And I don't know if I can keep this secret, one of many, for that long. Not when I know I'm going to see him.

"You two make the stupidest bets," I tell her with an evil grin and then lean in to confess to her in a hushed whisper, "And don't you know I'm a virgin?"

She outright laughs at my joke, even though it makes my heart pound harder.

"Nothing, absolutely nothing, is ready," Viv shrieks with a cracked voice before dropping her phone to the ground and falling onto the sofa across the bridal suite.

I take that as my cue, grateful for the distraction. Standing up abruptly, I'm quick to talk over everyone else, trying to comfort her.

"I'll go find the event coordinator right now." I can feel Lauren's eyes on me, but I ignore her and wrap the tie of my robe tighter so I can leave the room and feel somewhat decently covered. We all have matching scarlet robes, other than the bride's white one of course.

"What's her name again?" I ask.

"Sheryl," Viv's voice is weak but hopeful. She's not a bridezilla per say, but she's certainly emotional today.

"I'm sure everything is fine," I tell her and give her a small smile as I head to the door, "But I'll get a timeline and a checklist." With a firm nod, I exit and nearly collapse against the door. With my own emotions running wild, I lean against the hardwood and breathe for a moment, the faint chatter of voices muffled behind me, and the clanging of folding tables being set up echoing through the wooden ceiling above me.

Aiden is somewhere close. Somewhere smoking cigars and laughing with Jason, joking about how he's ending his bachelor days. I can do this I remind myself. I have to. After tonight, things will be different. No more hiding, no more secrets.

I don't know how they can't read it on my face.

I've kept secrets before, but not like this. But we all do foolish things for the ones we love.

CHAPTER 2

I'D RECOGNIZE HER VOICE IN A CROWD ANYWHERE, AT ANY TIME. Even the soft hum that spills from her lips when she's listening to a good story.

"And the centerpieces will be placed like this. She wants the larger candle on the inside," I hear Ella say calmly as I stand at the bottom of the stairwell. The florist gives me a simple smile as she continues to pin ivory tulle up along the railing. It looks like she's just gotten started.

I know the bridal suite is in the back, but I take the stairs one at a time, following the sweet voice as her words drift down the stairwell.

"I've got it all and it's all under control. Please tell her not to worry." A tall woman in a silver tweed suit with her hair up in a tight bun stands beside Ella as I peek around the corner, "It's all under control," she repeats.

My eyes drift to the short silk robe, and then lower to the tanned legs on full display.

"I told her that already, but now that I've talked to you, I'm sure she'll feel better," Ella smiles, her long brunette hair already pinned up and braided. Just seeing that gorgeous smile and the flush of her cheeks tugs at the corner of my lips. My gaze drifts down her chest to her slender fingers, and my cock hardens instantly.

I lose control around Ella, I always have. She has a way of bringing out a side of me that's possessive and unpredictable.

I'd do anything to have her and keep her. But what she does to me…

I groan low and deep in my chest as I watch the staff leave her all alone in the expansive room upstairs. There's not a soul in sight but her.

My jaw clenches, remembering how I lost control at the party, in the back laundry room.

Everything in the last two years disappeared into nothing and all I knew was that I needed her to be mine again.

I wanted everyone to know it. I wanted them to hear her scream my name. Instead, she clawed down my back and sank her teeth into my neck, leaving a bruised mark as I fucked her ruthlessly.

Precum leaks from me while remembering how good it felt to have her against the wall, pounding into her tight cunt while everyone we knew was just beyond a thin wall.

Before I can turn the corner, two men carrying a large white box enter, their simple black shirts have a cake on the front of them. And on cue, Ella claps her hands in delight, elated that the wedding cake has arrived.

"I'll go tell the bride," she tells them with a pep in her step that I haven't seen in so long. A darkness has clouded my judgment for years. I didn't know enlisting in the Army would change everything. Not just how I felt about Ella, but how I feel about myself and everything I've done.

I never questioned whether or not I would love her still. I always knew I would. There's nothing that could have taken me from her, or so I thought.

Ella disappears down a small hall, heading down the back stairwell, and so I turn around, going back the way I came.

Running a hand down the stubble of my jaw, I take the path that leads me to her. Taking my time so she'll be there before I am. *Although, I didn't come for her*, I have to remind myself.

My knuckles rapped against the door to the suite, knock knock knock.

"Who is it?" a few voices call out at once and someone tells me, "If it's the groom tell him to fuck off. He can't see her yet!"

A genuine smile is stamped on my face when the door opens two inches. "I'm serious," Lauren says, and I respond, "It's just me. Should I fuck off too?"

She cocks a brow and takes a peek behind her. I know she's looking to find Ella and the smile slips. Soon they'll look at us differently. They'll never understand, but they won't deny what she is to me.

Soon everything will go back to the way it was supposed to be.

"Her husband-to-be isn't anywhere near." I pick up the small black, velvet box from my pocket and hold it in front of me, "I just have a gift."

Vivian pushes Lauren out of the way, pulling the door open wider and staring up at me with wide eyes, "From Jason?" she asks breathlessly.

My brow cocks as I say, "Maybe 'gift' was the wrong word." I clear my throat and give her a tight smile as the excitement drains from her expression. "I was told the ring was needed. For the ring bearer?" Jason needed someone to deliver it, and I was more than happy to oblige.

I'm not sure Vivian ever liked me, even though Jason was my best friend for as long as I can remember. She took him away when we were in high school, but she gave me something in return during our first year of college.

Ella. Her friend she thought would hit it off with me. She had no idea how right she would be. Sweet and quiet, but full of vulnerability, Ella was perfect for me. It only took a single date, a single kiss to know it. Even if she did make me wait for months to have her.

Still, she was perfect and I knew one day she'd be my wife.

The thought splinters the barely-healed crack in my heart. The pain of losing her never leaves.

Vivian turns her back to me, searching in a large cardboard box for something, not bothering to tell me to come in, so I stand where I am, waiting.

When I broke up with Ella, knowing it was what I needed to do when I came back from the war, Viv didn't hide her hate for me. And I get it. She found out who I was related to on the same day. Ella told her everything, so she knew the moment that Ella knew. A sad smile tugs at my lips. Viv didn't know everything of course. How could she? She wasn't Ella; she couldn't read the truth between the lines like Ella could.

I wish I could take it back. I wish I could change it all.

It took years of therapy to learn you can never go back. You can only take advantage of the day you're living. Tomorrow is never promised.

"I'll take that," the bride's sister-in-law tells me, slipping closer to me and yanking the box from my hand. It's her son that'll be walking down the aisle. "I've already got the box," she tells me.

I can feel Ella's gaze on me, begging me to look at her, to speak to her, to give her more than I am now.

Scratching the back of my head and attempting to make Viv a friend again, I tell her, "You look beautiful, Viv. The blushing bride suits you well."

As if she truly wanted to play the part, she blushes shyly. "He's going to go crazy when he sees you," I add.

"We have a bet going that he's going to cry," Lauren says, leaning against the back wall and grinning.

"Do you really think so?" she asks genuinely and I nod.

"He's lucky to have you, Viv," I tell her and mean it. What they have is love. I know exactly what it feels like and what it looks like. When you can't go to sleep because you only want to sleep next to one person who's miles away. When you hear their voice and everything else goes quiet so you can focus on the cadence of their voice and try to remember the sound for as long as you can. Jason didn't join the Army; he didn't go through a long-distance relationship like Ella and I did. But he looks at Viv the same way I used to look at Ella.

The way I'm trying not to now.

My gaze scans the room and I tell them all, "You all look stunning." My eyes land on her, on Ella, as I watch as those sweet lips part and add, "Gorgeous."

CHAPTER 3

THE CAMERA FLASHES AS WE ALL STAND AROUND VIV IN FRONT of the window. The light floats across her features beautifully, highlighting the dress we're holding up.

My fingers pinch the zipper, half way up, as we pose for another shot. The camera clicks and flashes before the photographer looks down at it and then tells us she got the shot.

My heart hammers the closer we get to the wedding, but the buzz of champagne and the happiness clearly evident in everything Viv does is addictive.

I'm happy she's happy.

I want that happiness too.

"It's so beautiful on you," I tell Viv as I pull the zipper up and slip the fastener into place. "This dress looks like it was made for you." The lace and the deep V-neck, it's just stunning.

"My cheeks already hurt from smiling," Viv says teary-eyed. She's done a one-eighty in the last two hours. Ever since the crew started putting her dream wedding into place.

I had a dream wedding planned once. We'd been together for almost three years. It made sense to start thinking about church bells and all the white lace I could dream up.

Until Aiden broke my heart; twice.

The first time when he left me, volunteering to fight in the Army alongside his cousins and brother. Leaving me pining for him and worried every night of the two years he was gone. And bringing up memories I'd longed buried.

The second time was when he came back with his cousin in a casket and told me it was over. To stop sending him letters. I saw a broken man who needed love. He saw a way to hide in his regret, his pain, and even his anger.

I believe in true love and fate. And that's why I held on. He was the only one who knew me. Who really knew me.

In a world where I knew I didn't quite fit in, he was my counter. My other half.

I let him come in and out of my life. Sneaking in late at night to hold me and fuck me, but never giving me anything other than pleasure in the dark.

The first night, I don't know if he was aware that I knew he'd come in.

I heard the door open, the creak stopped me from crying so hard. It was only days after the funeral. Days after he'd ended it, even though I'd sent him letters for years, and he'd sent them in return.

He wasn't going back to war; his time was over. But he wasn't coming back to me either.

I gave him a key and told him I knew why he didn't want to see me, but that it was okay. I was forever attached to a sin that he struggled to accept. But that didn't change how I felt about him, or how he felt about me.

He crept into the bedroom, as quiet as he could be. I still remember closing my eyes and pretending to sleep. I don't know how long he sat in the chair, but I know he cried quietly.

I gripped the comforter, wanting to go to him, but I knew that's not what he wanted. The next night it happened, I wouldn't let him cry alone. Even if he didn't want to tell me what'd happened.

Even though he let me hold him that night, it took days before he came back and when he did, he told me not to let anyone know. That night I cried with him, for both of us, but agreed to keep his secret.

The moment I did, he kissed me like he was starved for me. He whispered along the crook of my neck that he never wanted to see me in pain, that he never wanted to miss me again.

But he lied to me, he would miss me again. And I would miss him. Because he only came every so often, and we went about our lives separately, keeping up the rumors that after years of waiting for him to return, he broke my heart and left me.

Some would call it pathetic, that I would let a man come and go, not giving me anything other than his heart at night.

But secrets have layers that run deep. Just as he needed me, I needed him, and that's a truth no one can deny.

CHAPTER 4

I'VE BEEN WAITING HERE FOR NEARLY HALF AN HOUR, WAITING FOR her to sneak out of the reception. The night air is crisp and sends a soothing chill up my jacket sleeves as I lean against the brick wall just outside of the back exit.

There's no one here as the sun sets along the trees of the forest behind the old brick building.

The crickets are louder than the music that drifts through the walls, and I know she could scream my name out here and none of them would hear it.

The door creaks open, the rusty hinges giving her away, my Ella, as she slips outside. Peeking up through her lashes, her hazel eyes are filled with nothing but desire.

"I thought you might be out here," she whispers and all I can do is watch her plump lips as she talks. I want them swollen like they are after a brutal kiss.

"I thought you'd never come," I tell her pushing off the wall.

"You lie," she whispers as I make my way to her, not bothering to wait for her to walk down the stairs. The steel steps clank as I walk up to her, wrapping my hands around her waist and pulling her in close to me.

"Never to you," I whisper against her lips before taking them. My fingers dig into the silk of her dress as I nip her lower lip and then groan at the sound of her moaning in my mouth.

"Tell me you're ready for me," I command her and then leave

open-mouthed kisses down her neck. I bunch the fabric of her dress up as I move my way down her body.

"Here?" she gasps, although her fingers spear through my hair as I cup her pussy through the thin lace hiding it from me.

"Fuck." The word rumbles up my chest, my cock instantly hard. "I can feel how much you want me; you're so fucking wet." My body is on fire, every nerve ending springing to life knowing I'll have her soon.

"Aiden." My name on her lips is a plea as I push her back against the brick wall. I muffle her protests with a hard kiss.

I can feel her chest heave in a breath when I finally break the kiss and lift her legs to wrap around my waist. Her neck arches back as I trail my fingers up and down her cunt before hooking the lace with my thumb and shredding it. It tears easily and leaves her bared to me.

"I wish I had time to savor you," I confess at the dip in her throat as I shove her panties into my pocket so no evidence will be left behind.

"Tonight," she whispers reverently in the cool air as I unzip my pants and stroke myself.

The head of my cock slips between her lips and it feels like heaven. "I've waited for you all day," I tell her as rub my tip against her clit. She writhes against the wall, her eyes closed tightly and she silences her moans by sinking her teeth into her bottom lip.

"Look at me," I demand and instantly her hazel gaze pierces mine and I thrust into her in one motion, all the way to the hilt. Her legs tense around me, her mouth drops open into that beautiful 'O' and I stay buried deep inside of her tight cunt to let her adjust.

"Aiden," she whimpers as her nails dig in deeper, trying to pierce my skin even through my jacket.

"Ella," I breathe her name back to her in the hot air, lost in her gaze until I can thrust into her again.

Her back tries to arch against the wall and I have to grip her wrists, holding them above her head, so I can pin her where I want her. One hand on her hip, the other on her wrists, I fuck her ruthlessly against the brick wall.

Her cunt spasms without warning and my toes curl, my balls draw up, but I refuse to let go. Holding my breath, I watch her cum, the blush rising up her cheeks, and her chest rising and falling with her chaotic breathing.

"I love you," she whispers in the night air. All I've ever done is love her. It's myself I couldn't love for so long. How could I not have known?

"Where is it?" I ask her, needing to see it. I have to see it right now. I have to know it means to her what it does to me.

"My necklace," she gasps as I rock myself into her, brushing her clit as I do.

Pulling on the thin chain of her necklace, the rings appear on the end of it. The engagement ring and wedding band. The set that was my grandmother's and now belongs to her.

The wedding rings I didn't want anyone to see, but the rings I needed her to have. That night she left the party, I wanted to leave beside her. I needed her hand in mine and for everyone to see. Instead, I watched her walk away until she reached for the keys to her car.

I decided at the moment I saw her pause at her door, the keys jingling in her hand, that my place was beside her and I couldn't hide anymore. I'm not the only one with secrets, and I know if mine is ever known, it may bring up her own. Still, she deserves more than what I'd given her, she deserved every piece of me. After all, she already had every piece I could spare in her back pocket. So, I grabbed her hand and pulled her away, and married her that night.

I made the woman I've always loved my wife. The world has yet to see it, but tonight she'll leave with me.

The light shines on the platinum bands as they fall to her chest and I let go of her wrists, letting my hands roam back up her dress so I can fuck her savagely, taking what's mine.

Her heels dig into my ass and she kisses me frantically as I piston my hips. I cum with her and only break away after her breathing has calmed and she can bear to stand on her own. I watch her as she sags against the wall and she watches me.

She's mine. She's always been mine.

"I love you too," I finally tell her and lick my lower lip to kiss her one more time, before smoothing her dress back down and helping her to fix her hair.

"You're the one who said we should hide it," she reminds me as I slip the rings back into place, hidden beneath the neckline of her dress.

"You're the one who said it would be wrong to elope just before our best friends' wedding," I counter. I'm ready for the world to know again. They can't know what happened in between. I wish I could erase it all, but that will never happen.

Ella whispers, "I don't want to hide anymore." And for the first time in years, I think it's safe. I'm willing to risk it. I need her back in every way.

"Thank you for loving me," I tell her as my throat gets tight with emotion, remembering how she said 'I do' at the courthouse. "For never stopping sending me letters." The letters held it all together. I wouldn't have known that she truly loved me without them. That she could look past the pain just to hold on to me.

"I told you I'd love you through the war. I know sometimes it doesn't end just because you came home." Her bottom lip wobbles and I know why.

"You know it was more than that," I whisper to her. Only the second time I've dared to hint at the truth allowed. But it's Ella, and she knows it was all for her. I would do anything for her.

She never told me what my cousin had done to her, but she didn't have to. I could see it in her eyes that day.

He hurt her, so I hurt him back.

The Army taught me how to kill; love taught me the power of vengeance.

Burying my head in the crook of her neck, I hold on to Ella, wrapping my arms around her waist and pulling her small body into my chest.

"You know I love you. I could never stop loving you," she whispers.

"For the rest of my life, I'm yours."

Our love story is dark and twisted, haunted by a past we didn't choose. But it doesn't make it anything less than the purest of loves.

EPILOGUE

Ella

Some secrets are worth keeping. Just as is some love.

The day I found out who Aiden's cousin was, as they sat together ready to enlist, is the day everything changed between us. He was my only, my everything, for years before. And in my heart, my first.

I've never told anyone what his cousin did to me, except the night it happened, but Aiden knew without speaking the truth. I didn't tell him; I didn't think he'd believe me. The way no one else had. Drunk at a party and underage with college boys, I should have known better. That's what they said to me back then. I didn't want Aiden to look at me the same way.

And so I never said a word.

The moment I saw his cousin, I squeezed Aiden's hand and struggled to breathe as it all came back to me. I couldn't hide my fear and shame.

Aiden left that week, the look in his eye changed and that day, I thought everything would be ruined forever.

I had no idea what would happen, or the man Aiden would be when he came back. I never stopped writing him letters, or worrying that he'd stop loving me.

He didn't tell me what he'd done when he came home, but just as he knew my secret, I knew his when his cousin's casket was lowered to the ground.

Neither of us could voice them and these secrets separated us. Almost broke us.

He struggled with the pain of what'd happened to me, but also what he'd done. He stayed away, not wanting to risk what would happen to me if we were together when his secret came to life.

I remember how he whispered in the dark when he realized I knew, *"If they find out, I'll never tell why. Promise me, you'll let me take the fall and never speak a word."* When I promised him, I wouldn't say a thing, and I'd stay his secret until the case was closed, I made a promise to myself as well, to never lie to him again.

But they never found out. No one knows and now he's come back to me.

Love has a way of turning you into a person you never thought you could be.

It takes time and distance to recover. More than that, it takes love. I would never have stopped loving Aiden, before or after the war, before knowing how close our secrets were.

People wait for love.

People die for love.

People kill for love, too.

Some secrets are worth keeping. And I'll keep his secrets forever, just as he kept mine.

But after tonight, no more secrets. I want our love back, to be his and for everyone to know it, always and forever.

BAD BOY
NEXT DOOR

CHAPTER 1

MY CHOPPER SLOWS, AND I PLANT MY FOOT DOWN IN THE gravel. The crunch of my boot and the October breeze blowing against my face make me grin.

I'm a good distance away from the address the boys gave me, and I take a hard look at it.

This place is fucking insane. It's not a house. It's a mansion. The corner of my lips kick up into a grin. This is gonna be one hell of a party.

I've got this damn coat on for this party, but it's a bit too hot for it. I didn't have anything else to wear for the Halloween party. I'm not one for dressing up in costume, but I'm not gonna ruin the vibe of the party either. So this jacket means I'm a hunter. That's as dressed up as I'm getting.

I wasn't gonna come even though the boys all invited me. But then I heard Catherine was gonna be there. It's a college party, although it's at some mansion owned by two professors that are brothers. I wasn't invited by the professors directly, so I guess technically I'm crashing the party.

And I haven't laid eyes on Catherine since I took off. I moved out two years ago and never looked back. Leaving my shit parents behind and getting my life on track is exactly what I needed to do.

I huff a laugh as I kick my bike back to life and feel the vibrations under my ass. They made sure I knew I was nothing but trouble growing up. And that's exactly what I am, but I'll keep it to myself.

I've got a business to run now, and clients that fucking love my choppers.

My parents can get fucked for all I care. I've moved on and accepted we'll never see eye to eye.

But that's not the part that sucked when I left.

It was not having my eyes on the good girl next door anymore. Catherine Parker. She's two years younger than me, and I never thought much of her as we grew up together, to be honest. Then one day, shortly after she turned seventeen, something shifted inside of me.

Suddenly she had curves where she didn't before. Her tank top would ride up, and the only thing I wanted to do was pull it off and get a better look at her sun-kissed bare skin. I was nineteen though, so I kept my distance.

I'd also just gotten my job at the mechanic shop and started realizing what real life was, and how abusive my parents truly were. I wanted to get out, but I can't deny that knowing she was right next door kept me there longer than it should have.

The day I left she was outside on her porch as I grabbed the two boxes of stuff I owned and put them in the back of my buddy's car.

That was two years ago, and I didn't take the chance to make her mine. I should have, but she wasn't even eighteen yet. And I was almost twenty. Besides, I was no good for her. I truly believed that back then. I wanted to ravage her, ruin her for any other man. I wanted to make her mine.

I'd never felt that way before, and that fear of wanting to completely dominate her and own her kept me from taking her right then. I didn't want to destroy her. I didn't wanna bring her down to my level.

Times have changed though, and I wanna get a good look at Catherine now.

Jake and Levi know her from classes at the university. I'm making their custom bikes, and I happened to overhear her name. I know I'm not one of them. Shit, they're jocks, and I'm a mechanic. But we share the love of bikes and that gives them a good name in my book.

The wrench slipped right out of my hand as her name rolled off his lips. I've been working on bikes for nearly six years; it's what kept me out of trouble all those years ago. But hearing her name got me so worked up, I couldn't remember how to do a damn thing. Lucky for him she was just his study partner. If her name had been dropped in any other way… I'm not sure what I would've done.

Being reminded of her brought back all those memories. It brought back a sense of regret. But everything happens for a reason. I hadn't wanted to leave the way I did, but I had to get away from my parents. And now I'm a better man. I still wanna ruin her though. That shit hasn't changed.

Hearing her name made me work a little faster to get those bikes done and keep in touch with them.

They said she'd be here. I wasn't too subtle about asking how she's doing. I'm sure they know what's up, but that's good, because I want everyone to know.

I'm known for getting what I want even if I have to destroy everything in my path to get it. And I want her. I've waited too damn long.

I park my bike and stride toward the mansion with purpose. Tonight she's getting a taste of the bad boy next door.

CHAPTER 2

Catherine

I TAKE ANOTHER SIP OF CHAMPAGNE AND LEAN AGAINST THE WALL of the dimly lit dining room. The music of the party is pumping, and the bass is making the walls vibrate slightly. I didn't have much to eat before I started drinking, and now I'm starting to get a buzz. I should be alright though. I had some of those pumpkin pie bites when I came in here.

I look over my shoulder to the foyer. I'm waiting. I've been waiting and staring at those damn doors ever since I got here. I feel slightly sick to my stomach with nerves. Maybe this buzz isn't from the alcohol at all.

I should be studying for my calculus test. I shouldn't even be at this party. But I had to know if he was really going to come.

I heard Ryker's going to be here.

My parents warned me to stay away from him. He comes from bad blood, they said. But they don't see him the way I do. Still, I know he'd only want me for a night. I can't give in to those fantasies. He's never wanted me anyway.

One of the football guys said he's coming. I've been helping Levi in class. I don't mind being his study partner. But when he started talking about Ryker Dean I swear I couldn't focus on anything else. I'm supposed to be Levi's study partner, but when we get together all I wanna do is ask about what Ryker's been up to. I can't believe he's got his own business now. He always loved motorcycles. I'm so fucking happy for him. But my heart still hurts.

He left me years ago and never said a damn word. It's not like I was entitled to even a simple goodbye, but it broke something inside of me when he left.

I feel pathetic for being so worked up over hearing his name. I'm no one to him. I should know better by now. I know all too well that men are assholes.

I take a deep breath and settle myself down. Not all men are assholes, and just because Ryker left doesn't make him an asshole.

After all, I would've left too if I had his parents. It hurts my heart to think about everything he went through. He was right there, right next door. I could hear them yelling all the time. It wasn't right. That's what my mom used to say. A few times she wanted to go over there, but Dad held her back.

He'd had words with Ryker's father more than a time or two. It put a stop to some of it, but not for long. Words weren't enough. Even calling the police when we heard them fighting didn't do a thing.

I clear my throat, trying to shut down the bad memories. I'm glad Ryker left. He didn't deserve that.

Maybe that's why I've felt like my heart belongs to Ryker. In a lot of ways, it does. I was right there hurting for him, but I couldn't do anything. I was just a girl. I wish I had been stronger. I wish I could've gone over there and stopped his parents from beating on him and saying all those awful things to him.

"Whatever mood you're in," Khloe begins, interrupting my thoughts as she points the cigarette holder in my face, "Knock it out." I stare back at her and bite my tongue.

She's wearing *my* costume. I wanted to be Audrey Hepburn. I was the one who bought that costume. I should've said no when she asked to wear it. She does this shit all the time. She twirls the pearls around her finger, *my pearls*, and purses her lips. "Come on. We're here to get drunk and get laid. And no one's going to come around us with that sad look on your face."

She tilts the champagne flute in my hand up toward my mouth. "Drink up!"

I got stuck with a shit roommate. A really shitty roommate. Next semester I'm moving out. She's so selfish, and somehow she always convinces me to give her whatever she wants.

I have to live with her, so I don't want to rock the boat. I'll just deal with this shit for one more month. One and a half, to be precise.

I throw back the small glass of champagne.

It's actually really good. And at least Khloe got me thinking about something else for a change. I don't need to think about Ryker or anything else other than relaxing tonight.

Just as the thought enters my head, I look over to the doors and see him standing there.

My lips part and I have to bite down on the inside of my cheek as my eyes travel over his masculine body.

Ryker looks different from when I saw him last, but in the best of ways.

He's taller, and his shoulders are broader and more built. He shrugs off the camo jacket he's wearing, and his clean white t-shirt is snug around his frame and thick biceps.

He runs a hand through his dark hair and and walks over to Levi and the other guys hanging around the table plated up with hors d'oeuvres. I was munching on them earlier. Liam and Marcel really went all out. It's a bit odd calling the Henderson professors by their first names. It's strange even being here for this party. But I fucking love it. It's thrilling to get out and have some fun.

I need to do this more often. But large parties just aren't my scene.

I hear Ryker's deep rough laugh as someone jokes about him coming in costume.

He shrugs his shoulders with a sexy grin on his face. "I'm a hunter." Hearing his voice again after all these years makes my heart skip a beat in my chest and my pussy heat with anticipation.

"What the fuck is he doing here?" Khloe spits out. I cringe just hearing her voice.

Ryker's head whips over to us just as I turn to tell her off.

My body freezes as I feel his eyes on me.

I feel like a nervous little girl all over again. I nervously try to pull my long hair into a ponytail. It's a stupid habit I have, but I forgot I'm wearing a damn headband with bunny ears, and it slips down off my head and over my eyes.

Stupid fucking ears.

I curse under my breath and try to compose myself as Khloe laughs.

I was a rabbit last year. I felt so cute. The ears are white, and I had a cute white dress with a puff on the butt for my bunny tail. I did my own makeup, all cute with little dots and whiskers.

But I spilled something on the dress, staining it at the end of the night last year.

And since Khloe came to me last minute, crying about not having a costume, I'm just in a white tank top and jeans. I don't even have a cute little puff on the butt. I just pulled these ears out of the back of the closet instead of getting a new pair. She should've been the damn bunny.

I did put some pink lipstick on the tip of my nose and drew whiskers on my face using eyeliner. But I don't feel nearly as pretty in this getup compared to last year's.

My cheeks heat with a blush. He's going to see me like this.

My fingers fly to my face to check if my makeup's okay. Which is stupid as fuck, 'cause as I look down at my fingertips which are now covered in black eyeliner, I'm sure all I did was smudge it.

I need to get to a bathroom ASAP. Khloe starts to say something while rolling her eyes, but I ignore her and head straight to the kitchen. I know there's a bathroom nearby.

As I walk away from her, I hear Levi call out my name. My blood heats, and I almost trip in these heels. No way. I am not going over there like this. It's been years since I've seen Ryker, and I need to make sure I don't look like a mess. Even if that's what I feel I am right now.

I keep walking straight ahead and pretend like I don't hear him. I don't stop until I reach the bathroom, quickly closing the door and leaning against it, sagging in relief. Holy shit.

He's really here. A broad smile covers my face as I push off the door and go right to the mirror. I slide the strap of my clutch off my wrist and pull out my eyeliner.

This is gonna be an easy fix.

I breathe out deeply and shake out my nerves. The smile on my face won't go away. I'm finally going to put my big girl panties on and make sure Ryker knows exactly how I feel about him.

CHAPTER 3

MY HEARTBEATS FEEL LIKE WEAK FLICKERS IN MY CHEST. I know she saw me. I fucking know she did. And what'd she do? She turned and walked away as fast as she fucking could.

Maybe I'm remembering all this wrong. I thought she was into me back then.

Maybe she's pissed. After all, I did up and leave without saying a damn word to her. Maybe she's just grown up and realized I'm not good for her.

That thought fucking hurts. Mostly because it's true.

When we were younger, I used to help her get through the woods in the back of our development. I knew I couldn't have her, but whenever she asked me for help, I couldn't say no.

She wanted a shortcut to the strip mall right behind the woods. So I made one for her. It took a few days, but I made her a nice little path. She was too scared to go by herself, and I used to hang out at the mall anyway, so I didn't mind escorting her. I used to wait for her to come knock on our back door during the week. My parents were hardly ever home until later in the day. Much later. And she was so predictable, coming by every day at four.

If my parents were home, she'd come out her back door late at night and throw rocks at my window to get my attention. She'd ask all sweet and shy if I was gonna go with her the next time she planned on making a trek. She always apologized. She never got over that, even the last time we went. I remember how she looked up at me with vulnerability in her eyes, expecting me to be annoyed or just say no.

I never did. I would never tell her no.

She was so fucking cute. If only she knew how much I looked forward to seeing her.

It was a guilty pleasure of mine. I knew I could never have her. She was too sweet and innocent, and I was just a lowlife who'd never amount to anything.

But I could at least enjoy her company and pretend like there was more between us.

That was years ago, and back then she didn't know any better.

She should know better now than to let me have a taste of her. My heart plummets in my chest, all the way down to my stomach. She does know better. That has to be why she walked away.

I don't realize I'm staring until Levi shoves a beer in my hand. It's ice cold, and the condensation on the outside of the bottle almost makes it slip from my grasp.

The guys are all looking at me, and I wanna smack the shit out of them.

"What?" I ask in a hard voice.

"Guess she didn't hear me," Levi says and shrugs. She heard him. Just like I heard that chick with the pearls ask what I was doing here. I think I recognize her from somewhere, but I can't place her. Maybe she was friends with Catherine back when I used to live next door. I don't remember any of her friends being like that toward me back then, but that chick in the pearls sure as fuck doesn't like me now.

This was a fucking waste of time. I shouldn't be here trying to blend in when I don't belong.

I open my mouth to come up with some excuse to bail, but Jake throws his arm around my shoulders. He's got his fake vampire teeth in his mouth, and it keeps throwing me off every time he smiles.

"She just went to powder her nose." His breath smells like beer as he leans into me and laughs. At first I'm pissed they're having a good laugh about it, but then he adds, "You gotta tell him what she said, Levi."

My heart does that stupid nervous shit again and I take a drink of my beer with my eyes on Levi. Jake chuckles and pats my back hard as I bring my arm back down. I don't want them to know how on edge I am. But damn, I really am sweating this.

I didn't realize how much I wanted her until right now. Until the idea that she didn't want me back popped into my head. I fucking hope that's not the case. I want her.

Levi's grin spreads across his face. "Dude, she fucking *wants* you."

"She said that?" The words spill out of my mouth, and I can't help it. They come out fast, and the guys have a good laugh over it. I let out a sigh and turn my head back to look to where she left the dining room.

Levi looks me dead in the eyes and says, "Fuck no. You think she'd just come out and say it?"

I huff and let the irritation grow on my face.

"Relax, bro. She *wants* you." Jake draws out the word and I just stare back at him.

"If you're fucking with me, I'm gonna beat the shit out of you," I say, deadpan.

Jake pats my shoulder and urges, "Go get her, man. I can't fucking stand the fact I lost the bet."

My blood heats, and I resist the urge to clench my fists. They made a bet about my girl?

"He bet that you'd be fucking her in a bathroom by now," Levi says with a grin.

"I knew you'd be classy and at least talk to her first," Mickey says to my left. This guy barely knows me, but at least he thinks I'm classy.

"It's so damn obvious you two want each other. Just go get her already." Levi's got a grin plastered on his face as he waits for me to respond. *Just go get her.* Like it's that easy. He must see the hesitation on my face.

"Will you two shut the fuck up if I go talk to her?" I ask them.

They all laugh and a smile finally cracks on my face. She wants me. Alright, I'm gonna go find her and get the girl I've wanted for so long. I down the rest of my beer and pass the empty bottle to Levi. He takes it and nods toward the dining room, which leads to the kitchen.

"Yeah, yeah, I know where she went."

Levi reaches his hand out to Jake, and Jake shakes his head. "No, we gotta make sure he gets laid, or you don't get paid." I chuckle as they get into it and take my leave.

As I make my way to the kitchen where Catherine went, a cute little cheerleader with glasses walks by. I look back over my shoulder at the guys as the argument ceases and they fall quiet. Jake's eyes are all over that ass. Those assholes can make fun of me all day, but I know they're just as caught up in getting their girls as I am.

CHAPTER 1

Catherine

I GET ONLY TWO STEPS OUT OF THE BATHROOM WHEN MY HEART stops at a voice behind me.

"Did you really come here as a kitten?" I recognize Ryker's voice instantly, and it does things to my lower regions I'm ashamed to admit.

I turn with my clutch held tightly in my hand. My heart swells in my chest. I give him a small smile, and feel a blush rise to my cheeks. It's almost like time hasn't passed. He's leaning against the wall and kicks off it, shoving his hands in his pockets before he walks over to me.

I try to remember what he asked and when I do, I roll my eyes and say, "I'm a bunny." I point to the ears. They're long and look nothing like cat ears. I love how it feels like we're just picking up where we left off though. It feels so natural talking to him. A stupid little voice that gives me false hope is screaming, *It's a sign! It's a sign!* I'm trying to shut it down, but I can't.

He huffs a small laugh. "I'm a hunter. I think you're in dangerous territory."

I scoff at him. "A cameo jacket makes you a hunter?" I involuntarily roll my eyes. Men hate this holiday.

He cocks a brow. "You do like to roll your eyes at me, don't you?" he asks in a low, threatening voice. It's a voice that would send shivers of fear through most people, but not to me. I know who he really is.

When we were younger and in his backyard, I saw his true colors. I saw him change into the bad boy everyone thinks he is at a moment's notice. Like he was putting on a facade.

Once I'd dropped an entire box of decorations for my parents' anniversary. A few tissue paper pompoms I wanted to hang from the deck blew over into the neighbor's yard, into his yard.

I was only fourteen at the time and he was a few years older, but I wanted him to notice me. My hormones were in full swing, as were the pimples on my face. And my mother wouldn't let me wear makeup. I cringe, remembering that fact about my childhood. How could I not want him though? He had a motorcycle, and his right arm was covered with tattoos. He'd clean up the weeds in their front yard without his shirt on, and those lean muscles and deep "V" at his hips made him the star of my dreams at night.

He never looked my way though, not that I expected him to. Of course he wouldn't have. I was the pimply, naïve girl next door. But that day he was out back with low-hung jeans and a tight white t-shirt that fit snugly over his broad shoulders. And my mom's pink tissue pompom flew right over to him.

My heart stopped in my chest as he bent down with his muscles rippling and picked it up, raising one brow and looking at me with the corner of his lips kicked up into a smirk.

I apologized and nervously tucked my dirty blonde hair behind my ear. I'm sure I was blushing, for no good reason other than I was thinking naughty things I knew I shouldn't have been.

He just chuckled and offered to help me decorate. 'Cause that's the kind of guy he is.

I remember that day just like yesterday.

I wasn't tall enough to reach the deck, so he helped me. I just sat on the concrete porch and watched the sweat glisten on his sun-kissed body. I felt like a pervert creeping on him, but he didn't look at me like that. No matter how much I wanted him to.

And then my father came outside.

In an instant, Ryker's features went sharp and dark as my dad bitched him out. He told him to get out, and stay out. I was mortified. He was only helping me. My heart tried to climb up my throat, and I didn't say anything. I felt like a traitor. Like I'd betrayed him.

Ryker dropped the pompom and shrugged like he didn't care. But I could see it in his eyes. It was wrong. I cried my eyes out and yelled at my dad after he'd left, but the damage was done.

I'll never understand how my father could talk to him like that when he knew just as well as I did the shit his parents put him through. But then again, my dad yelled at me, too. He said I should know better. I wasn't allowed to date boys, and especially not THAT boy. I knew what I'd done was wrong. But Ryker hadn't done a damn thing wrong. That was years ago, and he's definitely not a bad boy… he's a bad man now. Or at least that's how he looks.

I know he's still the same at heart. Even if he doesn't look the part.

"I do like rolling my eyes at you," I say back in a flirty voice. Normally I'd be embarrassed by how apparent it is that I'm into him. But I've got a nice buzz going on now. It's not like he'd ever make a move on me anyway. A waiter passes us with a fresh tray of champagne glasses, and I snag one off of it. I give him a small smile and clutch onto the drink for dear life.

I need liquid courage.

"I like to see you get all wound up," I say in a lowered voice, looking up through my thick lashes. I'm going all in. I hope it came out as sexy as I think it did.

Ryker's eyes heat and narrow as he tries to hold my gaze. I slowly lick my lips and bite down on the bottom one. It does exactly what I'd hoped it would. His eyes focus in on my mouth and I can practically see his dick jump in his pants.

Yeah, I'm not a pimply little girl anymore. Look at me now, Ryker.

"Careful what you're doing, kitten. You're gonna get in trouble." He takes a step forward and part of me wants to instinctively step back. He's trouble with a capital T. But that's not happening tonight. I take a step forward, closing in a bit more. I could reach out and run my hands down his muscular chest if I wanted to. Well, I do want to. My pussy clenches around nothing.

"I told you, I'm a bunny, not a cat." I shake my head and slowly bring my drink to my lips. I don't even taste it as I take a swallow and keep my eyes on his the entire time. "You should listen to me sometime, Ryker."

"That's not why I'm calling you kitten. And you should watch that mouth. You're really," he says as his large body cages me in, "gonna get your ass in trouble talking to me like that."

"By who? My dad's not here, Ryker." I surprise myself with how seductive my voice comes out. I must be *really* buzzed.

Ryker takes another step closer to me, and now we're so close we're only a few inches apart. He lowers his head and drops his lips down to my ear. His breath is hot against my neck, sending shivers down my spine. I close my eyes and tilt my head slightly. This is a fucking dream come true.

My heartbeat slows, and my lungs fill with his masculine scent.

But before the words fall from his lips, I hear a voice and my eyes pop open.

"Get away from her!" Khloe shrieks.

CHAPTER 5

"**W**HAT THE FUCK, KHLOE?!" CATHERINE YELLS BACK AT THE bitch in the pearls. I take a step back as Khloe grips Catherine's arm and yanks her away from me. Catherine's drink spills and splashes on my jeans and the floor. She looks back at her friend with pure rage on her face.

My heart beats frantically, and I resist the urge to pull Catherine back to me.

She's *mine*.

In my head she is, but in reality, I have no claim on her. And she sure isn't the sweet little thing next door anymore. The years apart have only made her more beautiful, and confident, and brazen.

I fucking love it.

The chick tries to pull Catherine away even though my kitten is fighting it.

They're talking in angry whispers, and Khloe pulls her farther away from me, trying to get her out of earshot.

Catherine rips her arm from her friend's grip and looks back at her with disgust.

"Get away from him!" Khloe says loud enough for me to hear. Khloe's eyes keep darting from me to her, but Catherine's focused on her friend.

"What are you thinking?" Khloe screeches.

I barely hear Catherine reply. "What are you doing?" she practically hisses.

"A guy like that is a lowlife thug. He's the type of guy you fuck for a night, and then you're done." Catherine's eyes go wide. I take in a slow breath and try to let the fact that she doesn't defend me roll off my shoulders. But I'd be lying if I said I was successful.

"You deserve so much better than that prick. He may be good for one lay, but you'd feel like shit afterward." Catherine turns her body slightly, rocking on her heels and says something I can't hear. "Trust me, I'm saving you."

There's a pause for a long moment while Khloe rubs Catherine's back, like she's consoling her. I start to get this sick feeling in the pit of my stomach. Like that's really what Catherine wanted. Like she's upset because Khloe is just trying to talk her out of making a mistake.

Mistake. Yeah, that's what I am.

"He doesn't belong here." She scrunches her nose and points a fake cigarette in my direction. "I don't know who invited him, but he needs to leave. Now."

I watch as Catherine's mouth opens wide and she stares at her friend. I wait for an entire minute, and it feels like a lifetime. I wait for something, anything. But Catherine says nothing. Instead she slowly closes her mouth and crosses her arms across her chest, then looks past Khloe's shoulder and away from me.

It's like a bullet to my fucking chest.

Catherine isn't a girl you fuck for a night. She's the kinda girl you keep. I always knew that. And somewhere in me, I knew I wanted to keep her.

But I know what she was thinking. She just wanted to go slumming for the night.

I don't say a word; I turn on my heel and walk out.

The music is blaring in my ears. My shoulder bumps into the streamers hanging from the ceiling and they stick to my shoulder, irritating the fuck out of me. I rip them down and let them drift to the ground as I head to the door.

I walk past groups of people talking and laughing in corners. A few girls are dancing and squealing with laughter. Jake's climbing the spiral staircase, holding hands with the cheerleader I saw earlier..

Fuck. I don't belong here.

As I turn the doorknob and open the door slightly, Levi's hand comes out and slams it shut. Fucker's about to get punched in the face.

"What the fuck, man?" Levi asks.

I keep my teeth clenched to prevent me from saying something I can't take back to a client. That's all he is. I was fucking stupid to try to make friends with him or any of them in here.

I was perfectly fine burying myself in work and staying out of trouble. Right now all I wanna do is pick a fight, and Levi's about to figure that out if he doesn't back off.

"What happened?" Levi asks with some hesitation in his voice. He's searching my face for something, but I don't answer. I'm not fucking telling him.

I'm angry. My body is screaming at me to lash out. To just take my anger out on him. But more than that, I'm hurt, and I don't wanna show it.

"Are you alright?" he asks. And that's the last fucking straw.

"Get off the fucking door," I say through gritted teeth and pray he does it. 'Cause if not, my hand's coming off the knob and my fist is slamming into his face.

I pull on the doorknob and he takes his hand off of it, letting the door open wide enough for me to get out.

I don't look back at him, and he lets me go without further fuss. Good move on his part. I walk across the grass rather than taking the path. I make a beeline right for where I left my bike.

I need to get the fuck out of here, and never look back.

It's better it happened this way. I was a fucking idiot to think I'd ever be anything to her. I still have my tats. I'm a Dean. I have my asshole parents' blood in me. I'll never be good. I'll never be worth anything.

It was stupid to think I'd be good enough for her.

I kick my bike to life and take off. I don't bother to look back even when I hear Catherine calling out my name.

CHAPTER 6

I CAN'T BELIEVE WHAT THIS BITCH IS SAYING. I CAN'T EVEN LOOK AT her. And now she's talking about him the same way his parents did. All the memories flood back at once. I feel weak and helpless listening to the way his own mother used to talk to him. I cross my arms over my chest and turn away while tears run down my cheeks. I force myself to breathe out deeply.

I'm taken back to a night when we came home together. He'd always wait for me at the food court when the mall had curfew. He knew I didn't like walking in the woods alone. Especially at night.

We walked mostly in silence. I had a cherry slushie, and I have no idea why because it was so damn cold outside. He laughed at me when I started shivering and took off his Henley. I remember how we stopped on the edge of the woods. The moon was out and it was bright. I could see all of his lean muscle and that "V" at his hips I used to dream about.

He handed it to me to cover myself with. I wore a thin tank top that cut off at my midsection. I'd worn it for him of course. I always made sure I looked cute if I was going to be around him. I was always hoping he would notice me.

I had to try hard to keep myself from looking at his body, and judging from the smirk on his face, he knew that. I remember how hot I felt then. I was a bundle of nerves and embarrassed for being caught looking. I expected him to make fun of me or put me in my place, but instead he just walked into the woods like normal.

He always walked faster than me, maybe because he's taller? But I remember he seemed to be walking faster than normal that night. I kept telling myself it was because he was cold. I offered a few times to give him his shirt back, but he insisted I wear it. It was obvious he just wanted to get home and get away from me. At least that's what I thought until I tripped over a tree root. I would've landed hard on my face. The damn slushie went flying and splattered on the ground.

I let out a shriek and prepared to fall in the dirt and land hard on the ground, but he caught me. Both of his strong arms wrapped around my waist and pulled me up until I was pressed against his hard chest.

I thought he was going to kiss me. My hands were on his bare chest, and the way he was holding me close made every nerve ending in my body burst into flames.

I remember how my breathing came in pants and I swear that even in the darkness I saw a heat in his eyes. But in a flash it was gone, like I'd just imagined it. And he set me down on my feet, leaving me confused and shaken.

He slowed his pace, and we walked home in silence. And it was an awkward silence. I kept my hands clasped to keep me from reaching out to him.

I felt fucking nauseated and practically ran to my house. I always entered through the back door so my father wouldn't see I'd walked through the woods with Ryker. He was my dirty little secret. My parents would have killed me.

That night when I walked in, I'd completely forgotten I was wearing his Henley. I walked right in without thinking.

I was bombarded with questions. I wasn't allowed to date anyone, and my father said it was unacceptable for me to be around Ryker, even if he was just a friend. He was in the middle of scolding me when we heard the neighbors. Ryker's parents were having a fight. It wasn't obvious at first. But then there was a loud yell of pain. I think his dad hit his mom. And then Ryker got in the middle. He always did that. He always defended his mom, even when she was the one yelling at him half the time.

The way Khloe is talking about Ryker reminds me of Mrs. Dean. It makes me want to slam my fist in her face.

I finally snap out of my recollection and look that bitch in the eyes.

"Fuck you." That's all I give her as I turn around and go back to where I left Ryker. But he's not there.

I walk quickly around the corner searching for him, but I don't know where he went. My heart races with worry. He left me? Fucking Khloe ruined it for me. Oh my god, what if he heard her?

"What the—" Khloe sneers as she puts her hand on my bare shoulder, digging her nails in so I'm forced to turn around. I don't even think about it as I clench a fist and punch her right in her face.

She lets out a wail and clutches at her nose with her hands.

My eyes go large. Holy fuck!

I can't believe I hit her. I mean, I've dreamed of doing it for so long. She's definitely had it coming. But still. Holy hell.

She's bent over, but then she stands and pulls her hands away from her face. There's no blood, but her face is all red, and her nose is starting to swell.

"You bitch!" she yells out, her eyes glassy with tears. I start to feel bad, but then I remember what she said about Ryker.

"You fucking had it coming." I almost leave but then I think to add, "Don't you ever talk about him like that again." As if she'll listen to me. I know she won't and there's going to be hell to pay for this, but I don't care. What she said is not okay, and I'm not going to pretend like it is.

She looks up at me with complete disgust and opens her mouth to say something. But two drunk girls come into the room and one doesn't see Khloe clutching her nose.

She tumbles right over her and they fall into a pile on the floor. There's yelling and pushing, and the other drunk girl is just staring wide-eyed.

I have no intention of staying to see the end of this. I head to the ballroom where everyone else has been hanging out. The music gets louder as I approach, and the lights are flickering in beat with the music.

I look all over, and each second that passes my heart slams harder in my chest.

He had to have heard. For a fleeting second I think maybe he was bored and is making out with someone in a corner. But I push those thoughts aside.

There's a reason I feel the way I do about him. The way he held me all those years ago did something to me. I know it did. Tears prick my eyes and they make me feel weak. I am not going to cry. I am going to find him, and I'm going to beat his ass for leaving me like that.

I nod my head as I leave the ballroom and see Levi by the door. I pick up my pace to ask him if he's seen Ryker, but I slow down when I get close and see his expression.

He looks pissed. I come to a halt as he walks toward me.

"What happened?" His voice is hard, and it's a demand. I don't like it. I don't like being talked to that way. I'm cool with Levi, but he better watch it.

"I don't like the way you're talking to me, and where's Ryker?" I say coolly.

Levi's brow scrunches, and his hard features soften.

"He took off."

My heart plummets, and my throat closes. He left me again. That fucking bastard. I bite down on the inside of my cheek to keep from crying.

"What happened?" he asks again.

"Khloe's a bitch. That's what happened."

Levi stares at me for a second before moving aside. "He just left, so maybe you can catch him."

A small bit of hope blooms in my chest. I race to the door and open it just in time to see Ryker on his bike taking off. I call out for him, but he doesn't hear.

I stand in the open doorway and watch him grow smaller in the distance. Motherfucker. I'm so angry and hurt and upset.

I take a deep breath, trying to calm myself and grip the door harder so I don't slam it over and over again like I want to out of frustration.

I'm just going to leave. I don't need this shit right now.

If he really wanted me, he knows where to find me, I think as I step outside and walk to the garage. But then I stop cold in my tracks and remember that Khloe drove. Looks like I'm walking home.

I unzip my clutch to make sure I have my keycard to the dorm. I do, but I don't want to go back there. I don't want to deal with her. For all I know she called the cops on me. It sounds like something she'd do.

I zip it shut and just start walking. I'll figure something out on the way.

I walk down the long, winding driveway and onto a busier road with street lights. It's a little chilly, but still warm considering the time of year. There's a permanent frown on my face that I just can't stop making. I hate that this part of the road is empty, but farther down there are more houses and a development. I try to walk quickly, but I don't want to. I don't have the energy, and I'm sure as hell not in a race to get home.

I didn't really want to go to that party anyway. I just wanted to see him, and I was too scared to go to the shop. I waited for him to come to me, and I can do that again.

I wrap my arms around my chest and rub my forearms to heat them up.

That's not going to happen. I already know it. He left me before, and now he's doing it all over again. If I want to see him, I'm going to have to go to him.

How pathetic. I feel so damn pathetic. I'm like some lovesick child who can't get over her crush who's probably not even into me.

My eyes go glassy and I don't care. The hot tears run down my face and I angrily wipe them away.

He was going to kiss me though. I know he was. But for him it was probably something else. A one-time fuck.

It hurts to think that, but it's true. I know it is.

I wipe my face again and look down at my hands. Shit, I forgot about the makeup. My hands are covered in black eyeliner with a smear of bright pink lipstick.

I quickly hunch over and scrub my face with the bottom of my tank top, feeling a cool breeze blow across my midsection as I angrily rub off as much as I can. As I do, the bunny ears slide down my face and I rip them off and throw them on the ground like a petulant child.

I stare at them for a second and decide to pick them up. I can't just leave them on the side of the road, even if right now I hate them. I see a trash can on the side of someone's house and walk quickly to it to throw tonight's offending evidence in the bin. Now it's right where it belongs.

I take in a staggering breath and keep walking. I have a good twenty to thirty-minute walk ahead of me still. But I need it. I must look like a mess. I'm sure my face is red and puffy from rubbing at it. My hair is all tangled, and I don't even have a hair tie to pull it back like I want to.

I hear trick-or-treaters squealing as they run on the sidewalk across the street. They're going in the opposite direction, and their parents are behind them chatting while the kids run ahead.

I look like a wreck, and I feel pathetic and disappointed with everything.

I just need to sleep, but I don't want to go back to the dorms.

Fate doesn't care about what I want though. That much is obvious.

She brought Ryker into my life again, only to dangle him in front of me one last time before snatching him from my grasp.

Fate's a bitch.

I close my eyes and shake my head. No, it's my fault. It was my fault back then for not doing everything I could to help him. And it's my fault tonight for not pushing Khloe away faster and leaving with him. I wish I'd seen him go. I would've gone with him.

Fate gave me a second chance, and I blew it. That's no one's fault but my own.

CHAPTER 7

Ryker

I CAN'T FUCKING RUN AWAY EVERY TIME I GET PISSED. But running is better than snapping. I can't afford to let my temper get me into trouble. My mouth is still slammed shut. I slow down as I approach a red light and look down at my hands to examine them. It's a habit of mine that helps me calm down. There's usually oil somewhere around my fingernails even if I scrub them clean. I don't see anything though.

I look over to my left at the kids in their little fairy and skeleton costumes screeching with delight, and then to my right at a 24/7 convenience store and gas station. I shouldn't be driving right now, not in this state. I just need to calm down for a minute. I pull in and park my bike, but I don't get off.

I'm not very good with conflict. I'm better than I used to be. Back then it was fight, fight, fight. Not that I wanted to fight that bitch.

I don't know what her problem was. It's been years since someone's talked to me like that. It still fucking hurts though. It wasn't even to my face, but at least it wasn't behind my back.

I thought I'd changed. I *have* changed. I know I have. I'm good enough for her. But either Catherine can't see it, or she doesn't want to.

He needs to leave now. I remember Khloe's words and they get me all pissed off again. That's when the memories hit me. Khloe's the chick who was dating that IT guy I hired.

I groan and cover my face with my hands.

Her being a bitch tonight is definitely because of me, but it has nothing to do with who I am.

She came into the office of my shop awhile back. I knew she was with him. I think his name was Joey. I can't even remember. I only hired him for a week to set up the new system. She came in at lunch to see him every day. And each passing day she showed me more and more attention. So much so that I felt bad for the guy.

And then she came into my office and closed the door behind her. I can't remember what she said verbatim, but she basically offered me a quick fuck.

All I said to her was, *You can leave now unless you want me to call your boyfriend in here and repeat what you just said.* I never saw her again. Not that I minded. But now her little rant makes sense.

A smile creeps up on my face. She's just holding a grudge and jealous I was giving Catherine attention.

I feel a small bit of relief, but only for a moment.

Catherine's gonna be pissed at me for leaving maybe. But she still didn't stick up for me.

That's what really matters. She could have, but she didn't.

She turned me down. Well technically she didn't, since I never even asked.

I went there to finally get the girl I've been lusting after. The girl I've been working hard to be good enough for. It's been two years, but I've been working steadily toward that goal. And as soon as it got rough, I walked away.

Fuck. I run a hand down my face. I can't believe I fucked this up.

My forehead pinches and I kick my bike back to life. The loud rumble fills the air as I make a left out of the gas station and head back to the party.

I'm tired of not being good enough. I want her.

I'm going to make sure she knows it.

As determination sets in and I rev my bike up, I almost crash the damn thing.

Catherine's alone and on the left side of the road. Her arms are crossed like she's cold, and she looks upset.

My heart sinks in my chest. What happened?

I have to wait to make a U-turn at the next light and pull up behind her.

I left her, again.

I need to make sure she forgives me. I need to make this right and most importantly, I need to get my girl.

CHAPTER 8

Catherine

I HEAR THE DULL ROAR OF A MOTORCYCLE, AND I HAVE TO CLOSE MY eyes and push out the image of Ryker on his bike. I don't think I'll ever not see him when I hear a motorcycle.

The rumble gets closer and closer, but then softer as whoever it is pulls up close to me.

My heart thuds in my chest, and suddenly I'm scared I'm here alone at night.

This is a good area of town, but crime happens everywhere. I'm too scared to even turn around as I walk quicker and closer to the edge of the sidewalk. But then I hear his voice.

"You need a ride."

My head whips around at the sound, and I stand dumbfounded.

"Ryker?" My blood heats, and anxiety washes through me. I take several steps closer to him, gripping my clutch tight in my hands.

My blood surges with adrenaline, and the exhaustion that was weighing me down before vanishes.

Fate gave me another chance. I can't blow it.

I walk to his bike and prepare to just put it all out there. Taking a deep breath, I say, "Ryker, I'm sorry."

"Catherine, I'm sorry," he says at the same time as me.

My breath stops, and my mouth opens slightly. I don't know what he could possibly be sorry for. He looks at me as though he's thinking the same thing.

He throws a leg over his bike and walks in front of me. A car's coming, but we're safe here on the sidewalk. He looks over his shoulder as the car drives by and watches as it drives away.

He takes a step closer, looking me in the eyes. I know how I must look; I'm a mess and I hate that, but all I see in his eyes is desire. It's like that night all over again.

He starts to talk, but I don't want to hear it.

I don't know if it's the exhaustion, the thought of losing him again, or the fact that he came to get me when I was so down on myself, but something pushes me to wrap my arms around his neck, get on my tiptoes and push my lips against his.

I kiss him with the desperation I feel. I can't lose him again. I can't let him leave again without him knowing exactly how much he means to me.

I catch him by surprise, and at first his lips are hard. Then they soften and mold to mine. His hand splays across my lower back. My tank top has ridden up some, and the feel of his warm hands on my bare skin is heaven. He pulls me closer to him as his other hand cups the back of my head, angling my head so he can kiss me back passionately.

I keep my eyes closed and moan into his mouth. My body arches of its own accord and my pussy heats for him.

I've waited years just for this kiss, but it isn't enough. I want more.

As the sound of another car approaching barely registers, Ryker breaks the kiss and moves us backward and onto the sidewalk.

He looks down at me with his chest rising and falling, and lust in his eyes.

My lips feel slightly swollen from his bruising kiss.

"You need a ride?" he asks in a low voice.

I start to answer, but then my eyes fall. I clear my throat. I don't want to go back to the dorm. I don't want him to just drop me off.

But I'm not going to tell him no.

"What's wrong?" he asks, searching my eyes before I can even answer. He cups my chin in his hand and forces me to look at him.

"I just want to go home with you tonight." I say each word slowly and carefully. My heart races in my chest.

I've never gone home with a man. I've never done anything with a man beyond kissing. And even then, it was nothing like what I just had with Ryker.

Ryker cocks an eyebrow and an asymmetric grin pulls his lips up.

He leans down and quickly plants a kiss on my lips.

"I'm not gonna say no to that, kitten." His rough voice sparks the desire in my core once again. My heart flutters in my chest as he reaches behind him and grabs a helmet off the back of his bike.

CHAPTER 9

I REV THE ENGINE A LITTLE MORE AS WE GET CLOSER. CATHERINE lets out a small squeal of delight, and her arms squeeze me tighter.

Her cheek is pressed against my back, and it's everything I thought it'd be.

We ride in silence as her warmth molds to my back and her arms hug my waist.

As we pull up to a red light, her hands slip down lower. She starts to slide them past the waistband and down farther. Her fingertips tickle my pelvis, and my dick jumps.

Fuck, I need to control myself. I wanna get off this bike and bend her ass over. She'd have it coming to her, teasing me like this. Instead I grip her wrist and put her hand back where it should be.

"You're going to have to wait, kitten," I tell her over my shoulder. I watch as she gives me a sexy little pout.

Now my dick is hard, and my girl is horny. Thank fuck my place is right around the corner. I can't wait any longer.

She's a good girl the rest of the way, but feeling her body pressed against mine and knowing she wants me has made my dick impossibly hard. Fucking her tight pussy is all I can think about as I pull up and climb off as quick as I can.

I help her off the bike, making the bike bounce slightly. She almost stumbles, but I right her and keep the bike from tipping. My little kitten is not graceful.

"Thank you," she says as I help her with the helmet and set it back on the end of the bike. I got that just for her. I wanted to make sure if she was there, she wouldn't have any excuse not to come back with me tonight.

"You live here?" she asks with slight disbelief. I take a look at the condo and second-guess myself. It's a nice little place, but it's basically a bachelor pad. I mean, it's not huge or in an upscale, gated community, but it's a nice place. A sense of insecurity runs through me. This never fucking happens. But with her it's different. I crave her approval for some unknown reason. If anyone else questions me, my belongings, or anything I do, I shrug it off. I don't give a fuck. But with her, knowing she approves is important to me. I don't think that'll ever change.

She pulls her hair over her shoulders and points over to the dorms behind the condos.

"I live right there," she says as she looks up at me with a small smile. "So you're still the bad boy next door."

I smirk at her and nod my head. Both my shop and my place are close to campus. A lot of business comes from the students. A bike is cheaper than a car.

"I could literally walk back to my place in like two minutes if that fence wasn't there," she says comically. I know right then I need to tell her what's up. I have to give her a chance to go, cause if she stays, she's mine.

"I'll take you back to the dorms if you want. But if you come home with me, I want you, Catherine. I've wanted you for years. And if you walk through that door, I'm not holding back anymore."

"You want me?" she asks with slight disbelief.

"That's putting it mildly, kitten."

"You never—" she starts to say, but doesn't finish.

"I never what?" I ask her, taking a step closer to her. "I never acted on it, no. But I wanted to. Every walk through those woods I thought about stopping and pushing your back against a tree and lifting you up. I wanted to feel that sweet, lush ass of yours in my hands. I dreamed about you wrapping your legs around me while I kissed you and fucked you out there where no one would find us."

Her chest reddens with a blush, and her breathing comes in pants. I see her thighs clench, and I know she's turned on as much as I am.

"But you didn't," she barely whispers.

"I wanted to do that back then, but I couldn't. I want you now though. And there's nothing holding me back. Tell me you want me."

"I want what you want, Ryker." Her whispered words make my dick hard as steel.

I've waited a long time for this.

"Get your ass inside, kitten." Her eyes heat, and she instantly turns on her heels. I smack that cute ass of hers, making her jump.

I'm gonna make sure she doesn't regret this.

CHAPTER 10

Catherine

I SHOULD TELL HIM. I KEEP THINKING OVER AND OVER THAT I should tell him I'm a virgin. But I know what he wants, and I know what he'll think.

I can't lie that a part of me has always wanted to wait for him to be my first.

He closes the door to his condo and locks it with a loud click. I turn around, standing in the middle of his living room. Suddenly it becomes all too real. My body tingles with excitement, but also fear. What if I'm not good? What if it's not what I've conjured up in my head?

I start to feel anxious and my nerves threaten to get the best of me, but then he turns around and reaches for his belt.

My pussy clenches with need when I see him unbuckle it and reach for his zipper.

My breaths come in pants as I drop to my knees.

He gives me a sexy grin and walks slowly to me.

I've never done this. But I want to. He shoves his pants down and his dick springs free.

It's so big. Oh my god. That's never going to fit in me. "Open up, kitten," he says as he strokes it. I place my hands on his bare thighs and I stretch my jaw as far as I can. He brushes the hair off my shoulder and pulls it into one hand, gripping at the base of my skull.

"You have no fucking idea how sexy you look right now." I look up at him as he pushes his cock into my mouth. I shield my teeth with my lips and try to push him as far back as I can. I barely get half of him in.

He groans with satisfaction as I push him deeper. I pull back and hollow my cheeks as I bob my head on his cock, each time trying to shove him down deeper and deeper. My eyes burn as I push him down my throat. I try breathing through my nose, but it's hard.

Just as I start thinking I can't do this, Ryker pulls away from me. "Fuck, you feel too good. I'm gonna cum before I'm done with you."

His confession makes me feel a little better. I nervously scoot backward and wipe my lips as daintily as I can as he steps out of his jeans and pulls off his shirt.

My eyes travel along his body. He's a fucking sex god. My panties are practically soaked as he crouches down in front of me and lifts me into his arms.

The movement is sudden, and I let out a small shriek.

"You're wearing too many clothes, kitten." Ryker slips his hand up my shirt and pulls it off of me as he carries me to the bedroom.

My heart beats faster and I try to soothe my nerves by crashing my lips against him.

He moans into my mouth and unclips my bra. I want to hold onto it and cover myself, but I let it fall. It's all or nothing. And I want it all.

He breaks the kiss and drops me on the bed, making me bounce. My arms instinctively cross over my chest. He opens his mouth and I know what he's going to say, but before it comes from his lips, I pull my arms away and let him look at me.

He gives me a wide smile. "Good girl." His eyes travel over my body with appreciation as his deft fingers unbutton my pants and pull them off of me. The rough jeans rub against my ass as I lift my hips and lie there in only my thong. He leans down and pulls my hips to the edge of the bed.

"I've waited too fucking long to taste you." He pushes his thumbs through the thin material, and the sound of the thin lace fabric tearing fills the room.

I close my eyes and lean my head back as he lowers his head to my pussy. I can't believe this is happening.

He lifts my legs over his shoulders and I feel a cool breeze against my heat. My nipples harden, and part of me wants to hide. Part of me wants to rock my pussy in his face to get off.

He takes a languid lick, and I have to open my eyes to watch. It's so gentle and warm, it's relaxing more than anything at first. But then he flicks his tongue against my clit, and my body bows and jumps at the sensation.

I look up as I hear the sound of him opening a drawer to his nightstand. I let my head fall back as he licks my pussy again and then pulls back to tear the condom wrapper open while he sucks my clit.

A rough chuckle vibrates up his chest as he grips my thighs and pushes me down, sucking my clit into his mouth. My mouth opens wide and my body tries to move away from the sensation. He suctions my clit and pulls back with a *pop*, and the sensation pushes me over the edge. I can't take anymore, and I cum violently. Waves of pleasure crash through my body.

I'm vaguely aware that he's pushing my body up the bed and caging me in. The heat and tingling pleasure rise and fall in slow waves.

"You look so fucking gorgeous when you cum." He cups my right breast and rolls my nipple between his fingers. My body writhes under him. "We gotta work on your control, kitten," he says with a bit of humor as he pinches and pulls my nipple. The slightly painful sensation is directly linked to my clit.

He lowers his lips to my ear as he lines up his cock, nudging the head between my pussy lips and he whispers, "Although I do love how responsive you are."

I barely have a moment to take in his words.

In one hard thrust he's buried deep inside me to the hilt. I feel a sharp pinch and my mouth opens as a silent scream is ripped from my throat and my head flies backward. He stills inside of me and pulls away. He braces himself above me and looks down at me with wide eyes.

I can hardly breathe looking up at him. *He knows.* I turn my head to the side and refuse to look back at him. My pussy hurts, and I just want him to move. But he's not.

A blush heats my cheeks as he grips my chin in his hand and forces me to look at him.

"You're a virgin?" he asks.

I nod my head slowly and swallow thickly. "Not anymore," I finally answer.

His eyes flash with a primal need as he lowers his face to mine and his tongue dives into my mouth. His fingers grip my hips and he moves out of me slowly.

It hurts. My forehead pinches, and I want to move away.

He pushes back in with a hard thrust and grinds his pelvis against my throbbing clit. The pleasure is so strong I have to break our kiss and release a strangled cry.

Fuck, my head thrashes around as my body heats. I feel so full.

He buries his head in the crook of my neck, kissing, licking and biting as he slowly moves in and out of me. His gentle touch is offset by the hard thrusts and his blunt nails digging into my hips.

He nips my earlobe and whispers, "I want to hear you say my name when you cum on my dick," sending a chill down my body and leaving goosebumps along every inch of my skin. Just hearing his dirty words has me on edge.

"Say it," he commands me.

"Ryker." His name falls from my lips instantly. I've dreamed of this a thousand times, but it was never like this. Never this intense and all-consuming.

"That's right, kitten. I'm gonna make you scream my name."

His lips clamp around my nipple and then I feel his teeth. He massages his tongue against the tender skin, and I feel the arousal between my thighs. My head pushes into the mattress as a low, radiating desire moves outward from the pit of my belly, threatening to paralyze my body.

But then he pulls nearly all the way out and I can barely stand it. The pleasure fades and in its place is the hint of pain from his taking my virginity. I need more.

Just as I think it, he slams back into me. His teeth pull against my nipple and I go off. I shatter beneath him. My pussy clamps around his dick, and my body heats with my release. My breathing stops, and I cry out his name.

He lifts himself up again and pushes his thumb against my clit, rubbing slow circles with soft pressure.

Oh, fuck. Yes! It feels so good. My legs wrap around his waist and my heels dig into his ass. I need more.

"Uh-uh," he admonishes me. His rough voice makes my eyes snap to his as he says, "You'll take what I'll give you." I can't reply to him. The only response I can give him is a soft moan as he slams into me again. The force of his touch on my clit makes everything that much better.

The pain slips away as he fucks my body like he owns it, playing with me however he wants.

"Look at me, kitten." My eyes fly to his and he holds my gaze as he pounds into my pussy. My body rocks with each hard thrust, but my eyes stay on his.

His mouth is parted and his eyes half-lidded as he continues his ruthless pace.

The height of my orgasm seems so high. Too high. I'm going to fall and shatter into a million pieces below him, but he doesn't care. He pushes my thighs farther apart and fucks me deeper, pounding me with a ruthless pace.

"Mine," he growls into my ear as he pinches my clit and I instantly explode under him. A bright white light flashes before my eyes as my body goes numb and then instantly blazes with pleasure.

I scream out his name as my back bows and my pussy spasms around his dick. I feel his thick cock pulsing inside of me as a warmth leaks out of me and drips down my thighs.

He groans in the crook of my neck and whispers my name.

I lie under him trying to catch my breath as he kisses my neck, my jaw and then my lips.

I feel exhausted and sore, wincing as he slowly pulls out of me.

As Ryker climbs off of the bed and heads to the bathroom, I pull the covers up and over my body. Insecurity quickly washes over me as the high of my orgasm dims. I clench my thighs, and the hint of pain makes me feel deliciously used. I don't regret it, not even for a second.

But this is Ryker in real life. Not the man in my dreams. I want more. But I have no idea what he wants. A pain settles in my chest, and I try to ignore it. To me this is more than what it is to him. I can't hold that against him though. I got what I wanted. And I got what I asked for.

I finally got the bad boy experience I knew Ryker would give me. And he has the piece of me I've always wanted to give him.

All I can think as I hear him turn on the faucet to the shower is, *Now what?*

CHAPTER 11

Ryker

I WALK BACK INTO THE BEDROOM WITH THE WARM CLOTH AND LOOK at the tinge of pink on it.

She waited for me. Never in a million years would I have thought she'd do that.

She's mine for good now. She's mine. I have an odd sense of pride that I can't let go of. I was her first.

As I walk back to her with a grin on my face, it falls. I stop to take a good look at her. She's got the covers wrapped tight around her, and she's not looking at me.

I don't know what's going on in that pretty little head of hers. But I'm not letting her go. It's not happening.

Whatever's going on, I'm making sure she knows I want her.

I climb onto the bed and pull the covers back. Her eyes widen and fly to mine. I can feel them on me, but I ignore her. "Spread your legs for me."

My dick jumps as she obeys my command. I see her wince with pain though, and I don't like that. I tried not to be too rough on her, but I lost control a bit.

I gently wipe the pink-tinged cum from her legs and ass. A bit's gotten onto the sheets, too. Her little pussy is swollen and red. I watch her face as I gently wipe the cloth against her sensitive flesh.

She closes her eyes, but it's a look of comfort. Good. I push her thighs closed and get off the bed enough to toss the washcloth into the hamper. The sheets will need to be washed too, but it can wait.

I lie down under the comforter and pull her body into mine. She's a little stiff, and I don't like that. She's feeling insecure. I don't want that for her.

"What's wrong, Catherine?" I ask her in a soft voice. "Did I hurt you?" I already know I did. It was her first time. I know she's going to be sore.

Her body relaxes some as she gently shakes her head and replies, "No, it felt good." Just good? She felt like fucking heaven. I knew she would feel like that. She tacks on, "Really good," and a small smile plays at her lips.

"What's bothering you, kitten?" I nudge her chin with the tip of my nose, and she turns in my arms to finally look at me.

"I'm scared." Her confession puts my guard on high alert. Whatever her worry is, I'll ease it for her.

"Tell me why," I say and keep her gaze, willing her to tell me the truth.

"I don't know what this is." Her voice cracks, and it breaks my heart that she's so insecure. I can't blame her. I fucking jumped on her the second I got her back here. It was selfish of me. I run my thumb along her bottom lip and think about what I should tell her.

I finally settle on the truth. "It's whatever you want it to be." I'll take whatever she's willing to give me. Maybe that makes me pussy-whipped. But I don't care. I just want her.

"Do you want me still?" she asks with a pained voice, and her eyes shining with vulnerability.

A soft smile turns my lips up and I lean down to kiss the tip of her nose. "I finally got a taste of you, I'm not letting go now."

"What if I want more than just sex?" she asks while looking down at the comforter and picking at nonexistent loose threads. Relief flows through me.

"That's what you're worried about?" I ask her, cupping her chin and tilting her face so she has to look at me.

"I—" she starts to say something, but then she moves her head out of my grip and looks away as she haltingly says, "I think I've loved you for a long time, Ryker."

My heartbeat slows, and my skin heats. I don't use that word, *love*. I don't believe in it. One minute my parents loved me, and the next they hated me. I know I need to say something to her to ease her worries, but I don't believe in that word. I splay my hand across her belly and pull her small body closer to mine. I kiss the crook of her neck gently. "I've wanted you for years, Catherine. Not just in my bed and screaming my name. But

I wanted you next to me. I wanted to be good enough for you. I wanted to be the man who deserved to have you." She looks up at me with her big doe eyes like she doesn't believe me, but it's true. Every word. "I don't know that I am right now. But I'm working hard to be that man, and I want you. Not just for tonight, and not just for sex. I want you to be mine. Period."

She surprises me as she takes my face in her hands and kisses me with a passion I wasn't expecting. It's a sweet kiss, but there's more to it than that. It's like all restraint has left her. There's nothing holding us back.

I pull away just slightly and nip her bottom lip. I look into her eyes and see nothing but happiness. That's better. I want her to be happy.

I let out a yawn and almost tell her to go to sleep, but then a thought pops into my head.

"How are you gonna tell your father?" I ask her. That worries me. Her father never liked me. Not that many parents did back then. And not that I could blame him.

She giggles. "He's gonna have a fucking heart attack. But he'll get over it."

"You think it'll be that easy, huh?" I'm not looking forward to that family dinner. My heart clenches in my chest. I can't split her up from her parents. They were good to her, and they were right to keep me away from her. I don't want to keep her from having something that I'm missing out on.

"I'm all grown up now, Ryker," she says with a hint of humor. "Besides, you should've seen my last boyfriend."

My body goes tense. I don't like the thought of her with someone else. "I'm kidding!" she says with a wide smile before nuzzling into my chest.

I let my body relax and run my hand down her side. My fingers trail along her skin and give her the shivers. I let out a small chuckle.

"Dad might never approve, but he'll get over it." I nod once at her words. That's true. And I'll do my best to show them I've changed. "What matters is that I want you."

I smile at her words. That pride fills my chest again.

It's a feeling I don't get often, and I want it every day from here on out.

"You have no idea how much I wanted you," she confesses. But I do. I knew she wanted me, but back then it wouldn't have been good for her. I wouldn't have been good for her.

I huff a laugh. "Well I've got a hold on you now, kitten." I kiss the tip of her nose. "And I'm not gonna let go."

EPILOGUE

Ryker

Two years later

I'M SO DAMN NERVOUS. I HATE THIS FEELING. I WIPE MY HANDS OFF with a towel and make sure all the muck's gone. Mr. Parker's gonna be here soon. Usually I'm proud looking at my choppers when they're all done. I look over the bike and love it. The design is hot. The chrome is shiny, and the leather smooth. Everything's perfect.

But it's for Catherine's father. Mr. Parker's approval makes me nervous.

I know I make my kitten happy now. There's no doubt in my mind. But her father's a different story.

Ever since that night at the party, she's been staying with me. That's how I want it. I need her in my bed and cumming on my dick every night. That's the way it should be. Even though Khloe got kicked out of school for public drunkenness, I wouldn't let her go back to the dorms. Catherine's my girl, she should be in my bed.

But I've also been going to their family dinners every other Sunday. And that's… fucking exhausting. It's getting better though. I can at least admit that.

At first I refused to go. Who the hell wants to go to their girlfriend's parents' house? Especially since I know her father, and I remember how he told me to stay away from her. It was years ago, but still.

It made her so upset though. So I caved and went with her to her parents' house. My parents aren't next door anymore. It's odd seeing the house

I grew up in. It looks different. New siding, and the current owners painted the shutters. They fixed the fence out back and put in large bushes on the edge of the sidewalk. It doesn't look like the place I grew up. Which is a good thing in a lot of ways.

It sucked being there that first day though. I haven't seen my parents in years. Not since they lost the house and came to me for money. That ended real quick when I told them no. I could see the look in my father's eyes. That same mean look he used to give me before the fights would start. But I didn't back down. If they want a relationship with me, they can have one. But if they just want money they'll have to go somewhere else.

It hurts still that they left and never came back, but it's for the best.

My parents are nothing like the Parkers.

Catherine was blessed with parents who really love her. They love her enough to be concerned about the fact that we're seeing each other, too.

They know she isn't at the dorms, which only makes it more awkward. That first night her father looked at me the way a man looks at the prick who's fucking his daughter. Can't blame him for it, but it didn't make spaghetti Sunday go by any quicker.

I had to grin when I overheard Catherine's mother scolding him in the kitchen. Janette reminds me a lot of Catherine. But there's no doubt I'm nothing like George.

Although he did order a custom build from me. So that means something. That, and he didn't put up much fuss when we told them we're buying a new house closer in town when Catherine graduates this semester. So those are good signs.

"Hey! You aren't dressed!" I hear my kitten come into the garage and practically stomp her little foot.

I turn around and smile at her. I've got a wrench in one hand and a towel in the other and say, "I'm going as a mechanic."

She rolls her eyes and walks down the two steps so she's on the concrete slab. "You gotta hurry, babe. As soon as Daddy leaves we need to get going, or we're going to be late!"

She's excited to see everyone from the party. Like it's a reunion of sorts. As if we even stayed that long last time.

I hope Jake and Levi have another bet going, 'cause this time I am fucking her somewhere in that house. With that cute little skirt and fishnets, fuck yeah I'm getting in that pussy as soon as we find an empty room.

My dick twitches, and I think about taking her ass up to the office real quick, but then I hear a car pull up.

If her father doesn't hate me now, he sure as hell would if he walked in on me fucking his baby girl.

I try to think of everything I can to get this erection down as Catherine walks over to her old man. He steps out of the car and looks back at me with a tight smile.

"You're going to love it!" Catherine squeals, pulling on his arm before he's even had the chance to shut his car door. He kicks it closed and keeps up with her pace as he comes into the garage.

"Mr. Parker," I greet him and put down the wrench and towel.

"I told you to call me George," he says.

Catherine rolls her eyes and says, "And I told you to call him Dad." I cock a brow at her. My little kitten is cute and sweet, but we're both giving her a look to tell her she needs to get over that wish. It's not happening.

Her father walks around the bike and I square my shoulders. It's exactly what he asked for, and then some. I'm confident in my work, and I'm damn good at what I do, but I still want him to like it.

He nods his head and smiles. "She's a beauty. Good work," he says proudly.

Catherine rocks on her heels with glee. "Told you."

I nod my head once and say simply, "Glad you like it." But that's an understatement.

"Mikey's in reception today; he can take that last payment there if you still insist on paying." I wanted to do it for free. After all, he's my girl's father. And I've got enough business that I'm not at a loss. But he's been persistent.

"I know where it is," he says with a smile.

"I'm getting a Coke," Catherine says, absentmindedly walking over to the vending machine. I swear she uses the machines more than the guys do.

I watch her walk easily across the garage and my eyes wander to that ass of hers. I want her today just as much as I did when I first met her, maybe even more.

"Walk with me, Ryker," her father says as he heads up the stairs to the receptionist's area inside the shop attached to the garage. I nod my head and walk behind him.

As soon as we're inside the building, he stops and turns to face me.

"It's been two years, hasn't it?" George asks me.

"Two years?"

"Since you and Catherine started," he waves his hand in front of him and purses his lips trying to think up the right word.

"Dating?" I offer. Although what we have is so much more than that. She's my everything, and I'm the same to her.

"Sure," he says as he turns to face me with his brow furrowed. "What I'm getting at is the fact her finger doesn't have a ring on it." My fingers itch to reach into my pocket. I just got one last week. He doesn't know, but I'm proposing tonight. My heart swells, and pride runs through me.

"Is that your blessing, George?" I ask him.

"It's the best you're gonna get, son." I nod my head and start to tell him my intention, but Catherine opens the door. I look over my shoulder and see her narrow her eyes as she says, "You two having a pow wow?" she asks.

Her father chuckles and says, "Just headed in now, sweetie."

He walks off down the hall and I turn to face Catherine. I'm gonna marry this woman. I'm a lucky man.

"What were you two talking about?" she asks suspiciously.

"None of your business." I hold her gaze as she clucks her tongue. She's deciding if she wants to push, but I know she won't.

She sighs and crosses her arms. "Are you gonna get dressed now at least?"

"Yeah, I'm heading back now."

We're going as school girl and professor tonight. Catherine's choice.

I kiss the tip of her nose. "I love you, kitten." She's showed me over the years what those words really mean, and I really do love her.

"I love you too," she begins in a peppy voice, "but I'm gonna kick your ass if you don't get dressed."

I smirk down at her and make sure her father's out of sight so I can pinch her ass. She squeals and jumps.

"Watch that mouth of yours," I warn her like I always do. "It's gonna get you into trouble."

She winks at me and saunters off, trying to be sexy, which she is. "I'm counting on it."

ONE HOLIDAY WISH

CHAPTER 1

Carla

THE LIGHT DUSTING OF SNOW STEALS MY ATTENTION AS IT BLOWS in the bright lights of my headlights and across the sidewalk. It's dark already, even though it's only six, but I'm wide awake with the nervous butterflies in the pit of my stomach.

The sound of the keys jingling is all I'm left with as I turn off my car and sit in the driver seat. Rustling in my bag, I find the stick of sheer berry lip gloss. It matches my nails that I just had done yesterday too. I spent way too long thinking about what I was going to wear. It's just a holiday party, and hosted by my best friend, Lauren. So it shouldn't matter.

Every other Saturday I park my car right where it is now, and head straight into her house without an ounce of makeup on and only in my PJs. I have no shame when it comes to girl's nights. And a holiday party of just close friends normally means making sure I'm wearing real clothes, complete with a bra—even though I hate bras. Not the designer skinny jeans and flowy white silk blouse I picked out just for this night.

My phone pings with a text from Lauren just as I'm smacking my lips together: *You here yet?*

Just pulled up.

My phone buzzes again with: *Shit, I have no red wine!*

My lips quirk up into a grin as I snap a picture of the two bottles in my passenger seat and send them to her with the line: *Got you covered.*

You are the fucking best. My smile widens but with her next message, it falls.

Now get your ass in here!

Deep breaths. Dropping my phone into my bag, I open my car door and grab a bottle of wine in each hand which means I have to bump my car door shut with my ass.

It thuds as it closes and so do my heels in the bit of snow.

My coat's not shut tight enough with the loose tie, but even with the chill, I'm burning up with nerves.

He's going to be there. I swallow down my anxiousness as my heels crunch down the snow and I get closer to the front door. I can hear the laughter, the chatter, the faint sounds of Christmas music.

I should be excited,—*merry*, so to speak—but I can't shake the apprehension, knowing Michael Davis, my high school boyfriend, my college on-again-off-again-can't-keep-my-hands-off-of-him-when-we-run-into-each-other-occasional-fling is going to be there.

All of these nerves because of one very important detail.

He's coming back home; he's moving in down the street from me, back into his old house. It was one thing when I could travel a thousand miles and put distance between us after we had a rendezvous. It's completely different when he's a block away and we'll run into each other constantly.

I don't know how I'm going to keep my hands to myself. I don't know if I want to try to pretend like I don't still want him.

Ringing the doorbell, I tell myself the scary truth that has me shaking in my cherry red heels, I don't know if he wants me at all now that he's back. That's the part that makes the butterflies in my stomach beat their wings a little too hard.

CHAPTER 2

Carla

"I T'S IRRATIONALLY HOT IN HERE," I tell the back of Lauren's head as I plop both bottles down on her kitchen table, knocking the bowl of Tostitos ever so slightly.

"Wine! My hero," Lauren drags the "o" way too long as she gives me a hug without wrapping her arms around me because she's got a Solo cup in each of her hands.

"You started without me," I jokingly scold her and slip off my jacket as someone comes into the kitchen from behind me.

"Pre-gaming was like hours ago girl. You and that bakery," she's back to filling the cups as soon as I let her go.

"I'll be in that bakery every day until I die," I respond and my words are full of pride. It's my family's bakery and I'm the one who inherited it from my grandmother. My mother's a nurse and my father married into the family with a career in law. So the bakery—and all the memories that come with it—are all mine. "I wouldn't have it any other way."

Lauren rolls her eyes at me but then winks and gives me a nudge to look behind.

Shit. I almost say the word out loud; I wasn't ready for this. I should be or maybe I should know I never would be. But dammit, I thought I'd at least have one minute… to down whatever is in that Solo cup in Lauren's left hand.

Michael is standing right there behind me, telling something to James that makes him laugh as the two of them open the caps of their beer and toss them in the trash can next to the counter. As Michael lifts his beer to take a swig, his eyes catch mine.

My heart pounds in my chest.

The second he lowers his beer; he smiles at me. Charming, sweet but he fails to hear whatever James said. My floosy of a heart picks up her pace.

"Are you listening?" James questions Michael, clinking the bottom of his beer against Michael's.

"What?" Michael's attention is stolen by James and it's only then that I let my own smile show. Even though I know the blush will stay right where it is and I won't be able to hide that.

"Dude," James shakes his head in disapproval until Michael nods slightly my way. I see him do it and stupidly, I stay put, a hand on each bottle of wine as if they'll save me from this awkward moment.

The movement doesn't go unnoticed and Michael lets out a soft chuckle before pulling his bottom lip into his mouth and biting down on it slightly, shaking his head at me.

Instantly, those butterflies move lower, so does every bit of heat in me. It's his broad shoulders, I think, that does it. Lauren and I narrowed it down based on my celebrity crushes. The way he hovers over me, dominating my space and closing me in. I am a helpless victim to it.

And that lip that's trapped in between his teeth right now, I'd like to bite it too. In fact, I have. On multiple occasions.

"Carla!" James is the first to speak. He and Michael roomed together at college. He knows every sordid detail of what Michael and I have done, and unbeknownst to Michael, he also kept me up to date when I wasn't there, filling me in on any and every detail of any girl Michael could have gone after. He never did date anyone else though, even when I broke it off, admitting that the distance was too much. He had school. I had the bakery. It wasn't going to work.

But James and his wealth of information are the reason I always fell into Michael's bed whenever Lauren went to see James, her brother, and she needed a travel companion, or whenever Michael came back here, to this small town. James is the one who told me I was all Michael ever talked about and said he didn't want anyone else.

I didn't want anyone else either. But when we hooked up that first time after the break up, I didn't want to put a name on what we were. So it was on-gain, off-again, whenever we were around each other, or miles away. Just hooking up, but I didn't want to hook up with anyone else.

"Hey, I heard you were coming back," I say off handily, peeking up at Lauren to save me, but she's busy gathering a bag of chips from the cabinet.

"So that's how you're going to play it?" Michael's question catches me off guard.

"What do you mean," I play innocent and peek at James just as Lauren bails on me, practically running out of the kitchen with a twinkle of mischief in her eyes and the widest smile I've ever seen. Michael asks James to leave us for a minute and before I can even turn around, we're alone.

"So you don't want them to know?" Michael asks and I stumble on my answer.

"Know what?" Adrenaline races through me. We've never talked about what we do and I sure as hell don't spread the gospels about how I still spread my legs for Michael.

It only takes three foreboding steps from Michael. One. Two. Three. Until he's standing over me, invading my space and making me crane my neck to look up at him. I can smell him, feel the heat radiating from him. I could taste him and that lip of his if I wanted to right now.

"That I fucked you last week on my sofa… and then my desk. And that you already know I'm coming home because I mentioned it before you left."

"They don't know." I answer him with a shake of my head. Michael's facial expression gives no hint of what he thinks about the fact that I kept it a secret. Whether he likes that I've kept it a secret or otherwise. His statement is simply matter of fact … and dripping in sex appeal. Until he clarifies with another question.

"So you haven't told anyone?" His eyes flash with something. It's gone as quickly as it came, and too soon for me to place it. Maybe guilt? I feel it too. Everyone in here knows what we used to be and I don't want them coming between what we have now simply because I'm happy with the way it's been. Even if we don't have a title.

Or I was… until he decided to come home. Still, we don't need the opinions of the peanut gallery.

If my nerves would calm the hell down, if I could breathe whenever Michael gets close to me, I'd be a better fighter in this battle of flirtation. But as it is, Michael dominates every piece of me the second I smell his woodsy scent, or see that dark stubble that lines his sharp jaw all the way down his neck.

"You're staring at my lips, Carla," Michael's voice is deep and husky, and the way he speaks sends a heat straight to my core. "You want something?"

I only nod, and let my fingers reach up to the last button on his long sleeved Henley. The deep groan that slips from him is accompanied by a roar of laughter from just on the other side of the wall in the living room. Lauren's house is small, it's all her own, but this is a tight space to hide something like what I want to do with him.

"You want to go upstairs?" Michael asks me, glancing behind him and I follow his gaze. No one's there but the shadows of people are coming.

The second I nod, his hand is on mine and I creep up the stairs of Lauren's two-bedroom townhouse as quietly as I can. "We won't have long," I whisper and wish I'd had at least one glass of wine so I can blame this on that, but the way Michael looks when he pulls me in closer to him at the top of the stairs has me drunk on lust already.

"We can be quick here," he leans down to nip my bottom lip before adding, "And then we have all night."

CHAPTER 3

Michael

I MISSED THE SLOWER PACE OF THIS TOWN AND HOW EVERYONE knows everyone.

I missed being able to walk everywhere and know that every single building has a story to tell.

I missed all of this when I left for college.

But most of all, I missed her. My Carla.

Pushing my hip against her belly, I back her up until her back hits the wall. Grabbing her wrists in my hand, I pin them above her head. No one can see us here, but if anyone came up the stairs, they'd have a view of everything.

Carla moans into my mouth and my cock is instantly hard. I rock it against her, making sure she can feel what she does to me.

She breaks the kiss before I'm ready, leaving my heart racing. As I trail my finger down her arm, still keeping her wrists pinned, I watch the goosebumps spread across her body and her nipples pebble through that thin bra and loose blouse she's wearing.

"Did you wear that for me?" I ask her and my voice comes out huskier than I meant. I have no control when it comes to Carla.

She nods and pushes herself against my leg, grinding into me. "All for you," she nearly whimpers as her back bows and she rocks herself harder against me.

Releasing her wrists, I cup her pussy through her jeans and my other hand goes to her hip. My lips trail down her neck until I can nip the lobe of her ear and whisper, "I need to be inside you in the next two minutes or I'm going to lose my shit."

Carla's eyes widen, as if registering what we're doing for the first time. Her lips purse as she glances behind us, to Lauren's bedroom. "We can't. Not in Lauren's room and the other is where her sister is staying."

I back up slightly, wishing a third room would appear when I see the wide hall closet. So wide it's two-doored. Not hesitating, I swing the closest door open and pull a string to turn on the old light. There are only a handful of coats on left side and plenty of room on the right to take care of Carla and the hard on that never goes down when she's near.

"I need you to be quiet," I warn her and open the door wider. it's not until she takes one last peek down the stairs before she grins at me. A mischievous and sexy grin that has my cock aching to be inside of her.

"I can be quiet," she whispers and lets out a giddy feminine laugh as I come in behind her. "Liar," I tease her and close the door behind me.

Before her back even hits the wall, her lips are on mine, sucking and nibbling. I don't waste any time either, pushing my hand up her blouse and rolling her hardened nipple between my forefinger and thumb.

She moans, loud, breaking our kiss and I pull back on her nipple in punishment since I know that mix of pain and pleasure is delivered straight to her core.

"I bet you're wet for me," I taunt her in a low breath.

"There's only one way to find out," she teases me back and as my hands find the button of her blue jeans, she does the same to mine.

The button, the zipper, the jeans in a mess around our ankles.

I groan in the crook of her neck as I tear off the thin lace that separates her hot cunt from my fingers and learn that I guessed right. "You're so fucking ready." I leave an open-mouthed kiss on her throat and then on the back of her neck as she turns around for me, slowly and with intent. It's more difficult with the jeans still around her ankles, but she does it well like the little minx she is.

"We've got to be quick," she whispers as I wrap my hand around my cock and stroke it.

"I should have stopped by the bakery before coming here." I'm only joking, but the serious side of Carla comes out when she answers me, "Not going to happen in the bakery."

The smirk on my face is uncontrollable. "That's what cars are for, baby." I playfully answer and smack her ass before telling her, "stay quiet," and shove my cock inside of her in one swift stroke.

Fuck, my eyes nearly roll back into my head. Not just because she feels like heaven, but because of the look on her face right now. Eyes closed and her mouth open with a silent scream of ecstasy.

With every buck of my hips, I brace her against me so her body doesn't hit the wall.

I could give two shits if they know we're fucking up here, but I know Carla doesn't want anyone to know.

I'm sure they're thinking we're doing something else right now. That I couldn't wait to ask her. And that's fine by me if that's what they think. They should know better at this point.

"The two of us can't be in the same room together without getting inside each other's pants," I whispers to Carla and as she smiles, I slam inside of her. Again and again.

She's trying to grab on to anything at all, but there's nothing but bare wall in front of her.

It's hard to control myself as I slam inside of her, still bracing her against the wall. Feeling her cum around me, the heat, her arousal, the way her cunt grabs my cock. Fuck. I'm going to cum and I'm not ready. I want to fuck her how she likes, rough and hard. For hours.

"Tell me I can have you again tonight," I barely groan the words out at the shell of her ears and she shivers, shivers from her shoulders and down, all the way down, in a way that leads straight to my cock.

"You can have me," she gives me just what I need and lets her head fall back against my chest. Her cheeks are full of color, her lips still parted and her eyes half lidded.

"One more," I whisper against her heated skin and reach down to rub the rough pad of my thumb against her clit.

Her hands come up to her mouth; she bites on her thumb to keep from screaming as I fuck her recklessly, harder, faster, waiting to feel her cum one more time.

The second she does, all the tension in her body leaves her and I feel my own release with her. Gripping onto her with a bruising force, I let go of everything and cum with her, feeling my balls draw up and the tingling in my spine. My toes curl as the pleasure rocks through me in waves.

I can barely breathe I cum so hard.

I pull out of her, wishing we had more time and use her underwear to clean her up and then shove them quickly in my pocket. She's still panting against the wall and I have to help her pull her jeans up. I have every curve of hers memorized. The way she leans her head against the wall is exactly how she does it on my pillow. And her fingers come up to rest in the little space below her collar bone, that little divot she loves for me to kiss. She does that every time too.

Time ticks too fast. I want to stay in this moment forever. But that's a holiday wish that won't be gifted.

"Is this going to be something we do one last time? I don't know that I can handle…" Carla asks me quietly, one hand on the doorknob and the other on my hip. Her eyes reach mine, and I hate that she has any insecurity. It's always been her. I knew if I didn't push, I'd hold on to her until I could come back and be here for her how she wanted all these years.

"Carla, I have one question to ask first."

My heart hammers in my chest. It's now or never. As my bottom lip drops to ask her the one question I need answered, the door to the coat closet flies open, bringing with it the bright light of the hall way and a not-so-shocked Lauren who somehow manages to bother grin and scream out, "I knew it!" at the same time.

Fuck.

CHAPTER 1

Carla

"Everyone!" Lauren's screaming through her house with a shit-eating grin that won't budge. The thud, thud, thud of her pattering down the steps as quickly as she can is far faster than mine because of these heels.

"Lauren!" I scream her name and add, "Don't you dare!" as I bend down on the third step to grab my heels so I can catch her barefoot before she can go shouting to everyone what she just saw. I have half a mind to throw them at her as she lands on the bottom step.

"Guys!" Lauren squeals as she rounds the corner, leaving me in a view of only her hand. My chest is heaving in air by the time I catch up to her in the small living room crowded with James and four more friends for years and years. Friends who have been my family and know every detail of my life. Including the bits about Michael. The very large bits that have made up most of my life since the tenth grade.

All of their eyes are on me, I can feel them burning into me as I hold up a heel at Lauren, ready to tell her to shut it just as she announces, "He totally gave it to her already!"

Gave it to her. My mouth drops just like the shoe in my hand. How could she? Betrayal rips through me like I've never experienced in my life and instantly tears prick my eyes. Were they betting on how long it would take before I fell back into bed with him? Fuck. That hurts more than anything ever has. Embarrassment doesn't even register. It just hurts.

"Lauren, I didn't ask yet!" Michael's voice booms down the stair case. I barely notice the thumps pounding down the steps and coming up behind me.

"Fuck," Lauren covers her mouth before closing the distance between us and grabbing my shoulders. "That sounded so wrong. I thought you two were up there because he asked you. I'm so sorry. Don't take those words like the way they sounded.

"You really put your foot in your mouth," James laughs at Lauren, no sense at all

"I thought he asked her!" Lauren raises her voice and directs her guilt on James who shakes his head comically. "You're a mess," he jokes and my friends in the room chuckle. Everyone still jovial as if nothing's wrong in the least.

"Ask me what?" I breathe the words and turn around to face Michael, his soft blue eyes piercing me like they always do.

"Oh my God he's going to do it now," I hear Lauren's words rush out of her mouth as she steps away, giving us room and letting everyone else see the two of us.

My heart beats fast, my body heats and my lungs stay perfectly still, refusing to let me breathe as Michael takes my hand with one of his, running the rough pad of his thumb over my wrist and reaches into his pocket to pull out a small black velvet box.

Oh, my fucking God.

My bottom lip wobbles slightly as my eyes glance at the box, then back to his eyes.

Michael lets out an uneasy breath, "I wanted to ask you in private." He clears the nervousness from her voice with a small cough before continuing. "I wasn't sure what you'd say, but I guess in front of all of our friends is a perfectly fine way to do it."

"You remember how you asked me what my holiday wish was?" he asks me but my mind still isn't functioning quite right and I can only stare back at him, feeling so much excitement, nervousness, so much hope that this means he wants the same as me. Michael glances at everyone behind me before leaning forward and reminding me, "Last week when I saw you, do you remember when I asked you and then you asked me back?"

Blinking away the buzz of this frenzy I nod vigorously and Michael smiles at me, it's a lop sided grin that makes him that much more charming. "You've got to help me here," he whispers just for me, "I'm nervous."

Rocking onto my tip toes I steal a quick kiss from him, feeling the blush rise into my cheeks, "Sorry, I swear I'm paying attention." He laughs as I rock back down onto my heels and look up at him with a warmth flooding every bit of me.

"You're my holiday wish." He stares into my eyes. "I just want you and this can be whatever you want it to be, if you want me too." His words come out faster as he goes on until he takes a moment to breathe, opening up the small velvet box for me to see. "A promise ring or more, I'm not sure," he lets out a long breath as I peek at the sparkling ring.

Tears cloud my vision of the rose gold diamond ring with floral details surrounding it. *Or more?* I never expected this.

"I'm not sure what you want, proposal or a promise, or to get married tonight. I just want you and this is for you."

"Tonight!" the word shrieks with glee from behind me and I look over my shoulder to see Lauren barely being held back by James. She covers her mouth with both hands and I have to laugh at her antics. She's always said we were meant to be together, that even a thousand miles wouldn't keep us apart.

"Not tonight," I say mostly to get that thought out of Lauren's head before looking back at Michael. "Not tonight," I repeat and hold his hand tighter. "And if it means I get another, this is just a promise ring," I bite down on my lower lip to keep my grin at bay, but it doesn't work.

Michael's shoulders shake as the tension around us eases and our friends laugh from my answer.

"Told you!" this time it's James who pipes up.

"I'll get you another then." Michael's voice is soothing, and the look in his eyes is everything right now. Devotion, love, the way he looked at me when we shared our first kiss, our first time, all of our firsts. And the way he looked at me when I left him, thinking I couldn't be the only one who felt this between us, but too scared to ask. "When you're ready."

"Let's just be us, for now."

"That's all I want." He lowers his nose to mine, and gives me another kiss as the chatter and cheers pick up behind us. It turns to white noise when he whispers though, "I love you Carla. I always have and I always will."

My lips press against his for a short kiss and then I whisper in the warm air between us, "I love you too."

COLLARED FOR CHRISTMAS

CHAPTER 1

Joshua

I SIGH HEAVILY AT MY DESK KNOWING I SHOULDN'T BE DOING THIS. But I fucking want to. I lean back in the leather chair, staring across the room with the tips of my fingers tapping on the Mahogany desk.

It's been years since I've seen her and now that I've had a glimpse of my sweet cherry, I can't get her out of my head.

What's worse is she didn't even see me. Or maybe it's better that way. I'm not sure.

It was her voice that made me turn. The soft cadence that spilled from those beautiful lips. Had I never heard her, I wouldn't have seen her. It's incredible how sometimes fate gives you just enough of a glimpse to change everything.

I close my eyes remembering the sweet sound of her voice. She ordered a salted caramel coffee and a blueberry muffin to go. I huff a small laugh at the memory. She always had a sweet tooth. Her pale pink, A-line dress flowed below her hips as she moved across the glass display case, smiling sweetly as the young man handed her the muffin.

She nibbled on the muffin as she waited for her coffee. Those plump lips parting ever so slightly as she pushed a stray crumb into her mouth and sucked gently on her finger. She'll never know just how tempting and sexy she is without even trying. The sight made my dick twitch. I remember how she wrapped those lips around my cock and owned me as she sucked me off. I groan in my chair trying to push the past out of my mind.

I was stuck there, in my seat at the far corner of the coffee shop, frozen in time, watching her as though I weren't really there. The paper in my lap and an espresso on the small, white table in front of me, I stared at her with desire.

I couldn't believe she was there right in front of me. As if the time hadn't passed and we hadn't parted all those years ago. I sat there in awe until she accepted her coffee with a smile, taking a sip as she strode to the front, shifting the purse on her shoulder as she pushed the door open and left, blending into the hustle and bustle of the city.

I smile at the memory, back when we were together, she never drank coffee. It doesn't surprise me that she ordered it flavored and added so much damn sugar to it.

I had no idea she'd moved to the city. I had no clue she was anywhere near me. *My Cherry.*

I'm ashamed to remember how I followed her to her office building. The winter air blowing in my face and the Christmas carolers already out in the morning on the corners of the busy streets. I walked into the sleek skyrise with shiny steel and tall glass windows. I've driven past this building a thousand times. I remember thinking there's no way she's been this close to me all this time.

I walked in behind her and watched as she walked through the marble floored lobby of Parker-Moore and confidently strode towards the elevator. I walked to the fountain in the center of the lobby and watched as she took small bites of what was left of the muffin, waiting for the elevator to ding and take her away from me.

I look back to the screen on my computer. All of her information is there. Alena Morgan. She's a chief advisor for a prominent sales company now. After years of schooling and a prestigious internship. Now she's back. Back in my life with her dreams accomplished.

And according to her background check, her name is the only one on the lease.

Which means she's single. As far as I can tell she is.

I fucking hope she is. I want her now even more than I wanted her then. I knew I'd hold her back, I knew she needed more from life than what I had to offer back then. Fuck, we were only just experiencing life and I wanted to keep her all to myself. I felt selfish and like an asshole for making her feel like she needed to run. And when she walked away, I let her go without fighting.

The day she left me tore a hole in my heart, filled only by my work. I worked in private security with a good friend of mine, Isaac. Every fucking day, I was working. Trying to ignore the fact that I'd let her slip away.

She was mine. Had I told her no, she wasn't leaving, I think she would have rebelled, but I could have disciplined her and she would have fucking loved it. She would have seen how good it felt. How much she wanted it as much as I did. We could have made it work. But back then, I wasn't the man I am now and I sure as fuck wasn't the Dom I am now.

She wouldn't have understood her feelings and I would have failed at explaining them to her. She was degrading what we had by thinking her submission made her weak. It doesn't make her any less of an equal to submit. If anything she has the upper hand. I'm the one who needs to know the limits, her limits. The limits that *she* sets.

But she didn't accept that. She wouldn't. She left me and I let her go, burying myself in work as a punishment more than anything else.

Until I met Lynn and created this place. *Club X.*

A smile curls my lips up.

I never dreamed it would grow to be something so … powerful. This lifestyle has always been a passion of mine. The darkness may have been hidden and subdued, but it's always been there. I didn't know how lucrative my expertise would turn out to be.

This rebuilt mansion is an escape to debauchery and sin for the rich and powerful. Our security and use of non disclosure agreements as well as the clientele make Club X unique and desirable. We're exclusive and that makes the members even more eager to join. Most only know of Club X through word of mouth. We don't have a website and we aren't interested in advertising. With a ten thousand per month membership fee, we don't need more business.

This club may be my profession, but it's so much more than that.

It's something I want to show my cherry. I know she'd love it. She's the most submissive woman I've ever met. She's confident and professional, but she craves an escape from responsibility. She loves handing over power to those she can trust. She may not be aware of it, but it's liberating for her.

I need that exchange of power. I need her back in my life.

I haven't had a steady relationship for years. I haven't even had a submissive or played downstairs for months. I haven't *wanted* like this in so damn long.

Not since she left me.

I click to my email and hover the mouse over send. But I can't do it. I can't let her know that I'm here just yet. I'm afraid she'll run.

I stare at the screen, feeling pissed off to even be in this predicament. I know one thing for sure, as soon as I get her in here, I'm not letting her go.

At that thought, an idea strikes me.

"Lynn?" I call out of my office and my business partner, the face of the business really, peers into my doorway.

We met years ago and hit it off right away as friends, good friends too. We aren't anything more than that, and we both like it that way. In this line of business, that makes what we do much easier.

"What can I do for you Joshua?" she asks, walking in but only taking a few steps into my office.

I don't want my sweet Alena, my Cherry, knowing I want her here. I want her to come here on her own.

I tell her, "I need you to send an email for me."

She tilts her head with her forehead pinched, "am I your secretary now?" There's a touch of humor, but also slight disbelief.

"It's an invitation and it can't come from me." I tap my knuckles on the desk, debating on whether or not I should tell her.

Judging by the smile on her face, she doesn't need to know more. Lynn is an expert at judging facial expressions and apparently I've given more than enough away.

"I'm happy to help," she says with a twinkle of mischief in her eyes.

CHAPTER 2

Alena

I SWALLOW THICKLY LOOKING UP AT THE LARGE WOODEN DOORS. This is for me. A Christmas present of sorts for myself. I'm finally going to go through with it. My heartbeat races and my palms are sweaty. I've never done anything like this. I haven't even been with a man in years.

As pathetic as that sounds, work has taken priority. I'm more than ready for this.

I had a boyfriend, Joshua, years ago, who made me want this. He was my first in every way. He teased me with the idea of being a submissive. Really, I teased myself. He wanted me to kneel, to crawl to him, to obey his commands and let him tie me up. I'm wet just thinking about him and his dirty words.

I was convinced that lowering yourself to be submissive was wrong and dirty. That it was degrading.

But I'm obsessed.

Even more, I'm turned on by the idea.

"Come here Cherry, be a good girl for me," his seductive words echo in my memory and I have to close my eyes and sink my teeth into my bottom lip. My heart clenches at the memory, so does my pussy. Joshua was good to me.

But he didn't last. Your firsts never do. We each wanted different things and moved on, going our separate ways. It was hard at first, even if it was my decision.

After all, I was falling for him, I was weak when I was with him. I craved to submit to him and I know how badly he wanted it. But I wasn't ready back then. I didn't know that I ever would be. Almost ten years later, ten years wiser and more established, now I know what I want.

And now I'm standing out in front of Club X. It's not well known. It's full of powerful men and rumored to be the hottest BDSM club there is. But it's secretive for a reason. From outside it almost looks like a mansion. It's large and intimidating, but aged with beauty. There are details in every aspect of the architecture and landscaping.

It's a gorgeous building, but I have no idea what it looks like inside. Pictures are forbidden. The only ones I've seen are from the emailed invitation I was sent.

And I certainly didn't focus on the architecture in those pictures.

I almost didn't open the email. I had no idea who Madam Lynn was and it's only out of curiosity that I clicked. It was a personal invitation. Somehow she knew what my dark desires were.

My blood heats at the memory. It's been two weeks since I got the email. Two weeks of warring with myself. But I'm a grown woman. I'm successful and I have everything I've wanted out of my professional life. But my love life is non existent and I don't even know how I'd find a boyfriend.

Nor if I'm interested in one. But I can't deny my curiosity.

It's only two on Tuesday, so I'm sure it won't be packed. I'm surprised they're even open.

I wanted to see what it was like on my own. I just want a small peek to see if I'm really tempted. I want to know if I can actually do this. The thought of being a submissive is intoxicating; it's a fantasy. I don't know if I can go through with it. But I have to try in order to find out.

I ball my hand into a fist and knock against the door. The cold air makes my knuckles hurt at the hard contact. It's only when I'm pulling my hand away that I see the black cast iron knocker.

I roll my eyes at my stupidity. But before I can dwell on it, the doors open and I sucked in a breath.

A large man, opens the door. I have to crane my neck to look him in the eyes. I am a step lower than him, but still, his broad shoulders and towering height are intimidating. He's handsome enough, but not really my type. He looks down at me and cocks a brow, "Are you a member?" he asks. "I don't recognize you," his eyes travel down my body, "and I'm sure I would had I seen you before."

"I-" I almost stutter from the nerves, my cheeks heating with a violent blush, but I clear my throat and grab a hold of myself. I shake my head, "not yet." I'm proud of how firm my voice is, but my heart is trying to climb up my throat and my body is humming with anxiety.

This is my choice. I can always leave if it's not what I expect.

"Welcome," he says with a smirk on his face, opening the door wider and allowing a warmth to flow through the door, urging me to enter.

Seductive music lures me inside. I give him a small smile and blush again when I catch him blatantly staring at my ass. My heels click on the stone floored foyer. The ceiling is domed and there's a large desk to my right, a coat check on my left. Beyond the foyer, the deep red carpet mutes the sound of my heels as I step forward, drawing me to the large open ballroom beyond the lobby. Or is it a dining room? There are tables and what looks like a stage behind a thick velvet curtain. I unconsciously step forward drawn in by the elegance and mystery and, to be frank, disbelief.

It literally takes my breath away.

"Miss?" A woman calls out after me. Her voice breaks me out of my reverie and I turn to face whoever's calling me.

A gorgeous woman walks towards me with a confidence I can only wish I possess in the boardroom. Her blonde hair is pulled back into a bun and her makeup is flawless and natural with the exception of a slight cat eye and thick long lashes that must be fake. There's no way those are real.

Although she's not young, she has a better figure that most and she strides towards me in her Louboutin heels as though she's owning a runway, the scarlet colored dress clinging to her curves the entire way.

Madam Lynn. She must be the Madam of the club.

I take a step forward and hold my hand out, moving my coat to the crook of my arm. "Madam Lynn?" I say, although it's a question.

The woman pauses, accepting my hand and smiling with a twinkle in her pale blue eyes.

"You've finally come." She says accepting my hand shake and taking me in. "Alena, correct?"

I nod my head and return her smile although my heart's still pounding in my chest. "Yes, I'm here."

"I'm glad you've accepted the invitation." She looks at my coat and then back to my eyes. "May I?" She asks while reaching out for it.

"Oh sure, of course." I hand her the coat and she immediately takes my hand and leads me back out into the lobby.

"I know you're going to want to look around and," she looks over her shoulder at me with a mischievous grin, "have some fun." She stops at the desk and waves over a young woman in a silk black jumpsuit, "but let's get you checked in first." My cheeks color with slight embarrassment.

"Yes, Madam Lynn," I say just beneath my breath.

She looks back at me with slight surprise and tilts her head. "Oh he was right about you."

I take in her words, letting them resonate in me slowly, as she walks behind the desk with the other woman tapping on keys at a computer.

Who is 'he' and what the fuck was he right about?

CHAPTER 3

Joshua

I WATCH ON THE SCREEN IN THE SECURITY ROOM AS DOMINIC LET'S Alena in from the cold and takes a deliberate look at her ass. It would piss me off if I wasn't feeling so fucking confident.

She's here because she wants this. She wouldn't have come otherwise. She had one day off this week and she chose to use it to come here.

I should be ashamed that I hacked into her emails, but I'm not. It's something that's almost natural at this point. With every application we do a background check. And that includes some digging that's on the other side of the law. But we have to be careful.

And with Alena, I had to make sure she was single and that she was still the same woman I once loved. The thought strikes me like a hit to the chest. *Love.* It's been a long time since I've said that word. With no family and no relationship, I haven't had a reason to. I huff a small laugh as I realize the last woman I ever told those three little words just walked into my club.

I remember her whispering it with such sincerity after I took her for the first time. It was slow and sweet and I hadn't revealed how much more I needed from her. I was desperate to have her and I wish I'd told her sooner. Regret starts to creep up on me, but I shake it off.

She's here now and that's what matters.

I watch the screens in the control room as she walks into the dining hall. She's beautiful in her cream chiffon pleated dress. She looks innocent and naive wearing that in here. If it were any other time, she'd be struck with surprise at how out of place she is. We usually don't let anyone into the building this early. Some Doms have keys to the private rooms that work from the entrances outside, but not in here.

When she emailed back asking to come, I allowed it. I'm already breaking rules for her. I'll break them all to get her to submit to me.

Madam Lynn is getting her set up. Watching the two of them interact makes me uneasy. Lynn knows how much this means to me. I turn on the volume for the mics and listen in as they walk through the hall and into the play rooms. There are several on the first floor, and even more in the dungeon.

Alena never struck me as a woman who'd care for the dungeon. She doesn't want pain. She just wants to give up control. Even if she doesn't realize it.

My thumb rests on my bottom lip as I watch the screen.

They're quiet as they walk into the first play room and she eyes the Andrew's cross in the back of the room.

There are two crosses as well as some other furniture meant for BDSM interaction.

I can see her tied to one. Bound and helpless. Her eyes widen slightly and I can see her breath hitch as she realizes that's what it's for. She pauses mid step and looks at the dark raw wood beams as though they may bite her.

I lean forward watching her every move and willing her to explore.

I don't want her to be scared off just yet. She would enjoy it.

As if hearing my thoughts, she takes a few steps forward and gently touches the wood. Running her fingers down the side of it and eyeing the leather cuffs attached to it.

I can see the wheels turning in her head and finally, those plump lips part with lust clouding her eyes. *Yes!*

She turns abruptly and clears her throat.

"How are the…" she looks away and then back at Madam Lynn. "How do the Dom's choose their subs?" she asks. My skin prickles with excitement.

"Well," Lynn takes a seat on the dark brown leather chaise and crosses her legs as she leans against the back of it. "Submissives and dominants are free to roam so long as they're wearing the bracelets that signify their interests.

"So as long as I have no collar and wear this," she raises her arm, showing off the three layered bracelet, silver, black, silver, bands. "Then the dominants will know?"

Black for carte blanche. A smile slips into place. I have so much to explore with her. So much to teach her.

Lynn nods her head. "That's correct." She gestures to the cross. "If you'd like to go up there, you can simply kneel by it and wait for a partner.

Alena's head whips to the side. "Just wait?" she asks with a higher pitched voice. Her face is etched with insecurity. "What if no one wants to."

Lynn laughs at the absurdity. It pisses me off that she thinks no one would want to accept the offer. She'd have men lining up for her.

My hands ball into fists. That's not going to happen though. I'll kick all those fuckers out before I allow that. *She's mine.*

My anger dissipates entirely as Alena asks, her voice laced with fear, "what happens if they just leave me there or-"

Lynn's quick to cut that off, and I'm relieved she's there to put cherry at ease. This was good. I was right to handle it this way. Lynn isn't intimidating in the least. This is the perfect introduction for Alena.

"We have security in each of the rooms at all times. All you'd have to do is safe word. If you're gagged, then you can use a hand signal."

I can see Alena taking in the information and letting it calm her down. She nods slightly and looks at the other trinkets and toys around the room. Most items are in packages because of the nature of their use. Vibrators, plugs, nipple clamps. Some paddles and whips aren't packaged. They can be wiped down and sterilized.

"You can always go up for auction," Lynn offers out of nowhere. Every hair on my body stands upright, the breath stolen from my lungs. Once a month we hold an auction. It's a one month long contract. Lynn's eyes meet the camera in the room and I know that comment was meant for me.

I grunt and sit back in my seat. Fuck that, cherry's not going up for auction .. although. If I bought her she couldn't say no. I'd have her to myself for an entire month.

She'd have to sign the paperwork afterwards though. And the next auction isn't for two weeks. I'm not waiting that long or risking her running when she finds out that I'm the one who bought her. Waiting this last week was too much as it is.

I've waited long enough.

She wants a Dom and I want her. That's all that matters.

I watch as Alena shakes her head, although her eyes are hazed with curiosity. "I don't think an auction is what I'm looking for." *Good girl.*

I rise from my seat. Muting the microphones and buttoning my suit jacket. It's time for me to take over the tour and show Alena what she really needs.

CHAPTER 4

Alena

THE SECOND PLAY ROOM IS EVEN MORE INTERESTING THAN THE first. It seems more private since it's smaller and there's only one of everything … but there are so many items I'm not sure if multiple couples play together or not.

"How many people are usually in here?" I turn to Madam Lynn and ask. I love the idea of being at a Dom's mercy. But I'm not sure how I feel about other people watching. Especially at first, when I'm just learning. All of this is overwhelming to see in person.

I just don't think I could do it if strangers were watching. And the insecurity of it all is making me wonder if I can do this at all. I swallow thickly and wait for her to answer.

She's been patient and I really appreciate the tour. I didn't expect it. I also didn't expect it to be so empty.

"The play rooms are usually packed." My lips purse and my brow raises. Shit. I don't think I can handle that. I look around the room at the benches and sex swing and try to imagine being fucked mercilessly while tied down and having people watch. The first part heats my blood and makes desire stir low in my belly, but the second … it kills the fantasy for me.

I can't lie. I've been mused about this for a long time. More so recently since getting the email. I've touched myself to the thought of what it would've been like had I let Joshua dominate me like he wanted.

It caught me off guard back then. I kept thinking it was wrong and that he must've thought less of me. But now that I look back on it, he never treated me differently. He was just more aware of what he wanted. He shared his desires with me and fear kept me from submitting.

I wonder what it would have been like if I'd let him cuff me to the bed like he wanted to. What he would have done to me. I stifle my moan at the thought of him strapping me down and spreading my legs while I'm bound and helpless.

Madam Lynn's cough makes a blush stain my cheeks. I turn and ignore the fact that my thoughts must've been obvious.

A frown pulls at my lips as I take in the room, remembering what we were just talking about. Coming here would be nothing like what I fantasize about. I'm not interested in an orgy or voyeurism. Whatever it is that they call it.

I was hopeful that this was going to fulfill my needs, but all this tour has done is fill me with regret. I wish I'd never ended things with Joshua. I let my fear push him away.

I bite the inside of my cheek.

"I wouldn't worry too much if I were you," Madam Lynn says, her seductive voice grabbing my attention and bringing me back to the present.

"Why's that?" I dare to ask.

She may be elegant and graceful, but Madam Lynn seems to be a woman of secrets. She has a look in her eyes and a manner of speaking that makes it obvious that she knows more than she's telling you. I'm not sure I like that, but considering her profession, it's admirable.

"I have a feeling you'll be spending most of your time in a private room." My shoulders relax slightly at the thought. Yes, I think I'd much prefer privacy.

I open my lips to ask to see the rooms, but my body freezes as my eyes catch sight of *him*. My heart, my blood, everything slows and heats to a nearly unbearable degree.

I blink a few times. Not believing he's here.

"Alena," Joshua steps into the room, proving that he's not a figment of my imagination. My entire body feels as though it's on fire.

Holy fuck!

Ten years ago he was a hot-as-fuck twenty year old. The years have aged him beautifully. His strong jawline and broad shoulders heighten the severity of his suit. Joshua has always radiated power, sex appeal and authority to me. But in this moment he is the epitome of dominance.

I almost take a step back as he walks closer to me, out of sheer instinct. But my lust for him has me frozen in place. I can hardly breathe as the images I was just conjuring flash before my eyes.

Prickles of want travel down my body, hardening my nipples.

Desire stirs in my core.

"I have more work to attend to," Madam Lynn says to no one in particular and not waiting for a response. she gracefully, yet quickly leaves me alone with Joshua.

This is not good.

As she closes the door behind her, the only thing I can think is that I am so fucked.

CHAPTER 5

Joshua

I EXCEL AT READING BODY LANGUAGE. AND RIGHT NOW MY CHERRY is looking to bolt, but more than that, she's turned on. I have to resist the urge to smile. I want her. I want her badly. And it's obvious that she wants me too.

"Do you want to try it out?" I ask her as she tries to right herself. She still hasn't spoken and I can practically hear the questions on the tip of her tongue.

There's a spark between us, a recognition of desire and want. But our past is in the way and all I want is for it to move aside so I can take her like I'm meant to.

"Joshua," she finally says my name as I walk closer to her, standing at a safe distance, but close enough to talk easily.

"How are you Alena?"

She nods her head as her fingertips roll the hem of her dress nervously and she glances behind me at the door. Her cheeks are colored with a violent blush that looks beautiful on her.

"How did you-" she starts to ask, but she doesn't complete the thought. It could be one of many questions.

How did I get here?

How did I know she was here?

I decide to lay it all out for her and let her choose what to do with it.

"I knew you were coming." I answer her. My heart races as her eyes widen. "In fact, I asked Madam Lynn to send you the invitation." I spot the large wing back chair and decide to take a seat. It will be less intimidating for her if I'm sitting.

Her lips part with a question and then slam shut. She blinks several times.

"I saw you a few weeks ago in the city and I couldn't believe you were here." I sit back in my chair, "I thought this may be better." I look her in the eyes and wait for a response. It may have been easier to stop her from leaving the coffee shop, to walk up to her at the elevator before she went to work. But that would have set the wrong precedent.

This is the relationship I want. And the one she needs.

Our needs have to be established. Without it, without her willing to give both of us what we need, this relationship will fail like it did before. This time I'm going to fight for it. I want her badly enough to convince her to give this a chance.

"I wanted to see you here. I wanted to offer you this." I gesture around the room.

She blinks several times and then a small breath leaves her and her eyes gaze with lust.

"You want this?" she asks me as though she's shocked by the truth. Her hands reach up to her collarbone and she looks at me with a raw vulnerability I've only seen in her eyes once. The night I first made her mine. All those years ago.

I nod my head once. "I want this with you."

She seems to come out of the lust filled haze and realize she's in a room with me, a man who she's hardly spoken to in years. But I'm still a man she once loved. A man who knew her better than anyone.

"You don't know me, Joshua," she starts to say although she's obviously bothered.

"I knew you well enough to know you'd want this." I know she's going to fight at first. She's not used to submitting, but I'll earn her trust, I'll show her it's worth it.

It's quiet for a moment as she takes in my confession. "Do you come here a lot?" she asks, changing the subject.

"I'm a partner in the business." Her mouth drops some and she looks around the room with more unease than before. Insecurity obvious on her face.

This is a turn for the worse and I don't understand why. I wasn't expecting it.

"What's wrong?" I ask.

She shakes her head and almost refuses to answer.

"What did I say?" although it's a question, there's a command in my tone.

She recognizes it and considers me for a moment. She may not know it, but this is just like any other submission. She can choose to trust that she can trust me and answer the question honestly, or she can blow it off or hide from it and run without giving me a chance. I wait with baited breath for her choice.

And finally she answers, "I just didn't realize you did this a lot."

It doesn't take me long to read between the lines. I stand and make my way over to her, holding her gaze. "Do you think I fuck a lot, Alena?" I walk close enough to touch her, but I don't yet. "You think this is a game for me and you don't want to be used and tossed aside?"

I know that's exactly what she's thinking. And why wouldn't she? I work in the business of selling sex and she's going to want a commitment. She needs one.

"I don't." I tell her the truth. "This isn't about a quick fuck for me. I'm not a playboy. I didn't bring you here to toy with you. I want to see if this can work between us." I'm not ready to fall back into the deep relationship we had before. Not just yet. But I won't lie and say it's not something that's on the forefront of my mind. I want her as a submissive, but I can give her more than that.

I can give her everything, if only she'll let me.

"What do you want from me then?" she asks.

"I just want a chance. One I never got before." I take a step closer and gently brush my hand along her jaw, leaning in so I can whisper against her lips. "I want to show you how much you'd love it."

Her eyes close and I know she wants the same.

As she leans in, I pull away slightly. I need her to submit before I can give her anything else. She opens her eyes instantly at the loss of my touch. Her breathing is heavy and I know she's feeling insecure. I don't want that. But I need this first. It's too big a part of my life and my desires.

"Do you want to try it?" I ask and gesture to the bench behind her. It's a spanking bench made of plush leather and steel.

She turns to look behind her, pushing her soft brunette hair out of her face.

"Right now?" she asks.

I nod my head once, "right now."

She may not be ready just yet. And I can wait, I can take it slow. But she's in need and I'm desperate to fulfill those needs.

"I don't know," she answers honestly.

"What don't you know about?"

"I don't think I trust myself right now," she smiles slightly letting out a small nervous laugh.

"You don't need to, just trust me." I look into her eyes and plead with her to give me this. To give *us* this. "I still want you Alena. I've never stopped wanting you."

She takes in a sharp breath, her hazel eyes heating with a lust that makes my dick harden.

"I want to," she whispers.

"What do you want?" I ask her.

"I want to… try it out." She barely gets the words out, but I heard them and it's all I need.

CHAPTER 6

Alena

MY HEART IS RACING OUT OF MY CHEST.

What am I even doing?

I feel drunk from the pure seductive nature of this atmosphere. And from *him*. He always made me weak and he's doing it again right now.

Seeing him in this very room is a dream come true. But it's terrifying at same time. I feel like a naive girl all over again. I close my eyes and walk over to the bench. I want to do this. This is why I came here in the first place.

This is for me. I need this.

I open my eyes at the thought and the look in Joshua's eyes pins me in place. It's predatory and full of lust. The desire evident on his face, but also… lower. His massive cock is hard and the outline of it is pressing against his suit pants.

I close my eyes again as he walks forward.

"Look at me, cherry." The command in his voice is hard and on edge. It's a tone he's only used with me once. I refused it then, but I won't now.

My eyes meet his piercing gaze.

"Yes?" I almost say sir. Simply because I know the language. I've done some research over the years. I'm familiar with this scenario and I want it. I want it desperately. Even if it's just for now.

Just this one time.

"I want you to lay down on your back on the bench." My body stiffens at his command. I'm not used to it. It's not what I anticipated either.

I turn to look at the leather seat as my hands drift to the buttons on the top of my dress.

"I didn't tell you to undress," my eyes snap to Joshua's at his words.

"Yes, sir." The title slips out without my consent and the look on Joshua's face makes me want to say it again. And again and again. He's obviously pleased and that makes pride and motivation flow through my body. I hold onto them as I gently lay down on the bench. It's angled slightly, so my head is lower than my ass and it feels a bit awkward.

"That's my sweet cherry." Hearing the praise in Joshua's voice and the nickname he gave me so long ago fills me with warmth. *Cherry.* I loved it when he called me that. My thighs clench and my eyes close at the sweet memories of what we once had and what I walked away from all those years ago. But now I have a chance to have it back. I can give him what he's always needed. I know I can.

As I think the words, he brushes his hands up my thighs and loops his thumbs around my panties. I lift my hips as the thin fabric slides over my ass and he slowly pulls them down my legs. Goosebumps follow his path and my body ignites with an intense need for more.

"If you want me to stop, you'll say red. Do you understand?"

"Yes," I breathe the word.

I can't breathe as he takes them off me and tosses them onto the chair behind him. Oh fuck.

I swallow thickly and wait for his next command. My clit is throbbing with need and my nipples are hardened into peaks. I want him so much, it takes everything in me to just lay here and wait patiently for him.

His large hands grip the inside of my knees and spreads my legs wider. I grip the edge of the bench harder as he lowers himself closer to my bared pussy. I'm fully exposed and feeling a mixture of desire and insecurity. It takes me back to our first time. It's just like that. All over again.

He pulls my dress up slightly over my hips and stares at my pussy with a hunger I've never seen on another man. My lips part with lust. I love the look in his eyes. I've missed it. I've missed *him.*

He kneels on the floor and grips my hips, moving my ass and tilting me so I'm where he wants me.

Oh, fuck. My neck arches and I want to watch and I want to run and hide all at the same time.

"Fuck, cherry," Joshua says as he trails a finger down my clit to the opening of my pussy. "You're soaking wet for me."

My clit throbs as he leans down and takes a languid lick. My neck arches and my mouth opens with the unexpected pleasure.

"Hold onto the bench," he says firmly and I look up at him and realize my hands are on his shoulders. I nod and quickly follow his command.

As soon as I do, he thrusts two thick fingers deep inside of me, making my back bow and sending spikes of pleasure shooting through my body. *Fuck, yes!*

My nipples harden and I instantly remember how he used to control my body. I know now why sex has never been the same. My body is a slave to his touch. *Only his.* I writhe on the bench, but his firm grip on my hip keeps me pinned in place.

I can't help the moans spilling from my lips as he strokes my g-spot over and over again, making me climb higher and higher. Soft cries fill the room as my head thrashes.

So close. I'm so close.

As he sucks my clit into his mouth, massaging it with his tongue, my body ignites, coming alive with a pleasure that's unmatched. White spots flash before my eyes as I cry out my release.

My back arches and my hands reach up to grab his hair and push him closer to my pussy, but I'm quick to go back to the bench and obey him.

I grip onto the bench as hard as I can while he continues to suck my clit and fingerfuck every last bit of my orgasm out of me.

I gasp for air as my head falls to the side. Every inch of my body tingling with desire. I struggle to breathe and finally calm down as I hear a zipper. I look down my body and see Joshua's thick cock and my heart stops.

"Turn over cherry," his voice drips with desire as he gives me the command. He holds my hips, steadying me as I quickly do what he says and get into position even with the intensity of my orgasm still racing through my body in dim waves.

His deft fingers quickly strap the cuffs to my wrists and ankles and my heart races. I trust him. I do. I'd be lying if I said I wasn't partially scared, but I want this. I want to get over my fear. I want to *enjoy* this.

His hot breath on my ass makes me want more. He leaves a kiss on my right cheek as the trembling in my legs settles.

I can hardly breathe as he kisses up my body, pushing the dress above my waist, his fingers trailing softly up my body. A shiver runs down my body and I just want him right now. I don't want to wait.

His soft touches are torturous.

"I want you Cherry. Let me have you just like this, with nothing in-between us." His voice drips with lust and desperation as he gently sets his hands down on my hips. It makes me feel powerful. Even though I'm bound, it's my limits that he has to abide by and the knowledge makes me yearn for more. "It's what I've always wanted." He barely speaks the words.

I've been dreaming of this for so long.

"I know you want it to," he whispers into my ear. His hot breath sending shivers down my entire body.

I pull against the straps and moan, arching my neck to let his teeth graze down my neck. I give in to him like I want to. I trust him and I want him. It's now or never.

"Yes, Joshua. Please. Take me."

CHAPTER 7

Joshua

I'VE WANTED THIS FOR TOO FUCKING LONG.

I line my dick up at her entrance and slam all the way in without hesitation. The bench tilts forward slightly, but it's bolted to the floor. I can fuck her as hard and fast as I want. And there's nothing to stop me from giving her just that.

She screams out a ragged cry of pleasure as I hammer into her tight pussy over and over again. I'm rough with her and ruthless, it's a hard fuck, but it's how I want her and I know she'll love it. The sounds of her pleasured moans and my hips slamming against her ass, fill my ears. I fucking love it.

I'm going to give her everything. I want her so consumed with pleasure that she can't think straight. I want her so sore tomorrow that she can't sit without remembering this.

She's mine.

I want her to know it with everything in her. I want to own this tight pussy. The thought makes me groan as she writhes under me as best she can although she's bound. It's a useless effort, but instinctual.

Fuck, she feels so good. Too good. I groan as I lean forward and nip along her shoulder, keeping up a relentless pace.

Her strangled cries of pleasure fuel me to push harder and deeper.

"Joshua!" she screams out my name as I push her limits. Yes! My name. Her breathing is ragged and I love it. The sound fuels me onward.

She pulls at the leather cuffs on her wrists and I nip her earlobe, "stay still while I fuck you just how I want." If she pulls any more, the leather could rub against her wrists. I don't want that. Even more so, I want her to obey me. I want to give her a command that she can obey, even if it is against her instincts.

She bites down on her lip as I pound into her over and over. Fuck yes! She's perfect. She's trying so hard to stay still. Her head thrashes from side to side and she's holding her breath as her mouth opens into a perfect "O". She's so close.

"Scream for me as you cum on my dick, cherry." At my words, she cries out my name, her pussy spasming on my dick. Yes! My name! Because she's *mine*. I ride through her orgasm, hammering harder into her as I grip her hips. My blunt fingernails dig into the soft flesh and I piston my hips.

"Joshua!" she screams again and sucks in a sharp breath and it only fuels me to go faster, to take her over the edge again. I want to give her everything.

I need to. This is my one chance to have her and show her how good this is going to be. How easy it is and how much she'll enjoy it.

I keep fucking her, over and over with hard, fast strokes, taking her to the edge.

My balls draw up and a cool tingling sensation grows at the base of my spine. Fuck, I'm going to cum. She's so tight and so good, I can't fucking hold it any longer.

"Cum for me again," I tell her with my eyes firmly on her gorgeous face as my hand reaches between the bench and I gently pinch her clit.

Her face scrunches and her body tenses as her orgasm rips through her body. She pulls instinctually at the binds, but she's quick to correct the behavior. Fuck, she's so good. Knowing that even as she's overwhelmed with pleasure, she's still trying to obey me, makes me lose it.

I bury myself to the hilt and pump short, shallow thrusts until we're both spent and left panting with our combined cum leaking onto her thighs.

My body is still humming with the afterglow of my release as I grab a few tissues from beneath the bench and catch my breath. I tuck myself in, watching as her legs stop trembling and the effects of her orgasm dims.

She was perfect. Everything I've dreamed of having in a submissive. From the moment she decided to walk to the bench and give this a real try, she gave herself completely.

I kiss the small of her back as I wipe the cum from between her thighs and then unbuckle the straps on her ankles. Her wrists are next and she immediately sits.

I pick her up in my arms and she leans into me, her body still trembling. I lean back and sooth her, running my hand down her back and kissing her hair. She's so beautiful. The years have only made her more of a woman. After a moment she moves from my lap, not looking me in the eyes. I don't like it. Aftercare is important, but I let her get up and move to the chair where her panties are.

I regret letting her get up when I see the look in her eyes. She's on edge and nervous. She's thinking too much. Worrying about what's going to happen.

If she was my sub she wouldn't have a worry in the world. And I want her to be just that.

She leans down and pulls her panties on and up her lush thighs without looking at me.

I bet she's wondering what this meant to me and if it's over.

I don't want her to wonder; I don't want her to think about anything at all but pleasing me. After all, I'm doing the same.

"I have a Christmas dinner tomorrow to attend for a client." The words escape my lips before I can think. Her forehead pinches and she's unsure why I'm even bringing it up. "I want you to come with me."

She stares at me wide-eyed and doesn't answer.

"A submissive doesn't question the commands." I pick my suit jacket up off the floor and wait for her response. "You know what to say Alena."

I wait with baited breath. This is about more than sex for me. And I damn well know the same is true for her. She just needs to give in.

"You came in here for a reason cherry." Her eyes dart to mine. "Let me give you what you need."

Her lips part with uncertainty.

"I want you. As submissive and more. I want you to be mine."

Her eyes focus on my lips and I know I have her. If nothing else, she loves my touch. But I know there's more to it than that. You don't hold on to this desire and these feelings if there isn't *more* to it.

"Just say yes, Cherry. Let me collar you, like you really want me to."

She says the next words in the sweetest voice I've ever heard, "collar me, Joshua. I'm ready."

EPILOGUE

Alena

I TWIST MY HANDS AND STRUGGLE TO MOVE. I'VE BEEN WAITING here on the bed, tied down by my wrists and ankles for at least twenty minutes. In the six months that we've dated, Joshua has never made me wait this long.

I'm naked and horny and so ready for him to take me. But I lay here quietly and wait. I know he's going to come in and give me exactly what I need. And I trust him to do just that.

A small smile plays at my lips.

The only thing I really need is him. I sigh with contentment, feeling warm and safe. He's my security in life. I feel complete with him. I didn't even realize how much I was missing from life until he showed me.

My eyes slowly open and my pussy clenches as I hear the door creak open.

My chest flushes and heat travels to my cheeks. I'm spread and naked and I know he's seeing everything. But that's the way he wants me.

"Cherry, you're so damn patient," he says from behind me as he walks into the bedroom.

"For you," I answer with a smirk. Really, he's the patient one. It took me ten years to accept that I wanted this. Ten years for me to let him show me how much I'd love it.

The bed groans as he crawls closer to me. He's hiding something in his hand and excitement courses through me at the thought of what it could be.

"I got you a present," he says seductively. I smile broadly and let my teeth sink into my bottom lip to try to conceal my elation.

Ever since our second night together, he brings me little gifts while I'm tied up. That second night was Christmas Eve and he gave me a collar. It's beautiful and I love it. I wear the necklace, another gift from Joshua, outside of Club X, but inside and in the bedroom, I proudly wear my collar.

"What is it?" I ask.

"Uh uh, close your eyes." I smile sweetly at him, my eyes darting from his handsome face to his closed hand.

I close my eyes and wait patiently. My blood heats and my breath stills as he leans over and slips a cold metal ring onto my ring finger. *Oh my god.*

"Marry me Cherry." Joshua says in a voice that has a hint of insecurity. I keep my eyes closed. Still in disbelief.

"Say yes." He gives me another command.

I slowly open my eyes and stare back at him.

"You're mine, Alena. And I want you forever and for everyone to know it."

Tears prick my eyes and I nod my head. "I love you," I say as he bends down, kissing me sweetly. He breaks our kiss and says in the hot air between us, "you need to say yes."

"Yes," I whisper. He takes my lips with his and groans into my kiss. I have to pull away and struggle against the damn binds pinning me down. I just want to hold him.

A rough chuckle rises up his chest as he reaches over and unties my wrists and then my ankles.

It's then that I get a good look at the sparkling ring on my finger. It's a beautiful cushion cut with perfect clarity and at least three carats. I stare at it in awe.

"I had to tie you down and make sure you'd say yes."

I shake my head, my shoulders shuddering with a small laugh, "you had to know I'd say yes." I've never wanted anything more than this. My life feels truly complete. "You collared me for Christmas," I jokingly say back to him.

He shakes his head and looks at the gorgeous engagement ring on my finger. "For life my cherry."

STOLEN MISTLETOE KISSES

CHAPTER 1

Vinny

THE BRIGHTLY COLORED MOUSE FACE ON THE PLASTIC PHONE IN my hands stares back at me. I remember this toy, with its primary colors of red, yellow, and blue, and the loud noises the buttons make. I can't pull the little phone out, but I know there's a thin red cord that's connected so little tykes can drag it along the floor. I huff a small laugh.

Same damn toy I had as a toddler, twenty-five years later.

Some things never change.

I set the box back on the shelf and look over to my left. This aisle in the toy store lines up with the door to the back room, which in turn leads to the manager's office. That's right where I need to go. I'm just waiting on the perfect moment to slip into the back and grab the spare key. The manager slipped out already; he clocked out early even though the store's still open. I don't blame him, since it's dead. In this small town, everyone's done their shopping early for Christmas.

The owner and him are the only two with the keys to the registers, but now they're both gone and won't be back till after Christmas, and I know the keys are back there somewhere.

The old lady behind me finally tosses something into her cart, making a small racket and a squeak. I turn to look over my shoulder and watch as she pushes her cart away. I take the chance, looking to my right and left as I make my way to the "employees only" door and confidently open it.

As though I belong back here.

My heart's racing, and adrenaline is pumping through my veins. This isn't the first time I've done something like this. It's been years since I've jacked a car or stolen anything. Back then I was a thief for hire. I'm not proud of it. But now I stay on the right side of the law. I peek into the break room and see it's empty. Stockroom is next and there's a girl bending at the waist digging in a box, muttering about how the color of the dress on the doll isn't gonna matter. I keep walking until I find the door with the Manager's Office plate on it.

Bingo.

I test the knob and it doesn't budge. But that's alright. I may be a reformed man, but I still remember how to pick a lock. I stare at the door for a moment, then look back to the storefront at the end of the hallway as I shove a bent paperclip in the lock.

This isn't about stealing for me. It's about doing the right thing. Maybe it's the wrong way of going about it, but it's the only way I know.

The lock clicks and I'm quick to open the door, walking in as swiftly and quietly as possible and shut it behind me with a soft low *snick*. My heart pounds, and I can hear the blood rushing in my ears.

I stalk to his desk and check there first. I need the keys to the register. I need that cash. I know this old toy shop doesn't have a safe. All the money's stored in the registers, and I need that fucking key.

It's not on the desk. I open one drawer after another, sifting through all the paperwork and looking under the stapler and pens.

Where the fuck is it? I know he didn't take it with him. He's got the key to the entrance doors though and I wasn't able to lift that like I would have liked. My eyes look up and hone in on something shining on the bookshelf filled with binders.

A smile crawls across my face.

The tiny key that's been a pain in my ass the last week to get is hanging on a keychain, and I don't hesitate to grab it. Finally. The last piece falls into place. I shove it in my pocket, knowing I'm one step closer to completing this task. Nothing's going to stop me.

I put my ear to the door and listen for anyone coming. I don't hear anything, so I open it slowly and peek out.

The chick who was digging in the box is walking toward the door leading out to the rest of the store with her back to me. She's empty-handed and muttering to herself with her hands balled into little fists. She huffs a deep breath like she's getting ready to go to war over this doll. I shut the door and wait a moment, listening for the telltale sound of the heavy door opening and then shutting. *Click.*

Once the coast is clear, I sneak another look and make sure.

No one's there. My throat feels dry and my face is heated, knowing I need to make a clean getaway out of here and back into the store.

I lock the manager's office door behind me and make a beeline for my escape. As soon as I'm back to the customer area, I feel a slight sense of relief. But I need to get the fuck out of here. One rule I always lived by back in the day, you never stick around to find out if someone saw you.

There's no security in this place though. I know that for a fact.

If there were, I wouldn't have to do this. They would've caught that bastard in the act, and it wouldn't be left up to me to get justice.

I walk quickly toward the exit, through a few aisles of toy trucks and stacking blocks, but I stop before walking through the large automated glass doors.

Cary Ann's standing at the register. Sweet Cary. The sight of her makes me stop before I can leave.

I've known her most of my life since we grew up together in this small town, but scoping this place out has made me see her in a new light. It's been years since I really *looked* at her. And now I can't stop. She's not the little girl who'd fawn over me on the school sidewalks. She's a woman now.

Her tight, faded jeans fit her figure just right and make my dick hard as a fucking rock. They leave nothing to the imagination, and I can just picture how the curve of her ass would feel in my hands. I don't know how it's possible that I ever looked at her with anything other than lust; she's fucking gorgeous.

Her white tanktop is low enough that a bit of cleavage is showing, but the red cardigan she has partially buttoned up over it makes her look a bit more modest. I crave more. I wanna see more of that sun-kissed skin. Every inch.

She's always popping that bubble gum, blowing big, round, cherry-red bubbles at the checkout counter. *Pop!*

It's like she knows she's tempting me with her sweet innocent glances. I don't even know what she's still doing here; she's better than this.

She's got her degree in social work, and I know she doesn't want to work here at the toy store forever. This was a side job for money while she was at the university. She shouldn't be here.

I clear my throat as the front doors open and an older lady walks out, clutching her cardigan.

Cary's a distraction. And she's sure as fuck too good for a man like me.

I thought she'd be gone by now. In the weeks I've been staking this place out, I never thought she'd still be here. But Christmas is around the corner, and she's not showing any signs of leaving or even putting in her notice.

That's a big fucking problem for me. I'm stealing every fucking dime in this place on Christmas Eve. She can't be here, but she's scheduled to be the one closing. All alone, too. I can't pull a gun out and point it at my cherry. The thought of putting fear into those innocent baby blues breaks my heart.

But I'm not the villain here; Jimmy Morose, the owner, is a greedy thief. He's practically the fucking Grinch. All the money that was supposed to go to the orphanage, he's already stolen. I'm getting it back though, and that means emptying these tills at midnight on Christmas Eve. It's the perfect time, right when the annual Christmas Eve parade will be happening and the police will all be there on the other side of town. It's then, or never.

But Cherry's going to be here… A grin slips into place. I could just steal her, too.

CHAPTER 2

Cary Ann

HE'S HERE AGAIN, AND HE STILL HASN'T BOUGHT A DAMN THING. Not that a man like him looks like he needs anything in this toy store. I think he's just coming to check me out. Or at least I thought he was. But he hasn't said a damn word to me. Maybe I'm just vain or getting carried away with the thoughts I used to have of him.

Vinny's a bad boy… or bad *man*, I should say.

I knew him growing up, and lusted after his I-don't-give-a-fuck attitude. He wore his leather jacket and rode that motorcycle everywhere. I wanted to be on the back of that bike. I wanted him to take me away. I shake off the thoughts and swallow down my childhood fantasies.

I was just a silly little girl. My parents would never have allowed it, and he was a few years older anyway. He wasn't interested in a girl like me. Besides, I'm better for it now. I have my degree in social work, and I've already nailed down the job of my dreams. I'm going to be making the world a better place.

I'm not saying Vinny would've held me back, but I'm damn proud that I was able to focus on school and my career.

And to be wise enough to know what's been going on around here.

Now Vinny's back, and he's tempting me. But judging by the puppy dog look on his face, I'm tempting him just as much.

My heart beats just a little faster, and my blood heats with lust. *Pop!* I blow out a bubble and hide my smile when I see him shake his head and smirk at me. My cheeks heat with a blush as I lower my head out of shyness and ring up the remote control car for the mom that's checking out.

"But I want it!" her little boy screams from the seat in his cart, and his loud shriek brings me back to the present.

He's a cute little guy in a snowman sweatshirt, jeans and little boots that look like they could take on a blizzard. But his high-pitched yells and him kicking the cart are driving me crazy. And giving me a headache.

"You want to just hand it to him, or do you want it in a bag?" I ask the mom. I feel bad that she's got two kids out here this late at night. That's gotta be a handful and even worse since they're obviously tired. She looks worn the fuck out. Her hair's pulled back into a ponytail and the little infant in her arms is trying to yank on her earring, which is a miniature Christmas ornament. I wince. That looks like it hurts.

The woman leans her head down so her baby isn't tugging on the earring, seething through her clenched teeth; the pain is evident on her face as she pries the little fingers off of the dangling jewelry. The little girl squeals with delight in her mama's arms and the woman gives the baby a small smile, but switches her to the other hip.

I don't know what good that's gonna do, since the little girl just focuses on that side's earring now.

"No thanks, can you bag it please?" she answers with a forced smile and leans forward to talk to the boy in the cart. "You have to wait, little man." Good for her for at least holding it together.

The boy comically crosses his arms across his chest with a pout, and I have to stifle my laughter as I ring her up.

Once she's done, the store's basically empty. And it's only a few minutes before close. Thank God. I'm spent. I'm ready to get out of here and grateful that so many people are shopping online. I yawn and cover my mouth, then look back to where Vinny was standing. He's gone, and the sight of the empty aisle makes a frown touch my lips. I don't know why, but I just want him to say hi. To just acknowledge my presence. He never did growing up, but I never talked to him either. I didn't have the courage back then. Now though… I need to suck it up and let him know I'm interested. I can do that. I should've already.

He's been in here three times this week, and he's never bought a damn thing. The knowledge makes my stomach twist in knots.

He's up to no good. I hate that I think that. That's what everyone said when he was growing up. They pretend like they don't know why he ended up doing shady things when they never even gave him a chance at anything else. From what I know, he's a good man now. He's got his life together. And I hate that I think anything negative about him at all. But why the hell does he keep coming in here?

I hated the way the parents and teachers all talked about him when we were younger, yet I find myself thinking he's gotta be up to something.

Or maybe I'm just projecting my own actions onto his behavior. My blood cools at the thought, but I can't focus on that right now.

I smile as I ring up the last two customers in the entire place. At least there aren't any more kids in here yelling. I've taken so much Advil the past week that I should really consider buying stock in them.

I'm leaving soon though; this job isn't forever. I just need to stay until Christmas. I have to. I need to be here and make sure everything goes the way it's supposed to on Christmas Eve.

With the store finally empty, I go through the daily closing checklist and take a peek down one aisle. It's a fucking disaster.

Cindy's crouched down, picking up dolls off the floor and shoving them back into place on the shelf. "I bet it was that little brat," she says under her breath when she sees me. I have to press my lips together and hide my grin. She's had a really hard day and given the fact that she only stayed on later because the manager ducked out early, I can see why she's pissed.

"I can take these if you wanna line up aisle three?" I ask her. I know she prefers the larger toys. They're mostly in boxes and easier to straighten out.

She sighs and looks up at me, shoving her blonde hair out of her face. "It doesn't matter really. I'm just tired and ready to go home." She looks fucking exhausted.

"Go ahead," I say with a shrug, "I got this." I don't mind taking a little more work anyway. *Besides, it'll give me a chance to get things ready for Christmas Eve.* The thought makes my skin prickle with nerves.

"You are a saint, Cary." She rises slowly and stretches out before giving me an unexpected hug.

"Thank you," she says and then doesn't look back as she heads out the front doors to the parking lot. For this town, nine o'clock is late for any place to be open. But for the holiday season it's worth it to be open another three hours on Sunday. At least that's what Morose thinks, but he's a liar, a thief, and an asshole. Judging by the lack of business, you can add dumbass to that list.

I have to straighten two more rows, all the while wondering if I'm going to be able to go through with my plan, and then I turn out the lights and lock the doors. I've been sick over this. I can't stand it, and I want to make things right.

But I'm struggling with what I need to do. I'm not a criminal. And what I'm planning on doing is a crime. I run my hand over my face, feeling torn and exhausted as I walk to the parking lot. It's late, and the street lights are dim. My heels click on the pavement, and my keys rattle in my hand. I look at the ground as I carefully watch my step, avoiding the potholes in the parking lot that Jimmy Morose hasn't bothered to get fixed yet. The only sounds I hear are my heels, and I think I'm alone, but when I lift my head, I stop in my tracks.

Vinny.

He's leaning against my car, his motorcycle parked behind him.

CHAPTER 3

Vinny

ICAN AT LEAST GET HER NUMBER, I think as I walk out of the store. Take her on a date. Maybe then I can convince her to quit. Or better yet, wear her out and make her pussy so sore she won't be able to work on Christmas Eve.

The thought makes me smile as I take out my cell and text Toni. I let him know it's all set for Christmas Eve and then sit on my bike watching the little boy across the parking lot say "please" over and over again to the mom who looks like she's gonna snap any minute. She's got a cart full of toys by her trunk, a little boy kicking the cart for enjoyment while begging for something, and the baby in her arms is throwing a fit.

Last-minute shopping doesn't look like it's treating her well.

"You need a hand with that?" I ask her, walking away from my bike and over to her minivan. The night air is crisp, and my boots smack against the pavement.

"Please," she says as she looks up at me, but it doesn't last long as her infant arches her back and lets out a shrill cry. "I thought they'd sleep," she says with desperation cracking her voice. Poor mama. I feel bad for her as I reach in the cart and grab a few of the bags in each hand.

She opens the trunk and then the side door before placing her keys back in her purse. "My husband had to work late," she starts explaining, as if she owes me that, but she doesn't. I get it. Sometimes we do shit we wish we didn't have to. "And he was supposed to do the shopping for his side of the family, and he never did." She talks while plugging her little one into the carseat. I can faintly hear the clicking of the buckles.

The rustling from a plastic bag makes me look up, and I catch her little boy trying to grab one of the bags.

She shuts the door and comes around the rear of the van with her hands on her hips. "Jaxon!" she yells out. The little boy looks up with big wide eyes and his lips in a perfect "O." He's been caught red-handed. And he knows it. The look of fear is evident in his eyes and the entire thing makes me chuckle, but I turn away so he doesn't think this is funny. Little rascal.

She snatches him out of the cart and moves to the other side of the van to put him in his carseat. He can't be any older than three. He's silent the entire time and looks stiff, like he knows he's in trouble. At least he's not throwing a fit.

I load the last few bags in and shut her trunk with a loud clunk and start rolling the cart back over a few parking spots to the cart corral to join the rest of them.

I look back over my shoulder as I hear the door close.

"Thank you," the woman says with a look of sincerity.

"No problem," I answer back, giving her a little wave as I shove the cart into the others.

"Merry Christmas," she says, grabbing the keys from her purse and walking to the driver's door, her boots smacking on the pavement. As she opens the door, I can hear her little girl wailing. I cringe out of instinct.

"Merry Christmas," I say, but I don't bother raising my voice since I doubt she can hear me.

I haven't had many people tell me that this season. *Merry Christmas.* I'm not used to hearing it anyway. Same with the rest of the holidays.

I grew up alone, and I'm fine with that. But it's nice to hear holiday greetings occasionally. I can't deny that. The older I get, the more I realize how much I want it.

I click my phone to check the time, shaking off the unwelcome feelings. Cary Ann's gotta be closing up soon, so I might as well wait for my cherry.

I tap the phone against my jeans, staring at the building. This is bad news. I shouldn't even be going after her, but I *want* her. Something about her is calling to me. I can't justify it. In fact, this can only complicate things. But still I lie to myself.

I can convince her to stay away. I can keep her out of danger by getting close to her.

That's enough to slip a smile across my face as I head on over to my bike and take a seat while I wait for her.

I get lost in my emails on my phone. Since I've been distracted with this heist, I've fallen behind on orders for my custom-made choppers. But I'm calling the delay a holiday break, and my customers don't seem to mind. They don't have much of a choice either. There's a reason they come to me. No one can build choppers like I can. If I'd known all those years ago that I could make good money doing this, I never would've gone down the path I did. I shove down the regret. The past is in the past, and I've moved on.

I look up as a sweet little thing strolls out of the store and walks straight to a beat-up, faded white Honda in the parking lot. It's not my girl, it's the chick who was getting all wound up in the back room. I smile to myself remembering how pissed off she was, and return to my phone, wondering if the customer even got the doll.

I stop what I'm doing when I feel her eyes on me. For a moment, I freeze. *Fuck.* I shouldn't be lingering out front. What if it seems suspicious? How fucking ironic would it be if I got caught because I was waiting for her? Something that has nothing to do with this shit I have planned.

The girl starts her car and sits there a minute, looking at me in her rearview before driving away. She looks back at me again when she gets to the stop sign and then pulls off as I meet her gaze.

No, that's not gonna happen. My cherry will tell them I was just waiting on her. I know she will. Yeah, that's just one more reason to pursue her. Now she's my alibi.

Every time I was here, it was just to see her sweet ass and work up the courage to ask her out.

I grunt a laugh, seeing as how that's sorta what happened, too. I'd feel pathetic over the thought if I really stopped to think about how this girl's got me twisted up in knots, but I stop that thought in its tracks.

It's the way she looks at me. I'm affecting her just as much and the moment she steps out of that store, I know I'm not gonna have any problems making her mine. As if accepting the challenge, she slips out of the building and locks the doors behind her.

I think about how easy it'd be to just lift them off of her. I could do that.

Maybe I should. If we had the keys, it wouldn't have to be a stick-up; without them we'd be left to break a window, and that would trigger the alarm. That's something we don't want. The thought lingers in my mind, but it's quickly replaced by the sight of her lush ass in those jeans.

Damn, I can't wait to get her writhing underneath me. My dick is rock hard as her hips sway and she strolls toward her car. I get off my bike and wait for her. She seems lost in thought as I lean against her passenger side door. She doesn't even see me at all. She should be paying attention out here alone at night.

Fuck, my dick twitches in my jeans. We could fuck right here and right now, and no one would ever know. This town is old and small. Everyone's home this late at night. And this shopping strip is mostly vacant and on the edge of town. We could get away with it.

My cherry's not that kind of girl though, I know she's not. She's not gonna be giving it up that fucking easy. And I'm fine with waiting. For a night, anyway. And then I'll make sure she warms up to me.

She finally looks up, and her eyes go wide as she takes me in and stops walking in her tracks. I give her a cocky smirk and nod my head. "You finally got off?"

She blushes at my words, and it's only then that I realize the double meaning. My sweet cherry has a dirty mind.

"Vinny, right?" she asks, swinging the keys in her hand and walking up to me full of confidence with a playful smile gracing her lips.

Fuck, I love that about her. Her confidence. I know she's a shy girl at heart, but she's got a way of putting it all out there for me. I fucking love that.

"Cary Ann," I reply and nod my head as I let my eyes roam down her tight body. I want her to see me appreciating her curves. It's pretty fucking cold out here, and her coat's hiding a lot of her body, but the plump part of her breasts is peeking up and flushed with the chill of the December night.

"What are you doing out here?" she asks as she moves around to her side of the car and I follow behind. She opens up the door and leans against it, giving me a generous view of her ass and taunting me. I adjust my dick real quick while she's not looking, and she actually wiggles her ass some. She definitely teasing me.

"Oh, don't tempt me," I warn her as she puts the key in the ignition and starts her car. It's not that cold that she's gotta warm her car up. It never gets that cold this far south, but I do appreciate the view.

She blushes and looks over her shoulder. "Oh yeah?" she says before sinking her teeth into her bottom lip. I wasn't actually considering fucking her against her car, but if she keeps this up that's exactly what's going to happen.

"Come on, Cherry," I say and lower my voice, "I'm trying to be good for you."

She straightens herself as I walk closer to her. She looks up at me, batting those thick lashes as she says, "I heard you were bad."

I stiffen at her confession, but she leans in and whispers, "That's what I like about you." Her hot breath tickles my neck as the sweet words touch my ear, and a playful smile spreads on my lips.

She pulls back with her eyes sparkling, and lust clearly present.

"Good. 'Cause I wanna take you out and show you a good time." I get right to the point before I do end up crushing her body against this car and giving us both what we want.

Her smile widens, and that shy side about her comes through as she brushes her hair out of her face and tucks it behind her ear. "I'd like that." A blush brightens her cheeks. "I was wondering when you were gonna ask me."

My brow pinches in confusion.

She gestures to the store and explains, "You kept coming in, but you never said anything." I swallow my nerves and smile back at her, but internally I feel like I'm suffocating. It's not good that she noticed, but this is the perfect cover-up.

I shrug it off and say, "I was just waiting till it felt right."

We both turn to face the entrance to the parking lot as the white Honda from earlier drives through and comes straight for us. The girl from earlier takes a look at me and then says, "Cary, you doing alright?"

Cary laughs a little, walking to her friend and bending over to lean into the window as she replies, "I'm fine, Cindy. Just getting asked out on a date," she says, staring at me over her shoulder and clearly looking pleased. It's a little irritating to be interrupted, but I have to admit it's a nice thing for her friend to do. I can't say that I blame her; I was looking a little sketchy earlier. The suspicious gaze she was giving me with narrow eyes turns into a surprised and somewhat excited look.

"Did you really drive all the way back here to check on me?" Cary asks with a hint of disbelief.

Cindy rolls her eyes and shrugs before saying, "Sue me for being a good friend and caring about your ass." She grins at Cary and gives me a quick wave. "Alrighty then, I'll leave you two to it."

A rough chuckle rises up my chest as she pulls away and my cherry walks back to me slowly.

"So, tomorrow night?" I ask her as the back lights from the Honda fade in the distance down the street, feeling cocky. My dick's already hardening at the thought of getting her under me.

"That's the night before Christmas Eve; I have a family dinner." Oh, yeah. I forgot for a moment. It's not like I have anything going on, but most people do.

She's looking all sorts of disappointed, like it really hurt her to tell me no. "Sorry. We decorate the tree. It's a family tradition."

"That makes sense." I don't have family traditions. You need a family in order to have them. Yet another difference, another reason we shouldn't be together. The thought takes me back.

I'm not planning a future with my cherry. I struggle for a moment to remember why I'm out here with her. Why I waited with the intention of seeing her and planning our little date. I need to get her out of the store on Christmas Eve. Yeah, that's the reason. I'm a fucking liar. I just wanna get her under me.

She shrugs and says, "It's early, and my mom's usually tipsy and passed out by eight."

She sways from side to side, shrugging. "I can skip out. Meet you a little later?" Her voice practically purrs on the last line.

"Fuck, yeah. It's a date."

CHAPTER 4

Cary Ann

THIS IS STUPID. I HAVE BUTTERFLIES AND I'M NERVOUS AND I feel so childish, but thinking about Vinny reminds me how I used to feel about him. I'd walk back home from school while he drove away on his motorcycle, just dreaming about being on the back, my arms around his waist. Imagining how he'd kiss me outside of school. I huff a small laugh and bring my beer to my lips.

Times have changed, but I can't help feeling the nerves from way back then.

I watch as a customer rings the little bells scattered along the holly on the bar. That, along with Christmas music, is really making it feel like the holidays. The holly also has fake snow on it, and there's a snowman spray-painted with more fake snow on the front window of the bar, too.

It's cute, but some asshole is running his finger through it and pissing off the bartender, who I'm guessing is the one who made the artwork. I look straight ahead and just ignore him. The guy's drunk, and the bartender doesn't do anything but shake his head, then continues wiping down the glasses. I imagine he's gotta spray-paint a new snowman every night.

"No mistletoe?" I jump a little in my seat and almost spill my beer when I hear his voice. *Vinny.*

I give Vinny a small smile and set my beer down, trying to remember what he asked as my heartbeat calms back down. His voice is so deep and rough that it makes desire stir in my belly.

My cheeks flush when I finally realize what he said. *Mistletoe.* I'm a strong, confident woman, but this man brings out a shy side of me that I haven't felt in years.

I start picking at the label on my beer bottle and shake my head with my teeth sunk into my bottom lip. "Not here," I whisper in the sexiest voice I can.

I dressed the part tonight, wearing a deep red dress that clings to my figure. I know it's tight and a bit provocative for this bar, but I want to look good for him. I want to show off this feminine side of me. I want to show him that I'm a woman now, and that I want exactly what he has to offer.

Part of me feels self-conscious, while another part of me feels slutty. But I don't care. I want him, and I'm not letting him go without trying.

He takes a seat at the bar, looking up at the college football game on the TV behind the bar as he slides off his leather jacket. All he's wearing underneath is a clean crisp t-shirt that hugs his broad shoulders tightly, and a pair of faded blue jeans. Fuck, even in casual clothes he looks like a million bucks.

Suddenly the expensive dress I wore makes me feel cheap. I stop picking at the stupid label on the bottle and finally take another swig.

"You look beautiful, Cherry," he says in a deep low voice that's somehow directly connected to my clit. I turn to look at him when I feel those baby blue eyes on me.

I'm not letting him go without making it damn well obvious what I want tonight.

He's my Christmas present to myself. If that makes me a ho, then I'll ho ho ho myself right to his bedroom. Definitely his, since I'm still at my parents' house until I start my new job. I visibly cringe at the thought.

Vinny laughs, and then orders a beer. "What, you don't like my nickname for you?" he asks me.

I let out a small laugh and smile, feeling the light buzz of the beer and accepting another as the bartender slides the glass bottles toward us on the bar.

"I like your nickname for me. It sounds dirty when you say it," I confess and blush violently at my own words and silently blame it on the alcohol.

He cocks a brow at me and leans in as he asks, "Is that so, Cary Ann?" His hot breath lingers on my neck and creates a shiver that slowly runs down my body, hardening my nipples. His lips barely touch the shell of my ear as he huskily says, "I didn't know you were a dirty girl… Cherry."

I laugh it off even though I'm all hot and bothered. I want him to know that I want him, but I'm not going to make it *too* easy for him.

"So what are your plans for Christmas Eve?" I ask casually, and then I remember my own plans. All the desire leaves me, and my mouth goes dry. I grip my beer a little harder. My heart races in my chest. I have to work, but more importantly, I need to make sure everything goes smoothly.

I need to stop the video camera footage first. My blood heats with anxiety. I'm not letting Morose do this again. That orphanage matters to me, and I know for a fact last year he did the same thing. The donations are truly needed, and that greedy fucker took it all. I saw the check he wrote to himself. I didn't want to believe it, but when I asked Mrs. Pilcavage if the check went through and she said she hadn't gotten it, my heart truly broke. She's an older lady and she believes what he tells her. It's so wrong. I can't stand it. I'm going to do the right thing, even if it costs me everything.

"Not much," Vinny says and shrugs and then seems to stare off at the television for a moment. I have to get my shit together. I take a deep breath, trying to calm myself down.

I've never done anything like this, but I'm not going to let anything stand in my way of making sure I take every cent from the registers and giving it to the orphanage where it rightfully belongs.

And on top of that, I have proof of what Morose did so he goes to jail for being the thief he is. But I'm not waiting on the law. I'm making sure those kids have the best Christmas they've ever had.

The last thought fills me with conviction.

Anger courses through my blood, but the sight of Vinny staring back at me changes it to something else. Something stronger, something hotter that I can't deny.

This shit is for me to worry about tomorrow night. Everything's going to go down perfectly. So tonight I'm going to relax. With *him*.

"So nothing for Christmas Eve then?" I ask casually and then set the bottle down on the bar. I remember he's from the orphanage, and my heart hurts a little. He grew up there for a few years before his aunt finally took him in. I can't believe I forgot. I take another drink to stop all the emotions from creeping up on me.

I have to change the subject, fast. "You looking forward to anything for Christmas?" I ask him.

He looks above me at the holly and asks again, "Mistletoe?"

I laugh a little, making my shoulders shake some.

"How about a kiss then?" he finally asks me, leaning in.

I smile shyly at him, but I'm not shy about this kiss. I'm more than happy to give it to him. I want *more* though.

I lean in slightly and he goes for it, but I put my finger to his lips and stop him. His eyes slowly open and they narrow at me, as if daring me to deny him. The hidden threat lying there in his baby blues ignites that desire full force.

"I'm gonna need you to take me home first," I whisper against his lips.

I gasp at the heat that blazes in his eyes. "That can be arranged, Cherry," he says. "Finish your beer, and then you're coming home with me."

CHAPTER 5

Vinny

I CAN'T RIP THIS DRESS OFF OF HER FAST ENOUGH.

Her fingers kept inching closer and closer to my dick while I drove her back here. We left her car at the bar and she rode with me on the back of my bike, her warmth on my back and her breasts pressed against me. I was already hard just feeling her curves, but then those hands…

My cherry is a naughty girl, and I fucking love it.

Her nails gently scratched at the waistline of my jeans until the tips of her fingers were buried inside.

"Cherry," I admonished her as we pulled up to a red light. But all she did was lean forward, taking my lips with hers and moaning into my mouth.

Fuck, my dick twitches thinking about how I wanted to take her right then and there.

I slam her back against the wall of my foyer, kicking the front door shut behind me and struggling to get these fucking clothes off. I should get a damn medal for waiting until I got her home behind closed doors.

Her lips press to mine, molding to my easy pressure as I slip my tongue into her hot mouth. She kisses me with a passion I've never had with anyone else as my hands roam her body.

I grip her ass in my hands and pull her up to me, her legs wrapping around my hips like a good girl.

Fuck, if I'd known how much she wanted me, I would've skipped the bar entirely. I pick her up and walk to my bedroom. No shame, and no fucks given. We're both adults with needs, and I'm ready to strip her down and relieve all this sexual tension between us. My hand's up her dress and caressing her smooth skin, while her nails dig into my shoulders and her other hand grips my hair.

"Vinny," she moans my name. I take the break in our kiss to graze my teeth down her neck and leave open-mouth kisses all along the exposed skin. As the front of my legs hit the bed frame, I throw her ass down on it and smile when she lets out a playful squeal.

I'm quick to take off my shirt and then reach over for the light on the nightstand. I slowly unbuckle my jeans and look back at my sweet cherry on the bed.

She's looking all kinds of hot and bothered, and a little shy, too.

She's still wearing her dress although her heels are gone, lost somewhere between the foyer and the bedroom.

"Take that off, Cherry," I say beneath my breath, looking at her with obvious hunger in my eyes.

She looks to the light switch and visibly swallows. "Can we turn the lights off?" she asks softly. Her confident energy is gone, and her insecurity is coming through. A part of me wants to give in and let her have whatever she wants, just grateful that a girl like Cherry wants to be with a man like me. But that's not happening. I wanna see her.

"No," I shake my head, holding her gaze. Her expression falls slightly and I shove my pants down and stalk over to her, buck naked. The bed groans as I crawl closer to her, my dick hard and ready. "I wanna watch your face when you cum on my dick, Cary."

My dirty words make her mouth fall open into a beautiful "O."

"Off," I give the command and she shimmies out of her dress and then hesitates to unclip her bra. But a cock of my brow has it coming off of her, leaving her in nothing but a skimpy pair of lace undies.

And those have got to go, right fucking now. I lean forward enough to shove my thumbs through the lace and tear them off of her.

I shouldn't have done it, but she'll forgive me. She gasps, but she doesn't protest. Her breathing is coming in short pants and her pale pink nipples are pebbled. She's fucking gorgeous.

I toss them off the bed and grab her hips in my hands, angling her pretty little pussy and taking a languid lick.

Fuck, she's so sweet. Just like I knew my cherry would be. Her fingers spear through my hair and she pushes my face into her pussy. I smile into her tight cunt at how greedy she is. I take her clit in my mouth and suck, making her squirm under me.

She needs more, and I know it. She's trying so hard to get herself off. But she needs me. I massage my tongue on her throbbing clit and I'm rewarded by the sweet sounds of her moans spilling from her lips.

I finally take my hand off her ass and shove two fingers into her pussy, stroking her G-spot and fucking her just like she needs.

"Yes!" she cries out, rocking her pussy into my face. I pull away and pin her hips down, staring at her with a serious expression on my face.

"You need to be a good girl, Cherry," I say and she looks up at me, her breath ragged. "Stop moving your ass, and stay still for me." I'm serious, too. I don't mind her riding my face, but right now I want to be the one controlling her pleasure.

"Yes, sir," she says back breathlessly, and it nearly floors me. Fuck yes. My dick's leaking precum, and I need to get her off quick so I can get inside.

I dive back between her legs and ravage her pussy like a starving man.

Her fingernails scrape along my scalp, but she's holding still for me, even as her back bows with pleasure. *Good girl.*

I suck her clit and push my fingers in, pumping in and out until her thighs are squeezing around my head. I move my face away, licking my lips and looking up her body to find her heated gaze.

"Cum for me, Cherry," I whisper the command, pressing my thumb down on her clit and she ignites under me. Her head falls back as she lets out a strangled cry and then moans my name. She's the most beautiful sight I've even seen. Her thighs are still trembling as I push her legs farther apart so I can fit my hips in between and line my dick up.

I slam into her before she has a chance to come down from her high, and her back arches from the intensity.

I groan in the crook of her neck, completely buried to the hilt and let her adjust to my size. She's so tight. She's soaking wet for me, but she's so fucking tight.

"Vinny," she moans my name again, and the soft sound spurs me to move. I grip her hips and thrust my own in a rhythmic pace, watching the looks of pleasure play across her gorgeous face.

The dim light in the room makes her soft features look even more beautiful.

"Look at me, Cherry," I whisper as I pick up my relentless pace, nearly out of breath.

She stares back at me, eyes half-lidded and her gorgeous lips parted. "I wanna watch when you cum this time."

She nods her head although she doesn't say anything. She looks like she's lost in pleasure and on edge, and I'm ready to push her over a second time.

I pound into her tight cunt over and over. The bed groans with each thrust and the harder I fuck her, the harder the bed hits the wall. But it only fuels me to take her further, to push her limit higher. I lean forward, nipping her lips and staring into her lust-filled eyes.

My spine tingles, and my toes curl.

Fuck, my balls draw up and I know it's coming. I hold my breath as I fuck her harder and faster. Mercilessly pounding into her and desperate for her to find her release with me.

Her neck arches and her fingers dig into me, but she never stops looking at me. She's so perfect. Finally, her mouth opens and I hammer into her just two more times and her tight walls are spasming on my dick.

The feel and sounds of her own release push mine over the edge. My body ignites with pleasure, tingling over every inch of skin as I fill her tight walls with my cum in thick, hot bursts. Waves of heated and numbing pleasure crash through my body as she trembles beneath me, shaking from the intensity of her own release.

I lean forward and kiss her sweetly. She moans into the hot air, holding me close to her, and everything in that moment feels right. It settles something deep inside of me, and when I pull away, it's still there.

I don't know what it is, and I try to shake the unfamiliar feeling as I walk to the bathroom and clean myself off before grabbing a washcloth for her.

She's still lying curled on her side in the bed, looking absolutely beautiful and vulnerable with her eyes closed as I wipe up her thighs.

She lets out a small satisfied sound as I clean her up and pull the covers around her. But that action seems to break whatever sensual spell she was under. She sits up with her eyes wide open and looks around the room the second I get off the bed.

She's looking for her clothes. She's already leaving? Damn, that's a first. I try to ignore the feeling in the pit of my stomach.

I walk to the bathroom and toss the cloth in the hamper as she starts gathering her clothing.

"You wanna stay?" I offer. I want her to. I wanna have access to that sweet body all night and wear her ass out.

The thought reminds me that she's working tomorrow. Shit.

Fucking her was a beautiful distraction, but the reality is slowly creeping back in.

"I'll make you pancakes in the morning. Give you a little sausage, too?" I try to make light of it, but I'm already feeling the high wearing off. I wanna just rewind, back to when it was just us enjoying the feel of each other.

"That thing is anything but little," she says comically, looking back up at me as she tosses her torn underwear into the trashcan by the desk.

A grin slips across my face. It's almost like tomorrow doesn't exist. Like what I have planned isn't important at all. But it is. It's life changing. Not just for me, but for those kids.

"So you staying over?" I ask her again. I want her here. I need to keep an eye on her, and I don't like the idea of not having control of that aspect tomorrow.

"I can't. I need to wake up early."

"For work?"

"Yeah," she answers. Fuck. I don't want her to go in. It would be so much easier if she wouldn't.

"I don't think you should." I try to say it teasingly.

"I don't think you should tell me what to do," she says with a smartass tone while slipping her heels back on. Her snappy response makes me walk straight to her and grab that ass of hers, pulling her over to the bed. She gasps as I toss her body down and I cage her in, her small body trapped under mine.

"And what if I want to?" I ask her, staring into those baby blues.

She's breathless and her eyes are heated with desire, but she pulls away. Damn. This time I let her go.

"Sorry, Vinny. I've gotta work tomorrow." She slips out from under my arms, and I groan in disappointment. My dick is so fucking hard again already.

"You gonna leave me like this?" I ask her, gesturing to my obvious hard-on with a grin. "Come on Cherry, I didn't think you'd do me like that."

She gives me a wide smile and leans in, putting her knee on the bed and planting a kiss on my lips.

"Maybe tomorrow?" she asks, vulnerability shining in her eyes. "Late tomorrow night?" She kisses me one more time. "I get off, and then you get off?" she asks, looking straight at my dick.

Fuck, I want that. So damn bad. But tomorrow night… she might know. There's no way she's not gonna recognize my voice. I gotta figure this shit out.

"You alright?" she asks with concern obviously written on her face and laced in her voice. I realize then that my expression has turned.

"Yeah, yeah Cherry." I give her a small, chaste kiss, my hand cupping the back of her head. "I'll take you back and see you tomorrow night."

CHAPTER 6

Cary Ann

Ever since I grabbed the duffel bag, my heart's been beating out of my chest. I have that ready, along with the tape with the evidence on it. I already wrapped and addressed the tape so all I need to do is mail it, and the video footage has been stopped. I removed that tape altogether and got rid of it, so they'll have no idea it was me. There's nothing stopping me from opening up every register with my PIN number and emptying out the drawers. There aren't even any more shoppers left. For the last twenty minutes this place has been dead. I'm waiting until we're closed though, just in case.

Being open on Christmas Eve is a fucking stupid thing to do in a small town. Everyone's done their shopping and they're either at the annual parade, or hunkering down and telling their kids Christmas stories as they try to settle them down for bed.

If I wasn't planning on using this situation to my advantage, I'd be pissed that I had to work.

But here I am, prepared to right a wrong and steal this money back. I click the button on my phone and see it's eight. Closing time.

I'm staring at the two cars in the parking lot that aren't mine. They need to leave and get out of here so I can do this and get it over with. I don't know why they're here. Nothing else is open on this strip, and the owners don't seem to be coming in. My palms are sweaty, and my heart's racing. I just want this to be over with. I'm sick to my stomach over it.

I tear my eyes away from the parking lot. I just need to stay calm and do everything with ease.

I close my eyes and take a deep breath, calming myself.

But then my eyes snap open and my heart sputters faster in my chest. Someone's come in. Fucking hell. My nerves can't take this.

I slowly turn, expecting to find Mr. Morose there, ready to thwart my plans because that would be just my luck, but instead it's worse. I'm frozen in place. Fuck. My heart slams against my chest so hard it hurts.

Much worse.

I should scream, but my lungs are paralyzed in my chest, and my legs are shaking. I grip the counter to stay upright as two men in black ski masks walk through the door and the second one locks it behind him.

Oh my God.

I shake my head in disbelief, every ounce of strength replaced with fear. My legs feel weak, and my body feels freezing cold.

"Stay," the first man commands, and some small part of me notes his very deep voice. They each have a gun in their hands, but neither are pointed at me. They have on gloves and masks and all black clothing. Oh shit. No! This can't be happening to me!

My eyes dart to the parking lot as I take in a shaky breath. Both cars are still there. Fuck. I bet they belong to them.

I shake my head, wanting this to all be make-believe.

"It's gonna be alright. You just need to listen and do what we say, and this will all be over with as soon as possible," the man on my left says calmly. His voice is lighter, and sounds more southern.

With the ski masks on all I can see are his deep chocolate eyes. Both men are tall, with broad shoulders. The one on the left is heavier than the other. Internally I start to track all the features that can be used to track these assholes down. I stand a little straighter, feeling my determination come back to me.

I'm not letting them get away with this.

The man on my right slaps a large black backpack on the counter as the man on the left says, "Just put the money in the bag and we'll leave." I stare at the black backpack, feeling the anger rise in my body as my hands ball into fists.

This money was supposed to be for the orphanage. I seethe in a breath through my clenched teeth and shake my head.

"No?" the man to my left says incredulously. He moves the gun from one hand to the other, and while it's still not pointed in my direction, it does the job of instilling fear in me. My heart thump, thump, thumps.

"Look sweetie, it's real easy. You just empty the cash out of each of the registers, or we will."

I shake my head again, feeling tears prick my eyes. The man on the right is stock-still, just staring at me with his pale blue eyes. "I won't give you my PIN," I say in a cracked voice.

This is stupid. It really is. But I can't let them do this.

I can't let yet another person steal from these kids. It belongs to them, damn it! They *need* it. Not these assholes who thought they'd rob a store on Christmas Eve.

The thought makes me even angrier, and I almost lose my shit. But the man on my right walks closer.

"This doesn't have to be a fight," he says beneath his breath. So low, but he sounds so familiar. He looks to his partner and adds, "We don't wanna hurt you."

Tears leak from the corners of my eyes, rolling down to my cheeks and I angrily brush them away.

"Besides, we've got the key," the man on my left says confidently as he holds up the manager's key. What the fuck? My face scrunches up in a mix of sickness and irritation.

They don't even need my PIN. Shit, I'm going to have to physically keep them away, and that simply isn't going to happen. But I still have to try.

I shake my head and outright refuse. "No," I say with a strength I hardly feel. "I won't let you." I close my eyes and try to summon the courage to continue fighting them.

When I open my eyes, I instinctively take a step back, the small of my back butting against the counter and forcing a small scream from my lips.

Oh fuck, he's pointing the gun right at me, and my heart stops entirely. His chocolate brown eyes stare back at me, daring me to resist further. I put both of my hands up as fear grips me. I don't wanna die. I take in a shaky breath.

"Don't you fucking point your gun at her!" the man on my right snaps. My heart stills, and my hands slowly drop. I do recognize his voice. I shake my head, not wanting to believe it.

But the second he looks back at me, I know it's him.

"Vinny?" I whisper.

CHAPTER 7

Vinny

IT'S A FAKE GUN, BUT TONI'S SCARING THE SHIT OUT OF MY SWEET cherry. I'm gonna beat the shit out of him.

I'm gonna spank Cherry's ass, too. Money isn't worth putting herself in danger. What the hell is she doing?

I was starting to feel like everything would be fine. We'd just have her step aside, grab the money and get the fuck out.

Easy peasy. I've got the two junkers out front to throw her off, and the cops too once they get here. They can't be traced to anyone, and everything would've been fine.

Shit, I was looking forward to consoling her tonight.

I know my cherry's strong, and she's wanting to do the right thing. But she shouldn't be risking her life like this.

My heart beats faster as she shakes her head no again. She's terrified, and all I wanna do is pull her into my arms and calm her down. I wanna let her in on what's going on. But she's not going to understand. She might not even believe me if I told her the truth.

The very thought that she'd think I was lying and that I'm no good makes my heart hammer faster in my chest.

I can't let that happen. I don't want this to come between us. There's something here, and I want more of her. I can't let this shit get out of hand.

"No," she says as she looks Toni in the eyes. Damn, my girl has some balls on her. "I won't let you."

She closes her eyes, and Toni raises the fake gun in his hand.

Fuck that. He's not going to scare her. I can't let him fuck her up like that. I've had guns pointed at me before. I won't let her go through that shit.

"Don't you fucking point your gun at her!" I scream at him, reaching over and smacking the gun away. I can't hear anything but the sound of my heavy breathing, I'm so pissed. He should know better than that.

I start to tell her to run, to get the fuck out of here before she gets hurt, to do anything but stay here, but she whispers, "Vinny."

My blood runs cold and I stare back at her, slowly facing her and watching the disbelief grow in her gorgeous eyes.

My palms feel like ice. Shit, this is the worst possible outcome.

She knows.

I raise my hand up, trying to calm her as she seems to get over her fear and starts shaking her head even stronger and harder than before.

"It's not what it looks like-" I start to explain myself, but she cuts me off.

"Are you fucking kidding me?" she practically spits out. She must really fucking trust me because all traces of fear vanish, replaced with rage. I was not expecting that. "Are you fucking serious?!" she yells at me.

She's pissed.

"Shit, shit," Toni curses behind me.

"Cherry," I say in a low voice. It's a warning. I know she's angry, but she needs to calm her ass down.

"You aren't taking this money! It's for the orphanage!" she screams as she walks around the counter to get in my face. "You of all people-" she starts to rip into me, but I cut her off, gripping the hand that she tries to shove into my chest. I need to tell her the truth, and she's not gonna like it, and she may not even believe it.

But she's gonna fucking hear it.

"It's not gonna go there," I say as she stands toe-to-toe with me. Completely forgetting the fact that Toni's right there, watching us go at it.

"The hell it isn't!" she yells back. "Take your mask off and talk to me!" She tries to smack my chest with the other hand, but I grab that wrist too and hold her still.

"Stop it, Cherry," I tell her in a low voice, with a threat just barely there. I'm not above grabbing her ass and taking her out of here like a tod-dler having a damn fit. Toni can handle this on his own. "The video sur-veillance is running, and I can't let them see my face." I know there's no audio, but there's video at least. I know that much. And even though I know Cherry knows, I still have faith she won't tell them.

"Fuck, man!" Toni yells behind me, slamming his fist down on the counter and pacing a bit. He needs to calm down.

"Everyone, just calm down," I say loud enough for both of them to hear.

"I already cut the feed. You're going to have to fucking kill me." Cherry pulls her hands out of my grasp. "I worked too damn hard to make sure the kids get what they need."

I try to take in what she's saying, but it doesn't make sense. She crosses her arms across her chest, looking at me with tears in her eyes. She's try-ing to be strong, but the weight of what she just said is wearing down on her.

I tilt my head and ask, "What do you mean you 'cut the feed'?"

She rocks on her back foot and looks away. Fear is creeping in. She's trapped in this store, and she's just said there's no feed. *Cherry.* She really does need me to spank her ass raw. What the hell is my sweet cherry doing admitting shit like that? She's not very good at staying out of trouble.

But then again, if she was, she wouldn't have been with me.

"Tell me." I give her the simple command, and that gets her attention.

"I can't let you steal this money." She says the words simply in a soft voice etched with pain. Conviction is there as well. I know why. She thinks this money is going to the orphanage like it's supposed to. But it's not.

"I'm taking this money to the orphanage," I tell her, staring into her soft baby blue eyes. "Morose is stealing." I take in a heavy breath as her eyes widen. She's gotta believe me. "It has to go there, Cherry. Just let us take it to where it belongs."

She blinks a few times and her breathing comes in short pants. "I swear to you, just let us take it to the orphanage."

"No fucking way," she says, and then my cherry takes two steps closer to me before she does the last thing I thought she would. She wraps her arms around my neck and presses those sweet lips to mine, moaning into my mouth.

I'm shocked, but she feels so damn good, I fall under her spell, letting her kiss me and setting the gun down on the counter behind her so I can hold onto her small waist, pulling her closer to me.

I could do this all night, but we can't. I try to pull away, but she just holds me tighter. My greedy girl. She doesn't let up until Toni snaps from behind me, "What the fuck is going on?"

CHAPTER 8

Cary Ann

I PULL AWAY AND LOOK AT VINNY'S FRIEND. THE SMILE ON MY FACE dims as I catch sight of his gun again.

I take another step back and look between the two of them.

"You cut the feed?" Vinny asks me.

I nod my head and reply, "Yeah." My heart is just too full knowing Vinny was doing exactly what I was planning on doing. I feel safe with him. Which doesn't make sense with his friend freaking out. It makes me really uneasy to see the guns.

"What the fuck's going on, man?" The guy pushes on Vinny's shoulder as Vinny takes his mask off.

"She's cool, Toni."

"So you were gonna rob me?" I ask Vinny, ignoring the prickle of fear running through me. I keep looking at Toni. I don't know him, and I don't like that he's here. For some reason it's so easy to forgive Vinny. Especially knowing why he was doing this.

"I didn't want to." He wraps his arms around my waist and pulls me close to him. My small hands land on his chest. "I didn't want you to be scared."

I scoff at him and refuse to admit how worked up I was and say, "I was pissed, not scared." He smiles down at me, like I'm being cute.

I look back at his friend who finally pulls the mask off of his face. He looks vaguely familiar.

"She your girl?" he asks with his brow pinched. "Would've been easier if this was an inside job," he mutters.

He shoves the mask into his pocket and walks over to the nearest register. Vinny's grip on me tightens as I try to pull away and watch Toni.

"So we're robbing this joint together?" Vinny asks me with a smile and then kisses my nose.

I purse my lips, not sure if I trust the fucker at the register.

"It's right across the street, baby. We've got twenty minutes before the parade goes through. We take the cash and slip it through their mail slot in the door." I nod my head. That's better than the plan I had, which was to drop it off in the early morning. Now is better. Get the cash and move it from one place to the next as quickly as possible.

I look at Vinny, and I'm pretty sure I know why he's doing this, but I don't know Toni's story. I watch him as he shoves the money into the bag. Vinny's completely at ease, and obviously trusts him.

"Why are you doing this?" I ask as Toni closes the first register and moves to the next. There are only three in the entire store. So this won't take long.

"I went there once." He looks up at me. He's got a baby face although he's built like a man. "To the orphanage. Without Mrs. Pilcavage I wouldn't be standing here today. There's no doubt I'd be locked up." He opens the next register with the key. "Those kids aren't gonna have the life I had." There's a hint of sadness in his voice.

"You trust me, Cherry?" Vinny asks me, pulling my eyes away from Toni.

"I don't know," I whisper although everything in me does. I shouldn't. I know I'm naive, but I do. I trust him.

"Shoot me, Toni," Vinny says, and my heart stops. Toni laughs and picks up the gun.

"Stop!" I scream out, pushing Vinny hard in the chest, but he's a powerful man and my strength doesn't do a damn thing.

My heart pounds as Toni pulls the trigger over and over again.

It takes a minute for my racing heart to settle. He's gotta be fucking kidding me.

"It's a squirt gun," Toni says before looking at his watch and then heading to the third register, "but there's no water in it."

"I knew you'd be working," Vinny says. "I couldn't bring a real gun, I couldn't risk even the slightest possibility of you getting hurt."

My heart clenches in my chest. I swallow thickly, not liking how strongly I feel toward this man. It's too fast, too soon, but all I wanna do right now is run away with him.

The last register closes shut with a large clank.

"It's not everything that was donated," Toni says, "but it's close." He zips up the backpack and clicks his phone to life.

"Fifteen minutes," he announces, throwing the bag over his shoulders and looking back at Vinny and me. "We gotta get this over there."

Vinny looks down at me, and I know he's going to tell me to stay here. But that's not happening. No fucking way.

"Cherry-" he starts, but I'm not letting him finish.

I shake my head and say, "No, I'm coming with you."

Vinny's eyes are hard, but the moment is broken by the laughter coming from Toni.

"Yeah, she's definitely your girl," Toni says.

Vinny puts his hand on the small of my back and leads me toward the doors as he says, "Let's go then. We gotta make this fast."

"Leave the keys on the counter so they know it wasn't Cherry," Vinny says, and Toni nods. He leaves the keys and then slips a note under them. I walk over and reach down to touch it, but Toni stops me, grabbing my wrist.

"No prints," he says easily, and I nod my head. I suppose they'd run fingerprints on employees first. I could see that.

"What's the note say?" I ask him.

An asymmetrical smile kicks the corner of his lips up. "Merry Christmas, Grinch."

CHAPTER 9

SHE KEEPS WATCHING TONI AND I CAN PRACTICALLY SEE THE wheels turning in her head. She doesn't trust him.

"Yo, Toni," I call out to him as we walk past the two cars we planted and head through the parking lot to the other side of the vacant strip mall. We drove Cherry's car around the block first. It added on a few minutes to the walk, but I don't want her car out front just in case they find the money gone before Thursday morning. I can't be too careful. It was awkward as fuck driving in the car. She's tense. But she'll be better once this is over with.

The orphanage is close. A five-minute walk if we step on it, and that's the perfect amount of time. But I don't like the way Cherry seems to be so damn uneasy. The faster we get this shit done, the better.

Toni takes a look over his shoulder, he's leading the way. We have to go this way to avoid the cameras. The direct path goes right through the convenience store, and there's surveillance in that parking lot. So we're gonna avoid that and take the long way around.

Cherry's keeping a safe distance from Toni. I wish she'd knock it off, but she has no reason to trust him.

"Whatcha want, Vinny? I'm not slowing down," Toni answers as he hops over the chain link fence on the edge of the parking lot and turns to wait for us.

It's a clear shot from here on over to the other street.

"Give her the backpack," I tell him. He looks at me with a bit of confusion as I swing my legs over the fence and hop over easily. My sweet cherry is struggling a little. She's on the petite side and I've got my hand out for her ready to brace her body, but she's gripping the chain links of the fence.

"Alright sure, it's a little heavy though." He walks quietly over to Cherry as she tries to right herself. She almost landed on her ass, but I've got a good grip on her waist.

"Here little mama," he says, holding it out for her to take. We're hidden behind the bushes, but as a car passes, we all freeze. No one's out this late on Christmas Eve unless it's to go to the parade on the other side of main street. There aren't any houses over this side of town either. The orphanage is basically on its own on the outskirts of town.

I hold my breath as the car passes, the lights from the headlights peeking through the bushes. I step in front of Cherry and Toni huffs a small laugh at me.

"Calm down, we're home free." He looks relaxed and happy. Truthfully, this is an easy heist. We're so close to being done. I can taste it.

The car passes without incident and Cherry reaches for the bag, her eyes on Toni.

Her expression falls as he drops the full weight in her hand and she hunches forward to get a better grip.

"Holy shit," she mumbles and then shakes her head, shoving the bag back at Toni. "You take it."

Toni looks up at me, and I give him a nod. I just wanted her to see that it's not about the money for him.

It was never about the money. It's about the fact that the town wanted those kids to have a chance. That money isn't for toys. It's for the electric bill, the hot water. It's to put food on the table and shoes on their feet. I know how much those simple things in life can make a difference. And I know that Mrs. Pilcavage is struggling and that she's worried about the money that was supposed to come from the donation, but never came.

My anger rears up inside of me and I lead the way, my hand splayed on the small of Cherry's back. "Let's go," I tell them.

I crouch beneath the low-hung branches of the trees across from the orphanage and look both ways. No one's here, and all but one light in the whole house is off. I look for a sign that someone's watching, but there's no one here and no one looking.

Quickly, we cross the street and head straight over to the side door on the house. The outside light is on, so if someone comes, they'd see us instantly.

"Hurry." Cherry's fear is evident in her voice as Toni swings the bag off his shoulder and quickly starts shoveling the money through the slot. I take Cherry by the waist and lead her in front of him, the two of us blocking anyone from seeing him.

"You look like you're up to no good," my cherry says in a low voice. And I think she's playing with me with that smartass mouth of hers until she pulls on my jacket. Oh shit, I almost forgot about the all black I'm wearing. I quickly shuck my sweater off, I was hot anyway, and toss it into the trashcan out front.

"Toni, you too." He rises from his position, shoving the last bundle through the slot and then the card wishing a Merry Christmas and Happy New Year to all the kids at the orphanage. I know Mrs. Pilcavage, we both do. She's a good woman and when she wakes up tomorrow and sees that money, she's gonna cry with joy and relief. I know she will. It makes me proud to be able to give her back a sense of peace that she gave me all those years ago.

The town clock chimes as Toni stands up and chucks his black jacket off, revealing a beige thermal underneath, shoving the jacket and the backpack both into the trashcan. We toss our gloves and ski masks into the next trashcan and keep walking.

No more evidence. It's done.

I finally feel like I can breathe. The three of us stroll down the street, heading toward the main road where we'll meet up with the parade and blend in. I wrap my arm around Cherry's waist, but she pulls away and runs to a blue metal post office box on the corner of the block. She pulls a small package out of her purse, covered in brown wrapping paper with an address written in black sharpie.

"What's that?" I ask as she drops it into the box. She smiles and says, "The video surveillance of Morose." Pride's written on her face.

I huff a laugh and say a prayer that Morose pays for what he did. At least we've done everything we can do. The rest is in the law's hands.

"You alright?" I ask her as Toni walks ahead. He's got his hands shoved in his pocket and he's breathing easy. I am too, if I'm being honest. Cherry's not, she seems tense and she's looking every which way like someone's just waiting to get us. She gives me a small nod, but I know she's still a little shaken.

I'm a reformed man, but this isn't the first time I've gotten away with this shit. It'll be the last though. I don't need this in my life. Toni turns back to look at us and gives me a nod when Cherry leans against me, wrapping her arm around my waist.

Toni doesn't need it either. This was the last heist for us. It's a good way to end this career.

I look down at Cherry as we stop on the corner, finally seeing the parade just two blocks down. A Christmas elf from the bank is leading the way.

"You think it's going to be alright?" she asks me.

"It's gonna be perfect." I kiss her hair and she seems to relax a bit. "I promise you," I whisper.

The crowd from the parade appears, and the three of us keep on walking. Soon we'll be blending in with them. Just another block to go.

Cherry stops walking as Toni jogs across the road. I turn to look at her, wondering what she's doing.

I look down at my sweet cherry and she points up.

Right above us on a street light is a bit of mistletoe. I let out a huff of a laugh and look back down at her. She's got a sweet smile on her lips.

"I'll give you that kiss if you stay with me tonight," she says softly.

"You already owe me a kiss," I tell her, cupping her chin in my hand.

"I owe you more than that," she says, batting her lashes. I lean down and take her lips with my own. The sounds of the parade are getting closer, but I don't stop kissing her until we're surrounded and the music and cheers envelop us.

She looks up at me with those sweet eyes when I pull away and I know she's feeling vulnerable and scared, but I'm gonna make everything alright. For her, I'll make it all up to her.

"Merry Christmas, my sweet cherry."

EPILOGUE

Cary Ann

One year later…

"Y**OU HAVE THE BIGGEST SMILE ON YOUR FACE, C**HERRY." I hear his voice from across the bedroom. I blush at Vinny as I sit up in bed and rub the sleep from my eyes.

"I'm just happy today," I say easily. I'm so full of warmth and so excited. I love this time of year.

He crawls on the bed closer to me, balancing a cup of coffee in his hand. Peppermint coffee, my favorite this time of year. *Mmm.* I reach out and take the hot mug from him, giving him a sweet kiss before taking a sip.

Coffee is my life source now.

I work nonstop, but I love it. Being a social worker has made me feel like I'm finally giving back in the way I was always meant to. I feel complete in my career, even more so with Vinny in my life.

My engagement ring clicks on the ceramic mug and the bright light from the morning sun shining through the windows makes it sparkle. Every time I look down at the ring, I feel whole. I love Vinny more and more with each passing day.

Ever since that night, we've exposed ourselves completely to one another. I never believed in love at first sight, but all those years ago, that feeling in my chest was special after all. It had to have been love for us to fit so perfectly together. I know it.

We're gonna start trying to have a baby on New Year's Eve, but the wedding comes first. *A Christmas wedding.* The thought makes me practically shake with delight.

I set the mug down on the nightstand as he curls up next to me, pulling my back into his hard chest. My ass nestles into his crotch and I wiggle a little, wanting him to know that I want him.

I always want him.

His rough chuckle vibrates up my back, and his soft breath tickles my neck.

"Careful what you wish for, Cherry," he warns.

I bite my lip and roll over in his arms.

"So what do you want for Christmas?" I ask him. I already know the answer though. He told me he wanted to donate toys to the orphanage, so that's going to be our tradition every year. And that's all he wants. Even for our wedding, in lieu of gifts we asked for donations to the orphanage. Especially now that my work deals with a few of the kids there.

No one ever found out what we did last year. We got away without a single soul knowing, and Morose went to jail for the crimes he committed.

Sometimes everything just works out perfectly.

"I already told you," he says softly before leaning in for a kiss.

I smile against his lips.

"All I want is you," he says again, and it makes me feel so full of love.

I brush his hair away from his face and say, "I love you, Vinny."

I whisper the words, and I mean them with everything in me.

He kisses me sweetly and says, "I love you too, Cherry."

A SINGLE NIGHT

A SINGLE NIGHT

"**D**OES IT SCARE YOU?"

Does it scare me? Does the fire licking along my skin scare me?

Not like he scares me. It's not a fear of who he is or what he could do to me. The fear is deeply rooted in the knowledge that I lose myself around him. That the background fades to blackness and all I can see is his masculine physique.

"No," I dare to whisper. It's so quiet in the vacant room, that all I can hear is the click and then the hiss of a tender flame that grows larger and then brighter, the lit candle coming to life.

Stripped down to nothing, lying against the leather, I wait for him with baited breath.

My skin is already sensitized, the edge of knife he used to shave down my body made sure of that. The blade glints from the simple steel cart behind him. Everything he needs for his fire play hides away in that drawer.

"Not like it did at first," I admit a truth and the innocence of it doesn't escape me.

With the candle in his right hand, his left caresses the pinkish skin of my waste. "Even if there was so little, it would singe," he speaks as he trails his fingertips from the curve, up to my belly and then lower.

He prefers a knife to a razor and a candle for a flame. First he strips me, leaves me here in the chill of his absence, and then it begins.

As his fingers slip lower, past my belly and even farther still, his satisfied groan disrupts the heavy breathing that's lingered between us. "Already wanting me," he comments as the tip of his blunt nails slip down my most sensitive nub.

"Part of me wants to be selfish." His tone is even, deep and with the soothing cadence that calms me. His thumb slowly, teasingly, spreads me and then moves back to that most sensitive place, where he spreads my arousal. The spike of heat and want stir in the pit of my stomach, the desire escaping me in a gasp that parts my lips. "Part of me," he continues as he reaches for the ethanol, "doesn't even want to play tonight."

My voice is strained and it takes great effort to open my eyes and meet his soft gaze. I swear the vulnerability that shines in the bright light of the flame wasn't there days ago. It echoes back to me now, making my throat dry as I remind him, "Whatever it is, the clock is running."

Wherever the alcohol is placed, the flame will dance. The fuel of it, the trail placed on my skin, dries so quickly, licked clean by the bright light, that it's only a flash. Only a moment of the heat that threatens to burn.

The air between us thickens and the flame drops and the bead of wax drips slightly. Gripping the table harder, my back arches and the sudden heat is met with my moan.

"You're ... needy, wanting..." Parting my closed I catch sight at his tongue darting across his lower lip. "Tempting... I imagine I could blow, and you'd reach your limit, wouldn't you?"

As he walks to the end of the table, letting the wax melt as he goes, allowing it to drip carelessly, recklessly down my already sensitive skin I wonder if he'll do it. I wonder if it's all too much for him like it is for me and he'll take me now like my body begs.

I don't know at what point the need changed, but it's as if it's all different now. At least in this moment. Locked in this barren room for him to do as he wishes to me. I don't know when it happened... but everything has changed.

"Tell me what you want?" he murmurs, his lips brushing against my inner thigh, his warm breath giving me just enough, to stop the chill of goosebumps from taking over. With no heat, not a single bit of it, my body aches for the void to be filled.

The flame and the wax aren't enough.

With a single low breath, he blows against my core and then higher. My lips stay parted and I'm fully aware my expression gives it all away. The arch of my back as the tenderness of a burning need sends me higher.

"I need an answer," he murmurs his left hand gripping my right thigh and as he holds me still, dripping the wax at the same time that a languid lick sends my orgasm over the edge.

"You," the word is begging, desperate even, as it's torn from me.

The spike of my release has barely waned before he's ripped me from where I lay and positioned me, a fist of my hair at the base of my neck, the candle recklessly dropping to the floor.

He enters me without warning, swift and ripping a strangled moan from my throat. I don't recognize myself or my own voice as he takes me, my back to his chest. The fingers of his other hand gripping my hips and the relentless thrusts deepened by my hips pinned to the table. With no place to go, I'm his to ravage and that's exactly what he does. My nipples pebble, the cool air no match for his skin scorching my back.

He's rough … but only for so long. Only until I'm limp, the pleasure rocking through me, taking from me, draining my strength to do anything but call out his name in mercy as my body sags against the warm leather.

With his lips trailing down my neck, he parts them ever so slightly, and a trail of goosebumps linger where his gentle touch has been. The intensity of such a gentleness, brings the onslaught of my climax higher and my back arches as he finds his release. His rough groan of utter satisfaction is accompanied with a final thrust that he holds deep inside of me, forcing even more from me, more than I can handle. My nails dig in his corded forearms, in a weak attempt to stay grounded as we both fall from the highest high and my orgasm crashes around me, like the burning rubble of a fixture engulfed in blistering flames.

My chest rises and falls recklessly with my heavy breath as reality slips back. The table groans as he readjusts, and I expect him to leave me, and for the chill to settle in. Instead he braces himself on his forearms and places a kiss just beneath the tender spot beneath my ear. He whispers, "Bethany," softly and with a delicate cadence that brings the goosebumps back, beginning where the word was breathed and slowly trailing down every inch of my sensitized skin.

Even though there are moments I despise his entire being and the part he's played in my pain and other moments where the intensity of what he could do to me and what I'm all too aware he's done in the past chill me to my core, I can't deny there's a tenderness now. There's a scorched section of my twisted heart that has been scarred and branded. Not from his harshness, no, he scarred me with this side of him, the side that brings out a pain and longing I've never felt before.

I find my lips parting with my gaze caught in his and I whisper with the same reverence his just held, "Jase."

Until the debt is paid, I am his.

I hope you enjoyed this alternative scene from my A Single Glance trilogy. Jase and Bethany's complete story is available now if you want to read their story!

BEAUTY AND
THE BEAST

PROLOGUE

"**S**IR, ARE YOU SURE YOU WANT TO DO THIS?"

Alessio's hesitation is personified by weakness.

It was different when I started. We were all different back then, and I know my driver longs for the days where my reputation didn't send shivers of ice down the back of spineless men.

Maybe I'm more callous than I once was when wealth flowed freely, and my partners held more respect for me than they did fear. That's what happens when a man is forced to become a beast.

As the limo comes to a slow stop in front of the castle bathed in the dark night, my thumb runs along my hard jaw line, skimming over the deep scar that made me who I am. The glittering candlelight and floral scent that filters in through the cracked tinted windows doesn't hide the ruthlessness of the men attending tonight.

The elite and upper class, better known as the devils in Armani suits that run this city, don't hold a flame to my brutality. They can hide behind the masquerade of tonight, their flutes of expensive champagne and cloaks of luxury, but we all know who we really are. I don't intend to hide behind a damn thing. Just like they don't hide their unease around me.

One of the few partnerships and personal relationships that hasn't changed since then is with a man named Carter Cross. He took what he wanted when it came to *all matters*. I've decided I'm no better.

Annabelle will leave the ball with me tonight. There's nothing that will change my mind of that.

She's beautiful, and the opposite of the beast I became. More than that, the business deals I can acquire with her father's reputation … well, he owes me, and I've decided beautiful Belle is what I want in the place of his debt.

Am I sure I want to do this? I answer Alessio with the grim reality, "I've never been more sure of anything in my life."

CHAPTER 1

Annabelle

I T'S UNCOMFORTABLE ENOUGH IN THIS LACE DRESS THAT HUGS nearly every curve without feeling so many eyes on me. *'A deep red will compliment your complexion,'* my father's public relations director suggested. *'Go dark and sexy, make a show of it and have fun.'* I still remember how she shrugged like it didn't really matter. If it didn't matter, she wouldn't have stepped in at all.

My heels click on the large black and white marble tiled floor in the entry way. Although I can barely hear that over the pounding of my heart as it wrestles against my rib cage to escape.

The chandeliers drip of wealth in this castle. As if the tables topped with ridiculously large bouquets and hors d'oeuvres served on polished silver at every turn of this massive place didn't give it away. It's a masquerade ball set back in time. This elaborate party is ideal to present the newest member of an elite family who runs in my father's circle. As I catch sight of truffles dusted with gold, I wonder how much they spent on renting this castle … or if they own it and all this décor was added simply for the show of it all.

I don't belong here for one very important reason. My family is broke, but no one knows it.

The Constantines have money … so much more than we do. Which is why PR informed me that I must be present, I must stand out, even, to ensure that stream of money continues to flow into my father's business ventures.

"Miss?" I attempt and fail to hide my shock at the innocent voice at my left. The man dons a simple black mask that only covers his eyes and down to the tip of his nose. All the waiters are wearing them to match their black tuxes. "Champagne?" he offers, and clearing my throat as politely and lady-like as I can, I graciously accept a glass. I'd love about three of them, but I settle on just the one.

"Beautiful mask," he compliments me before nodding and quickly moving on. I don't even have time to thank him. With his back to me, my gaze wanders, but it's quickly diverted when I meet the gaze of a group of men. With their masks on, I'm not sure who is who, but I'm certain they're aware who I am. My mask doesn't conceal my identity in the least. By design of course. *I must be seen.* The dark red ribbon of lace is hardly a mask at all.

I'm a seductive red rose from head to toe. The designer whispered it with a delighted smile on her face. I could only offer her the same smile and thank you I offered the waiter knowing how much my father needs this.

The champagne is rather bitter on the first sip.

Keeping my clutch close to my side, I walk easily to a lone table and try to decipher who is who. It's impossible, though, with the masks. The vibration against my hip alerts me to a text from my father.

How is it going?

I'm to be the ambassador of sorts for my father. He's older now, and it's simply better to have my face in front of the crowd. Even if they are all older men. Businessmen supposedly, but I've run the books for my father long enough to know.

I'm to look pretty but not speak … with that thought in mind, I graciously sip the alcohol. And then a bit more. I'm certainly going to need it.

I've just arrived. I answer him, then silence the phone, slipping it back into the clutch we can't afford. If he wants me to mingle and drop his name and the investments, I can't be on the phone with him.

"Another glass, Miss?" A second waiter, or perhaps the same, they look so alike, holds out his silver tray.

"Thank you." At least I can offer my gratitude this time around.

"I'm so very sorry for your loss," he adds, before dipping slightly.

My heart does a tumble, and my lungs stay still, just as surprised as I am.

"Thank you," I repeat the words spoken in exchange for a glass of champagne as he walks away. They're the only words I seem to know tonight.

My throat is tight, and the next sentence doesn't come. *I appreciate your condolences.* That's what I should say, and I'm aware, but they're too professional … too cold. Even though my father and I knew it was coming … well, you can never prepare for something like that. My mother's death wasn't sudden, but it was brutal.

As the waiter leaves, a group of three men walk past me, nodding their greetings and hushing whatever conversation they were having.

"Hello, gentlemen," I offer and tip my champagne to them, memorizing their masks and noting that they're at least friendly enough to approach later. I don't know a number of the men here, although some of them are somewhat familiar.

Time ticks, and the crowd thickens. I stay where I am, gathering my composure and forming a plan. Approach, laugh, be conversational, but when the time is right, mention the investments.

I only get one glance around the room, searching for someone who's off on their own, before seeing a face I certainly recognize.

Without the mask, he stands out more than the others. Ever since the books a few months ago. Six to be exact. When my mother became too ill, I took over the finances for my father. It's something only she'd done before.

And when she passed, my father made a deal he shouldn't have, taking out a loan that he couldn't possibly pay off. My fingers slip around the stem of the champagne glass as I take in the man the debt is owed to. Even if we liquidated everything, there's no way Harrison's debt could be paid.

My father never should have done it. The only blessing is that no one here knows. So here I am, to smile and look pretty, and hopefully, new deals will be made in the coming weeks. Even if they are a few weeks past due.

From the whispers I've heard, I would have thought Calum Harrison would stay in the shadows. I thought he'd wear a mask on the half of his face that's scarred.

There's no attempt at hiding from him in the least. With his sharp dark gray suit, tailored perfectly to fit his large muscular frame, he'd stand out even if he tried to hide.

Everyone keeps their distance from him, or so it would seem. He stands alone, swirling a glass of whiskey in his hand as his gaze sweeps across the room.

He's taller than I thought, more handsome, too. With stubble gracing his skin, I can barely make out the silver line that runs from his cheek down to his throat. It's not the scar, though, that alerted me to who this man is. It's the very air that seems to bend around him.

He is the epitome of dominance. Dark, sharp eyes and a hard jaw line only add to his powerful presence. In a group of ruthless, cutthroat men, he stands out from all the rest.

He can only be the beast. The debt that's owed is owed to this man. The one man in the room I'm not to approach. A direct order from my father.

Like the air around him though, I feel drawn to him.

Until his eyes meet mine, and he steals my breath. My gasp is silent, but the heels of my shoes aren't as I grab my clutch and flee as quickly as I can.

I cannot speak to him. I cannot approach him. I remember the last warning my father gave me: He is a monster.

I repeat the warning in my head as I slip through the crowd. 'Excuse me' is uttered every few steps as I pass guest after guest and questioning gazes through jeweled masks. I nearly trip on the expensive rug leading to a glittering garden away from the main dining hall. It's quiet in the garden, away from prying eyes and away from that man.

It's only once I'm able to sit that I let out a tortured breath. With the shock and innate instinct to run waning, I question what the hell I've just done.

Running all because a man looked at me. But when he did, when that piercing gaze hit mine, I swear he did more than just look at me.

Thank goodness for the champagne.

A deep breath and a sip. I blame my reaction on my nerves and the importance of tonight, until a darkly masculine voice alerts me that someone is here.

Turning slowly, I face the glass doors I've just come from to find the man I was hoping to avoid standing with that same penetrating gaze pinning me in place.

"You weren't invited here." His statement is simple and cutting. If he looked threatening before, all the way across the hall, he looks so much more so in the dim moonlight of the garden. The shadows dance across his handsome face.

"My father—"

"You are not your father," he cuts me off.

With every ounce of strength I have, I answer calmly, "I am here in his place." My palms heat with anticipation, and it's only then that I realize all the ways I react to him. *It's not fear that makes my body bend to his.*

A smirk ticks Harrison's lips up, charming yet cruel in its intention. As if he knows exactly what I've just realized.

Although my thoughts race, I gather my composure and clear my throat. Swallowing thickly, I inform him, "I'm here on my father's behalf, and I can assure you, your debt will be paid."

Harrison's gaze wanders down my body and then back up to meet my own. He makes no response, no sign at all that he heard me.

My body tenses, and I've never felt more like prey caught in the eyes of a hunter.

When he takes his first step, it's not towards me like I thought it would be. Instead, he moves his attention to a blood-red rose and plucks it. My heart races as I watch him move, stealthily and with purpose. There's no one here but us.

"I know it's past due, but I promise he will have every cent to you before the start of the next quarter," I lie, and even to my own ears it sounds like a lie.

He stares at the rose that he twirls between his deft fingers as he speaks. "Do you know the men here?"

"Know them?" I whisper the question, my brow pinched.

"Do you know what they do?" he clarifies, and my heart races.

"They are executives," I speak clearly, although inside I'm screaming.

"Don't lie to me." His voice isn't harsh, but his tone is threatening.

With a tight swallow, I stay calm in my composure and take a single step closer to him. In the moonlight, his gaze shifts to my shoes, then back up. The shards of auburn and gold in his eyes shine back at me.

I answer again. "They are the men who run every aspect of this city. Drug dealers, murderers, and yes … executives. They control the wealth and the elected officials. They control everything."

"Wrong." The single word is rushed from his lips and he mirrors my action, taking one step closer to me. "*I control everything.*"

A cold sweat lines my skin, a shiver running down my spine as a gust of wind blows by us both. The smell of roses mixes with his masculine scent, and it's heady, nearly dizzying.

I can only nod, "Yes. I know."

"I could have your father killed."

My heart lurches. "No. Please." I nearly go to him, rushing to him to beg him not to, but he closes the distances between us before I can make that move.

Thump, thump, my heart protests, but my body stays right where it is as he towers over me. Slowly, ever so slowly, his hand reaches for my throat. His fingers wrap themselves against my pulse one at a time. And all I can do is look into his eyes. There's so much that swirls in that dark gaze.

"You lie to me."

"No." The attempt at shaking my head in denial is thwarted by his strong grip tightening. It's only a warning.

"You just told me he could make his payment."

My eyes open slowly, but I don't make an attempt to respond.

"I should kill him and set an example. When men take my money and can't pay it back …"

"Please," I beg him again. My clutch falls from my grasp to the stones beneath our feet. My trembling fingers reach up to the fine fabric of his suit. "Isn't there anything you want instead?" I question, and I'm very aware that the offer is leading.

So much so that when his eyes drift down my body, I'm certain he can see the hardened peaks of my breasts. I'm not a whore, and I've never offered myself to a man … but the tension between us is thick and undeniable.

"Yes, there is. You can take his place."

"Not to die, I hope," I make an effort for my statement to sound as if it's a joke. But with his hand on my throat and the knowledge of what he could do to me, I can't deny fear lingers under the lust.

Leaning closer to me, Harrison drops his lips to the shell of my ear to whisper, "There are many things a man like me requires. I'm sure you can think of something."

CHAPTER 2

Calum

THERE ARE ONLY TWO THINGS THAT KEEP ME FROM FUCKING Annabelle on the leather seats of my car right now.

Alessio, my driver; I'm not sharing her moans of pleasure with him or anyone else.

And the second thing … my phone going off in my suit jacket. The vibrations haven't stopped since I escorted Miss Belle out of the party.

I've never been harder in my life, walking behind this beautiful rose with everyone's eyes on us. There isn't a single guest that didn't watch in silence as her heels clicked and my hand rested on her back.

Speculation and rumors have already started. I can only imagine what they've conjured up in their heads.

Not a single one of them has the balls to ask though. Maurizio is the only soul who's called. Time after time, his calls have been persistent, and I'm certain his voicemails are riddled with concern. Perhaps threats at first. Maybe indignation. There's no doubt in my mind that he'll be begging for an answer and to know she's all right in the last message he leaves tonight.

"Harrison." Belle's soft voice grabs my attention. Without the laced ribbon across her face, she's even more alluring. With soft curves and long brunette locks that sweep across her slender shoulders, every inch of her was made to tempt me. She has classic beauty.

Even the way she says my name, questioningly and submissively … the desire to take her raw right here and now may win out. "It's Calum …"

She clears her throat politely before asking, "Did you know?" There's a brazen tone to her voice that gets my attention.

"Know what?"

"That my father wouldn't be able to pay you." Her lips stay parted just slightly. Her thighs tighten every single time I look her in the eyes.

I could answer her honestly and admit I knew he was a losing bet. I could lie and hide the truth from her. Instead, I settle on something else. "I knew I wanted you. But I didn't know the foreplay would be this … enticing."

Her chest rises, and a deep blush blooms in her cheeks.

My phone rings again, interrupting the moment, and I don't hide my annoyance.

"You're a smart girl," I compliment her as I press the ignore button on my phone, sending her father's call straight to voicemail.

"If I'm smart," she practically whispers, her delicate fingers gripping the edge of the leather. The seat protests as she readjusts, attempting not to squirm under my gaze. Licking her lips, she continues, "Then I should know this … trip to discuss terms is more than just a trip to discuss terms?" She says each word carefully, and only once she's finished speaking, making her very true statement sound as if it's a question, does she look me in the eye.

The air is thick between us. She already knows the answer.

There's nothing else I want more, and there's no way for her father, Maurizio, to pay.

A text comes through on my phone just as I decide a simple 'yes' will suffice. It halts my answer.

I stare down at the message from Alessio even though Belle's gaze stays on me:

I'm not certain this is for your best interest.

My answer is immediate:

You said yourself, I'm viewed too harshly, too much of a beast. No one comes to us out of fear, and if I don't soften, I'll lose everything.

His answer comes just as quickly, and I ignore it as the red light in front of us changes to green.

You think blackmail and extortion is softening?

He can call it whatever he'd like. The men I deal with are weak when it comes to violence. Bloodstained streets is how I acquired a good portion of my wealth. They need to see me in a different light, and a woman like Belle by my side will do just that.

"Calum?" Belle whispers my name again, and I'm reminded of the strain against my zipper. Her red-stained lips are parted, and all I can envision is slipping my cock between them.

"Yes. This is much more than discussing terms. You'd be smart to know that," I finally answer her, and this time when my phone vibrates, I simply turn the damn thing off.

CHAPTER 3

Annabelle

MY SHOULDERS SHAKE WITH A SHUDDERING BREATH AS THE cold breeze from outside is quelled by the front door closing. Calum's estate is massive, and I stand in the grand foyer in awe.

Riches and wealth drip from every detail of the structure. Yet, it's nearly empty, and the expansive room, heated by a crackling fireplace, still feels cold.

The thud of the locks behind me are what rip my attention away from the carved wood details of the double winding staircase and massive crystal chandelier that shines down from three stories up.

His large hand rests on the small of my back, just as it did when we left the party. Far too early and abruptly. I can only imagine what the host and guests think.

With Calum leading me, I walk forward, towards the warmth of the fireplace lined with slabs of dark stone that travel from floor to ceiling. I've never felt so small, surrounded by burgundy crushed-velvet furniture and the smell of polished hardwood.

Everything is clean, in its place, and luxurious.

A subtle change forces a small gasp from me. Calum's hand slips from the small of my back to my hip and then slightly lower. Possessively and making no attempts to hide what he wants.

"Shall we have a seat?" he offers, but his gentlemanly question is laced with sin. His front presses against my back as his hand rests on my shoulder.

I'm certain I can feel his length against my backside. Sucking in a sharp breath, I wish I could gather the courage to speak.

I've always been a bit too shy to go for what I want.

But that's what led me here, to the mercy of this man. Listening, obeying.

The thought is what convinces me to turn where I am, still close enough to him that we touch, only this time, it's my front to his. With his head lowered and mine raised, I ask him, lust coating my question, "Here then? On the sofa?"

His eyes flash with primitive need, and for a moment I know I've shocked him. He's quick to regain his position, placing his hands on my hips, gently so.

"For now ... until I have you on your knees on the floor. Or would you rather we get right to it, Belle?"

"On my knees?" The vision flashes in my mind. The crackling of the fire, my knees and palms burning against the rug as Calum takes me from behind, his blunt nails digging into my hips.

A rough groan travels up his chest, once again making me feel as if he's read my mind. "Yes," he answers, "Let's get the formalities over with, and then I'll have you that way first, your ass in the air as I fuck you on all fours."

I couldn't blush any harder, but with the barest grasp on the last bit of dignity I have, I manage to speak. "Is that the deal? My father's debt for tonight?"

Calum's head tilts, and a threat laces the single word he speaks. "Tonight?"

The raging of my heart heats my body, as if I've said something wrong. Instinctively, I take one step back, and he's far too quick to keep us close, matching my step with his own.

"What do you want with me? If not ..."

"Oh, I assure you, Belle, what you're thinking is precisely what I want." The desire in his tone is reflected in his gaze, and the lust that rushes in my blood is the only thing that keeps the fear from taking over.

"Then ... I don't understand." I honestly don't.

"It's going to take much more than a night to pay off your debt."

CHAPTER 4

Calum

"**H**OW MUCH MORE?" SHE QUESTIONS, THE DESIRE SUBSIDING, overtaken by the details. "How long is this … Arrangement?"

"I'll decide that." Irritation rolls through me, tensing my body. She's already thinking of limiting her time. "I want everything from you. Including your time. As much of it as I desire."

I could give her everything and anything she wanted, but all she wants is to know when it will be over before it's even begun.

"I need to know."

"You don't need to know anything other than how I want you." My words are harsh, and I'm quite aware. She was eager and ready, but panic has reached her eyes.

For the first time since I met her eyes and stalked her steps at that party, regret lingers in the air between us. My anger quickly dissipates, and the hint of fear bleeds into my thoughts. I almost have her. Ever since I saw her years ago, I've wanted her. I can't let a minor detail take her away from me.

"Did you think one night would pay it all off? That in one night I'd have my fill?" Slipping my hand around the back of her neck, I nip her bottom lip in admonishment, ramping up the desire I know she has for me.

"Calum." Her throat tightens as she swallows. "Please, I need—"

"You need to do as I say," I command her, and my tone resonates, but still she hesitates. I fucking loathe it.

"I will," quickly spoken, her eyes wide and her body willing. "I promise I will. But I need …"

"Make it very clear and be quick, Annabelle. My patience is running thin."

"You want to use me, fuck me, and I swear I want you too. How can I agree to letting you do as you please with no way out and no way to stop this …"

"When I'm done with you tonight, that won't be a worry. Now, get on your knees."

She gasps, the sound both alarming and tantalizing.

The image embeds itself in my memory.

"You can only have me at night."

"No."

"You expect me here for how long?"

"When I'm here; you're here." My voice is firm. "This isn't negotiable. You'll be taken care of and you'll be ready for me whenever I need."

"And my life?"

"It is owed to me."

"For … for however long you decide?"

I can see the likelihood of the next series of events. The fear, her wanting out. She'll make it difficult. More difficult than it needs to be.

"I would prefer not to give you a date. I'd rather give you a word. If you feel the need to be alone. To be without me for a moment. You will come back, and you will continue to be mine in all ways. But if it becomes too intense …" My pulse races as she slowly unravels under my offer. The way her eyes turn darker and peer into mine and her lips part just slightly inform me that she's willing, that the offer tempts her.

"Give me a word. Or a statement. Tell me what you'll say if you need … a moment. I'm only willing to give you a moment."

"I say this word and you'll let me go?"

"For a day. I'll give you one day and then you must come back."

"A word …"

"Or a phrase."

"Deep red rose."

"Deep red rose," I repeat.

"So the terms are: I'm yours to do with as you please. But if it's too much, I have one day if I tell you 'deep red rose.'"

Nodding, I hold her gaze, refusing to let it go as she stands in front of me, taking it all in. Did she really think I'd only want her for a night?

"I've grown tired of terms, Belle."

With a sudden inhale, she nods slightly and the tips of her fingers play at the hem of her dress. "How would you like me?" she questions, and I swear I couldn't get harder if I wanted to.

"Good girl," I commend her and take a chance, stalking around her in a slow circle to her back. When I rest my hand at her neck, brushing her hair out of the way, she shivers, and her head falls back slightly. Her quickened breath and the sound of her dress unzipping is all that fills the room. The heat from behind us swells until her dress falls to the floor, followed by her undergarments, and I leave her standing there, bared to me as I unbutton my shirt behind her.

She steals a glance over her shoulder, and I allow it. Taking my time as she stands nervously waiting.

When I unzip my pants, she shifts her weight, her thighs clenching and the blush turning darker against her skin.

With puddles of cloth beside us, I circle her again, gripping and stroking my length. Precum beads on my head and I spread it, stoking myself again.

If I wasn't already an arrogant man, the sight of her eyes widening and her lips parting with a gasp when she stares down at my cock would certainly turn me into one.

With my other hand, I test the weight of her breasts, holding them for a moment and running my thumb against her hardened nipples. Her soft whimper begs for me, and she leans in slightly until I tsk at her.

She's quick to correct herself, even if need is etched into every aspect of her expression.

Her reactions and obedience are perfection. I didn't make a mistake. I was right that she was the perfect one for this.

"Down on your knees and lick," I command her, and she's quick to do just that. I grip myself at the base as she leans forward, gliding her tongue along the veins of my cock. A shudder runs through me as her scandalous tongue slips between my slit, gathering the precum.

My toes curl against the carpet, and my pulse quickens with need. Just as she parts her lips to suck, not lick, I scold her and command her to get on her hands and knees.

The curve of her ass is only outmatched by the glistening folds that await me. She's ready for me. I don't need to run my fingers along her pussy to know it. But I do. Just to feel her arousal. That small insignificant touch, my fingers drifting from her center to her clit, elicits the sweetest sounds from her. Her eyes close, and she bites down on her lip until I scold her once again.

"I want to hear what I do to you." My wish is spoken as I slip my middle finger inside of her warmth, feeling how tight she is. A strangled gasp fills the air, and I swear I can't take anymore. She's sensitive to every touch.

I could take her slowly, but I have needs, and she should know I'm not a gentle lover. I won't do her the disservice of pretending that I am.

I steady her with one hand gripping her hip, and her body tenses. In a swift stroke I fill her, burying myself to the hilt. Her gorgeous body bows, and she cries out the sweetest sound of pain mixed with pleasure. Staying deep inside of her, I wait for her to adjust, and I'm barely able to contain myself. Leaning down, I rest my chest to her back and kiss just below her ear. With a deep inhale, she peers back at me, looking up through her thick lashes.

Her lips stay parted and her eyes are on mine as I pull out ever so slowly, watching how her eyes dilate and the dangerous cocktail of sinful pleasure rolls through her.

Another thrust, and her head falls forward. With both hands on her hips, I take her brutally and roughly, just as I promised. I groan in time with the sound of our flesh meeting, and Belle cries out her pleasure. It's not long before she tightens around me, nearly making me come before I'm ready as she finds her release.

I allow her another, holding my breath and fucking her until she can no longer stay on all fours. With her front on the carpet, I piston my hips, loving how she writhes under me. I forcefully take her again and again until she cries out my name as if it's a plea. Only then can I finally find my release.

Still recovering and breathing heavily, I lay gentle kisses along the center of her back, running the length of it up to her shoulder. Once I've met the crook of her neck, I slip out of her, and she winces.

Using my shirt, I clean what I can between her thighs. All the while I kiss her, and she turns, facing me and exploring with her own small touches.

Her fingers travel up my chest, her nails slipping gently along the grooves of muscle.

"Calum," she moans my name, maybe still lost in the pleasure. I love the sound of my name slipping from her lips. My kiss meets hers, and if only I was still hard, I'd take her again, right here in front of the fire.

In an effort to run her lips along my jaw, she parts those sweet lips, but I back away. Even with the dim light and the stubble, she'll feel the indentation, her soft kisses will travel along the scar. It's a sharp knife of betrayal that pushes me away from her touch.

"Deep red rose?" she says the phrase I loathe, her escape, but before I can fully absorb it, she corrects herself. "Is that your limit? That's what I meant. You don't want me to touch your scar?"

"No. I don't see why you'd want to."

"Can I?" she questions, her voice full of exhaustion. Ignoring her question, I lift her limp body to the sofa and lay her down.

"Let me get you a blanket … or rather…" Not finishing the thought, and not bothering to dress myself, I leave her where she is. Replaying the last moment obsessively.

She doesn't flinch, doesn't seem to have any fear at all when it comes to the scar. She doesn't cower at the man I am. Her gentle touch is at odds with everything else. After dressing, I grab the box and return to the living room to find her spread out under the simple throw from the back of the sofa, her hair in a halo, her curves hidden under the luxurious fabric, but still very much on display.

"Can I touch you now?" Her sultry voice carries through the room.

"No."

"Is holding me after out of the question?" she asks, not hiding the longing in her voice.

"Needy girl," I comment, sitting on the end of the sofa where her head rests. The furniture protests with a groan as I take my seat, then I lift her head and set it down onto my lap.

A moment passes of quiet, the glow of the fire our company, and the only conversation the crackling and snapping of the wood.

"How long have you lived like this?" She whispers her question as I pet her hair. How many nights have I sat here alone, lost in work and thoughts of vengeance?

"Like what?" I ask to clarify.

"Alone in such a large place."

"It doesn't matter."

With a saddened tone, she responds, "Small talk never does."

Disliking the way her eyes close and the very idea that she's done with the small talk itself, I answer, "All my life."

It's quiet again, and all I can think as I steal glances at her, with her eyes closed and her dark red lips resting nearly against my leg, is that she's going to say 'deep red rose' any minute. I need to be careful with her, or she'll run.

"You want me to stay here." It's a statement, not a question. She's already thinking about it. I never should have offered that clause.

"Yes.

"And you won't tell me how long?"

"… No. But I gave you my word. Your one condition I'll allow." My voice is hard, in stark contrast to hers.

"That's dangerous."

"You'll stay here. You'll do as I like. And the debt will be forgiven."

The fire snaps and hisses with my treatment of her.

Turning slightly on her side, she toys with the blanket between her fingers. Her bare breast peeking from just under the throw.

Lowering my lips to hers, I whisper, "I already want you again."

That gets her attention, and a bit of shock too if her wide eyes peering up at me is anything to go on. They're a beautiful hazel, not unlike the amber fire before us.

"I like that you want me, Mr. Harrison." She hesitates … and I wait for it with bated breath. Her escape clause to be uttered from between those gorgeous lips I've yet to use to the fullest.

"I think I like it a little too much. I think you're going to ruin me."

Let me ruin you. The command goes unspoken, and it's only when she rests her head again that I look up at the clock on the mantel, an ancient thing, but the tick of it is barely audible, and so it stays.

"You have a phone call to make."

"My father?" The cadence of her answer is dreadful.

"Yes, but before that … I got you a gift." She's forced to sit up as I pluck the box from the coffee table. This moment is a disturbance, but so long as this is taken care of, I'll have more of her and more of this tonight.

The box leaves my hand and rests in her lap as she sits cross-legged next to me, the throw pooling around, falling slowly, until it's nothing but a puddle of chenille.

It's been a week since I purchased the fine garment and had it delivered. She holds the matte-black box adorned with a satin ribbon.

Instead of opening it, she only runs her fingers along the silk. "You just met me tonight." She tilts her head, questioningly and accusatorily. It stirs something inside of me. Her obedience mixed with curiosity is alluring. I want more of it.

"I knew you'd be there. I knew you'd come home with me."

"You said you knew I wasn't invited."

"I say a lot of things to get what I want." My answer seems to satisfy her. She unties the ribbon and lifts the silk.

"A silk robe? Rather presumptuous." She doesn't look me in the eyes until the final statement, her slender fingers still running along the fine silk.

"I prefer the term 'confident'. It was only a matter of time, Belle."

"You went through all of this … for me?"

"I said I wanted you."

"Why me?"

"Because I saw you, and I imagined something different than what I had for the first time in years. Now put your robe on, it's time to call your father."

It was years ago. For years I've wanted her. If she thinks she can create an end date for this arrangement, she's so very wrong.

"Tell him you're staying here indefinitely."

CHAPTER 5

THERE'S A FINE LINE OF PLEASURE AND FEAR MIXED WITH sadness. Not for me, but for Calum.

We walk the ornate hallway of his home. He could stride past me without any effort. The man is so tall.

His wealth is so vast, this place could be littered with help, yet it's vacant and quiet as far as I can tell.

Calum Harrison could have fucked me in a hall closet of that castle, and I would have loved every second without a single regret.

He could have offered me this deal regardless of my father, and I imagine I would have taken it. Especially now, knowing the divine pleasure that's left me deliciously sore.

The thick wallpaper of deep red paisley lines the hall from floor to ceiling, and although I know this call is going to prove exactly where I stand, I wonder how Calum could even question it.

"You didn't have to do this, you know." I whisper the confrontation. His steady strides that he kept to walk beside me halt, leaving me a hair in front of him. I turn where I am, the fine silk of the evening robe grazing along my skin. Wearing nothing else, it'd be rather scandalous if there were maids or butlers hiding behind the corners.

The little touches he's been giving me make me very aware that Calum enjoys seeing me like this. Wrapped in fine cloth that barely hides a thing from him.

I enjoy it too. In fact … I love it.

"It has to happen. You'll call him, inform him that you're with me."

"I don't mean that." I'm aware I interrupt him, but he misunderstood. "Of course I have to call my father."

Content with my response, Calum places his hand on my back, a gesture that we're to continue.

"I would trade anything for my father's life … but you could have had my body regardless."

"Your body?"

"You certainly paid a steep price for it."

"Is that right?" he questions, peering down at me. My heart flutters when he looks at me like that. With genuine curiosity. "You think it's only your body I want?"

"No." My answer doesn't come out half as strong with his darkly spoken question. There isn't a doubt in my mind what Calum craves. My submission, my pleasure belonging to him. I have to clear my throat as the dirty thoughts of what he's going to do to me for however long he wants runs a shiver of want down my shoulders.

"You realize this is madness and unnecessary."

"I wanted you and I would do *anything*," he stresses the word, "to really have you."

"But like this?" I can't help but to push.

"I do what I have to do." His hard response doesn't add to the image of the man everyone else sees. All I see in his gaze is desperation.

My heart breaks for him. Truly.

I wonder if he would have gone about it this way before the accident, back when no one referred to him as a beast. Back to articles with him laughing. Back then … would he have sought out my father and offered him that deal at his lowest just so he could maneuver a way to keep me in his grasp?

"Do you pity me?" Calum questions, turning towards me and taking a dangerous step closer. The air around him forces me to take a step back, pressing myself against the fine walls of the hallway.

"Pity? No," I answer. He's an enigma, one that my mind wants to dance with. His hand cups my jaw, holding me captive as the back of my head presses against the wall. "Do you know it turns me on?" I question him back in a whisper. His strength, the force of his entirety. "I've never felt more alive." I only hope he feels the same.

"I could break you."

"I know," I whisper in response to his threatening tone.

"I could do whatever I want to do to you." His lips are closer now and the desire rises up from the pit of my belly.

It only turns me on. *Maybe there's something wrong with me.*

"I saw you years ago," I finally confess to him. "And I made a wish that night; that you would do exactly that." Whatever he wanted.

Calum takes his time slipping the robe from my shoulders. This time when he takes me roughly against the wall, he lets me kiss his scar afterwards.

CHAPTER 6

Annabelle

"**I** DON'T CARE WHAT YOU TELL HIM; I'M SURE HE'LL HAVE FIGURED it out anyway."

The sound of the first ring is ominous. It seems to slow as my heart races frantically.

Tell him the truth or tell the lie Calum wants to hear. As the phone rings once more, I make the decision simple. Which is the choice I won't regret? Because of the three of us, I'm the only one that will have to live with this decision forever.

"Harrison," my father hisses, and my heart hammers. "If you touched her, I'll destroy you and every—"

"Father," I interrupt him, feeling the ball in my throat grow spikes as I do.

"Annabelle." Relief is evident, but so is fear. "Where are you?"

"Father, please." I swallow and close my eyes at the sound of the hardwood floors creaking behind me as Calum shifts his weight.

Although my father protests, telling me to answer him and questioning where I am again, Calum's hand wraps around my front, splaying across my belly, and he pulls my back into his broad chest.

"I need you to listen to me." My voice is softer, easier with his touch.

All I'm given in response is a curse of frustration. Until he screams, "I'll fucking kill him for hurting you!"

"He didn't hurt me," I object. "I left with him last night because I wanted to." Calum plants a soft kiss below my ear in that sensitive spot that elicits the sweetest of chills down my shoulder.

There is only silence on the other end of the line.

"I'm going to stay with him for a while. I want a break, and I can still—" Just as I'm offering to still do the book-keeping, my father's voice turns questioning.

"If I didn't know any better, I'd think you have feelings for that beast of a man …"

"It's something like that …"

"This isn't going to end well for you." His voice is foreboding.

It's a tale as old as time, isn't it? Instead of speaking, I offer him silence as Calum breaks away from me, only watching from behind.

"You're making a mistake." My father's tone is harsh.

"I'm making a choice. I want more than this life." I don't know exactly what lies ahead, but it's something more. It's something I never knew how badly I wanted.

"This life?" my father questions with distaste, and then ignores me and what I've just said. They all do. They always have, and I'm tired of being ignored. "Did he threaten you?"

"No."

"Does this have to do with the debt?"

"No." *Lie. Lie after lie.* But I want the beast. I want to live in his dark castle and let him do whatever he wants to me.

"I'm with Calum now. I only called to tell you. I love you."

"Belle, please." Stress lingers over the line from my father's plea. It doesn't matter what he says though, I want this. I want to be captive to Calum. I want him to leave me deliciously used. It's not quite a fairytale, but it's certainly my fantasy.

"I'll call again soon." The old phone clicks as I set it down on Calum's desk, staring at the antique wood and wondering what I've just done. What fate I've chosen.

"Does he believe you?" Harrison's darkly murmured question catches me off guard. I swear this place holds a spell over me. With both of my hands gripping the desk behind me, I face him, the beast I've chosen.

"Does he believe what?" *What were my lies? I* can't even remember. The chill that runs down my spine when Calum peers down at me with his sharp hazel gaze is warmed by the simple touch. At first, it's only the rough pad of his thumb trailing down my jaw. Then it's his hand on my throat, wrapped around it, but not too tight as he plants a single kiss against my lips. The warmth flows just as the desire does, lower and lower to the pit of my belly. When my eyes close, his masculine scent wraps around me, and I can barely breathe.

"It doesn't matter, Belle," he whispers against my lips, and his warm breath travels down the crook of my neck as he plants a kiss there.

The unbuckling of his belt forces my eyes open only to be staring straight ahead at the faint scar along his jaw. Goosebumps travel down my heated skin as he plants one more kiss at the sensitive bit of my neck, just below my ear. My whimper of need is accompanied by his hard chest brushing against my breasts. He whispers, his lips at the shell of my ear, "Get on your knees."

Looking for a darker romance? *Merciless* is the book for you. Inspired by Beauty and the Beast it's a modern crime family retelling. Read it for free today!

FLIRTING WITH A GOOD NIGHT

In our small town, all of my friends have found their soulmates
and here I am, moving from one crush to the next but never
actually settling down. The reason why is standing only a few feet
from me now. He's joking with my best friend's husband, as I sit
on their sofa trying not to stare. With his sleeves rolled up, the
tattoos he got while he was away in the marines are on display,
curved around his toned muscle that flex with his rough chuckle.

Cade was years older and left right after high school. I never told him
how I felt, we were so young and there was no way he'd ever go for a
sophomore like me. Times have changed and now he's back… and I can't
stop staring and pining over the man I've been longing for.

And when he looks my way, with that handsome smirk, rough stubble
and gorgeous baby blue gaze…

CHAPTER 1

Sharon

"**J**UST SMELL IT."

Magnolia's command is murmured with aww, even if it does crack me up. Both of us take a deep inhale that has my back pushing against the cream sectional sofa. Her eyes are closed, her nose just a centimeter above the practically bald little one's head. He has just a small smatter of dark brown hair at the very top of his noggin and with the little jostle, he coos, putting a wide-eyed Autumn on edge.

"There's nothing like it in the whole world." Magnolia's statement is met with both another coo from Cameron, the two-week old little one fast asleep in her arms, and a long exhale of relief from his mother. Autumn's arms are still up as if she was getting ready to snatch her newborn and quickly rock him back to sleep if he woke from the two of us taking a nice long whiff of that baby smell.

I bite back my smile, unable to not see the humor in the room with Magnolia completely missing Autumn's stress.

"Seriously," Mags presses, "There's something about the way they smell…" I finally let out a laugh when Mags closes her eyes and lays back with the little boy.

"If you keep creeping me out, I'm taking my baby back," Autumn's response is given with a broad smile. You'd never know she just went through almost thirty hours of labor earlier this week.

There really is something about that sweet baby powder like scent, though. I have to agree with Mags, pulling my legs up on the sofa and then resting my pointer against Cameron's little cheek. "He is freaking adorable Autumn," I murmur and feel my heart swell with happiness for her and Trent and their other two boys.

"I want another baby." Mags cradles the baby closer and Autumn's eyes go wide.

"If you wake him, you keep him," she comments while dragging the basket of clothes across the kitchen island to be closer to her. She's all the way at the end of it, now perched on a stool, while the two of us, strike that, two and a little a bundle, are huddled at the end of her sofa where the living room meets the kitchen.

Our Wine-down Wednesdays have certainly changed recently. Mags with her … shall I say love life dilemma, and Autumn with her ever-growing family.

"I'm not going to wake him up," Mags admonishes Autumn then makes an 'oops' expression as Cameron wiggles in her arms.

The little man has only been on this earth for less than 2 weeks but he knows how to make the whole world stop as he nestles in tighter.

"I would steal him away from you," I start and then we all hear the front door open and the sound of several boot steps filter in through the house. "But I have to get going," I finish as the sight of two men interrupts the conversation.

With a charming smile, the first man pauses to cup the little one's head. Giving me the perfect comparison of father and son.

Cameron looks just like Trent, Autumn's husband. His little nose and those large brown eyes. They are all Trent.

With a pout from Mags, and her pulling the baby into her arms playfully, as if to say 'he's mine, off,' Trent chuckles and makes his way to Autumn, planting a kiss on her cheek before setting down a number of plastic bags on the counter next to his wife.

What is it with men and carrying every single bag from the grocery store in at once?

"Thanks for giving him a ride while his car is in the shop," Autumn's gratitude is met with a little nod from the second man.

The one who has my heart stuttering from my place on the sofa.

"No problem," his deep voice echoes and I take the chance to drink him in.

In our small town, all of my friends have found their soulmates and here I am, moving from one crush to the next but never actually settling down. The reason why is standing only a few feet from me now. He's joking with my best friend's husband, as I sit on their sofa trying not to stare. With his sleeves rolled up, the tattoos he got while he was away in the marines are on display, curved around his toned muscle that flex with his rough chuckle.

He was years older and left right after high school. I never told him how I felt, we were so young and there was no way he'd ever go for a sophomore like me. Times have changed and now he's back… and I can't stop staring and pining over the man I've been longing for.

And when he looks my way, with that handsome smirk, rough stubble and gorgeous baby blue gaze… Lord, have mercy.

"Cade Jameson," Magnolia calls out as she gently sets the infant down for the first time since she snatched him from me. The little bundle lays effortlessly into the rocker at our feet.

With a gentle touch, I rock the little one, still bundled in a 'choo choo', blue plaid, train swaddle and look anywhere but at the man who's become the center of conversation.

In my periphery, I gauge the friendly hug between them. It's nothing more than polite. Well maybe a touch comical considering how short she is and how he has to bend down to hug her in return. She's a bit petite and Cade is a wall of muscle, taller than most.

"It's good to have you back. You staying long?

"I am," he answers proudly and I only notice that I'm staring, waiting with baited breath for his answer, when his gaze lifts past Mags to where I am.

I'm quick to look away although I continue to eavesdrop about how he'll be home through the holidays and how he's stationed here now, hopefully permanently.

My little heart pitter patters at the thought of him being back home for good.

"You staying for dinner?" Autumn questions and it takes me far too long to look up and realize she's asking me.

"Oh, no. I have to head out and I already ate." I answer her but then realize once the words were spoken that she already knew that. I told her the moment I got here and stole Cameron from her before Magnolia could.

"You're walking home?" she questions further, the room of eyes on both of us. I ignore the heat that comes with Cade's prying gaze.

"That's how I got here," I cock a sarcastic brow Autumn's way and wonder why she added concern to her tone. I always walk to her house, she knows that. It's one of the reasons I love this neighborhood so much. As I stand, I stretch out my back slightly, focusing on the cream throw I'm folding rather than the man whose gaze is falling down my body.

Years ago I thought the tension between us was imagined. Or at least one sided. But this is the third time I've seen him since he's been back and I swear it only gets more and more obvious that I can't keep my eyes off of him and I know he does the same. Stealing glances each time we've had a run in together.

"Why doesn't Cade take you home?" Autumn offers, folding a tee-shirt in her lap and then adding it to a pile on the counter.

Oh, the betrayal. She doesn't have the decency to look me in the eyes. Instead she focuses solely on Cade as my heart completely halts in my chest. "You can take her home on your way, can't you Cade?"

Alone with this man? In his truck? Late at night with my ovaries still doing flip flops at the sight of a newborn?

Oh, no, no, no.

"Of course I can," he answers easily, a touch of southern hitting his last word as he slips his hands, which I already know are rough from years of manual labor, into his jean pockets. His asymmetric smile greets me, "Ready when you are, Shar."

Shar. It takes great effort not to swoon just from the way he says my nickname.

CHAPTER 2

There's nothing like the autumn leaves, hues of gold and red, being carried down the gravel road of this old town. Or the smell of the apples and the laughter of kids playing at the edge of the orchard that lines this half of the neighborhood I grew up in.

Nothing like the soft sigh that comes from Shar's plump lips either or the way the wind blows her brunette locks as I help her into my truck.

It's all a part of home to me. A home I missed dearly for years.

Her hand is small in mine and the blush that rises up her chest and into her cheeks is certainly from my hand on the small of her back rather than the chill in the air. I've always had an effect on her, one that forces a hint of a chuckle from me and she peeks up through her lashes and then finds her place in the passenger side.

"Thank you," she whispers shyly, letting me shut her door after giving her a small nod and a "no problem."

Shar has no idea how much I thought about her while I was overseas. How the stories Trent would tell me, keeping me up to date on this town, always seemed to come back to her.

It didn't matter what news was filtering through the town gossip, I needed to know about her and what she was doing, if she was with anyone. I had no right, she doesn't even know how I feel about her, but there was a piece of me that needed to hear she was doing alright without me.

Coming home every so often and catching up with a beer and friends was never complete until Shar idled in. Her confidence hitching just like her breath did every time she saw me.

I felt it, whatever it is that crackles between us now, but I never acted on it because it would only be days until I was gone again.

That changes now though.

The truck rocks gently as I pull my door shut after helping her get in on her side.

"You know you don't have to," Sharon speaks first as I bring the truck to life with a rumble and turn down the music so I can hear her caressing voice that much better. "I could walk."

My window's already rolled down and I set my elbow there, resting my chin in my hand, my pointer running along the rough stubble of my jaw as I stare at her and wait for her to look back at me.

"I like the opportunity to be a gentleman when I can be."

"Mm," she murmurs. "You imagine you're some kind of gentle beast, huh?" she jokes, but there's a breathlessness to her taunting. Both of her hands find her lap and then fall between her knees, which makes her thighs part.

A gentle beast? I'm not so sure of that. Not with the thoughts running through my mind right now. Imagining how I'd part those thighs of hers, barely covered by her burgundy cotton dress.

"I might be all brute, I think," I comment back, half-jokingly. "But I at least try."

She laughs gently, her chest rising and falling easily. With her hair swept across her shoulder she leans back, closing her eyes and listening to the faint music.

"Well thank you, Cade."

My cock twitches just from her saying my name. It's too rough a word for her seductive lips. Readjusting, I put the car in drive.

"Blue house on the corner, right?" I ask her and she nods.

"Right across from the lake."

"Yeah I remember now. It's been a year since."

"Since you dropped me off when I was wasted?" she questions and shakes her head, her beautiful gaze on the auburn leaves that blow in the wind as we drive by. "Thank you for that by the way… It was not my best night."

"We were all wasted," I attempt to appease her. If I was being fully honest, I'd admit to her that I'm glad she was too far gone that night. My fingers itched to hold her and if she'd been more sober, I'd have leaned in for a kiss. I'd have wanted more. Only for me to be called away the very next day. It was meant to happen, to give us more time for when it'd be right.

A time like now.

I lay my forearm on the center console, daring to get a little closer to her, my hand only inches from her.

"Seriously, thanks for that night. It was …"

"A good night," I stop her from finishing the word 'embarrassing.' "I love coming home and getting to hang out with you." I almost say 'you guys,' but I cut it off deliberately, choosing not to hide anymore. Not to hold back.

"Oh, is that right?" Shar swallows thickly, the sound of it bringing my attention to her slim throat and the dip just beneath it that begs me to lay an open kiss right there.

With the heat climbing in the cabin, no matter that our windows are both open, I pull up in her drive and park the truck. "You like hanging out with me?" she asks, a hint of reverence playing in the sweet cadence of her question.

I can only nod, my grip slipping slightly on the wheel as my palms turn sweaty.

"I like the way you look at me," I push her gently, calling her out and finally being a man when it comes to her and what's between us.

"I look at people, yeah," she tries to play it off.

"You blush the same way too? When you look at other people."

I'm only given a deeper hue of red as she sits in that seat, biting down on her lip. A lip I'd like to suck while my hand roams between her legs. I have to shift in my seat and I notice she squirms in hers too.

The crickets and nightlife are the only backdrop as I turn the keys in the ignition and let the silence take over.

"You don't make me blush, Cade," she lies and then stares out her window to correct herself. "Well… you make all the girls blush so it's not the same."

"I don't notice it with other women. I don't notice anything about them."

"Now you're just trying to prove a point and make me blush," she accuses.

"Tell me you didn't look at me different from the other guys?" Damn, it's odd how much thinking that's a possibility hurts. The pain vanishes the second Shar looks up at me with wide eyes.

"I feel like you always did," I admit.

Her breathing is shallow and her lips slightly parted.

"Do you want to come in?" is all she says, her fingers digging into the leather of the seat beneath her, as if she has to cling to it to keep her seated there.

"And why do you want me to come in Shar?" I don't know why I tease her, why I prolong the tension, other than that I need her to admit it too.

"Because I don't want to be alone tonight?"

"You answered that like you were asking another question."

Her gaze drops and insecurity flashes in her gorgeous eyes.

"Come on, Shar. Tell me the truth. Tell me all of this isn't in my head and something I just made up."

My heart rages against my chest and my pulse races, waiting for her to answer.

She shakes her head gently, swallowing first, and then admitting, "If you mean the fact that I've wanted you for years and that I've dreamt what could have happened that night a year ago… then no. It's not in your head."

"Then, yeah, I want to come in."

CHAPTER 3

Sharon

HIS LIPS WERE ON ME SO FAST, HIS HANDS ON MY WAIST, PINNING me against his truck. The only reason my eyes aren't closed as he devours me is because I need to see it, to know I'm sane, and that this all isn't a dream.

Cade Jameson, the boy who stole my heart in high school and left with it for years is back a man, demanding the very thing I've wanted since I first laid eyes on him.

With his large hands at my hips, his lips drifting down my neck and the chill of the autumn night air leaving goosebumps along my exposed skin, I can barely breathe, let alone believe this is real.

It's the site of my neighbor, Miss Clare Jane peeking through her blinds that snaps me out of the haze.

All hot and bothered, I'd feel shame if I wasn't living out a fantasy I'd trade all my modesty for in a heartbeat.

"Cade, inside," I whisper at the same time he rakes his teeth up my neck and smiles at the shell of my ear.

He whispers, "You have no idea how long I've dreamed about doing just this." His grip on me loosens and with a gentle hand in mine, helping me find my balance, he leaves a kiss just beneath my ear and adds, "But I was more of a brute than a gentleman in those dreams, Shar."

Pulling back, he gives me a charming smirk, "I'll mind my manners until we get through that front door of yours."

Oh, my… not a single word can finish that sentence. None come to mind even.

All the heat that had gathered between my legs burns its way up my body as I somehow find the ability to walk at a seemingly normally pace to my front door.

I'm already on edge just from knowing he wants me. Just from that short moment he had me pinned.

His strong hand wraps around mine, his deft fingers slipping against mine and caressing in soothing circles as I open the door.

The chill behind me isn't from the night air, it's from his immediate absence as I walk in and turn in my foyer, the light from the porch shining a light on his hulking body as he stands in the doorway.

"I have to apologize," he starts and with a quick intake, my heart betrays me, squeezing tight at the thought that he isn't going to come in. But then he does. A single step and then another. Each one of his, is met by one by me, luring him deeper in the house, until my back is pressed against the wall and the front door closes with a resounding click.

"I swear next time I'll lay you down right," he whispers although his words scream in my head, the lust making the quite polite words sound dirty. It's his hungry gaze that seems to tear my clothes off even though he's not touching me. His careful steps as if I'm his prey when he's aware I'm willingly already his.

"But tonight, I have to do this," he finishes the thought that seems to take forever to complete all the while my body heats and the desire takes over.

He's on me in an instant, my back arching from the intensity of his kiss. His lips press against mine as his hands roam down my body, lifting up my skirt and pushing my underwear aside.

My lips mold to his and I moan in his mouth as his thick fingers brush against my swollen nub and then drift lower, through my slick folds and to my heated core. He groans, his head falling back for a moment before he rests his forehead against mine. His lids are still closed and I stare up at him, my heart racing, needing more. My entire being depends on the words that are sure to fall from his lips.

"You're so fucking wet for me," he comments with reverence and before I can respond, I'm in his arms, my legs wrapped around his hips. With my back against the wall, he balances me there, his left hand pulling at the strap to my dress which falls carelessly, seemingly also affected by the unfair spell he's always had over me.

If I could speak, I'd tell him that. I'd admit I've been ready for him for longer than he knows. I'd confess how much I want him, if only every nerve ending wasn't lit along my skin, making his harsh touch filled with desperation ignite a craving both of us need to satisfy this very instant.

"Cade," I cry out his name as he rakes his teeth down the curve of my neck and pulls my dress down lower, taking my bra strap with it until I'm exposed to him.

"I promise next time I'll give you more attention," his calm words, force the haze of want to subside for only a split second, just enough to hear the unzip of his jeans. Then I'm gone, gone far away and higher than I've ever been with my lips dropped into the perfect "o" as he fills me in a swift motion, his thick length stretching me.

With my heels dug into his ass, my body freezes, paralyzed by the sudden wave of pleasure that holds me hostage.

"I'll give you time," he groans against my neck, still buried deep inside of me. My thighs tremble around his hips, my core stretching to accommodate his size.

"This is how I pictured it," he murmurs and I half wonder if he's telling me, or confessing a sin. "This is exactly how I've wanted you," his rough timber vibrates against my heated skin.

If I could speak, I'd admit the same, but he rocks just then, his pubic hair pressing against my clit and sending a moan to take over the words I dared to utter.

His lips find mine again as he rocks in and out, a gentle beast for a moment, before his pace picks up. My fingers dig into his skin, raking down his back and I find myself clinging to him, surrounded by his masculine scent. He fucks me, hard and rough until I have to silence my screams by biting down on his shoulder. The sudden movement awards me with a deep rumble of a groan that spurs him on. Faster, harder, relentlessly until I'm crashing hard against the wave of my release and he's doing the same.

He's gentle when he sets me down, although my legs are weak.

My head's dizzy and my body's numb all too soon. The climax still wracking through my body and leaving me so limp I nearly fall to the floor.

Nearly, but I don't. Disbelief still forcing me to have some semblance of grip on reality.

I just slept with Cade Jameson… No, no, Cade just fucked me against the wall of my foyer. They're two very different things and all I want from him now is *more*.

"Do you want to stay?" I dare to ask him, not even waiting to catch my breath. "You want to stay with me tonight?"

Cade lifts his gaze to mine as he pulls up his jeans, buttoning them and already appearing put together. It's not fair, because he's left me shattered and I know I look the part.

I'm a well fucked mess and his tussled hair shows the evidence of what I've done to him, but nothing else does.

Insecurity wraps its way around my heart until he speaks.

"I'm a pretty easy-going guy, Shar. This could be one good night. It could stay between us. It could be more."

Leaning against my foyer wall, still feeling him inside of me, it takes everything for me to believe this really happened. It's happening right now.

"I want it to be more, but that only matters if you want that too. So you tell me." Vulnerability shines in his light blue eyes when he asks, "You want me to stay?"

If you loved this sexy little short, you'll devour the first novel in this small town romance world. Start reading *Tequila Rose* today!

LOVE
YOU FOR
ALWAYS

CHAPTER 1

H E'S ALREADY DRESSED, SKIPPING BREAKFAST AND HEADING out the door. Every weekend has been like this. I barely see my husband in the blur of busy days and tired nights.

I wish we could go back to the Golden Coast. To barefoot walks on the sandy beach and times when kisses came easily. Nearly a decade ago, back to the days when Tristan always held my hand. We slept in and cuddled in bed, which always led to more.

Back to the days I was shy to kiss him before brushing my teeth—because back then we would kiss first thing in the morning.

"You're already going?" I ask Tristan as he pours from the pot of coffee into a thermal tumbler with the company logo on it. I blame his work for all of these emotions that keep me up at night, his side of it cold and empty.

Standing in our kitchen, the granite counters clear of clutter except for a single pile of mail, mostly containing bills, and a vase that's been empty since Valentine's day last year, my husband looks up at me. Sympathy echoes in his piercing blue eyes and when he swallow, the cords in his neck go tight. It makes the stubble on his jaw look all the sexier. "I have to Honey." I'll always melt at that nickname.

I'm a sucker for him. He had me the first night he ever laid eyes on me. Tall, broad shoulders that make even a plain white tee shirt look divine on him… I never had a chance with this man.

"I made you coffee though," he offers as if I'd rather have a cup of joe than him. My bare feet pad on the dark gray tiled floors as I make my way to him. They're cold and that makes me all the warmer when he holds me in his arms. Nestling my head against his shoulder, I take in the smell of his cologne, and the feel of his muscular chest as he kisses the crown of my head.

"I wish they'd never sold the company," I say just beneath my breath.

Four years ago, his company sold to another. Nearly everyone lost their jobs. We were the lucky ones because they transferred my husband. He kept his job, but it moved him three states away for most of the week.

My heart squeezes when he doesn't say anything other than, "me too."

I hate how little I see him. I hate that I'm stuck here, with a teaching job I worked my ass off to get, so I barely see my husband. I should be grateful and for a while I was. But distance makes things harder and time can change anything.

"Are you sure you have to go?" I question him when he releases me. I tighten the sash on my robe and fold my arms over my chest.

Years ago, at the Golden Coast, he held my hand on our honeymoon and told me he'd love me forever. I love this man with everything in me, but I don't know how much longer we can survive this.

"I have to. I wouldn't leave if I didn't have to."

My throat's tight when I nod in understanding.

It's a Saturday and I'm in nothing but a robe, while he's fully dressed in a slate gray suit. I want to sleep in and kiss him and love him, to feel him in ways I've desperately been missing. And he says he has to go to work.

"Will you be home for dinner?" I question, finding it hard to keep his questioning gaze.

"Of course," his answer comes out with a careful cadence. Like he knows something's wrong. "You okay?" he questions.

"I miss you," I admit my voice cracking; but he already knows I miss him. It's gotten harder to be away from him, not easier.

"Let me take you out to dinner tonight," he offers. "A date night. Like we used to do."

Hope flutters in my chest, and a smile slips onto my lips until he adds, "I just have a few things to wrap up."

Late nights and constant work comes with who Tristan is. He's always been this way.

"I'll see you tonight then," I answer, closing the distance, getting up on my tip toes to plant a kiss on his lips.

I don't expect his hand to splay on my lower back, keeping me pinned to him or for him to deepen the kiss. But, oh how I love it. His teeth scrape gently against my bottom lip until I part my lips for me, granting him entry. The warmth spreads through me, from my tippy toes all the way up to my cheeks where I can feel a blush blooming.

When he breaks the kiss, he whispers in the way air between us, "Love you for always."

I love him for always too. That's why this hurts so much. It wouldn't, if I didn't love him the way I do.

CHAPTER 2

Ana

COLLEGE IS SUPPOSED TO BE WHERE YOU SOW YOUR WILD OATS, or at least that's what my grandmother used to say. Back then, when I first laid eyes on Tristan at a pub on main street at the university, I thought he'd be a fun time.

And I thought that's all it would ever be.

We burned hot together. The casual glances that held on a little too long, the small touches with the passing drinks as a football game played in the background that neither one of us seemed to care about although the rest of the bar roared with excitement or disappointment every other play.

He was tall, dark and handsome. I was wearing my tightest jeans and a flowy top that gave away a little too much cleavage. I thought the moment he leaned down to kiss me, his lips tasting of pale ale and all male, my hand gripping his bicep through a polo, that we'd have a wild night together. One to remember.

I didn't expect him to call me the next day and tell me he was taking me out that weekend. He didn't even ask me. He later told me, he was terrified I'd say no if he asked. So he took a risk.

That night I wore a red dress, red is supposed to give you more confidence. And a matching shade of red on my lips for lipstick courage. Complete with my best black heels and a little clutch.

That was the first night he told me I looked beautiful.

A week later was the first morning he made pancakes before I woke up and told me I wasn't allowed to sneak out in the morning like I had been.

A week after that, he told me he had feelings. Seeing each other every few days, turned into every other, which turned into us spending fairly equal time, always together, at each other's place.

A month went by before I told him I loved him and he told me he knew, before admitting he loved me too.

I remember it all. Every moment we had. First kiss, first night, first date, first everything.

Each one felt like I wasn't worthy. It's scary to fall in love.

He's the one who said, "I love you for always first."

In the kitchen, at our first apartment together, he brushed his nose against mine while we were making dinner together and he said it.

I believed him because it felt like it was meant to be. Like we were simply made for each other.

My phone vibrates on our bed and I barely hear it, the distant memories of our past still lingering, but I do. As I toss the red chiffon dress onto the bed, I don't know why I was crying. I guess it's the pregnancy hormones and the fact that I don't know how I'm going to tell Tristan. We didn't plan it and I don't know how to tell him. But I have to.

How did we get like this? To the place where we have another first we've both wanted since we got married, but I have no idea how to tell him?

Taking the phone in my hand, I smile at his text: *I'll pick you up at seven.*

CHAPTER 3

RED IS ANA'S COLOR.

Something about the shade just suits her. The allure of it, the strength in such a bold choice; she wears it with elegance, even if her fire has dimmed.

As I turn up the radio in the car, it doesn't go unnoticed that she's barely spoken to me. Nervousness pricks its way along the back of my neck. I know she's unhappy and she's been that way, but I'm doing everything I can and tonight I can finally make her happy again.

"You look stunning honey," I compliment her over the hum of the radio.

I still think I have her, she's still mine because every compliment still makes her smile, that beautiful blush coloring her cheeks to be nearly as dark as the clothes she wears.

"You look pretty darn handsome yourself," she whispers and it's then that she places her hand on my thigh as I keep driving. I was waiting for that. Her little touches are everything. I've missed them so much.

With my left hand on the wheel, as I slow at a red light, I lift her hand with my right and kiss her knuckles, one by one, and then turn her hand over, giving her wrist a kiss before the light turns green.

Her small hum of satisfaction and the way her shoulders relax is everything that I needed.

"Where are we going?" she asks me and I tell her it's a surprise but she won't have to wait much longer.

"Oh," she perks up in her seat, a wide smile on her face, "the Blue Grill."

"Our first date as a married couple was here," I remind her.

"How could I forget?" she answers with a smile, her hand still on my thigh as I park the car.

"We sat at the bar because it was so full…"

"My hand may have slipped up your skirt a time or two," I complete the thought for her as I put the car in park and lean over to kiss the crook of her neck. She squeals with delight and I love it. I love everything about her. What we had and, more importantly, everything to come.

We walk side by side, hand in hand through the large double doors of black glass into the elegant foyer of the restaurant.

When I give my name to the host and he leads us to the private back-room, she squeezes my hand and whispers, "What's back here?"

The wooden doors open to a private room, with a single round table in the center, the chairs seated close together. The white table cloth is already laid out with candles, a vase with red roses, and a note on one of the plates. A note I wrote for her.

"Tristan," Ana's voice is tight with emotion and I simply kiss her cheek and pull out her chair for her.

As she scoots in, I take my own seat and rush things more than I wanted to do. I'd planned to make her wait. To wine and dine her like I used to before telling her. But the look on her face, seeing her break down like this, I can't wait. I have to tell her. She's been through enough. These years apart have been so much harder on her and I need her to know that we don't have to do it anymore.

"Read it," I whisper as she stares at the crisp white envelope. "I'm not much of a poet or anything, but I have something to tell you."

She reads the note out loud, her eyes watery, so she dabs them first with the corner of the cloth napkin.

I hope you know I don't take you—or us—for granted.

I miss you every day.

When I said I will love you for always, I meant it because that's all I want to do.

I've only worked so much, to get back home to you.

The moment she reads, back home to you, her hazel eyes widen and she whips her gaze to mine. "What does that mean? You're coming home?" Nervousness and hope wind together in her voice.

Strands of brunette hair fall from the elegant bun on the top of her head. I brush them behind her ear and keep my hand there, cupping her cheek as I tell her.

"I got a job offer in the city. Only forty minutes from our home." Her gasp is covered by her delicate hand. "I've had a few interviews the last few weeks I've been home. That's what I've been doing but I didn't want to tell you. I didn't want to get your hopes up until I knew for sure. I know this has been hard on us and I can't be away from you anymore."

I knew she would be happy, but I didn't expect the tears. I didn't realize she was so emotional about it all.

"I never would have stayed away if I'd known it made you this upset." At my admission, she shakes her head, reaching out to my cheek and cupping it like I do her.

With the tip of her nose brushing against mine, she steadies herself, giving me a peck on the lips before looking back up at me.

"I'm glad you're coming home because this baby is going to need both of us."

The moment she says baby, her hand moves to her belly and shock and then elation hit me harder than I could ever imagine.

"You're pregnant?" I question her in a single breath and her wide smile is joined with a nod.

I hug her and she hugs me back, both of us clinging to each other, both of us surprised in the best of ways.

There are ups and downs in marriage, there are good times and there are bad, but moments like these and all of our other firsts that we've shared and will share in our lives are so worth every dip on this wild ride.

"I love you," I tell her and kiss her, crushing my lips to hers before she can even say it back.

I love you for always.

MY SECRET

She's my secret. Mine and mine alone.

CHAPTER 1

I DON'T PITY THE MEN AND WOMEN WHO LINE THE BAR TONIGHT. As the snow falls behind the paned windows, barely visible with the darkened sky, they lift their glasses. Alcohol drowns out the thoughts of family and friends they aren't with during the holidays. The din of the bar is far from somber though, the occasional laugh ricochets off the paneled walls of this old place.

It may only be a rundown bar off the interstate in the tristate area, tucked away beneath the overpass, but it's warm and feels like home to many. It's my last name on that sign out front. My bar. My home.

It's sure as hell home to me and the only thing I have left from my family. At that thought I peek over my shoulder, a rag in one hand wiping down the glass in the other, and peer at a black and white portrait. My grandfather always had a Coors Light in his hand and it's there lifted in cheers at the grand opening of this very bar.

That photo, and the occasional postcard from my mother, are all that I have left of my family. She took off when I was five, came back when I was seventeen and my father passed suddenly, but she didn't stay long.

So the sight of Jackson at the end of the bar, his phone always in his hand, and Mr. Richards at the other end, his thinned hair as white as the foam in his beer, feel like home to me. Even on Christmas Eve.

"You're all dolled up tonight," Chrissy comments, her voice is a bit raspy from years of smoking. The stool drags on the floor as she pulls it out to sidle up to her brother.

"This old thing," I respond with a smirk. The deep red shift dress matches a shade of lipstick I put on hours ago. No doubt it's faded by now, but he told me once he loved the color on me.

And I know he'll be here tonight. He told me he would and he's never lied to me. Never let me down.

Chrissy huffs a laugh and then elbows Teddy, saying something about getting out of there so she can hang lights on the tree for her grandkids.

Every minute that passes feels as if it drags for hours. Each beer that hits the bar, every clink of the glass and grinding of the stools against the floor is far too loud.

I'm waiting for one man to walk through that old heavy walnut door.

"Another?" Jackson calls out, lifting his mug in the air and I mindlessly follow suit although my eyes lift to the door at the sound of the chimes.

And there he is.

A warmth spreads through me although I don't show it. My heart pounds and races, my blood heats at the sight of him.

The black flat cap is dusted with snow as he removes it, making his way to the far corner booth. He takes his time slipping off the black wool coat and I only watch him, my gaze shifting from the beer mug filling at the tap to his broad shoulders straining beneath the gray Henley.

In black boots and worn jeans, he sure as hell didn't dress up tonight.

There's a little dance of anxiousness that swells deep in my chest knowing I'm overdressed. "Here you go," I tell Jackson, and don't give him a second look or wait for a response as I make my way to him.

At least I'm in ballerina flats and not heels, but still, heat dances along my skin.

"Your usual?" I offer, my voice wavering as his pale blue gaze reaches mine. He pins me there, the world blurring behind him. Even the air bows down to this man. Dirty blonde hair and a ruggedness tell me he's blue collar, but I know he's more than that.

I've known it for years. He's dangerous. He's a man I once feared. Every instinct told me I should stay far away.

And I would have, I had decided I would.

Two years ago, when I first saw him and he ordered what he'll order now, a gin and tonic, I swore I'd avoid him. It's not just that he looks like a man who's been through hell, that smirk on his lips and that charming smile whisper a secret: he proudly runs the place.

His gaze slips down my body, slowly and deliberately.

In this room that's riddled with onlookers, it feels as if he undresses me. Heat creeps into my cheeks.

"I've missed you," he whispers lowly in a deep baritone that triggers a primal need. It surprises me, he's never said a thing like that until the place is closed up and everyone else is gone.

It's what happens every time. I wait for him and he waits for the bar to close.

And then he takes me however he wants, which is exactly what I crave.

This dangerous man who could do whatever he wishes. He fucks me like I've always been his.

I'm not given a moment to answer, before he nods and raps his fingers on the old wood table. "The usual."

With a nod, I turn my back to him, my fingers fiddling with themselves until I can grab a tumbler for a gin and tonic.

"You closing early tonight?" Jackson calls out loud enough for the bar to hear him.

With wide eyes, I stare back at him, still reeling from the comment: *I've missed you.*

I nod, without thinking twice, "thirty minutes or so," I tell him. "Snow's getting deep."

The excuse raises Mr. Richard's brow who glances over his shoulder at the devil himself. The man who brought that lie to my lips.

CHAPTER 2

THE DEEP RED HUGS HER CURVES AND EVERY INCH OF HER soft skin I've been fantasizing about. It's been over a month, the winter nights getting colder and lonelier without her warmth in my bed.

My cock aches, hard and straining against my zipper as she sways left and right, wiping down the bar.

It's like this every time, she ignores me, just a patron in the corner, as she closes up.

I leave like the rest of them as if she's not the only reason I come to this run down town every chance I get. As if she won't be crying out my name with the strangled pleasure I'll pull from her tonight.

There's no such thing as coincidence. Two years ago I came in here, following a lead and needing a moment to cool down before I did something reckless and stupid.

There she was, staring back at me like I was going to hurt her, like she should fear me.

Smart girl wrapped in a delectable package.

I would have left her alone. Taking another deep gulp of gin, I remember how very much at war I was with myself at the sinful thoughts that plagued me that night.

There's not an ounce of good in me and the things I've done would have her running from me if ever I confessed. But like I said, there's no such thing as coincidence and that night, I craved her. I needed her like I needed the air to breathe.

I waited for her to close down the bar, I followed her, needing to know what the hell it was about her that drew me in.

I heard the footsteps before she did, the clink of the glass bottle being tossed into the trash before some dumb fuck and his buddy cat-called her. Their whistles were sickening.

I'll never forget the look in her eyes, the fear was sobering as she stared at two men who made their way to her. Keys in her hand, she tried to play it off, waving back to tell them to have a good night before she picked up her pace.

All it took was one of them picking up their pace before I stepped out under the street light, calling out to her.

She stopped where she was, caught right there, my prey, not theirs.

My muscles coiled and I memorized their faces, every detail I needed to find them later, after I'd taken care of my poor little Scarlet.

Caught between the two of them and me, she was paralyzed. They took off when I opened my jacket, letting the light glint off my gun.

"Don't hurt me." The plea was spoken softly as the two pricks left us alone, at three am in the vacant parking lot. "Please," she whispered.

Her hazel eyes shone with more than a prayer for safety.

"You think I want to hurt you?"

"I know you could if you wanted," her response came back without any hesitation.

"That doesn't answer my question." The fear slipped away, quickly replaced with a simmering heat I'd felt from her all night. There's a thin line that separates desire from despair and it had played between us all night.

I lowered my lips to the shell of her ear, the tension crackling between us. "What if I wanted to do something else?"

When I backed away, her eyes stayed closed, her chest rising and falling with heavy breaths. "If you wanted... I imagine you could do whatever you wanted to me."

"Is that you giving me permission?" I murmured in the cold dark night, knowing full damn well I was going to fuck her raw and hard. First against her car, with her breasts pressed against the metal and her skirt barely lifted. And then again back at her place.

This beautiful woman, easy prey and tempting in every way, came on my cock and kept me from making a mistake that night. She may have called me a God that night, but she was my savior.

CHAPTER 3

Scarlet

A T FIRST, I FELT LIKE A WHORE. NOT IN THE MOMENT, BUT after. Once he'd gone and I could still feel him between my thighs, taking me like no man ever had.

Not that I was a virgin, but he was brutal, relentless, he was all consuming.

I slept with a man I didn't know at all. One who chilled me down to the bone, yet with a single look lit every nerve ending inside of me on fire.

He didn't even give me his name or a number. One night, he was mine and the next he was gone. I woke up naked, with both a noticeable ache and disbelief.

All he left behind was a note and a burner phone he must have bought while I was sleeping.

Use only this phone. My number is in the contacts.

He called himself Grim. I remember laughing when I saw his name under the contacts. There was no way it was his real name, but I liked it. It fit him. It suited what had happened.

The shame came shortly after. When I realized all I had was an old phone and a fake name.

The questions bombarded me and I hesitated to message him. I didn't know what to say or how I felt about what happened.

It was everything and yet I felt like I was left with nothing.

I'd planned on not messaging him at all, but every night, I pulled the phone from the drawer of my nightstand and I debated it. Three nights passed before I sent the first message, if for no other reason than to know the truth.

Are you married? I asked him.
No. I don't believe I ever will be.

It's an odd feeling that came over me, partly relief, partly sorrow.

Then why this phone?
I would rather not say. You may ask questions that I won't be able to answer. I have secrets but what I do is to protect you. You need to know that and be okay with some of your questions not being answered.

Over a series of days and messages a number of things became clear.

I was right, he was a dangerous man.

More importantly, which he made clear in no uncertain terms: he wanted me.

And lastly, I wanted him as well.

Every doubt I had, he vanquished. It was as if he knew what I was thinking before I did. From the very moment I felt like what we were doing was wrong, he'd do something to prove I had no reason to worry.

Every night he wished me to dream of him.

Every Sunday he sent fresh red roses.

If I told him I missed him, he would tell me he'd come for me at a certain time, within the next day or so and he was always there. Exactly when he said he would be.

Even if he told me very little, every small secret he confided in me felt like he'd trusted me with his world and I did the same, telling him every secret I had, knowing he'd keep it.

It was like a trance, like some magical spell had been cast. One day this man laid his hands on me, showed me pleasure I didn't know existed and told me I was his.

And suddenly, that's all I was.

My days in and days out hardly changed, apart from my thoughts of him and what he'd do to me when he came back.

It's been nearly every other week for two years now. It's not the romance story for a princess' tale. He's a dark knight with a tortured soul.

I'm not the one who needs saving in this story.

The keys jingle in my hands as I turn the lock and test the door. The harsh night brings a chill that sends shivers down my spine but I welcome the cold.

With the snow crunching beneath my feet I make my way around the side of the bar, to the parking lot where a car is parked next to mine, running but empty. He stands beside it, waiting for me.

Waiting for a night of debauchery with a man who holds secrets and pain I'll never know. A man who craves me and who never leaves me wanting anything but more of him.

He takes three large strides as I near him, eating up the distance and crashing his lips against mine under the street lights.

With my head tilted back, his hand splayed on my lower back, the other slipping between my legs, I shiver and then moan into his mouth.

His answering groan is sinful as his fingers push past the elastic of my underwear and meet my hot center. He whispers against my lips, "You'd be a liar if you said you didn't miss me too."

CHAPTER 4

Grim

I THOUGHT LONG AGO, THAT WHATEVER WAS BETWEEN US WOULD wane. When we first started this, I imagined she would grow tired of it, that I couldn't possibly satisfy her beyond the novelty of a stranger wanting to please her, thoroughly and roughly until her throat was sore from crying out in the dark night.

I anticipated the way she would end it, with a simple request that I would obey. Whether it be because she needed more than I could give her, time and transparency. Or whether it would be because she fell for someone who could provide her with normalcy.

As my thumb rubs soothing circles along the bare skin of her thigh and I drive back to her place, I realize just how addicted we both have become.

She is the only thing I have to look forward to. These moments where I can get lost in her and she can do the same with me. They are the heaven to the hell that is my life.

My scarlet angel.

It's silent in the car for the fifteen-minute slow drive back to her place. The backroads aren't plowed and the snow comes down heavy.

Her hands roam as much as mine do, resting on my jeans but the devilish bit of her reaches up a little higher, feeling my need hard as steel beneath my jeans.

A soft murmur of want slips from her lips but I tell her to wait.

It's agony not to give in right this moment, but I want her beneath me, writing and struggling not to fight against the pleasure. I want that vision of her so much more than I want those sweet red lips wrapped around my cock.

The moment I park the car, the keys still in the ignition and the car still rumbling, her lips are on mine. Leaning over the console, her lips meet mine with a desperate need.

It amazes me, that a woman like her could want the broken shell of a man I am. I'm quick to push the seat back and pull her into my lap. Her body fits perfectly right here in my arms.

With my hand on her neck, I brush back her long dark hair from her pale skin and leave opened mouthed kisses there. My other hand pushes aside the silky fabric of her dress and reddens her ass in a demanding grip. She rewards me with a sweet moan I know by heart now.

It's the most blissful sound in my world.

My teeth scrape down her neck, as her head falls back. Nipping and sucking, I leave a trail along her body, but it's far too soon that the cold slips between us.

It's bitter cold and although her house is buried deep in the woods, with the privacy we need, I want her inside, the doors locked and reality a world away.

"Inside," I command her before her pants of need get any heavier.

She crawls off of me, leaving the cold to slip between us, and we both hurry to get inside.

My pulse rages, my cock already leaking precum as she pushes her front door open and I follow her in.

The old house is dark, the floorboards creak and apart from fresher paint, and contemporary décor, the bones and fixtures haven't been touched since the sixties. It speaks to the old souls we have that must've once loved each other.

I don't bother with a light and neither does she. As her shoes fall to the wooden floor in the foyer with a dull thud, I lift her into my arms. A hand on her ass and the other bracing her back.

With a small yelp of surprise and then a soft hum of a laugh, her legs wrap around my hips and her hands find my hair.

Although the back and sides are cropped short, her fingers play and tug at the top of my scalp, giving me just a hint of pain. I fucking love it.

Letting out a short grunt of a growl, I nip her neck again, kicking off my shoes and making my way to her small living room.

There's a small fireplace I'll light when I'm finished with her. I've dreamed of laying on her sofa, her back to my front, her hair a messy halo and her cheeks flushed from a night of sin. The fire flickering and crackling as sleep takes us.

That's what I want with her tonight. If I could, I would have her that way every night.

Greedily, my hands roam her body, unwrapping her as if she's a gift fate left just for me. The deep red fabric slips off of her and falls to a puddle on the worn rug beneath my feet.

Her hands slip up my Henley, her fingers running along the divots of my muscles. She plays with me as she likes, as she always does, until I lay her on her back, the sofa groaning with my weight.

She falls easily, bouncing slightly, completely bared to me.

Without hesitation, my lips fall to her breasts and my fingers press inside of her.

Her back arches from the immediate onslaught of sensation and her nails rake down my back. If she wanted to scar me there, leave her mark, I'd gladly let her.

My tongue swirls against her hardened peaks and then I pull back, sucking and plucking her nipples. I'm not gentle and I don't take my time. It's been too long and I'll have all night to savor her, for now, every act is one of a famished man.

Curling my fingers, I press the rough pad of my thumb against her clit and stroke the front of her walls as I finger fuck her pretty little cunt. She's hot and wet, and those sweet little sounds she gives me are everything I've wanted. Her body tenses around me all too soon, and I don't let up, dragging out her release even as she pulses around my thick fingers.

Heat dances along my skin, even if the old house carries a draft. With her, like this beneath me, my world is lit with fire and it blazes between us.

Between sweet murmurs and heavy pants, she pushes her hair away from her face as I stand up and strip. All the while she watches, her small hands drifting down my body along every inch I've kissed myself.

With one knee on the sofa, I lift her legs up, hooking her thighs under my arms and spreading her for me. With a mewl of protest, her hands rest against my chest.

Her lips stay parted but she doesn't tell me no. She doesn't tell me to go easy on her. She wants this as much as I do.

I'm merciless as I slam into her with a single swift stroke. Her breasts press against my chest as she reaches up, clinging to me. I wait a moment, deep inside her, loving how she pulses around me and wait for her to stretch. Taking my time, I pull out slowly, not all the way though and then slam back into her.

She cries out, her head pressing into the sofa cushion and her eyes shut tight. "Please," she murmurs and I do it all again, not knowing what she begs for.

My thrusts come faster and faster, a cold sweat lining the back of my neck as I push her pleasure higher and higher, waiting for the merciful fall.

The sound of me slamming into her over and over combines with our heavy breathing and it fuels me to fuck her deeper and faster. To take her with the primitive need that drew us together from the very beginning.

My toes curl as I fuck her deeper and harder, needing more of her as I get closer to my own release. Not yet. I bury my head in the crook of her neck, grinding the back of my teeth and needing her to come again on my cock before I can even think of giving in.

"Fuck!" she cries out and I mute her cries with a bruising kiss, not relenting my pace in the least. The sounds that pour from her lips are barely audible as her fingers dig into the cushion, as if she needs something to hold on to.

My heart pounds harder with every thrust.

"Come with me," I command her, my voice strained. Pushing her calf to my shoulder, I angle her deeper and bring my thumb to her clit, ruthlessly rubbing and bringing full on screams of pleasure to her reddened lips.

And that's how we come undone, rushed and desperate, raw and tangled, bared and lost in one another.

CHAPTER 5

WITH MY BACK TO HIS FRONT, HIS HEAVY ARM DRAPED OVER the curve of my waist, we both watch the fire. His lips rest in my hair as he murmurs again how much he missed me, how much he craved this.

It feels as if I am his everything and the words tumble over themselves in the back of my throat: he feels like my everything.

The warmth of the flames lay over my exposed skin until Grim pulls the knitted navy blanket over us. It's barely enough to cover us, and I bury my feet beneath his calves.

There's a rough chuckle that comes from him with the act and then another kiss at my temple.

I could stay forever like this. Not a care outside of this room. Just wanting to be held by him, all the while, my hand lays over his, our fingers laced.

My heart beats along with his when his phone rings, the sound muffled from his jeans laying over it. The sofa groans as he leaves me, checking it and answers, "Walsh."

There's a pang of pain as he does. With the floorboards protesting his steps that lead him away from me.

I lay waiting, wanting him to come back to me while thinking of the many names others have called him on the other end of that phone.

Cody. Marcus. Walsh.

I asked him once why some people call him Cody and the others

Marcus. He said it's because they don't know him and that's the way he wants to keep it.

Before I could pry any further, he told me, I only want to be your Grim. And I believe him.

Because all I want to be is his scarlet angel.

My throat is dry when he comes back, two tumblers of whiskey from my kitchen in his hand. I accept one and take a deep gulp, letting it burn in a soothing way as he settles back behind me.

"Are they stealing you from me again?" I question him, watching as the fire licks up the log, cracking it and leaving blackness in its wake.

He hums a yes that's deep and allows the regret to linger.

I wonder if one day he'll stay. My fingers slip back around his, his warmth quickly wrapping around me as my cheek falls against his bicep. He pulls me closer and I let my eyes close when I ask him, "How long will they keep you?"

He nuzzles the crook of my neck, the tip of his nose tickling that tender spot before whispering, "not long. I promise."

His hand slips out from under mine, and he grips my hip, startling me as he flips my body over so that I'm on my belly. Hot desire overwhelms me as he tilts my hips up, his erection pressing against my core. A shiver runs down my spine and I hold my breath, wanting him and needing this more than I need anything else. His large frame casts a shadow down on me as he whispers at the shell of my ear, "I want you again."

Thank you for reading this sinful little short. Need more right now?
Check out This Love Hurts and get lost in the Merciless World.
For my dedicated readers, this story takes place AFTER
the This Love Hurts trilogy.

STAY RIGHT HERE WITH ME

I can't tell you how many mistakes I've made sitting in this very spot in this small town bar. Watching the iron doors swing closed as the broad-shouldered man who just walked in sits across from me, I already know he's on that list of, "I shouldn't have done that…"

CHAPTER 1

Lysa

"**M**AKE IT SHINE," MY GRANDMA USED TO TELL ME THAT whenever I was cleaning the bar top. I had a habit of it when I was only four years old. She told me all about it when I got my first job here, the bar called Brick's that used to belong to my grandfather. I thought she was lying at first when she told me, but the customers remembered it too. I'd take the little cloth rag from the little tykes kitchen in the backroom and I'd climb up the wooden barstools and get on top of the already polished bar top and mimic my father. Three small circles, then one large. My little arms couldn't reach all the way across, but I kept going when Grandma told me, "Make it shine."

With the fresh smell of pine and lemons lingering, I make three small circles against the hardwood top, worn down from years of doing its job, and whisper, "Make it shine," with the last swirl.

I've spent long days and even longer nights in this bar. It used to only be the weekends but now it's every day for almost three years now when the bar got passed to me. It should never have been mine at the young age of twenty-two, but life throws all sorts of things at you, and you just have to do your best to catch them. Yet another piece of advice from my grandma.

"You good wrapping this up?" Andy asks me on his way out. With his worn leather jacket in one hand, its creases matching the ones around his eyes, and his car keys in the other, the old man waits for me to tell him what I always tell him at 2 am.

"Darn right I am. Have a good night, Andy." His gray beard leads the way as he gives me a smile. I've nearly turned away when I hear a sound of surprise come from him.

"You may have company," he informs me with a raised brow and I'm already saying, "We're closed," from across the bar to the heavy front doors but then I get a peek of who it is on the other side.

Flip, twist, a little somersault happens inside my chest. His blue eyes meet mine first, even though he's nodding a thanks to Andy as he takes his baseball cap off. His stature is dominating, as are his broad shoulders, when the man walks in, his boot steps taking their time and thumping right along with my heart.

Tall, dark and handsome, with a slight southern charm on his tanned skin. Jeans that look broken into, boots made for working, and a simple dark gray Henley stretched across his shoulders fit his frame and spell out my kryptonite. The man of my dreams is a real thing.

"It's alright Andy… I think I can serve up one more drink." Pulling out a bottle of beer from the fridge underneath the bar, I keep my eyes on the man who just walked in. In a deft motion I uncap it, the piece of tin falling into the bucket beneath the bottle opener screwed into the bar top and place the glass bottle down onto the bar, listening to it fizz. "As in I can open a bottle of beer. I'm not washing any more glasses tonight."

I've made a number of mistakes in my life and one time my father said they could all lead back to my attitude. He laughed when I reminded him that it's his attitude I inherited so technically they could all lead back to him.

Maybe I am no-nonsense, but when you grow up in a bar you learn not to take any shit and to know your limits. I'll be damned if I'm cleaning anything else tonight. Besides, the man of my dreams is an IPA kind of man.

"Thanks," his voice is deep and has a draw to it that I love. It echoes down into the hollow of my chest and I find myself raising my hand to meet the vibrations.

"Have a long night?" I make small talk with him as I tidy up the place. Technically we're closed, technically I'm not working anymore, technically Mr. Tall, Dark and Handsome shouldn't be here.

In my periphery, I watch him fiddle with the torn edge of his hat before tossing it down onto the bar and taking his seat. "Long week," he finally tells me with a heavy sigh. "Just got a lot better though."

I pay his compliment back with a small chuckle that warms me from the inside and ask back, "Oh, did it now? A beer can turn it all around for you."

I stare at him, letting his gaze sink into mine and feeling the longing and the heat there.

He only offers a boyish grin, answering, "Something like that," with the bottle neck of his beer at his lips before taking a long swig.

"How about you?"

"How about me what?" I ask him, blowing a stray stand of hair out of my face. I note that his is long on top, just long enough to make it look like he doesn't care. Like he's just rough around the edges. *I like that.*

"Long night?" he asks.

"Always," I answer, finally taking a seat behind the counter. My back hurts, my body's sore, but we did good this week. I put everything I have into this bar. Keeping it alive and just like it was in every way that I can remember. It's my constant, my life really. Everyone I ever loved has memories in this bar. So it can have all of me. I'm fine with that.

"You ready to go home? I don't want to keep you up."

Home for me is just a walk next door. My dogs outside stay in the back behind the bar and the German Shepherds walk me down the stone path to my little raised ranch. They're my babies and the only family I have left.

The second that house next to the bar went up for sale, I bought it. I was only twenty and my dad had to help me, but it's mine and it's the perfect set up. I have my dogs, the bar, I have my house, and I have the people who have been here all my life in this small town. And then there's this man right here.

I try to ease his conscious, "You aren't keeping me up."

"You look tired."

"Hmmm," I hum and lean back so I can get a good look at him.

"I don't mind walking you home and helping you get to sleep," he offers with that smile I love.

"Dean Andrews, you are the biggest mistake I ever made." I love saying his name. Dean Andrews. Grandma loved it too. She always shooed the guys away, but never Dean. I could curse her out for that with the way he's played with my heart. But then she'd slap me silly and I was always taught to respect my elders anyhow.

"Made as in past tense?" he offers me a charming asymmetric smile. "I was hoping you weren't done with me yet." That smile is one that knows how to bring heat to my cheeks, a blush rising up my temples. No man has ever made me feel like he does. Maybe that's why I just can't say no.

I don't answer him, wiping down the rest of the liquor bottles, even though I've already wiped them down once, with my back to him. Very well aware that my hips sway just slightly with every movement I make. Let him watch. Let him want me even though he's not able to have me. It's only fair.

"You come into town once a month for a weekend, maybe twice a month at most… and you think you aren't a mistake for a girl like me?" I question him, peeking over my shoulder just in time to see him gaze shift from my ass up to my stern gaze. He knows I'm all his. He knows I'll bring him home and my bed will be filled with both of us tonight. This push and pull is just a game.

A game that's going to break my heart one day. Since I gave it to Dean Andrews and he doesn't even know. Shoot, I didn't even know I'd done it until it was too late.

CHAPTER 2

I**T'S BEEN AT LEAST FOUR YEARS SINCE I FIRST SAW LYSA HART.** My father was showing me *"a hole in the wall"* bar he'd found. Since I was a little kid, every summer I'd gone with him in his truck for the rides during the summer. My dad's a truck driver, my uncle, my brother. So it just made sense to me that I would be too.

I was twenty-three and I'd had my own truck for a while when my dad brought me in here four years ago. Craft beers, football games, a pool table and a small town vibe that made you feel at home. That's what he told me it was like, but when I walked through those doors, there was only one thing that felt like home to me.

It was her laugh that I heard first, and I caught her swinging her hair around to the other shoulder and telling someone to 'shut their mouth' before swatting them with an imaginary towel. Her long hair matched her deep brown eyes and her smile… her smile was everything.

It only took one look… and that was years ago. Just before her life changed forever.

I work on drinking the beer quickly, knowing she's got to want to get out of here.

"How long have you been on the road?" she asks; she only ever makes small talk. The thing I learned about Lysa first was how guarded she was. She could make friends with anyone, but to get to know her took time. And I know her, I know every little thing about her. Because after I'm inside her, after pulling down all of those walls and giving her everything I have, she bares it all. Heart and soul.

"Came in from Georgia, so a little while I guess," I joke and she winces, the idea of spending nearly ten hours on the road isn't her kind of fun. I don't mind it. With the audio books and the sites along the way, it's been good to me. But she's better.

Every time I come back, Lysa's made at least one change to the bar, this time the felt on the pool table's new. She does that, trying to keep the place updated… but a few things never change.

"Still have the photos up?" I question although the answer is clear. The photograph paper is yellowed from decades and decades of simply existing. Lysa's done a hell of a lot to fix up the old bar, but she's stuck in the past in a lot of ways. Understandably. "You could move them to the backroom you know?" I suggest for the second time. The first was a year ago, maybe more. I know she wants to move them because they just look dated, but she's dead set on the fact that they belong there.

A brunette lock slips out of place from her bun of messy hair, falling gently against the curve of Lysa's jaw when she turns to look over her shoulder.

I know her body better than I know the backroads. And damn do I miss it every time I leave. I spent my life in a truck, she spent hers in this bar. Both of us taking after our fathers.

"I just don't want to move them; you know?"

"I get it, it just might help bring the bar up to this decade… or," I offer up, "You could take it back. You know, make it look like a speakeasy or something? Isn't that the look that your grandpa went for back then?"

I've been thinking a lot about this bar and what Lysa could do on little money and even short time.

She laughs at me, "No. It was not a speakeasy. It was a biker club." The hint of a smile at her lips is addictive.

"Make it a biker club then," I shrug knowing damn well what she's going to say.

"In a small town with no bikers, I bet that would go over just wonderfully."

"You know what they say, you build it and they'll come."

She shrugs it off, tiredness forces a yawn out of her.

I finish off the last bit of my beer and the empty bottle clinks when I set it back down.

"You want to get out of here?" she asks me.

No. I don't want to get out of here. I want to stay with her and bring that smile, sweet and innocent, full of hope, back to her beautiful face. Just like it was when I first saw her. I want to stay here and fix this with her. Sometimes though… all a person can do is stand beside them and wait.

"If you do," I answer her, lowering my voice and letting my gaze drop to those lips of hers. Lips I dream about kissing every night. She parts them just slightly, taking in a sharp inhale. "Yeah," I tell her, pushing myself off the stool and grabbing my cap. "Let's get out of here."

CHAPTER 3

I**T'S QUIET BETWEEN US ALL THE WAY TO MY HOUSE, THE DOGS** padding along as Dean pats them and occasionally scratches their backs on the way.

The crickets are out, the early autumn night has just a slight chill to it, but still warm enough. And the moon is clear, shining down and giving me enough light to see the rough stubble on Dean's jaw.

He keeps his arm around my waist the entire walk and it makes me feel weak because all I want to do is lean into him.

The backdoor shuts with a loud groan and I lock it, feeling Dean's eyes on me. The house has charm and features from a century ago. Just like the bar. It's expensive to maintain, but every penny tile, and carved molding feature is worth it.

Some people say I'm an old soul. I just think I have good taste.

Dean doesn't waste his time taking off his boots and stretching out his back. Maybe he's trying to hide it, but I know he's tired too.

"You want to just go to bed?" I ask him, feeling a ping of vulnerability. He could stay at the truck stop, and sleep in the back of his truck like I know he used to. He could get a hotel. Or he can come here, where I give everything to him freely. My girlfriend Laura had something to say about that a while back. Two years ago before she moved to Texas with her boyfriend, now husband.

I told her then, I do what feels right. And Dean… everything about him feels right. Up until he's gone, that is.

"I want you in bed, if that's what you mean." His strong muscles coil as he pulls his shirt off, dragging it along and revealing himself to me inch by inch until the shirt is nothing but a crumpled ball of cloth he tosses carelessly on the floor. The way he looks at me, like he wants to devour me, steals my breath.

His barefoot self only in blue jeans making his way to me forces me to take one step back. This man is too much. He has a power over me like no one else.

My back hits the door at the same time his strong hands grab my hips, pinning them there, and his lips meet mine in a heated kiss I've missed for far too many nights.

Everything is hot instantly, my body dying to be touched, begging him to press against me, so I can feel him and only him. I don't want to feel anything else.

His left hand stays where it is, but his right roams up my body, slipping up the curve of my waist, barely touching me and teasing me. All the while my lips part for his deepening kiss, letting him take me as he wants.

With a deft flick of his fingers, he undoes my bra and before the straps can even slip down my shoulder beneath my shirt, his large hand cups my breasts and he moans into my mouth with need. His cock hardened and pressing against my lower belly through the denim of his jeans.

When he pinches my nipple, pulling it ever so slightly, I have to break the kiss to throw my head back. I writhe under him and he doesn't waste another second, pulling me into his arms and taking me to my bedroom, a room he knows all too well.

Even though his gait is large, and his steps swift, he peels the clothes away from me as we go, until I match him in attire.

I can't help but to let out a small squeal of surprise and glee when he tosses me onto my bed. The moonlight peeks through my curtains and that's the only light I have to see him as he kicks off his jeans, along with his boxers and stands in all his glory.

"Pants off," he tells me, stroking himself. The sheen from precum already leaking from him has me licking my lips as I obey. He spreads it around his thick head though, pushing me onto my back even though I got on my knees to lick him.

"Not now, I need to be inside of you," he groans when I mewl in protest.

What this man does to me… I just don't know how or why but he plays my body like it was made for him. Bracing himself on top of me, one forearm above my head, he spreads my legs and I spread them even wider in response, tilting my hips for him.

His hand cups my heat and when he presses his palm to my clit, my back arches from the sudden touch and instant desire. "You're so fucking wet for me, baby," his whispers the rushed words out, his lips finding my neck as he pushes two thick fingers inside of me. With his stubble tickling along my neck, his kisses roaming carelessly as he fingerfucks me, the heat inside of me intensifies, burning along my skin and igniting every nerve ending that I haven't felt since he's been here last.

Curving his fingers, he hits that sweet spot inside of me, and rubs my clit with his rough palm at the same time, turning over the waves of pleasure until they finally crash inside of me.

"Dean!" I cry out his name like I need him, like he's the only one I've ever needed as my toes curl and my neck arches with the pleasure rolling through me.

He doesn't wait for me to finish, he doesn't give me a moment to catch my breath. He slams inside of me to the hilt and I scream out in utter rapture. He pistons his hips and it feels like it's too much. My body instinctively curls around his, my legs around his hips as he picks up his pace.

His breath is hot along my neck and every small touch, every deep groan, every thrust from him takes me higher and higher, prolonging the pleasure and keeping me on the edge of falling until he finds his release with my second for the night.

I can't breathe, I can barely move onto my side to close my legs when he leaves the bed to go to the bathroom. The heated waves leave me and the cool air would give me shivers if he hadn't pulled the sheets up around me.

When he comes back, he makes sure I'm alright to fall asleep, before climbing back in.

If tonight is anything like the other nights, he'll have me again in just a little while, and I'll wake up to another round, longer and more gentle, but with just as much pleasure in the morning.

If only I could have him always. If only I knew he wasn't going to leave again…

The thought keeps me from sleeping. It keeps me from feeling the comfort I usually have with him.

Everything just feels out of place. Like something's horribly wrong.

"You're my worst habit," I shake my head, brushing my hair out of my face. I need a shower or even better, a nice long bath with him beside me in that large claw foot tub. But right now, all I want to do is lie here beside him, before he gets up and leaves me again.

"Now I'm a drug?" he chuckles, deep and rough.

"You're a mistake," I correct him, hating the truth that's there. I wish it was only ever a joke. It's not though. The way my heart already hurts and he's not even gone yet… he is a mistake and I know it. I just can't say no to him.

"That's the second time you said that tonight."

Unless I'm mistaken, a hint of his cadence sounds wounded. When I roll over on the bed, still naked and my bare shoulders showing, the sheets roll with me but they don't cover my upper half. A simper dances along my lips when his gaze lowers to my exposed breasts. Part of me wants to tease him, to tell him, *I hope you like the view*. Instead I hold my ground, saying something I've been thinking, every time he leaves me here with only a parting kiss and not even a date when he'll be back.

I whisper, not hiding the pain in the truth, "How could this not be a mistake?" The rustling of the sheets mixes with my words as I lay myself down onto his hard chest, just wanting my skin to be touching his. As if the words I just said aren't going to make him climb out right this second. Contrary to my initial thought, he stays perfectly still. Only for a fraction of a second and I stare at my pillow he's laying against, the masculine scent of him filling my lungs. "You could have a girl like me in every town," I try to joke, to make my voice teasing and force a smile to my lips, but I fail.

"I told you I don't and I don't like you saying that," his voice is hard, but the way his hand comes down around the back of my head, smoothing my hair down is nothing but gentle. "I only have you." Every breath he makes is deep and his chest rises and falls with my cheek on his hot skin. I turn my head ever so slightly, just to kiss his chest. Because a statement like that deserves a kiss at least.

I only have you. It sounds so romantic, but he has me for a weekend and that's all. Then he's gone and I get a call every once in a while, a text here or there, but we're both busy, we live two different lives. The fact that

I need to end this weighs on me heavily. This isn't what I want. I don't want a hookup every once in a while. Even if he says all the right things. Even if the smell of him on my pillows lulls me to sleep when he's gone.

"Dean, I—"

"You what, Lysa? You miss me when I'm gone?" he questions me in a tone I don't recognize and it forces me to look up at him. In the depths of his sharp blue gaze there's something there I haven't seen before. Something raw and wounded. "Cause I miss you too. I miss you so much that I don't want to leave."

In this moment, my heart twists. I swear everything stops because my heart can't pump when it's in a knot like it is. There aren't words to fix everything. He asked me once to come with him, to take a vacation and just ride with him. I can't leave the bar though. It's the only piece of my family I have left. It's all on my shoulders.

"I'm tired of missing you," I confess and nearly choke on the words. "I'm too lonely to miss someone who chooses to be gone." His expression doesn't change but his grip on me tightens. I lean forward, needing to be closer to him, praying he understands I just hurt too much when he's gone. My bed creaks with the shift in our weight. "I get it, I do. I swear I understand the family business and—"

Dean's thumb stops me from speaking, pressing it against my lips as his other fingers grace my jaw and he cups my chin, shushing me. I'm not a girl to be shushed though. He leans his head down, in an effort to rest his forehead against mine, but I pull away. I need it to be over. I am addicted to him, but this is killing me.

I think I love you. And it kills me that you don't choose me. It's what I want to say to him. But the words tumble over each other at the back of my throat. My face is hot and my eyes prick with tears and I have to get away and get off this bed to put space between us.

"Lysa, baby, stop," Dean's quick to snatch my wrist, jumping out of the bed and pulling my body against his. He's so much taller, and warmer, every inch of me wants to mold to his masculine form. With soft kisses in my hair, he says something… something that sounds like I love you, but it can't be that.

I try to pull away again, but his strong arm wraps around my waist, pulling me in close again. With both of my palms against his chest, both of us still bared to one another, I'm caught in his heated gaze when he tells me clear as day, "I love you Lysa. And if you'll have me, I want to be here with you. I sold the truck, I left the business. I just want to stay right here with you."

"What?" I'm breathless.

"I sold it, invested the money and I have some left over I thought…" shaking his head, Dean looks past me for a moment then licks his lower lip, his grip loosening on me and vulnerability shining in his pale blue eyes.

"But that's all you've ever known…" the words come out as a murmur.

"No. There's something else I know," he looks down at me with nothing but love. "Something I value more."

"Dean—"

"I thought I could help you with the bar. I don't need you to pay me, you can treat the money like a loan or a gift, whatever you want. I don't need the money, I have enough on my own. I just want to be with you."

Everything blurs around us as the silence passes. Time slows and I know I'll remember this moment forever. I dreamed a thousand dreams over the years, wanting to confess, but he always wanted me to run away with him, like I wanted to do that first time I saw him, back when my father was still here and he would be there to take care of the bar. "Did you say you loved me?" I have no idea how the words manage to escape my lips in a whisper, or where they even came from.

For the first time that I can remember, Dean blushes. With his large hand running down the back of his neck, he grins at me, a boyish grin. "I might have. I might have said I love you so damn much it hurts."

His grin falters slightly until I lift up onto my tip toes to press my lips against his and give him all of me in that one touch.

I don't know when I gave my heart to him, but right now, I vow to give him all of me.

"I love you Dean." I love him so damn much it hurts too. "You promise you'll stay with me?"

Wrapping his arms around me and pulling me into his chest, he brings me back to bed. "I'll stay with you Lysa. I'm here with you. I'm right here. And I'm not leaving anymore."

He repeats, "I love you."

THE THINGS YOU DO TO ME

THE THINGS YOU DO TO ME

The snow falls slowly, drifting in the wind along the once-dark tree line. With the blankets of snow covering every inch that I can see from the large kitchen window, everything shines brightly.

Parting my lips, I close my eyes and down the last bit of sweet red in the stemless wine glass. I've never been fond of the cold, but this ache in my chest today… it's not from the feet of snow that keep us locked inside the house.

"He's out there," I whisper, feeling the brooding shadow of the man I call my husband behind me.

"Yes, songbird, our son is out there and just fine."

With my long hair falling from my shoulder I turn around to face Carter. "When are they going to be home?"

With all of his hard features and dark gaze, Carter still manages a smirk that lights a fire in the pit of my stomach. It rages for him to deny the fact

A sigh leaves me and a part of me knows that ache in my chest is because my little baby boy is growing up. He's on the move and wanting to play.

I miss the late-night cuddles and the way Anthony used to wrap his chubby little fingers around my pointer.

"I just wish I could see him…" I comment, making my way to the large polished counter where, upon inspection, the wine bottle I was going to get is now empty.

"You didn't want to go. Miss 'I don't love the cold.'"

I stare down at my glass as if it's a traitor and somehow it swallowed up my wine before I was able to drink it.

Two large hands grip my shoulders tenderly. Carter's thumbs rub soothing circles along the blades of my upper back and then higher, where they dig in deeper, soothing my sore muscles.

With his lips at the shell of my ear, he whispers, "You're stressed."

I swallow thickly and admit, "I know."

"You're a good mother and he's in very capable hands."

"The house is empty…" I stress. Everyone else left to enjoy the snow. This house, typically filled with the sound of so many family members, is now silent.

"Yes," Carter's voice deepens. Moving his lips to the crook of my neck, he lets them fall and lays a kiss right there, sending a pulsing wave of desire through me. My back to his chest, he pulls me in closer and I drop the empty glass to the counter, bringing my hand up to run my fingers up the nape of his neck as he kisses me again and then says, not hiding the lust, in the shell of my ear, "We have the house to ourselves. We should take advantage of that."

Carter

My worrying wife is beautiful. She's always radiant and poised. When that soft smile hits her lips, life itself seems to melt away into nothing but peace. That's what this woman gives me: a life I never thought I'd have, let alone deserve. One I want to share with her forever. I'll give her everything to keep that smile that lingers on her wine stained lips in place, right where it belongs.

"Let's get you another bottle…" As I take a step back, my songbird places her small hand in mine, letting me lead the way. After three years together, there's no fight for power, no resentment at the way we came to be. I led her away from a pain and darkness that kept her trapped and she did the same for me. There is only love that remains and from me, a gratitude I'll forever be in debt to her for giving to me.

In a dark blue, silk to the touch nightgown she glides to the wine cellar door, opening it with a soft creak, but only inches before turning on her heel in her bare feet to look up at me.

"Cross," her voice turns tempting, with a hint of sin that dances from her tongue. "Are you trying to get me drunk?"

A deep chuckle rises from my chest and the hint of a smile lingers on her lips… "*Mrs. Cross,*" I emphasize her name and remember a time when the idea of me responding in that way would have been an impossibility. A time when she called me 'Cross' out of pure resentment for who I was. "That goal is a little too easy to achieve for a man like me," I tease her back, watching the simper on her beautiful face grow as the blush rises from her chest to her cheeks and she shyly looks away.

With a swat of her hand against my broad chest, Aria shakes her head. "Well if he's not coming home tonight and we're making the most of this," she speaks as she peeks up at me through her thick lashes, "I think I'll have one more glass."

My hand splays along her back and I pull her in close to me, feeling her warmth and softness curve around me. She gasps when I nip her exposed shoulder, "Well go get it then."

Aria

The cellar door closes with a click and with only the dim illumination, Carter's brooding frame takes up too much of the light.

"I can manage to grab a bottle," I tease him and make my way to the back of the cellar and to the right. The wine cellar is far too much, with four rows of wine lining the aisles from floor to ceiling and a bricked floor made to look worn, hints of brown matching the dark wood and iron accents in the space that's much larger than most bedrooms. I love it though.

"You could," Carter starts as I round the back corner, aiming for a section of Cabernet that Addison and I are both fond of. My breathing halts when I see the cream throw blanket laid out on the floor. Two glasses of red are already poured, waiting next to the blanket and chocolate covered strawberries are piled in a balanced stack on a silver tray. "Or we could make the most of tonight."

Carter's whispered answer forces me to turn from the scene and stare up at the man I love so dearly.

Taking one step closer to me, he asks, "Do you remember that spot? When you were first here and what you told me, drunkenly as you stared up at me wanting things to change?"

Tears prick my eyes and I shake my head. I try not to remember those times if I'm honest. I don't tell Carter that, I only shake my head. It's not often my Beast turns into a Prince. This is so unexpected, so sweet and it takes me by complete surprise.

"I don't."

An asymmetric smile picks his lips up, "It doesn't matter, really, what matters most is that I never wanted you to leave. And now I have you forever."

Shaking off the wave of emotions, I gaze into his dark eyes watching the flecks of gold that brighten when I smile up at him. "Forever and always," I whisper as I get on my tiptoes to plant a kiss on his lips.

There's a groan that escapes when I lean back just slightly. A deep sound of approval but also of want.

"Lay on your back and close your eyes," he gives the command with his own eyes closed. Restraint showing in the way he lets go of me and his body goes still, waiting for me to obey.

I don't hesitate, quickly finding my spot on the already smoothed out throw blanket. With a slight chill in the air, my nipples are already hardening. I'm careful not to knock the glasses or tray as I lay down, and wait.

Anticipation rolls through me, from my toes up to my neck and then higher, forcing my breathing to come in faster.

"Dessert tonight is going to be exquisite," Carter comments as he pulls the button-down shirt over his head, only unbuttoning the first few. He's eager. In past times he's made me watch as he's undone every button, showing off his taught skin and muscles that coil beneath the expensive fabrics of his shirts and suits. Not tonight.

Tossing the shirt behind him carelessly, he comes closer, taking his time to round my body but never taking his eyes off of me, as if I'm his prey. He takes more time undoing his pants and letting them fall along with his boxers. Towering above me, naked and with a deep hunger etched in his expression, my heart picks up its pace, no longer wanting to stay where it should. The *thump, thump, thump* heats my entire body.

He kneels at first, letting his deft fingers linger on my collar and then slipping down the strap to my nightgown. He exposes one breast, groaning once again that deep primitive sound, before sliding the remainder of my nightgown down to my hips. He pauses then, dipping his head between my breasts and letting his tongue run hot circles along my tender skin. He bites down ever so gently around my nipple and my back arches involuntarily.

"Still, songbird," he commands, not lifting his head and only pausing in the torturously pleasurable act enough to remind me that I'm to stay still.

I already know, but my body doesn't obey. It takes focus to ignore the need to writhe under him as he plays with my body. His fingers just barely touching my skin as he glides his hands down my curves and removes the garment completely.

Still on his knees he rakes his gaze along my body, balling the silk fabric and then dropping it to be nothing more than a puddle on the floor behind him. Naked beneath him, I should be cold with the chill of the cellar, but I'm hot and greedy for more.

He takes his time, leaning over me, but not touching a single inch of skin to mine to take the first chocolate covered strawberry.

"One small bite," he demands, tracing the tip of it along my bottom lip. The chocolate is sweet and decadent as I bite into it and the strawberry even sweeter. It's heaven on my tongue.

But what Carter does next is even more delightful. Letting the bitten part of the berry travel down my skin to leave a trail of juice in its wake, he licks behind it. Starting at the tender under-side of my chin and working his way down my neck and chest, the cool touch of the berry is quickly followed by his hot tongue. When he gets to my breast, he pauses placing the strawberry at my lips again and once again I take a small bite, but he commands me to take a larger one and so I do. As I swallow, he finishes off the fruit and takes another, repeating the act over and over, half a dozen times, causing every nerve ending in my body to spark.

He works me up, but never finishes me, never touches the one place I ache the most for his mouth to linger.

"Tell me what you want songbird," he commands, the last strawberry in his hand as he stares down at me.

"I want you," I beg him and even to my own ears I sound as if I'll die if he doesn't enter me right this second. My hands clench at my sides, hating that I can't simply take from him, but knowing it's so much better if I'm patient.

"Don't bite it," he tells me, sliding the strawberry halfway into my mouth. I keep my gaze on him as his broad shoulders travel lower, his strong hands gripping my inner thighs to part them. He settles between my legs, his shoulders propping up my thighs until the balls of my feet are on the floor. His warm breath trailing along my most sensitive area.

He takes one languid lick of my pussy and my head falls back from the wave of pleasure.

"That sound," he groans at my heat, "I fucking love it when you make that sound." With the statement still in the air, my sex-driven mind slowly comprehending his words, Carter sucks on my clit, massaging his tongue against it and I disobey him, biting into the berry and pushing myself into his face.

He grips my ass, pinning me down and continues to suck and lick and dive his tongue inside of me as the waves build and the pressure mounts and then finally, all at once and so much faster than I expect it to, pleasure erupts inside of me. Rolling from the tips of my fingers down my body and back up again.

With my heavy breathing making my chest rise and fall, I stare up at Carter, ready to apologize for biting into the berry. But he doesn't give me the chance.

My beast of a husband parts my legs wider and thrusts himself inside of me without warning, to the hilt. My palms hit the ground as my back bows and the orgasm I thought had subdued rages inside of me, growing hotter with every pounding thrust of his hips.

"Carter!" I scream out, feeling the overwhelming loss of control as he pistons himself inside of me.

"Yes," the word falls from his lips as a hiss and he drops his body to lay across mine, although his forearm, braced above my head, supports his weight. "Cry out for me, Aria. Scream my name."

Losing all sense of control, my heels dig into his ass and my hips tilt, letting him fuck me deeper and harder as I scream out his name like he told me to and like everything inside of me wants to do.

He's ruthless and relentless as he takes me, fucking me until we find our release together.

Lying beside him, I wince when I turn over, still feeling him inside of me. "I bit the strawberry." I whisper and the small admission awards me a chuckle from the spent man beside me. Deep and masculine and everything Carter is.

With a wicked smile he stares down at me, "I'll prepare for your punishment tonight."

I can only smile back, so aware that it would be impossible not to keep the strawberry where it was while he did what he did to me. He can play these games, he can lead me wherever he deems fit, and I will follow loving every step of the way.

"I love you Carter Cross."

"And I love you, my songbird."

To experience Carter and Aria's story from the beginning,
read *Merciless* today!

TOO MUCH WORK & NOT ENOUGH PLAY

CHAPTER 1

KEYS, WALLET: CHECK AND CHECK. MY MENTAL LIST DOESN'T stop there as I glance at the clock in my office of the bar. I'm going to be late. *Fuck*. Grace is going to kill me.

Flipping through each of the order sheets, listening to the tick of the clock and trying to focus on this stack of papers and not the others, all I can think about is the last time I was late.

I missed our son's entire appointment. My gaze involuntarily darts to a photo of our little man in a simple black frame on my desk. Besides a pen that states: World's Best Dad, the picture is the only thing personal in this room. That and the framed photo of Grace and I on our wedding day. It's almost been a year and time has flown by. The days seem shorter and the years faster. I don't know how to slow it all down.

I've already missed more than I ever thought I would.

With the faint smell of beer and the clink of bottles being carted through the bar on the other side of the closed door of my office in Mac's bar—my bar—I remember how Grace smiled and said it was okay. It's not a real smile though, not one that reached her eyes.

So when she tells me over and over again that she can't keep doing it all herself, I know she can't. I know things have to change.

Knock, knock, knock. The thud resonates in my office and I clear my throat before telling Maggie she can come in.

With both fists on her hips, she stands in the doorway, her hair swept into a wild bun on top of her head.

"Yeah?" I question, noting that her apron must've just come out of the dryer. Either that or its brand new. *Eric did say we needed new ones; did he order them?*

"What the hell are you doing here?" Maggie's head tilts with her question and her dark eyes narrow. "Your mother will have a fit."

My wife will too. I keep my comment to myself, my lips thinning into a straight line as Mags crosses her arms.

Behind her the chatter from the bar is barely heard, but the clanking from the kitchen and a laugh from James lets me know the bar is in full swing.

"Are you sure you've got this—"

"All taken care of?" she finishes my question for me and then tells me to get lost and go have some fun.

"Alright then. I was just leaving." Letting the stack of papers fall back onto my desk with a dull thud, I check my back pocket again and then grab my keys.

"Tell Cheryl I said hi," Mags tells me and then turns, but quickly turns back, her hand on the door jam and asks in a hushed voice, "Is she pregnant again?"

Ooh how this small town loves to whisper.

"Have a good night Mags," I answer her, well not so much answer as shut her down, with a grin and scoot past her.

The new equipment in the kitchen makes the old oven look even older. It's the only thing back here that hasn't been updated. I make a mental note to ask Eric about that too.

Too many changes, too many moving parts to keep up with now that the bar has expanded. A sigh leaves me and the keys in my hand jingle.

Time to see my wife, the thought brings a smile to lift my lips up until I see the time.

Shit.

I love Grace so damn much and I want to be the husband she deserves and the father my son needs.

CHAPTER 2

"**I** cannot believe it's been a year," Ali leans back in the plastic lawn chair, the front legs slipping up in the thick green grass of Cheryl's backyard. "It's crazy," she murmurs.

"It's been one wonderful year though," Cheryl replies, lifting the water bottle in a mock cheers to Ali, who in turn lifts her pink vodka lemonade cocktail up and the two women wait for me.

"Cheers to that," I join in, balancing the punch I have in my left hand with the bouncing baby in my lap steadied with my right. Little Dean. "Happy Anniversary Ali," I add sincerely.

"Almost a year for you too!" Her smile broadens and she taps the paper cup on the table before lifting it back up for another drink.

I opted for the punch, thinking it wouldn't be as strong as what Ali's drinking. She was already a little tipsy when we got here at a quarter to 6. It was my mistake though. Joseph must've poured an entire bottle of rum into that bowl.

Another sip and my eyes squint. I'm going to have to be careful when I pour this red concoction into the grass and then I'll have what Ali's having.

"Yes, all the summer anniversaries," Cheryl squeals, holding her belly and searching across the yard for her little girl Evie, who's squealing joyfully and chasing bubbles from a bubble machine. My mother-in-law, Cheryl and Ali's mother, is watching Evie. She offered to watch Dean too and snuggle with him, but he needs to nap first. Resting his head on my shoulder, the sigh is audible and he goes into his routine of that little hand holding on to my thumb as he nestles down.

"Velcro baby," Cheryl whispers and it makes me smile. Ma, as my mother-in-law told me to call her, gets my little man during the day every day practically, so this nap is mine. All the snuggles.

"Yeah it's all going according to plan," a familiar voice speaks over my shoulder. I glance, along with Ali and Cheryl to see both Eric, the manager at my husband's bar, tall and lean with dirty blonde hair and soft wrinkles around his eyes from too much time under the Atlanta sun and next to him, my husband.

As handsome and charming as ever. His broad shoulders show themselves off in his simple white tee, stretching the thin fabric that puts his biceps on display. Almost a year of marriage and a sleepless 3-month old hasn't changed the spark between us. Maybe the honeymoon phase is waning but I think that's because both of us work far too much which leaves little time for just the two of us. They're going over business more than likely. With a deep breath in, I continue rocking Dean, who's nodding off to sleep, completely unaware that his father is just behind him. If he knew, he'd shoot right back up and fight off sleep just to look at his Daddy. He loves his father, he should after all, he looks just like him.

"Do you even want to know what time it is?" Ali asks under her breath practically shooting lasers out of her eyes at Charlie.

"We knew he'd be late," I comment half-heartedly. I can pretend it doesn't get to me, but he's missing so much of Dean's life. His first appointments, his first smile, which happened when I showed little Dean the picture of Charlie hanging from his mobile before trying to get him to sleep in his crib.

"We're both tired, just trying to balance it all," I give the excuse to Ali although I can't look her in the eye and opt for another swig of that punch.

We've been working so hard we barely had a Christmas, a New Year… any holiday at all. I suppose that's what happens when two workaholics get together.

"Almost a year since my shotgun wedding and I don't think he's shown up on time to a single thing since then."

That gets a laugh from the gaggle of women around the table under the white tent. The fresh scent from the gorgeous bouquet of hydrangeas engulfs me as a decent breeze blows by. It's a little on the too-warm side for a July evening, but the company makes it all worth it. The spiked punch and the shade from the tent don't hurt either. Even if the rum is already hitting me.

"Shotgun schmotgun," Aliana comments. "You were swept away in a… what do they call it?"

"A whirlwind romance," Cheryl answers with her hand splayed over her heart and a faraway look on her face. *She's such a romantic.*

I don't want to admit it, but sitting here now, thinking about that honeymoon phase, maybe some of that spark has faded. Too busy to… well to get busy. It used to be that he couldn't keep his hands off of me. I still want him though. I still love him… even more now than before.

"And this little one is already such a big boy," Cheryl gratefully changes the subject and my mind focuses on what she said rather than what I was thinking.

"You have lost your mind. Dean is only 3 months old. Keep my baby a baby, Aunt Cheryl."

"Time is flying isn't it?" The women reminisce and my worries come right back.

CHAPTER 3

OVER THE SPAN OF 20 MINUTES AND AFTER ONLY SNEAKING A peck on the cheek to both my son and wife, both of my brother-in-laws have come to the same conclusion.

I need to fuck my wife.

No shit. The bastards think it's funny. She saw me but didn't make a move. Didn't say hi, barely even gave me a smile. My nerves pricked when I made my way to her after Eric finally let me go. I snuck in a kiss on her cheek and one on a sleeping Dean and since then, all I've done is take crap from these two.

"What's keeping you from having baby number 2?" my brother-in-law nudges my ribs and the other lets out a chuckle before calling 'hey now' at my little niece who takes a tumble while being chased by my pa. His words register, but I focus my attention on Grace.

"Burgers almost done?" Joseph questions Michael and the spices from sausages and grilled meat join the breeze as the men open the grill.

I can't hear what Grace is telling Ma as she rocks in place, tapping a sleeping Dean's bottom. I'm certain she's asking if my mother wants to cuddle with Dean or if Grace should tuck him in inside. There's a play-pen just inside and the baby monitor is already hooked up with the other piece of it sitting on the outdoor foldout table the ladies are all gathered around.

Grace is utterly breath-taking in that yellow dress. I heard someone one night say yellow is a happy color, it makes you happy to just look at it.

I don't know if it's true, but the butterflies in my chest are more than pleased when I take her in. Another part of my anatomy is also more than pleased. When Grace turns with a smile, her dress swaying as she heads to the backdoor with our son in her arms, I toss the empty bottle of beer and ignore my brother-in-laws as I follow Grace inside.

The screen door creaks and I stop it from shutting so I can come in. That's the moment Grace notices me and she shushes me, still cradling our son.

As if I didn't know he was napping. Giving her a nod, she keeps moving, a simper gracing her gorgeous face and those doe eyes softening just for me.

If she was mad that I was late, she doesn't appear to be now.

"We'll just let him sleep for an hour," she whispers after gently laying Dean down in the playpen.

"Sounds good to me," I keep my voice low and my eyes go wide for just a moment when Dean stirs. My heart freezes and my lungs hold steady until Dean coos in his sleep and snuggles down.

"Oh thank goodness," Grace's shoulders shake with a small laugh and her hand splayed across her chest and a wide smile on her lips.

She tries to leave the way she came, but my arm wraps around her waist.

"Not yet," I whisper in the crook of her neck and plant a kiss there. Her gasp is audible and I can't help but to glance at Dean.

"What are you—?" she tries to question and I pull her along behind me. There's a guest room in this house.

As I tug her hand and we stop in the hallway, Grace smacks my hand away. "What are you thinking Charlie?"

I'm thinking desperate times call for desperate measures, but I don't tell her that.

My hand finds the dip in her waist and I look my wife in her eyes to tell her, "I miss you. I need you. And I want you right fucking now."

"Charlie," she gasps again and the tension between us sparks. Every inch of me hotter and needing to be inside her, making her moan, watching her eyes go half lidded. I need that. She needs it too.

"Remember at the wedding, my sister's wedding?" I question her, my memory taking me back to a certain coat closet where everything about us changed for me. My heart locked in on her and right now having her and making sure she knows I love her and I want her just the same now as I did then is more important than going out in the backyard to chat with family we still see every Sunday night.

"Charlie," Grace admonishes me, but her lips stay parted and lust coats my name on her lips.

"Yeah sweetheart," I question, taking a half step closer to her, and letting my hands fall to her ass. "Are you going to make me beg? Cause I'd rather hear you begging me for more if we've only got a few minutes."

The blush I knew was coming lights up her cheeks, nearly turning them the shade of red of her gorgeous locks.

"Come on, I urge her, looking past her towards the back door of the house to see no one's there and opening the door to the guest room.

It's not dark at all with the bright light shining through the white curtains. But there's privacy. No one to see us, no one to hear us, the window is closed shut. Seeing the bed made perfectly, I decide in a split second, I'm fucking her against the wall.

"I think-" Grace starts and I close the door behind her, locking it and pressing my lips to hers before she can say another word. She's shocked at first, but her lips mold to mine quickly and she moans into my mouth as her seam parts, granting me entry and her hands find my hair, spearing through it.

Gracing my fingers along the smooth skin of her legs, I let them drift up her dress and find her underwear. When I slip them down, I have to break the kiss and Grace takes that moment to let her head fall back against the wall I'm about to fuck her against.

"We really shouldn't," she breathes the statement with her eyes closed, her skin already flushed and her nails digging into my shoulders.

"You want me?" I question her, already unbuttoning my pants and then the sound of the zipper dropping fills the silence and brings her deep gaze to mine.

"Always," she answers in a whisper and I'm quick to grab her ass with both hands, listening to that sweet gasp of surprise that's only muted by another heated kiss.

It takes a moment to bring her dress up around her hips and position her how I want her.

Grace's heels dig into my ass as my jeans fall to the floor. "It'll be quick," I tell Grace in between nibbles of her bottom lip. Her chest rises and falls with quickened breaths and she nods and then steals a kiss I intended for her throat. She knows what she wants. My sweetheart always has. I should have listened to this woman sooner. So many different times and for so many different reasons.

Fisting my cock, I press the head against her lips, parting them and slowly pushing myself inside of her. The sweet strangled moan from Grace that mixes with our warm breath fuels me to go slower, to make love to her for as long as I can before fucking her raw and hard like I so desperately want to.

I take my time, feeling her tight and hot around me. "Always so fucking wet," I groan in the crook of her neck, loving the pleasure she gives me and loving how she makes those little moans of sweet satisfaction as I rock myself inside of her.

Her teeth graze along my neck when I kiss her just under her ear, right at the sensitive spot she loves so much. It sends goosebumps along her skin and the way she writhes as I pull out and then push myself deeper inside of her, begs my body to thrust harder and faster, but I take my time.

"Charlie," she mewls and that right there is why I don't rush it. I love it when she begs for more. More of me, more of us.

"Yeah sweetheart," I pull out of her nearly all the way and bracing her against the wall with one arm, I move the pad of my thumb to her clit before she can answer.

Capturing her gasp with my lips, I spread her arousal around her swollen nub and piston my hips just a bit faster.

Her body tightens around me, her breath hitches and those heels dig harder into my ass. It takes everything in me not to rut into her faster, but the wait is worth it. It's always worth it with her.

Her silent scream is complete with her hand slapping against the wall, a strangled yes leaving her lips and her release feeling like heaven on my cock.

"My turn," I warn, the words slipping against her lips as her eyes find mine and I fuck her against the wall like we don't have a second to waste.

I take my wife like I did that night in the coat room of the wedding.

I fuck her like I'm going to lose her if I don't make damn sure she knows she's mine.

She is today, she was back then, and she always will be.

When I find my own release, she comes again with me, and we're lost in a heated kiss that's not at all lust and all love. Every little piece of us finding its place where it's supposed to be.

CHAPTER 1

Grace

How long has it been since I've held my husband's hand? I wonder as we quietly leave our still napping baby boy, and gently shut the screen door so we don't wake him.

Charlie's thumb rubs soothing circles on my knuckles, the rough pads remind me how hard he works, but also how hard he loves.

"Love you sweetheart," he whispers as the bright sun and chatter of the barbeque greet us and we part ways with a simple kiss that makes its way all the way down to my toes. I can still feel him and I love it. The second he's gone though, back to where the men are grilling, stacks of burgers on a plate surrounded by condiments on the small table beside them, I wonder if it's written on my face what we've done.

With a quick breath, I don't look anyone in the eyes and I go straight for the punch. One sip and I can hear the laughter from Evie. Another and I make my way back to my seat with my sister in laws.

"Did he wake up?" Cheryl questions, the girls, now joined by Charlie's mother, all stop talking and wait for an answer, their eyes expecting something right freaking now.

"Yeah," I play it off even though my head shakes, subconsciously denying the lie. "The second I laid him down, he woke up, but we were able to get him back down in no time."

Even though I catch a glimpse of the monitor on the table and Ali's raised brow, I double down with, "He's out like a light," and my third sip of punch. It's not so strong now and I wonder if someone added more of anything other than rum to dull it down.

None of the women push for more, but my two sister-in-laws both smile into their drinks as Ma continues, informing me that she's giving the girls the recipe to her pasta salad.

"Well hello beautiful," Charlie sneaks up behind me, his hands landing on my hips and a kiss landing on my cheek before I even see him.

I can't help but smile. "Hello yourself," I answer with a little more flirtation than I would if I was more conscious of the fact that all three women are staring. "You might need this if you were drinking the punch," he passes me a bottle of water and I let out a shy laugh.

"You might be right."

"I have one little surprise if you ladies," he raises his voice to address his family, "don't mind if I steal her away."

"You just had her but okay," Cheryl rolls her eyes and I try to keep mine from widening at you just had her. They don't know, I tell myself with every step I take to the side of the property with Charlie, where the sunflowers are tall and blooming.

"Okay, now that I have you sweetened up," he starts, and I smack his hand playfully. His rough chuckle vibrates up his chest and I land a quick kiss on his lips.

"What do you want, husband of mine?"

He sucks in a deep breath, his expression going serious and for a moment worry comes over me. Until he says:

"We didn't have a Christmas so I decided a little July surprise… would be nice."

"Oh yeah, it's Christmas in July?" I question him, my brow knitting. *What's my husband up to?*

"I thought Ali could come with us since she's got time off… and kind of volunteered… maybe on a trip to wine country? She can watch Dean and we can have a second honeymoon."

I can only blink several times, my heart going all soft.

"You won't be away from Dean… although he will be in a different room," he explains, the water bottle in his hand moving from his left to his right as he shifts on his feet in front of me. "I miss you all alone, flirting at the bar. I just thought…"

"What are you thinking?" I press him for more, reaching out with both hands to hold on to his shirt and looking my husband in the eyes.

"We have at least another 18 or more years of mom and dad life, and I love it. I really do, but I want some nights where it's just the two of us, so I can tease you. Eric is hiring another manager. I'm stepping back. I'm going to be the owner, instead of a worker. I'm stepping back like you wanted sweetheart. I promise I am."

"Can you do that?" I'm breathless with anticipation and shock.

"We can afford it," he answers with a single nod.

"I mean *can you* do that," stressing the question.

My husband takes a half step forward, folding his arms around me and pulling me in so he's only a handful of inches away from me. "What I can't do is continue to come home after my son is already in bed. I can't keep missing you either. Missing us and the memories we should be making." He adds, "Your weekends are with the family and now mine are too."

"You promise?" I can't believe he's actually doing it. I'm so happy I could cry. I know it may take time though. The bar was his baby before I came along and stole him away.

He states proudly, "I'm also declaring Fridays date nights and between your mom and sister, Maggie, and my sisters and mom, we have plenty of sitters…"

I stop him here, kissing him like a mad woman, my arms flying around his neck. When I break the kiss, I tell him I love him.

He doesn't have to tell me he loves me too; I know he does, but he says the words just the same.

We had a whirlwind romance and all I want to do is hold on to it forever.

If you haven't read *Knocking Boots*, Charlie and Grace's standalone sexy, contemporary romance, you can read today and get caught up in their sweet love story.

THEN YOU
KISSED ME

A Filthy Quickie

I thought I had life all figured out… and then you kissed me.

Then You Kissed Me is a prelude to *Tequila Rose*.

CHAPTER 1

Brody

I'M NOT SUPPOSED TO BE HERE, IN THIS BAR, TO FLIRT WITH A GIRL *I don't even know…* it's all I can think when I notice her.

Her curves are not why I'm here, although they're exactly why I'm standing in the middle of the bar, stopped in my tracks before I can even sit down. *She's* not on my to-do list tonight.

Even with the internal voice scolding every thought I have, I know the second I lay eyes on her, perched on a stool with a faraway look in her striking hazel eyes, that there's something about this girl that makes it harder to keep walking than it should be.

"You can seat yourself," a hostess, with a tight but kind smile and three tall menus for the Blue Room wrapped in stamped black leather, tells me as she walks past at the pace of a woman who's busy as all hell in this crowded bar. "Thanks," I answer the back of her white dress as she heads off.

This place is made to look like a modern day speakeasy with the clean décor but darkened corners. And packed at that. Makes sense, I guess, since it's a college town. It's amazing there's even a seat open at the bar. Especially one next to a woman like the one in that tight red dress.

My good friend Griffin told me about this bar. He said it was a good place to think since it's always busy and the chatter and ambiance makes for decent white noise. He knows the shit I'm going through and a beer and good atmosphere will do wonders to take your mind off things you'd rather not deal with. Well according to him.

Taking a glance at the far end of the bar that separates the large space into two halves, I'm sure Griffin didn't have that blonde at the bar in mind when he said I should go clear my head. Sit down. Have a beer. Watch the game. Those were my marching orders.

Getting lost in her is exactly what I'd rather do than spend the night drinking alone, waiting on Griffin to be done his … whatever the hell he had to do. Of all the people in here, she's the only one I really notice. Although it's obvious she did that by design.

She's alone at the bar, even though her short, red dress is a show piece. The way the silky fabric rides up her thigh and she blushes when she notices… it does something to me. The mix of sultry and innocence. Like she's not sure how much she should give away. She's not used to doing this. This young girl on the hunt for a good time charade.

If nothing else, I know if I don't sit next to her, someone else will. If I don't take her home tonight some other asshole in this place damn sure will. The moment that realization hits me, I know there's no way in hell I'm going to let that happen.

Smirking, I watch her throw back the pink cocktail and make my way to her as she watches the crowd. I'm no knight in shining armor, but I know how to buy a girl a drink.

I've decided, after less than a minute of watching her, that she's on the prowl, but too damn cute and innocent to know what she's doing. Telling myself that's all this is, I drag out the bar stool and ask her if she needs another drink.

Her eyes hit me first then the blush in her cheeks rises all the way up to her temple. My blood simmers and travels lower. I was right, she's a shy little thing to be sitting alone, wearing a dress that's meant for a good time.

She keeps looking at me, her fingers fiddling with the rim of her empty glass. Even that small movement is sexy as hell. The smile is sweet and the fact that she's too busy eying me up to realize she hasn't answered makes me laugh.

That gruff sound that comes deep from my chest turns her cheeks to an even hotter shade of red. I might be man candy to some girls, but damn she doesn't hide it at all.

"Yes please, if you're offering," she finally answers, twirling the ends of her wavy hair around the tips of her fingers flirtatiously. Her voice is soft, and gentle, but with a playfulness that's undeniable. And her lips… fuck, my cock is already hardening.

Better than that, she can barely keep her gaze on me without smiling even harder.

She's fucking adorable. The perfect mix of sweet and sexy. Just knowing I get to her makes the black tee shirt that's already tight on my broad shoulders even tighter. I know I look blue collar; I can't hide that rough side of me. Dark jeans and a black tee shirt are about as dressed up as I ever get.

This girl looks like anything but that.

But the way she fidgets and keeps glancing at me like I'm man candy she hasn't tasted, lets me know she's as interested in me as I am in her.

Thank fuck. I'm not from around here, never went to college, and it's been a while since I've dated anyone.

She's not eye fucking me, she's eye glancing me because she's too bashful to outright stare at me. Everything about her makes me smile. She's too damn cute to be here alone.

Small talk is easy with her. This girl named Rose. It suits her with the red dress and delicate features of her slender neck. Throughout the night, all I can think about is kissing her there. Every time her hand slips down to my thigh. Playful and seemingly innocent but I know she knows what she's doing.

Every hour that passes, the place empties out more and more. She doesn't seem to notice or care. She's too busy asking me questions that are far too sweet and demure to elicit anything more than a laugh and more of those stolen touches. *What's my favorite color? What's my best friend's name? What's a joke I'd never tell my parents?*

Until she asks what brought me here since I'm not in college. Saying I came to visit a friend worked the first time, but she pries deeper so I hit her back with the same kind of question. The kind of question where there's a piece of it you don't want to exist.

"What brought you here tonight? In a red dress, sitting all alone?"

Her slender fingers slip on the straw in her glass of water and her gaze drops to the bar. At first, I think she's not going to answer, but she surprises me. Her bottom lip slips out from her teeth, grabbing all my attention to her kissable lips before Rose answers me, "I wanted to meet someone tonight."

"Is that right?"

"Yeah," she nods, the tension that was there for a split second when I asked her the question vanishes and her small hand lands on my thigh again, doing all sorts of things to me that the simplest of touches shouldn't be capable of doing. Thump, thump, my blood pumps harder as she brings her lips to the shell of my ear.

"I kind of want to go home with you tonight," her warm breath sends a shiver down my neck, past my shoulders and doesn't stop.

"You're tipsy," it's only a comment, but there's an invitation hidden in my tone. I give her the way out though, just in case it's only liquid courage. "I could take you home, drop you off if you want?"

"You're cute," Rose whispers around her drink as she peeks up at me with her thick lashes. My grin is easy. All of tonight has been easy. I haven't thought about a damn thing except what she has to say. When the lights turn on behind the bar, the music turns off and the check hits the table, I slap the cash down, tipping the bartender well.

I ask this sweet Rose as she climbs off the stool, standing next to me a head shorter and her gaze focused on the dip in my throat, "What do you want to do?"

She sets her finger right where she's looking, her touch gentle and her voice nearly lost in the air between us, "I want to kiss you right here."

That does it. Wrapping an arm around her waist, I pull her in close and revel in the feel of her soft body against mine as her heels hit the floor and she squeals in delight.

She doesn't let go of me, and in the cab she fucking tortures me, kissing me just below my ear on that tender spot I thought about kissing her.

"Not yet, my wild Rose," I half scold her in a whisper but as she pulls away, I capture her lips in mine. The kiss is searing, that first one in the back of the cab, with the taste of temptation and tequila mixing. My blood runs hot, my fingers inching up her thigh the way she did it to me all night. The only difference is I'm touching bare skin and the light, tender touch isn't enough.

Her gasp fills the cab when I pull away and when the cab driver looks back at us in the rearview, I keep my gaze forward, as if nothing at all is going on back here against his black leather seat.

As if I don't want to rip off her dress and push my hand between her legs, and rock my palm against her clit.

"You're already hard," her whisper comes with a hint of awe as she grips me through my jeans. Fuck, my head falls back and I close my eyes when the cab driver tries to meet my gaze again, his eyebrows much higher up on his forehead.

"Wait just five more minutes, Rose."

"I don't want to wait." Her protest is adorable, but there's no way this driver is getting a show.

"You're killing me," I groan and decide I should satisfy her before I come undone and take her right here.

With my fingers spearing through her gorgeous blonde locks, I mold my lips against hers, stealing her surprise gasp and loving the soft moan of pleasure she gives me when I kiss her again. Her fingers play along the back of my neck, her tongue dancing with mine and I make sure to keep my hands right where they are on the small of her waist. One move, and I swear I won't be able to stop.

I've never been so relieved to hear a cab driver tell me "we're here" and hand over the cash.

Rose's cheeks are a gorgeous hue of pink that travels down to her chest.

Griffin's not here when I unlock the apartment door. She's in my arms, her legs wrapped around my waist, her ankles hooked behind me with her heels digging into my ass before I can even kick the door shut behind me.

This girl knows what she wants and I've never been so eager to give it to her, to satisfy every sordid thought I know she had back at the bar.

I don't bother turning on the lights to Griffin's bachelor apartment, barren of everything that makes a home a home considering his student budget.

She doesn't need to see any of this place, she doesn't want to either. All she wants is to get in bed and as I kick my shoes off, our lips still locked in place, I'm just fine with that.

Her ass fits perfectly in my palms, but this damn dress is in the way.

My desire to shred it is only tamed by the fact that I know this is all she has to wear when this is over and I sure as shit know Griffin doesn't have any chick's clothes here.

When I toss her on the bed, the faded light shining through the slits in the blinds and casting the most beautiful shadows along the curves of her neck and breasts, she takes in a deep inhale, arching her back like she's been deprived of breath all the while.

That's when I realize the heavy rising and falling of my own chest, and sharp need to be buried inside of her that overrides any other sane thought that might come to me.

My jeans are off, my shirt ripped over my head and tossed carelessly on the floor in seconds. Her dress and lace underwear are quick to join my pile of clothes.

"I love the way your hands feel," she moans as I cup her breast in my hand. Her chest is small but full and when I run the pad my thumb over her hardened peaks, her head falls back, her lips part just slightly and her eyes close. I let her lose herself in the pleasure I give her, skimming my hands over her body, kissing every inch of her until I find her hot and glistening between her thighs.

With my breathing finally calm again, and hers ragged as she lays under me, I pump my cock once in my hand to get her attention. Her eyes go wide and that seems to wake her up.

She doesn't say anything, but her gaze doesn't leave my length and she stills on the bed.

Fuck. That is not a good sign.

"You alright?" I ask her realizing something is very fucking wrong right now. Please don't back out. Please, for the love of all things holy, I need to be inside this woman more than I need to breathe.

Licking her lower lip, her body relaxes only slightly when she looks up at me and says, "You're… you're really big." I don't break her hazel stare.

"I'll go slow."

She nods and gets settled, the sheets rustling as she lays down, far more aware than I think she's been all night.

Nestling my hips between her thighs, she spreads her legs wider for me. The first kiss I give her is in the crook of her neck, that spot I was dying to kiss before. With the head of my dick pressing against her warmth, I let the tip of my nose run up her neck and take my time kissing her again.

The warmth comes back to her body, every small touch bringing her closer and closer to the edge of writing under me. I nip her lower lip and she kisses me desperately.

That's my cue to enter her in a swift but slow, deep stroke. I stare down at her as I push all of myself into her. Her nails dig into my back, her reddened lips, swollen from kissing me, making a beautiful little "o".

And her gaze stays on mine as her heart pounds in time with mine. I stay that way, letting her stretch and get adjusted until she finally breathes again. It takes longer than I thought it would, but every second is worth it.

The next stroke is faster, deeper and then harder. Working my way up to taking her like I want. The slapping sound due to her arousal and my pistoning hips stirs with her strangled moans of pleasure. She tilts her hips every time she comes and it lets me in deeper as her pussy flutters around my cock.

I want to come more times than I can count, but I can't get enough of the feeling when she gets off. The sound of her crying out my name. The pleas she makes not to stop. Every little thing she does is mesmerizing.

When I finally have my release, it's four o'clock in the morning and her breathing comes in chaotic pants, her body well spent and well fucked.

"Can I crash here?" her voice is a whispered wish, sleeping dragging her down deeper into the covers. As if I'd kick her out. *What kind of men is she used to?*

"Yeah, of course," I answer her, pulling the covers around us both. I'm rewarded with a small smile on her gorgeous face and a hum of satisfaction as she scoots closer to me. Apparently, she's a cuddler. A piece of me is more than satisfied with that side of her and the feel of her against me and the easy way she lets me hold her.

Her body molds to mine, her soft curves not leaving an inch of space between us in the bed. The bed protests with a groan at every small movement we make. The dim light that slips through the blinds, provided only by the street lights, lays against her soft skin, and begs me to kiss her again. Right there in the crook of her neck, just to see if she'll shiver again at my touch. If it wasn't for her steady breathing and the angelic look on her face as she sleeps, I'd wake her again and take her again. There's something about her that's addictive. Something that calls to a deeper side of me, telling me she needs it just as much as I do.

Lying beside the messy halo of her blonde locks, with the floral and fragrant, I drift off. Sleeping beside her lures me to sweet dreams of her soft moans as I take her again and again; I sleep better than I have in months.

I'm not prepared to wake up alone. Finding her side of the bed long gone and cold is a bit of a surprise to say the least. I want her again. I dreamed of the sounds she'd make early in the morning. Her legs wrapped around my waist as I pounded into her. Fuck, I can't wait to hear her cry out as her nails scraped down my back. There's no better way to start a morning than a good hard fuck. But the house is empty.

She didn't even leave me a note, my wild Rose.

That realization makes me laugh as I shake my head and pour myself a cup of coffee. She must've left before the sun was even up. I remember her asking if she could stay last night and I wonder if she's been kicked out before and didn't want to go through that again.

That's the first sign of unease I feel, but I shake it off, feeling confident that I'll see her again at the bar tonight.

It was a wild night and missing her only makes me want her more. Just like the red dress at the bar, she knew what she was doing. Playing hard to get.

I thought she was toying with me. I was so damn certain I'd see her again.

I only went to that bar to look for her. I only stayed in that town an extra week, waiting for her. Every day that passed, the disappointment grew deeper. I decided one day we'd meet again, and I'd make her ass pay for not saying good bye. I got a lot wrong in my life, but I've never been so grateful that I was right about running into Rose again. Even if it was four years later, in another town.

Even if she'd kept something from me that changed everything.

I thought I had life all figured out… and then she kissed me.

FALLING AT FIRST SIGHT

His smile is what got me.

It was charming but held a hint of the sexy thoughts I was hoping he had in his head like I did with only our first glance.

He may be tall, dark and handsome but I'm telling you, it was his smile that got me. I'm sure of that detail.

Too bad all I did was avert my gaze and let a blush rise up to my cheeks, outing me for having sordid thoughts about my son's preschool teacher.

Trent Morgan was everything I ever wanted, but there was no way I was ever going there.

Even if I had fallen at first sight …

PROLOGUE

Autumn

"I**T'S HIS ASS AND YOU KNOW IT.**"

Magnolia has to cover her mouth as she laughs and haphazardly sets the wineglass down, doing her best not to lose any of the sweet wine with the motion. I'm awful glad I waited to take a sip until Renee said what she wanted to say. She's the comedic one in our group of four. Twirling a lock of auburn hair, she leans back, her wicked hazel eyes glinting. Renee is sharp and shameless.

But it's definitely not his ass. *At least not for me.* My comment remains unspoken because we're discussing Sharon's crush, after all.

"Renee, you know darn well I am not a butt lady. I couldn't care less about what's good on the backside."

"But he has a really nice ass," Renee insists, completely ignoring Sharon.

With the mason jar string lights hanging above us, Sharon's patio offers plenty of light, even as the southern sun sets in a beautiful hue of marigold and rose. Add in the wicker furniture, a touch of salt in the air plus the smell of fall surrounding us, and I'm all for Wine Down Wednesdays starting up again with this group of friends. It's been too long and I've missed them.

"What does Henry think of Mr. Morgan?" Sharon asks me and I instantly feel the telltale sign of a blush rising up my chest and making my cheeks flush.

My mother always told me I couldn't hide a thing from anyone. My face gives away the truth every time.

"What does my son think of your crush?" I respond with a question and quickly take a sip of my wine, then another, buying time. Sharon called dibs on Trent Morgan in before I had even walked my son into the preschool for his first day. That was almost a full year ago.

Now that school has started back up, I have to see that handsome face every day, my words stumbling and my laughs coming a little too often every time he talks to me.

He's off-limits. My son's teacher and my friend's secret infatuation.

Truth be told, even if Sharon hadn't claimed Trent in our group of single ladies, I wouldn't have the guts to make a move.

Single mom and a little shy is what would be on my dating profile … if I had one. I'm rusty, to say the least, and haven't been on a date in over a year, other than horrible disasters which are "events that shall not be named," according to this particular group.

They're all still looking at me, waiting for an answer. Does my son like Trent Morgan?

Finally I shrug, setting my wineglass down and leaning back in my rocking chair. "You know all the kids love Mr. Morgan. He's the fun one who makes the best airplane sound effects."

All eyes are still on me as if they can tell exactly what I'm thinking, so I add a little comment: "They don't like him the same as you, though." Chuckles lessen the nerves racking me.

Little nerves that wish I'd make a move. Little nerves that pine from a distance just to see that smile again.

CHAPTER 1

Trent

Any minute now. The exhale after my first sip of coffee, with just a touch of cream and a touch of sugar, is long and impatient. Any minute now she should walk through that door.

The doors open, catching my attention, but the person who enters isn't who I'm waiting for.

"Morning, Mr. Morgan!" Savannah sings out, not bothering to slow down in her race with her brother Liam as the sibling duo run to their designated room.

"Good morning, Savannah," I say, smiling broadly when they both get to Stacey, who's waiting for them in her section of the first floor. There are already two dozen children playing and laughing, getting their excitement out, and another half dozen to go. My class is the first one, closest to the front door, filled with a mix of kids who are four and five years old, and shared with Miss Sandy.

There's one student in particular whose absence forces my gaze to move back to the clock on the far wall. Any minute now and Henry will walk through those double glass doors. He'll probably press his hand to the painted print of his palm that we did last week to decorate for September. It forms a pattern of fall leaves and is taped to the lower half of the door.

That moment is what I'm waiting for. He'll let go of his mom's hand

and she'll peer through the window, and those beautiful green eyes will meet mine.

With an asymmetric grin, fate gives me exactly what I ordered. Little Henry, with his dark, thick floppy curls falling in front of his forehead, races to the front door. It's not quite a mohawk that Autumn gives her son, since it's just a little higher on top. She told me it's because she loves his curls. His skin's a bit lighter than mine; a tawny brown. Henry's treasured Iron Man backpack hits the cement and the woman I've been waiting for bends down in her sundress to scoop it up for him.

With a simper on her lips, she moves her gaze from her son to me. Those green eyes spark, her smile widens and I can hear that feminine sigh that I know she just let slip from those full lips as she looks away.

The first thought I had about Autumn Holloway is far too inappropriate for this setting. As is my reaction every single time I see her.

Last year, she teased me, giving me mixed signals. Watching her gather Henry as they enter, I remember how I asked her out almost a year ago. She declined. Clearing her throat far too many times and that rosy hue that drives me wild staining her cheeks.

I gave her space, but every day since then she's given me that same shy smile paired with covert glances. Every. Single. Day. This year, the tension is even thicker and my longing for just a chance is even worse.

The front door opens, bringing in a refreshing fall breeze. "Mr. Morgan!" Henry yells although he's not paying me any attention at all as he races past me to the gate where Miss Sandy is already waiting for him.

"Miss Sandy!" he calls out with the same enthusiasm as I tell the five-year-old good morning and watch Sandra take him back. He's a happy kid and reminds me of my own son, Chase. Who just happens to be his best friend.

"Sorry I'm late," Autumn says, holding the backpack with both hands.

"No worries," I respond and hold out my hand for the backpack. I have to grin when she stares at my hand for a moment too long and then shakes her head with her eyes closed. She opens her eyes, her gorgeous green gaze finding mine before she passes over her son's backpack.

"Right, right." Her smile widens, beautiful and filling me with warmth as she stares back at me and says, "You'd think I'd remember this from last year." With the backpack now in my hand, I swallow thickly.

"No worries," I tell her again and inwardly scold myself. *Say something else. Damn.* This woman does something to me. I co-own the preschool and I don't want to push boundaries, but I want her.

I've never wanted a woman like I do Autumn. Her sweet blushes, her shy smiles, her luscious curves—I want it all.

As she signs her son in, I can't take my eyes off of her. That is, until her hand whips around, pen still between those fingers, to point at me and say something. She doesn't get a word out though other than "shit."

My disposable coffee cup was practically filled to the brim still and luckily only lukewarm since some of it splashed onto her forearm.

"I'm so sorry," she says, obviously in distress as she pushes out the words, frantically wiping up the mess with a stack of tissues she pulled from her purse. Mom-ready.

I almost say "no worries" yet again as I grab some paper towels, helping her clean up the mess that I could and should take care of by myself to put her at ease. Almost. Almost but I don't.

Stopping myself, I wait until the chaos has left her beautiful gaze.

"Looks like you owe me a coffee date," is what comes out instead. The casual maybe-joke, sets a tension between us as I clean up what's left of the mess and shy Autumn pauses her movements to peek up at me.

I swear my pulse slows and every noise around us fades to nothing when I watch her reaction. The way her mouth parts slightly and then her teeth sink down into her pouty lips. The swallow that follows makes her neck seem that much more tempting to kiss.

"Mr. Morgan," she barely says my name in a breathy voice and then clears her throat, the nerves getting to her. *They get to me too, beautiful.*

"Are you asking me out on a date?" she half teases back and the two of us toss the soaked paper towels in the trash can.

"Yes," I answer her and that playfulness evaporates. "Just coffee," I tell her, holding my ground, and then I hold my breath.

Wide eyed, her gaze drops to my lips for just a moment. I'll be damned if this woman doesn't want me. "Please," I add for good measure, plastering a smirk on my lips. The smirk that always makes her shift in place from foot to foot.

"Just coffee?" she asks softly.

I can only nod, because I'd rather do that than lie.

As two more youngsters enter, breaking up the moment when one of them cries not to be left by her father, I worry I've lost her. And that she's going to politely decline.

Instead, she tucks her hair behind her ear and agrees to the date by saying, "I think coffee would be nice."

CHAPTER 2

Autumn

MY PHONE IS BLOWING UP AS IT LAYS ON MY SOMEWHAT made queen bed. I never tuck in the sheets, but the off-white comforter with a gray paisley pattern is pulled over enough that when I tell my five-year-old son it's time to make his bed, he can't point a finger back at me.

Ting, ting. The phone chimes and buzzes again, and I'm quick to read the updates from Mags followed by the response from Renee. Magnolia's life could be a story line for a soap opera. Or a Lifetime movie maybe. I've thought it for years but especially now given what's going on in her love life.

I'm quick to reply and then silence it, but not before catching Sharon's comment. Just seeing her name on the screen produces guilty tumbles in the pit of my stomach.

What do you do when your friend and you like the same man? You don't touch him. You certainly don't go on a coffee date with him over the weekend.

I don't even see what Sharon replied or know what position she's taking on Magnolia's situation. All I know is that I said yes to coffee with a guy I know she likes.

"Ugh." The groan slips out as I pull my sundress down and then blow a few strands of curly, dark blond hair out of my face. Makeup is done, this dress is brand new and I love how it flows, but my goodness, I cannot get past this feeling of betrayal. No matter how excited I am.

"You look pretty, Mommy." Henry's voice catches me by surprise. The door creaks as my son pushes it open even more. "Pretty for date." His tone is mischievous.

My bottom lip drops and my mouth opens with shock for this little cutie staring back at me as he climbs onto my bed. His little fists grab a handful of bedding and I help him, scooting his bottom up until he's on the mattress.

"It's not a date, sweetie," I tell him and there's practically a scold in my tone. Maybe that's why he arches that little brow of his at me. It's nearly comical. He's always had a mind of his own.

It's between a glance in the vanity mirror and a glance back at him that I see his true intentions. "Nope," I say and snag my phone just before he can reach it. The last time he got ahold of my phone, I had about 100 pictures of his mouth and up his nose in my camera roll.

Before he can protest or reach for it, I change the subject. Distraction is my best parenting weapon. I think it was Maggie who told me that if a kid wants something, offer them something else while taking what they want out of view. It has worked like a charm for years.

"Do you want Aunt Renee to come by and hang out this morning?" My voice takes on a bit of a sing-song quality as I set my phone down on the dresser. "She might have said something about ice cream sandwiches."

Now it's my son's turn for his mouth to drop in surprise. As he chants "Auntie Renee," my smile grows and all those nerves take a back seat. Until I check my phone again.

Aunt Renee spilled the beans in the chat. With a grimace, I read the texts.

When are you bringing my little man over so you can go on your coffee date, Autumn? She sent the text only a minute ago and the other two ladies in the chat pile on:

Ooh, a date?

With who?

My stomach drops when Renee answers Sharon's question regarding who this coffee date is with. *The hot preschool teacher with the nice butt.*

Sharon assumes wrong, typing back, *Mr. Harding?*

And frozen in my spot, I watch the horror story play out in real time with Renee correcting her: *Nope, she snagged Trent.*

Before my eyes close, I catch sight in my periphery of Henry jumping on my bed while chanting, "Date, date, date. You date Mr. Morgan. I date Renee!" His gleeful song is accompanied by the squeak of the bed frame and more vibrating in my hand from the phone.

Oh my God, kill me now.

CHAPTER 3

Trent

K EEPING IT PG IS HOW MY BUDDY HARDING WOULD DESCRIBE this coffee date. He's far more experienced than I am on the dating scene and if he was here now … he'd enjoy laughing at me.

Autumn and I snagged a coveted table on the patio outside a mom-and-pop coffee and cake shop. There's not a cloud in sight and the breeze is just right. So right that when it blows by, Autumn's dark brunette hair sweeps across her shoulders.

Yet this date is less like a date and more like small talk between two people who are both waiting in a doctor's office for a rectal exam. Yeah, Harding would laugh his ass off right about now.

"Our boys get along real well," I say and take a sip of my coffee, my thumb tapping rhythmically on the edge of the generic white ceramic mug. I don't know what it is about this woman, but I have no game whatsoever with her. Even less so this morning. Maybe I just need more coffee.

"I know, Henry talks about Chase all the time." She mimics the way the two boys say, "best buds for life," then lets out a small laugh. Very short and riddled with the same kind of nerves that won't settle in my gut.

I know she already knows that the boys get along. The two of them hit it off Henry's first day of preschool last year.

Even though I can't manage a conversation outside of the weather, the cinnamon cake on the table, and our boys, I still think it's going well be-cause when that wind blows and she has to retuck her hair behind her ear, she smiles down into her latte that smells so sweet and then peeks up at me, all shy-like.

Maybe I'm not the only one affected.

"So you took over the preschool from your mom?" Autumn asks. The conversation is still steadily in the category of small talk.

"Don't tell her that," I joke with a huff of laughter. "She still says it's hers."

That gets a broader smile from Autumn. "I mean, her name is on it. So … Ann's ABCs and123s Preschool."

"Well, she would kill me if I change the name." Again she smiles and lets out a small laugh. I know this small town likes to talk, but I have no idea what all she knows about my past. "I have my master's in education but I never thought I'd run a preschool. That was my mom's thing."

"A master's?" she asks and doesn't hide the surprise. "I almost went back for mine before I got the editor position."

"You like that? Working for the town paper?" I could see Autumn doing anything at all. She's personable and charming, but smart and driven. It doesn't take more than a handful of conversation to know that.

"Well, like you, I never thought I'd be an editor. I was always a math and science kind of girl, but I love it. I wouldn't change a thing."

It's easy to smile at her response. Everything between us is easy all of a sudden and I'm grateful for that.

"What were you going to do with your master's?" she says.

Shrugging, I admit, "Administration of some sort was the long-term goal. But when Chase was born and his mom passed, I wanted to be more hands on. I had to be, really. With my mom's vision going … it just made sense to take over the preschool and be close to him."

Autumn's tone holds her condolences. "I'm so sorry to hear about her passing."

"Thank you," I reply automatically. It's been years since I said goodbye to my ex-wife, but my throat still gets dry whenever she comes up in conversation.

"Does Chase ever talk about her?" Her question catches me off guard but it's the genuine concern that resonates with me.

"Occasionally. He has some questions, but he's still so young and never knew her."

"It was cancer, right?"

"Yeah," I say and my voice is tighter than I'd like. I loved Candace and I wish things could have been different, but I know Chase and I make a duo she'd be proud of.

"I'm so sorry," she repeats, her voice gentle and comforting.

"What about Henry's dad?" I ask her to change subjects and move to lighter topics.

"We're on really good terms. We should have only ever been friends, to be honest."

"Just didn't work out between you two?" I already know that's what the town says. They were young, their son a blessing that came from a disastrous pair.

She shakes her head, setting down her mug and pushing it away gently. "We actually broke up amicably before I found out I was pregnant. We tried to make it work but it we're much better off not being …" she trails off and scrunches her face in distaste rather than finishing.

"And no boyfriend now?" I say, leaning forward. The way my voice lowers yet is still full of hope causes that blush to come out full force.

Shaking her head, she asks me the same, "And you don't have a girlfriend, Mr. Morgan?"

"Not yet I don't." I let the statement add to the brewing tension between us.

There's a moment of silence and then I say, "So, two single parents … meeting up at a coffee shop on Saturday afternoon."

"Oh, the scandal," Autumn jokes mockingly with a broad smile.

"I'm just saying … us single parents, we have to stick together."

"Is that right? Is that why you asked me out?" she asks and it's the first bit of flirtation, *real flirtation* from her since we sat down. The nerves have finally settled as another couple slips by and heads into the coffee shop with the telltale ding of the two bells above the door announcing their entry.

"I thought it was because you tipped over my coffee but—" Covering the embarrassment on her face with both hands, her reaction stops me from finishing the thought.

"You're a cute mix of sweet and shy," I say and I don't know why the confession slips out of me, but it does.

She doesn't blush, though, like I thought she would. Her smile stays put and her eyes flash with something. Something that tells me it's okay to keep pushing her.

"You think I'm sweet?"

"I know you are, but what do you think of me?" I dare to ask.

"Handsome. I think you're just my type, Mr. Morgan. Tall, dark and handsome … I would put good money down that you're just about every woman's type."

A rough chuckle leaves me as I reply, "But I don't want to be out here with *any* woman. I only asked one to coffee."

Setting her mug down on the white rattan table, she wraps both her hands around the cup. "Speaking of which, mine is almost gone."

"Well, you have been clinging to it like it was going to save you from having to make conversation."

"Did not," she says, the beautiful smile never fading even with her rebuttal. "Although I'm glad I was able to get you a coffee. Since I did spill yours and all."

"Well … actually, I asked you out for coffee so I could ask you out for dinner."

Her laugh in response is light and the sound is music to my ears. "You are something else, Trent."

"As are you, Autumn." An asymmetric smile pulls up on my lips. It doesn't escape me that she doesn't respond to the invitation. My pulse picks up and I swear there's a hard thump in my chest when she looks away for a moment.

"We could do tomorrow night?" I offer her. It's a holiday weekend and we have Monday off for Labor Day. Tomorrow is perfect for a real date.

"Tomorrow? So soon?" she asks as if it's a joke, but I think there's something real about her hesitation.

"Is there a rule against having a dinner date right after a coffee date?"

"There are lots of rules against that," she answers with all seriousness. Before she can deny me, I slip my hand over hers, which is still laying innocently on the table. There's a spark, a heat between us that's met with a small gasp from her lips. My dark umber against her fair skin. My thumb runs soothing circles, but all it does is stir up that heat, making it hotter and hotter.

"When I want something, I go after it. And I want you."

"Trent," she says and my name is a plea on her lips. She lets me lift her hand in mine and I take my time, letting my intentions be clear as I plant a single kiss on the inside of her wrist. The smell of her sweet perfume and the little sigh that slips from her, a sigh of coveted lust, does things to me that a coffee date never should.

I pull away easily enough, but Autumn still seems caught in a trance.

"Tomorrow night?" she asks after a moment, her voice low and full of the sexual tension that resonates in every inch of me.

I only nod and in response, she gives me a sweet smile and agrees, "Tomorrow night."

I leave her by her car with a small, chaste kiss. Tomorrow night, though … if I'm going to kiss her, it's not going to be on her cheek.

CHAPTER 4

"I. Have. A. Playdate. With. Chase." Henry smacks his hands with each word from the back seat of the car. "Mommy. Has. A. Date. With. Mr. Trent." My eyes roll hard as we sit at the red light on Main and Sixth Street. A row of cute houses is to my right and the coffee shop I sat at with Trent is to my left.

Even as I let out the frustrated breath, I stare longingly at the white rattan table we sat at. The table where his lips first touched me like I've been dreaming about. And everything inside me blazes. He may be my son's teacher … but there's no doubt that Trent Morgan could teach me a thing or two.

Turning down the music as the red light changes to green, I question Henry to get his mind anywhere other than the date I have with his pre-school teacher.

My phone pings and I wait until I'm at the next red light before I peek at it.

Sharon wants to know if I like him and how the date went.

Ugh. Those nerves from before rattle inside of me and I struggle to come up with another response. I know she knows I do like him and that the date was "just fine" because that's what I wrote in the group chat.

Not only was it "just fine," it was a low-key icebreaker that somehow turned scorching hot out of nowhere. I've been imagining all sorts of things for over a year but what I wanted to do to that man on top of that little table is downright deviant.

I'm surely not going to tell Sharon that. My plan is to drag my feet as long as I can until I know if there's really something there between Trent and me.

One kiss really. It's all in the kiss, isn't it? That's what they say, so … just one kiss. A real one. Not a peck on the cheek to say goodbye after a coffee date, but the type of kiss that slows down your whole world as you kick up one leg and turn to jello.

Nodding my head in agreement with … well with myself, I realize I've been ignoring Henry.

"Right, Mommy?" Henry says.

"Yes, that's right," I answer and immediately regret agreeing without knowing what I'm agreeing to.

"You like Mr. Morgan! Mommy likes Mr. Morgan!"

Ping. My phone goes off again as I roll up to the address Trent texted me.

I'm just curious! Sharon wrote and I know I need to write something back so I settle on a sort-of truth: *He asked me out tonight so we'll see!*

And with that response, my phone is turned on silent.

The inner voice in my head is anything but, though. With a heavy breath out, I lie to myself. I'm not a bad friend. She had a year. A full year. There has to be fine print in the dibs clause and if she was upset, she would have said so.

All the nerves that nag at me vanish the moment my gaze lifts to the dark blue front door of the raised ranch house. Standing there in the yard and staring straight back at me is the man I can't get off my mind.

In a crisp white button-down with the sleeves rolled up to his forearms and dark blue jeans, he looks impeccably handsome. That look in his eyes when our gazes meet, and the way his lips kick up into a crooked grin … morphs his clean-cut look into that of a tempting devil.

It's only when his mother calls his name that I'm snapped out of it and unbuckle my belt. As I gather Henry and his bag out of the car, I can barely hear their conversation.

"Is this your partner in crime, Chase? The one you've been telling me about?" Mrs. Emma Morgan's glasses slip down the bridge of her nose as she speaks, but even still the woman is a force. I used to think age didn't know her name; she could be Trent's sister if the whole town didn't know any better. She practically raised half of us.

The past few years may have added some lines around her eyes and as she smiles, some new wrinkles rest there too, but his mother is still the woman I remember.

Which makes it a little … odd to show up and ask her to watch my son while I date hers.

"Mrs. Morgan, how are you?" I give her the largest smile I can and do my best to pretend that there isn't anything at all weird about this.

"Wonderful," she says and her gaze slips down to my dress. "Don't you look as pretty as a peach in June."

The smile on my face is genuine when I tell her thank you and then add, "And thank you for watching Henry."

"Trust me," she says and stands upright, watching Henry run off to the flower bed where Chase is currently stacking rocks and knocking them down with some Transformer or other plastic figure of some sort I'm sure cost twenty bucks or more. "It will be easier on me for Chase to have a friend to keep him occupied."

"I really appreciate it."

"You don't have to keep thanking her," Trent says and slips a hand on my lower back as he adds, "She'd kill me if I let someone else watch him on her weekend with Chase."

His mother gestures with a hand before I can say anything and she writes us off with a wave as she says, "Enjoy your date."

There's this thing about a small town and how people talk. Word spreads and even the most innocent of things can turn scandalous.

That's probably why the only words I can think of right now are that it's not a date. But I know very well it is, so instead I stand there, watching the woman who used to watch me take a seat in a lawn chair and call out for us to have fun.

This is the specific time my friend group calls *the moment*. The one where you know you're really on a date and it's happening. So either you turn back, or you run full steam ahead.

"Your car or mine? I would immediately go to mine, but since it's not a date-date …"

"What?"

"You just muttered it's not a date-date," Trent says jokingly and with him next to me, standing there, I have to crane my head to look up at him. Even in these wedge sandals.

Standing there in the late summer warmth that's quickly fading into an early fall evening chill, I'm lost in his amber eyes for just a moment.

"If I had it my way, it'd be a date-date, you know?" he says, the confession sounding like it's something sinful.

The boys yelling out on behalf of the toy men in their hands breaks me from the spell Trent is so darn good at putting me under.

"Henry is already chanting that we're dating." I'm busy tucking my hair behind my ear when Trent replies, "That's my little man."

I can't deny it does something to me, listening to him talk about son like that. Little butterflies make my stomach flip and I can see a happily ever after with him. Already. I haven't even had my kiss yet.

As he asks me, yet again, whose car we're taking since I still have my keys in my hand, I come to a very real observation.

Dating a man you really want to hold on to for more than one night is completely terrifying.

CHAPTER 5

WITH DIM, CANDLELIT LIGHTING, MODERN FURNITURE draped in plush velvet, and the other guests dressed to the nines, Blue Bay is the fanciest restaurant this town has to offer. And the only one I can imagine taking Autumn to tonight. Even if she did drive and refer to this evening as not a date-date, this is an official first date. And judging by her shyness and the quiet thank you as I push her chair in, Autumn is very much aware of that.

With the din of chatter and clink of silverware surrounding us, the waiter takes our drink order.

A glass of chardonnay for Autumn. I make a mental note of which wine she's having. If my father taught me anything before passing, it's that love is in the details. Small gifts that bring memories will go a long way. I intend to have that with the woman I share my life with.

I'm almost certain it's Autumn.

Every moment with her, the tension gets thicker.

Every moment without her, she's all I can think about.

"This is a really nice place," she says and her voice is gentle with more than a hint of gratitude as she lays the napkin across her lap.

"This is the only place I thought to take you tonight."

"Really?" She sounds surprised.

"You're a single mom and from what I can tell, a workaholic." I answer her with complete honesty. "When's the last time you treated yourself to a night out?"

"I have my friends. We do get-togethers … but not like this."

"Exactly."

"So you want to spoil me?" She lays the question out as if it's a joke.

"Most definitely," I answer with as much charm as I can manage. The nerves are gone, the fears of ruining this with her nowhere in sight. It's just me and her and a date that is long overdue. "I really like you and I wanted to make sure I made that clear tonight."

There's a pause as the beat of my pulse and everything else slows when she looks back at me. Until she answers with five little words, "I really like you too."

The waiter is silent as he drops off our drinks, interrupting the moment, but it's pleasant enough and we place our dinner order.

The atmosphere mixes just right with the jack and Coke and her glass of chardonnay.

After a moment, Autumn seems to remember where the conversation was and picks it right back up. "As my son might say," she says and the words leave a beautiful smile on her lips as she sips the sweet-smelling wine that carries all the way across the table. "I kind of sort of, maybe, quite possibly, like you a lot."

"Is that flirtation I sense?" I tease her and she lets out a small hum of amusement as she nods her head.

"How am I doing? I may be a bit rusty."

"Well, this is a compliment I never thought I'd give, but I like you rusty."

Her shoulders shake with the laugh and her hair flows over her shoulders. In this moment, she's beautiful and I know I was right to wait for her to finally come around and give me a chance.

"Oh, aren't you just the charmer," she says but lays her hand on the table, palm up. I'm quick, but not too quick, to lay mine on top of hers and she threads her fingers through mine.

The conversation flows easily, a bit of laughter, a bit more of deeper conversation.

The only interruption comes when she checks her phone and then peeks up at me.

"You don't get out much, do you?" I jokingly scold her for checking on the boys again. "My mom has some experience here, you know?"

"Oh, come on, just text her and ask how they're doing."

"They're fine. I'm sure."

"Please," she says as the waiter refills her water goblet.

"You could message her," I say just to tease her. "I'll send you her number."

"I'm not texting your mother while I'm on a date with you."

"Ooh, so you admit it? We're on a date?"

Bright red stains her cheeks but she doesn't waste any time flicking her cloth napkin at me and saying, "Just ask her, please."

"She already messaged ten minutes ago and said they're watching Batman and the two of them ate an entire bag of popcorn."

Her smile grows and she slips her phone back in her purse with a simple thank you.

Before I can tell her she doesn't need to worry, before I can remind her she's on a date, she tells me, "You're lucky you have your mom. I don't have much family and none of them live around here anymore."

"I know I am. She loves watching Chase."

Her eyes spark as if she's about to say something daring. "So, I'm just going to put the obvious out there … if we were to do this thing, really date I mean. I think we'd make a cute little family."

I take a moment to let it sink in that she's considering things I've considered. This may be our first date, but it's not like we didn't already know what we were getting into.

I voice aloud a thought I've had ever since she agreed to that coffee date. "People might think Chase and Henry are twins … not the identical kind, but because of their age."

With bright eyes and a soft smile, Autumn replies, "So that didn't scare you? Because if we do this, really do this … I don't want just a fling."

"Men aren't scared off by the thought of a family. I know what I want, and I'm not looking for a fling either."

She bites down on her plush bottom lip and all I can think is that I want to do that nibbling. With my cock hardening, I readjust in my seat and thankfully, I'm saved by the waiter.

"The rib eye," he says as I lay my napkin across my lap, "and scallops and medallions." Nodding toward our drinks, I answer him before he can ask the question, "Another for each of us, please."

Autumn looks giddy staring down at her plate with a small hum of satisfaction. One thing I hadn't realized before tonight was how laid back and easily pleased Autumn is. She's all smiles all the time although there has to be something that gets to her.

"You look like a kid at Christmas," I say as she pops a roasted potato into her mouth the second the waiter is gone.

"I love good food." Autumn doesn't hesitate to cut into one of her scallops. "You're going to wish you got these," she taunts playfully, the chunk of caramelized scallop speared on her fork.

"I think I'm going to be just fine with my steak."

"It does look delicious," she says and eyes my meal like she may steal it if I don't eat fast enough.

"Where do you even put it away? You're a tiny little thing."

"All the way down to my toes," she says and the joke makes me grin. "So ... this is a date-date?"

"It's a date-date," I say, nodding in agreement.

All she does is smile at my answer and I comment, "You like to smile, don't you?

Her head tilts with a small nod. "Happiness is a choice."

"I want to be happy." I don't know why the words slipped out, but they do.

"You aren't now?" she asks with all seriousness, giving me her full attention.

"Happier," I say, amending my statement.

"What would make you happy?"

You. The word stays at the back of my throat and I shrug, taking a swig of my drink rather than answering. "Life is good, but I just want make sure it's everything it can be for Chase."

"I don't know a lot of single dads, and only a few single moms. But I know you're doing a good job. Chase is a sweet kid and he's happy."

"So is Henry."

A smile instantly blossoms on her lips and she tells me thank you.

"So ... since this is a date-date, can we agree to one thing?" she asks, changing the subject.

"What's that?"

"Can we can go slow?" she asks me.

"Slow?"

"I just think it's best, with the boys and all."

"Slow it is then."

And just like that, the serious tension is gone, but both of us know what the other wants.

One small problem, though: there's nothing about the two of us that I want to do slow.

CHAPTER 6

Autumn

"You're the one who said let's take it slow." Trent makes the comment as I catch my breath and lay my head back on the driver's side seat.

Dinner and another drink at the bar after, and then some more flirting and small touches, took most of the night. It's dark outside of the car. The moon is almost full, the stars on full display in the midnight blue sky.

Trent can't get the grin off his smug, handsome face.

"And yet …" He lets the words hang in the air as he gestures to my house. I drove to my house after dinner. Not to his where his mother and both of our boys are.

Freudian slip is all I can say in defense.

"You just wanted to take me home. Admit it," he teases and with his rough chuckle I can't help but laugh.

He's not wrong, though. Not in the least.

Something changed at dinner. My heart won't stop thumping for this man.

I just hope it's as real for him as it feels for me. Every time he breaks our kiss, I remember something Renee likes to say that serves to answer that nagging little question: *You'll find out by morning.*

With a grin pulling at my mouth, I lean over the console and lay another kiss on his lips. Our hands don't stop roaming. Both of us feeling up the other and enjoying the kind of making out I thought was only for high school and puppy dog love.

I suppose romance has layers. And I happen to really enjoy all of Trent's layers. Every last little bit of every single one.

Very few cars have driven by but when they do, we've paused, caught our breath and teased the other for starting up the kiss again. It starts with a little touch, then inching closer … I just can't get enough of him.

Ping. His phone goes off and this time I groan in protest, until I realize it's his mother.

He reads the text out loud. *They're both fast asleep so stay out however long you want. Go to a movie or something.*

"Are movies even playing this late?" I ask.

"She doesn't have to know all the details."

His words hang in the air. The pull between us only gets stronger as the seconds pass.

It's his turn to lean in and kiss me, which he does. His right hand on my thigh, his fingertips grazing against my bare skin and then higher, pushing up the hem of my dress.

I moan into his mouth as my left hand does the same to him, slipping up his collared shirt and finding his taut muscles beneath the fabric as our kiss deepens. He's got me every kind of hot and bothered.

It's only when a pair of headlights flashes and drifts by that the kiss is broken, leaving me breathless and more than that, wanting.

A million questions about how we're going to make this work and if it's going to last bombard my mind, but the only one I ask is, "You want to come in?"

CHAPTER 7

Maybe it's because I've wanted her for over a year. Maybe it's because her hands roam freely down my body like I've dreamed about. Maybe it's because her kiss tastes like lust and sweet wine and everything I ever wanted.

Whatever the reason, the second we're through her front door, I pin Autumn to the wall, my lips never leaving hers, and my hands reaching below her dress.

The sudden gasp from her lips only fuels me to deepen our touch. Her small noises are the only sounds I can hear apart from the blood rushing in my ears and my heart pounding inside my chest.

"Trent," she moans my name against my lips, our warm breath mingling. I don't know how she has any time at all to speak. I want all of her, in every way, without any thing between us. Not even words.

My fingers inch up her thighs, the soft fabric taunting me until I reach the thin lace of her panties. Her smile against my lips is sultry and sinful, just like the words she whispers. "Tear it if you want."

Fuck. As if I couldn't get any harder for her.

The thin fabric shreds easily enough and I let it fall before pulling my shirt over my head. Her hands fumble with the buckle on my belt and I swear it feels like first love all over again.

Each of us wanting, needing, and desperate to take this to the next level. With half our clothing a careless heap piled next to us, I make a move to lift her dress, but she stops me, breathing out heavily and taking in the cool air.

"Bedroom," she murmurs against my lips and I never knew I could hate a word so much. Not daring to put space between us, I lift her in my arms and take the stairs two at a time. The lust still clinging to every inch of us, I rid us of the remaining clothing before falling onto the bed with her beneath me. With my forearms braced beside her head, she seems so small beneath me.

The windows are opened just inches, the curtains blowing with the cool evening breeze that dances along our bare skin.

Slipping my hand between her thighs, I run my middle finger up her slick seam, finding her hot and glistening with arousal. As I spread it over her clit, I leave gentle kisses along her neck and let her mewl and writhe under me.

I'm hard and eager, but I want this to be perfect.

It's not until she's begging me, whimpering both my name and the plea, that I stroke myself and rest the head of my dick against her sweet center.

I kiss her once, watching her lashes flutter down as her eyes close. Readying myself, I can barely push my head inside of her. Fuck, she feels like heaven, but the expression on her face tells me I'm the only one feeling this pleasure right now.

Pausing to give her time to adjust, I nibble her lip and wait for her expression to relax.

"It's been a while," she says, the confession leaving her in a whisper.

"I told you I'd go slow," I answer with all sincerity, but a worried smile and a huff leaves her.

"That's not quite what I mean," she says, her voice low and holding questions I don't have the answers to right now.

Her heart races against mine as I hover over her, leaning down with a kiss to silence her.

With her lips still on mine, I thrust forward, as easy as possible. Her lips part as she holds her breath, feeling every inch of me until I'm buried to the hilt.

The mix of pleasure and pain stirs in her gasps and moans, edging closer to pleasure with every thrust. I take my time, pulling nearly all the way out then pushing myself deeper and harder each time. It doesn't take long before her nails are digging into my shoulders, her legs wrapped around my hips and her heel digging into my ass to fuel me on.

"Yes," she begs and I happily oblige. *Harder. Faster.* I fuck her into her mattress like I've dreamed of doing. Each time I get close to finding my own release, I slow, pressing myself as deep inside of her as I can. She loses herself, pleasure racking through her body and her back bowing in ecstasy.

She's so tight I can feel every bit of her orgasm as she pulses around me, screaming out my name. I don't give her time to come down from the sweet high. Instead I fuck her mercilessly, pistoning my hips and riding her harder. She angles her hips, taking it all and clinging to me as her head presses back into the mattress and she cries out in pleasure.

This is what I've dreamed of for so long, but even my dreams weren't this good. This is perfect.

When I finally let go, I bury my head in the crook of her neck, kissing her there and giving us both a moment to catch our breath.

Falling to the side, I lie there next to her and hold her close, recalling how our night unfolded. With my hand on the small of her waist, I run soothing circles over her soft skin with my thumb and kiss her hair.

Sleep could take us both, and as much as that would make me happy, life and responsibilities are calling.

I'm not the only one thinking it.

"Time to go pick up the boys," she says and her voice resonates two things. A longing to stay just like this. And a resignation that this night is over.

Peeking down at her, she's still vibrant and beautiful, but I know she loved getting away tonight. Her gaze is lost until she closes her eyes and she plants another kiss on my chest. She needs time to know I'm serious— hell, she needed a year just to let me take her out for coffee. I'll give her all the time in the world … tomorrow. But right now?

"Not yet," I tell her, positioning myself on top of her again. The bed groans and her bottom lip drops open just slightly. "I'm not done with you yet. Spread your legs for me."

CHAPTER 8

I T'S NOT A WALK OF SHAME. NOT AT ALL. THERE ARE NO RUMPLED clothes or a hangover. Nope. My pencil skirt is practically pressed within an inch of its life and my blouse fits exactly like it did on the mannequin at Macy's. Yet as my heels click on the pavement and Henry runs up to the glass doors of the preschool building, it feels just like that.

There is not a single doubt in my mind that every soul over the age of eighteen in that building knows I hooked up with Trent Morgan two nights ago. Deandra's daughter volunteers in the newborn section; she's only sixteen and I bet she knows too.

The blush that won't go the heck away is writing out the details on my face. I'm sure of it.

Still, I make a beeline right for him when I open the door and Henry takes off toward Chase to show him the pinball keychain he hasn't stopped talking about all morning.

"Good morning, Henry," Trent calls out to Henry's back when he zips past him and right to his friend.

"Well … it is a good morning, isn't it?" Trent's gaze flows down the length of my body, sending goosebumps over every inch of me. He's discreet and no one else heard, but still.

"Not here," I say, scolding him beneath my breath, although my smile seems to disagree with the sentiment. "I haven't told my friends yet."

There's only a hint of guilt in that confession.

"When are you going to tell them?"

"Soon?" My response is a question too. I need to rip this bandage off.

"Well, you better tell them before the rumor mill does." His warning is all too real in this small town. With a quick kiss, I tell him to have a good day and any nerves are gone, replaced by butterflies wreaking havoc in my chest.

The last person I expect to see when I turn around is Sharon. She doesn't have kids. There's not a reason in the world for her to be here. Well … except for the fact that she's telling Maggie's little girl to have a good day and appears to be signing her in.

I bet Mags had something that had to be done and Sharon's just helping her out.

"You all right?" Trent asks at the same time Sharon peeks up and beams as she says, "Look at you two."

Pen still in hand from signing in Magnolia's daughter, she raises it in a friendly gesture.

"Have a good day, Sharon. Nothing to see here," Trent jokes to her before whispering to me, "You have a good day too." The way he says such innocent words sounds scandalous to the point that my ears burn.

With the heat of a blush still rising, the tap of the pen from Sharon gets my attention, but even more than that is the wide grin she's trying to contain.

I only get a couple steps in before she squeals in delight. "Oh my God," she mouths and I'm quick to pull her out of the building before embarrassment of my not-walk of shame fully takes over.

"You two look so cute together," she says and her statement is as easy as her walk.

The guilt that ate away at me seems to subside. "I really like him," I admit to her because it's the only thing I can think to say.

She speaks as we make our way to our cars in the parking lot. She parked right next to mine. "One, you can tell. The tension is thick."

A hint of a laugh escapes me, but the nerves are still there, waiting for her approval. Waiting for one of my best friends to tell me it's okay that I took the guy she had dibs on. Freaking please have mercy because I really, really want to be with him. "He's not some fling for me and I know you called dibs—" The excuses tumble out of me and I wish I could stop them.

Seriously, if I could pluck the words back, I would. I'm so embarrassed and sick to my stomach over this.

"Whoa, I was just joking," she says and both of Sharon's hands fly up.

"I call dibs on every hot guy in this town. You know that … don't you?" The look in her eyes reflects exactly what I feel. It's the fear over being a bad friend.

"I just felt bad because I should have told you guys, but I didn't want to if there wasn't a connection in case … in case you really liked him."

"I was never going to go after Trent. Look … I can prove it. I texted Renee last year sometime," she says and scrolls through her phone without missing a beat. After a moment she adds, "You can ask her, because I can't find it." Looking me dead in the eyes she confesses, "I told her the two of you were going to hook up and then a couple months later I got drunk and asked her what was taking you so long.

"You guys have always had tension and you look so cute together. We all wanted it to happen. But Renee said not to push. With, you know, kids involved and you working on your career. So I stayed out of it."

Leaning against my car, I let the truth of what she just said wash over me.

"So … you're not mad?"

"Heck no, but we need details. Wine Down Wednesday?" she says, opening up her car door. I check the time and note that I'm going to be late if I don't get moving.

"Yes, definitely."

Wednesdays are for girls' nights, but Fridays are date nights with Trent. That was decided on the ride home last night, with his hand in mine.

There's no reason not to choose happiness and go for what you want. My only goal is to not overthink it and let us fall into place. Which oddly enough, seems to be right where we are now and right where we're meant to be.

"Oh my God … and did you hear what happened with Magnolia?" Sharon easily moves the conversation into new territory as she says, "We need to bring her a bottle just for herself … or rather, two of them."

"That bad?" I ask, both of us still standing although our driver car doors are opened.

Sharon smirks. "If you ask me … that *good*."

A LITTLE BIT IN LOVE WITH YOU

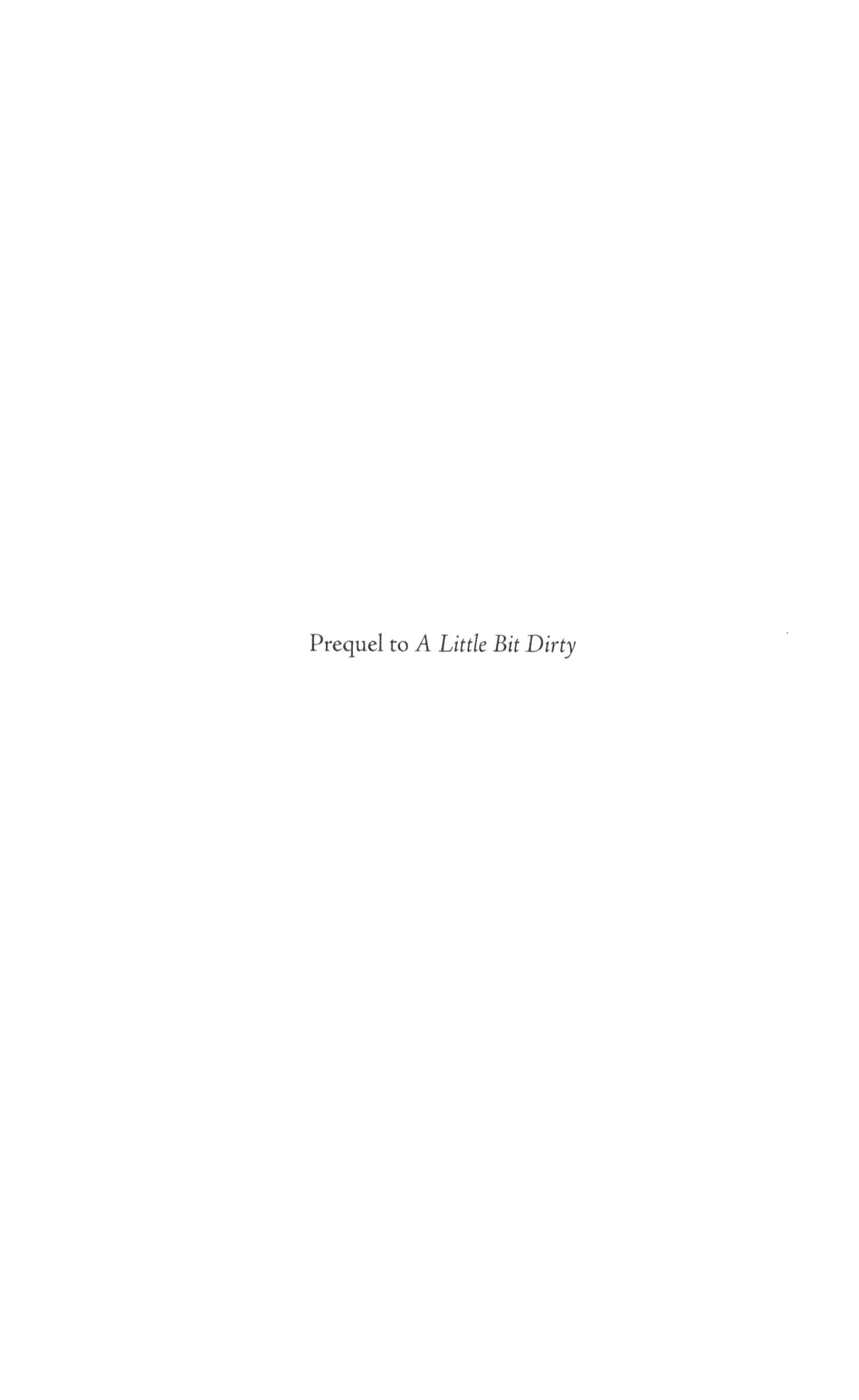

Prequel to *A Little Bit Dirty*

CHAPTER 1

IFORGOT HOW HOT IT IS BACK HOME. PULLING MY TANK TOP OUT in the center of my chest offers a cool bit of air to filter down, but the relief is lost on me. Until I see Asher and tell him exactly how I feel, there's not a damn thing that's going to ease this anxiousness inside of me.

Nearly slipping in a pot hole I didn't see in the long gravel pave up to his parents' house, I let out a hiss of irritation. It's too darn hot for August in Beaufort South Carolina. The coastal sea island is supposed to keep this place from hitting the high 90s, but there isn't a breeze to be found.

My jean white jean shorts are a bit too tight since I gained a little weight my first year of college. Freshman 10 and all that. I huff, feeling my cheeks redden in this heat as I turn the corner of the backroad surrounded by thin threes that don't offer any shade and the airplane hangar in the distance.

I haven't been back home for more than 48 hours and I'm already miserable. Although if Asher was answering his phone, if he would just talk to me, I know it would all be okay.

We didn't spend three years together to be off and on and constantly fighting because we're long distance now.

I love him and he loves me. Letting out an exaggerated exhale and pulling my dark brown hair up into a makeshift ponytail, I pretend I'm stopping right in front of his house just to catch my breath and cool down before I pull back the flimsy screen door and knock on the old worn door to the farmhouse.

We've been together all through high school, heck half of my memories are from that airplane hangar that doubles as a mechanic garage on the lower level. My first sip of beer… even though I'm only eighteen. Our first kiss… our first, everything.

My throat closes up tight as I tighten the ponytail and wipe the beads of sweat from my forehead.

I'm sure I look a mess, but that's exactly how I feel, so … I suppose it'll have to do.

With one step, the gravel crunches under my feet, but then I halt.

The screaming from inside makes my already hammering heart go into high gear. Asher yells at his father in return. The two of them are going at it.

I take a hesitant step forward, unwilling to turnback and needing to know what the hell is going on. The two of them have had their issues butting heads, but the rage in their tones is something I've never heard before. He didn't tell me anything was going on.

I can't quite make out what they're saying, apart from the cuss words and his mother begging them to stop.

My body goes cold and begs me to stop as I near the wooden porch steps.

Swallowing thickly I pull my phone out from the back pocket of my shorts and check my messages.

He didn't respond to the series I sent him:

Hey I'm sorry. Can we talk?
I miss you.
You know I love you right?
Please talk to me.

Emotions swarm me as something is thrown from inside, glass shatters and I instinctively step back, my mouth parted in both shock and fear.

Are you okay? I'm here.
What's going on?

My fingers fly across the keys and just as I hit send, Asher storms out, nearly ripping the screen door off as it bangs against the house.

He gets three large strides out the door before he sees me. His tanned skin and rough around the edges decorum fits his blue collar ways to the T. His hair is a bit messy on top, his piercing eyes hitting me with all the intensity in the world. First the anger and hurt, then the recognition and with it a touch of shame. Like he didn't want me to hear that and he's very aware that I did.

Only I'm not sure what the fight was about.

He slows his pace, turning to look back once, and then focusing his gaze on the porch floor before looking back up at me. He licks his lower lip and all I see is a wounded man. Worn blue jeans and a graphic dark blue tee complete the image.

"You okay?" I whisper. Cause really that's all that matters.

His parents don't come after him. It's far too quiet for far too long. He doesn't answer me, but emotions filter through his expression and every second that passes it crushes me more and more.

"Want to get out of here?" I offer, feeling the heat at my back and knowing right now the only thing I need in life is to get that look off his face.

I can't even try to count the number of times Asher has held me while I cried. Fights with my friends, with my parents, losing my grandparents and so many other things throughout the years.

I've never once seen him cry and I'm not sure he's going to now, but I think if I wasn't standing right here, right now, he'd have gone up to the apartment in the hangar and… and I don't know.

"I wanted to talk, but we don't have to, we can go anywhere you want," I offer him when he doesn't respond.

All I want to do right now, as the porch creaks with his shifting weight, is love on him.

However he needs and never leave his side again.

CHAPTER 2

Asher

"**Y**OU SHOULD COME WITH ME," SHE PLEADS WITH ME.

My hands fist at my side, a cold sweat lines by back although everything inside of me is do damn hot. Anger forces adrenaline to surge through me.

None of it is for her. Not an ounce of this is for my Bri. I hate that look in her eyes. That hurt and even sympathy she has for me right now. My face flames with embarrassment.

My throat's tight as I swallow and attempt to calm down. With a tension ringing throughout my body, I attempt to answer her without any of that shit back there being shown to her.

"What all did you hear?" I question.

Her head shakes, that ponytail sways and her gorgeous green eyes widen as she tells me she couldn't make out what we were saying, but she heard us arguing.

I love this girl more than anything, but I don't want to share this with her. I can't. I can't let her know what happened.

Heaving in a breath, I take a look behind her and I don't see her father's car.

"Did you walk?"

"Yeah," she whispers at the same time that there's a commotion behind me. Probably my dad pushing the sofa out of the way. A heat flows over my body and I move before either of them can come out here.

She can't see this.

"Come on," I pull her by her elbow as I walk passed her. All I want is to get to to my car and get the hell out of here. Her flip flops catch in the gravel as she tries to keep up.

"Shit," she curses beneath her breath.

My sweet little Bri cursed. *Fuck.* I stop everything and turn to face her fully.

"You alright?" She's bent down, those little shorts creeping up as she grips her toe and hisses.

"Fine," she mutters, her expression scrunched and then she reaches up, grabbing my hand in hers. That right there. There's a shift, an immediate change.

It feels like breaking down though and I'm quick to turn back and head to the car. Focused on keeping my shit together.

I can't speak, I'm barely conscious of opening the car door for her. But I'm all too aware when I squeeze her hand and she squeezes back before letting go.

After I close the passenger door, I nearly stop before heading around to the driver's side. Just so I can deal with this shit before getting in. Just a moment.

I just need one fucking moment but it never comes.

Pushing through it all, I get into the driver's seat, turn the ignition of the Chevy and drive off. As the car is pulling away, I peek up into the rearview to see my father walking out onto the porch. Arms crossed and a beer bottle dangling from one hand.

I hate it here.

I hate him sometimes too.

"You okay?" Bri asks, her small hand landing on my thigh as I turn down the gravel road, my family home from view.

Words tumble at the back of my throat, all the thoughts that have been weighing me down compete to be heard. I don't know what to say. That's the God's honest truth. But I settle on one thing as I flick on the AC to high.

"I just want to leave sometimes." It's far too simple. But at least it's true.

"Where do you want to go?" The innocence and surprise isn't hiding in her question.

"I don't know." Truth is, I've never even let myself think of where. Because the moment I think of leaving, I know I can't. I barely passed high school.

I put all my savings into the garage to start my own mechanic shop … and I can't leave my mom.

"I don't know, but right now I just need some space I think," I tell Bri honestly as I drive down the long road to get to town.

I could go to Robert's. I could stay there. He'd let me just like I've let him for years.

"Please don't say that," Bri whispers.

I have to take my eyes from the road to look at her. It's a quick glance but then I take another. I love Bri, I've always loved her, but she keeps at it with needing more from me that I can give her.

Hell, I have nothing. No way to come see her across the damn country and that's all she wants from me.

"I don't know what you want from me," I tell her. The last she text me, she gave me an ultimatum. Come up to see her or we're over. I almost tell her, as far as I knew we were done, but that vulnerable look keeps the thought locked in the back of my throat.

"I want you to come with me," she murmurs. Her hand shifts on my thigh and I think she's going to take it away, but she doesn't. She turns in her seat to face me, the leather of it groaning.

"Just come up north with me."

"And how am I supposed to do that? Really Bri? I don't even know if we're together anymore." I can't help it as my hand twists on the steering wheel. It just flies out of my mouth. "You change your mind every five fucking minutes."

"Don't cuss at me," she scolds and takes her hand back to cross her arms. Just like my father just did.

"Don't—" I start but bite my tongue. I'm frustrated and worked up. I know better.

"I'm sorry," I apologize and she doesn't react other than to soften slightly in her seat.

I glance up and see the sign for main street but I drive passed it. I don't even know where we're going.

"I'm sorry too," she tells me after a moment. And her hand comes back, I'm quick to grab it and steer with my left.

"I need you right now," I don't know where it came from, but I'm guessing something in me had to tell her that truth too.

"I'm here. I'm right here."

CHAPTER 3

Brianna

MY PARENTS WENT TO THE MOVIES. I KNOW THEY'RE DOING a grocery run when they're done that. The back door to the patio slides open easily as Asher and I sneak in. The thought hits me for a moment that it's crazy of us to *'sneak in'* at all. We're nineteen and there's no reason at all to not go right up to the front door and waltz in… except that this town likes to gossip. They make a big deal out of everything.

Whether or not Asher and I are going to last is a topic of conversation in the hair salon according to my grandmother. With the floor creaking as the back door closes softly, all I can think is, it's none of their damn business.

Asher's hand, hardened from years of working in the garage with his father, slips into mine. The lock clicks up into place at the same time that I peer up at him.

We've been together for years and I've never seen him look at me like this. With a hurt that can't be covered up by an asymmetric grin or a half-hearted, dry humored joke. The dark circles under his hazel eyes tell the story of him not sleeping well. We're only just learning what life and being adults really is, and it's so very apparent that it's taken a toll on Asher and I have no idea why.

Turning fully to face him, I ask again, "Can you tell me what happened?"

Instantly his gaze is ripped from mine and he tries to pull his hand away, angling his body towards the kitchen.

"Let's go upstairs," I'm quick to push the words out and grip his hand tighter, adding my second hand as well and giving him a gentle pull. "We can just lay down and if you don't want to talk, that's fine."

"Just lay down," he repeats my words with a hint of humor and a smile that doesn't reach his eyes. "Since when do we just lay down?" he jokes.

It awards him a playful smack to his chest and in return I get a rough chuckle and he squeezes my hand back. There's a shift, something more natural and more 'us' that happens with the small moment.

I cling to it and to him as we climb the stairs. Taking them slowly. Every step he gets closer, to the point that when we're at my bedroom door, his arm wraps around my waist like it's supposed to. Leaning back, I fall into him slightly, until the door is opened and I make my way to the bedroom, kicking off my flip flops.

"Hasn't changed a bit," Asher comments. He's right. I've had the same off white furniture since high school. The poster of the boy bands I love are still hung up, the stacks of fantasy novels haven't budged except the top one, my comfort read, and the matching off white desk is still cluttered.

"Mom said they might paint it and if they do she's going to rearrange somethings for me," I tell him easily.

"Your parents love you," Asher slips his hands into his jeans and looks around as if he hasn't been in this very room a thousand times before.

"Come on," I urge him. The bed groans as I climb in and crawl to the side pressed against the wall. It's not a large room, my older sister got the biggest room apart from my parent's.

"I don't know that it's the best idea, Bri," Asher confesses with a shrug and a spike of fear races through me.

Sitting up, I stare him down. "Just come lay with me," I request and when he hesitates, shifting his weight, I add, "please. Please just come lay down."

I nearly add that we don't have to talk but he asks me, "Do you even want to be with me or do you just feel sorry for me right now?"

Emotions swell in my throat. "How could you think that?"

"Don't be mad… for all I know you were coming over to formerly break up with me."

"Firstly, I'm not mad and secondly—"

"You didn't answer me Bri."

Tears prick my eyes as my voice raises. "Answer what? Do I want to be with you?" I've never felt regret like I do now. "It's been hard not seeing you," my bottom lip wavers and I strengthen my voice, "but all I want every day is to see you. To be with you. To have you more in my life. Of course I love you and I want to be with you." Every sentence his expression softens. The resistance is all but gone when I'm finished. "Come here," I pat the bed and take in a deep steadying breath. "Please, just come here and lay down with me because I miss you and I love you and all I want is to make us right again."

"Can you stop giving me ultimatums?" he asks me and my head feels light and dizzy. "I know I don't come to see you like I promised I would but I need you to be with me if we're together. Really be with me and not sending texts at three am that if I don't do x y or z we're done."

"I'm sorry," both hands raise and all the reasons I've been upset with him this last year races to the forefront of my mind but I push them away. Summer break is almost here and then I'll be home and we can figure those things out. "I won't," I promise him. Right now I just need him to be okay and for us to be okay … and then everything will be okay, won't it?

Asher swallows thickly and that hurt from downstairs comes back. "You sure you still love me?" he asks and for a moment it looks like his eyes glass over but then that emotion vanishes.

"I love you, I'm in love with you and every way you can say it." I confess and ball up the floral navy comforter in my hand. "You?"

"I might be a little bit in love with you," he answers with a smirk and a grin spreads across my face as I grab the closest pillow and chuck it at him.

That's how he told me he loved me for the first time behind the bleachers at gym. *I might be a little bit in love with you.* The pillow thuds as he catches it and a small genuine laugh is rough and masculine as he smiles back at me. Before I can press him for more of a reassurance he says, "I'll always love you Bri. Even when you're mad at me and overthinking everything, I love you."

CHAPTER 4

Asher

FIRST I PULL THE SHIRT OVER MY SHOULDERS AND DROP IT TO the floor, then I pull the covers back. I keep them up so Bri can get it inside me. I know every little movement she'll make as she slips in. How her shoulders do a shimmy when she nestles down beside me and the contented little sigh that slips from her sweet lips as she rests her head on my shoulder and I lay my arm over the covers and over the curve of her hip when she's settled.

We've done this a hundred times before, and I'd take this every day for the rest of my life if I could. I love the moment when she's right here and everything is safe and still. There's not a worry in the world. Just me and her.

"Are you trying to sleep?" she questions and my heavy eyes open as I tile my head to peer down at her. The comfort rustles as she lets the tips of her fingers skim over the rough stubble lining my jaw.

"I'm exhausted but no," I joke and tighten my grip on her. I worked all morning to finish the jobs that were due to be done by my father last night. "I only slept a few hours last night," I tell he and leave it at that. My father was screaming at me for taking over his job—I can't have peace in that house. Not if there's beer in it and my father's reddened face and clenched fist. There's never any peace anymore.

She's quiet a moment, before she says hesitantly, "Was it because of my text?"

My throat tightens, I don't even want to think about her texting me that I needed to be a better boyfriend. I can't. I'm barely hanging on as it is.

"I promise you I'll do the best I can, Bri. You know that right?"

"I know." Her head falls to my shoulder and I know there's something she wants to ask. It's from the way her lips stay parted and how she glances up at me before down to my chest where her fingers play in the bit of hair there. I almost tell her I bought a ring. I almost ask her to marry me right here and now, but I don't have it on me and I don't want to propose like this. All I want to do is give her the security she's begging me for and I may not be able to fly out to see her every weekend, but I show her she's mine. I can show her I'm serious.

"You smell like you just got out of the shower," she changes the subject and I let out a huff of a laugh. "I love the way you smell," she murmurs and then kisses me on my throat. My cock stirs slightly from how tender and soft her touch is.

"Bri baby, don't…" I warn her.

"I'm not doing anything," she teases under the covers.

"I know that hip roll"

"Which one?" her tone is tempting. "This one?" she mocks and a grin forms on my face before both of us laugh. She's just playing around and I pull her in closer, kissing her temple before she settles back down.

Everything about her is warmth and comfort. Before I can stop myself I tell her, "I missed you."

She doesn't hesitate and doesn't hide the agony of longing in her voice, "I miss you every day Asher. Every single day you're not with me, I miss you."

She's quick to kiss me again and this time it's on the lips. It's short and isn't meant to tease me but she does.

I kiss her back if for no other reason than to soothe that bit of pain. But one kiss turns into another. Testing and tempting, her soft body never leaving mine. I'm cock's hard in an instant and when she kisses me again, I deepen it. Slipping my tongue along the seam of her lips until she parts them for me. The moment my tongue strokes against hers, she moans into my mouth, her thigh slipping around mine until she's straddling me under the covers, her forearms resting on either side of my head.

When I break the kiss, I look up at my gorgeous girlfriend. Her sun kissed skin and the kindness in her green eyes. "I thought you said don't?" she questions teasingly.

With an asymmetric grin, I wrap my arm around her waist and flip her under me in a swift motion. A squeal leaves her as she grips onto my shoulders in surprise. The moment her back lands and she's under me, that smile hits her face.

The genuine one that I wish I could see every day. That thought forces me to take her lips back, mid laugh of hers and kiss her with everything I have. She moans again, this tortured sound of need that I fucking love.

Her legs are spread for me, her heels digging into my ass. As I rock myself against her, she writhes against me.

"Too many clothes," I scold her playfully as I pull back. The heat around us more than working us up. I work her shorts off first, letting my fingers glide down her skin as I do. A beautiful blush hits her cheeks when I move my hand between her thighs, the thin lace that'll go next separating my palm from her pussy.

"Already wet for me?"

Her gaze rips from mine as her cheeks redden even further. Leaning up, I nip her neck and her entire body tenses with a wanton gasp. "Answer me baby," I command.

"Yes." She whispers.

"Yes, what?" I look into her eyes and she stares back. There's a skip in my chest, one beat and then another that's harder and more needy. Like she can control the beat of my heart.

"I'm ready for you."

Knowing what this woman does to me makes me pause as I realize I can never lose her.

"Take your hair down," I tell her and she obeys. Then I help her with her own shirt and flick the snap of her bra undone. The moment her breasts are exposed, I tease her nipple, suckle it into my mouth. My tongue flicks against them as they peak and harden.

I take my time toying with her, but my girl is needy and so damn ready. She pushes against my jeans with her feet, as if they could be enough to rid me of them.

"Too many clothes," she mocks me with a lust filled gaze as her chest rises and falls more heavily than before.

It's tense between us, the pull not letting me take my eyes off hers as I kick off my pants. I stroke myself once, a bead of precum already at the head of my dick. Slipping myself between her slick folds, I tease her clit as I kiss her.

The way she gasps with my lips right there is everything. It's all I want and need.

"Bri," I whisper her name as I line myself up.

Her questing look meets mine. "I love you."

With both of her hands splaying in my hair, she tells me she loves me and kisses me with every ounce of sincerity there is in this whole damn world.

Her lips press and mold to mine and I slam into her in one swift stroke, filling her and forcing her head to fall back from the sudden sensation.

She's tight as all hell. So I give her a moment to adjust. A mewl leaves her and I rock against her, not moving just yet and kissing down her neck. It doesn't take long for her body to remember mine and I pull out then thrust back inside of her in an easy rythym, then harder and faster.

A cold sweat lines my skin as her nails gently scrape along my back. As I fuck her deeper and her small cries of pleasure fill the room, she tightens and spasms on my cock. Coming undone so easily for me.

I ride through her pleasure, kissing along her jaw and she clings to me. It's only when my thumb finds her clit again, that her piercing eyes find mine and she moans my name.

"Asher," my name on her lips is wrapped in desperate need for love.

And fuck do I love her. We nearly say it at the same time and I take her again and again, not wanting this to end.

I've learned my lesson before, so before I go down the hall to get what I need to clean her up, I slip my jeans on. She's still as can be on her bed, trying to keep the evidence of what we've done from getting onto the sheets.

I can't help but smirk as I stare down at her with that just fucked look. Her hair is a messy halo and her chest is still flushed.

Once all is taken care of, I get back under the covers to cuddle with her again, and it's not long before reality sets in.

"When are your parents going to be home?"

"You thinking of going back to the hangar?" she answers me with a question of her own.

"I don't know," I answer honestly. I don't want to go back home at all "I know I don't want to be naked and in your bedroom when they do come home though."

"We could go downstairs and turn something on … would that—"

"I'd love that," I cut her off. We have time to go from cuddling on the sofa to sitting up right when her parents come home. We've done it a thousand times before.

As I gather her clothes for her, I can't stop thinking about what's going to happen when I do go back home. They'll both probably pretend it didn't happen. They won't talk about it and if they do, it'll be a promise that it won't happen again.

My expression my show my thoughts, because Bri looks back at me with nothing but concern. I'm far too late to hide it from her.

"Asher?" she questions and I just kiss her. A quick peck as I hand her the bundle of clothes for her to put back on. That doesn't satisfy her though.

"Are we going to be okay?" She's the only thing in my life that is okay in this moment. I can't lose her. I love her too fucking much and I need her more than she could ever know.

"Of course we are. I love you and you love me. That's all that really matters."

"You promise?"

"I promise you, Bri; I'm going to love you forever."

Craving more of Bri and Asher's story? There's far more to it than this sexy little short. Have a look at *A Little Bit Dirty…*

I've got a thing for men who work with their hands.

I thought I learned my lesson years ago. But here I am, back in the small town I grew up in, staring down the man who broke my heart years ago.

I intended to tell him off.

My plan was to flip him the bird and prove to both of us that he hadn't ruined me.

I sure as hell wasn't going to sleep with him.

Until he tells me he's sorry.

Until he gives me that smoldering look I still dream about.

Until he whispers just beneath the shell of my ear… His breath trails down my neck and he leaves an opened mouth kiss right there, in that sensitive spot.

"You have no idea how much I've missed you."

My treacherous heart wants more. More of him. More of us. But there's a reason it didn't work before and when you don't learn from your past mistakes, you're bound to repeat them.

ALL I
WANT IS A
KISS

CHAPTER 1

THE BUTTERFLIES IN MY STOMACH JUST WON'T QUIT IT. I'VE searched the lobby with baited breath, but he's not here. Nick's all I could think about the entire flight. I was so convinced I'd step in through those double glass doors behind me and see him standing right in front of me, not this thin crowd of people I don't recognize.

The entire flight I pictured him at the end of the mahogany bar, seated on the leather stool with his gray tailored suit. He knows the one I like; it brings out his steely eyes. They're such a pale blue, I swear sometimes they're silver. At least they look that way under the dimmed bar lights late at night in this very hotel.

I imagined coming up beside him at the bar, and casually ordering a drink, pretending not to recognize him. As if I wouldn't know his cologne, his confident, dominating demeanor, that rough stubbled jaw in a heartbeat. I swear my body can recognize his in a crowd a mile away. I'm simply drawn to him. I even changed into this red dress that clings to my curves at the airport and touched up my makeup, just for that moment. Last time I saw him, he told me I look gorgeous in red. Pouty red lips. Check. Sultry red dress. Check check. Man I've been dreaming about for days? Nowhere in sight.

Sighing, I roll out my shoulder, letting my luggage bag fall to the crook of my arm for only a moment. It gives me enough time to take in the place without thoughts of *him* making me an anxious, excited mess.

The gust of cold from behind me urges me forward, away from the front entrance and back to reality.

It's bitter cold in the Pennsylvania mountains and I happen to despise the cold. We aren't friends. No way, no how. But the fireplaces in the ski lodge resort this hotel is based in, made of large stones and surrounded by plush leather couches? We may as well be old lovers.

"There you are!" Over the din of chatter from the crowded bar across the lobby. I recognize Autumn's voice instantly.

"Hey, hey love," I greet her with a peppy voice and a tight hug when we meet halfway. Her embrace is only half assed, but she's got a good reason. Standing two inches shorter than me with big brown eyes and a brunette bob, Autumn has a wine glass in each of her hands. Red for her, and white for me. The red in her glass matches her soft chenille sweater perfectly too. As if she did it on purpose.

"I freaking love you," I say gratefully, tossing down the weekender duffle and graciously accepting the glass. If I can't have him, my heart flips in protest at the thought, at least I can have a little wine to take the edge off.

"I'm telling you," my friend of over a decade is always "telling me" something. She's also typically right. Maybe always right, I'm not sure, I don't have the mental energy to keep track. She's the creative one, I'm the workaholic. Together we kick ass. "It's so much better when you come a day early."

"I seriously wish I could, but—"

"Work," she finishes the sentence for me and rolls her eyes when she does. "I know," she comments before sipping her red wine. Her bottom lip is already slightly stained, but it only adds to her charm.

"You would think with the way you said 'work' that you don't know we're actually here for work." With my glass in my left hand and my luggage in my right, I make my way to the elevators.

"A conference is different and you know it." Autumn follows behind me, offering to take my glass. With a smirk I tell her she'll have to kill me to get it from me. It's chilled and delicious and exactly what I need after a long flight. I thought I would be here hours ago, but the flight was delayed, and here I am arriving at eleven at night with tired, dry eyes. A glass of wine is exactly what I need.

"Fine, give me your bag," she insists, downing the rest of her red. I want to ask her if she's seen Nick, but I don't. I keep my lips sealed tight, grateful that she's at least here to greet me. Besides, I know she knows I'm looking for him. I always am at these events. If she saw him, she'd tell me. The simper on my face wavers slightly, but only slightly.

A lobby attendant passes by and collects the now empty wine glass from her just as the door to the spacious elevator opens. "Thank you," she offers the uniformed gentleman. Maybe it's the uniform, or maybe I'm just really in need, but the guy is *hot*. Like he came out of a People's sexiest men alive list, *hot*. His smile is charming, a little too wide and Autumn actually blushes before pushing me into the elevator.

"You aren't kidding," I tell her as the doors close and I take another sip, "I really should have gotten in last night." The smile that creeps onto my face is fitting for the Cheshire cat.

Autumn only laughs. She's all sorts of good bundled into a beautiful little package. "Oh fuck off," she jokes back. "I wish I had the balls for a one-night stand."

There's a little blip in my chest, and heat rolls down my shoulders, yet it gives my arms chills at the thought. I was hoping for a one night stand with a man I've had plenty of those with. Disappointment lingers, he knows I'm here for the conference and every time I come to the East Coast, we meet up. Every single time. One to two times a month for nearly two years now. He's not my boyfriend; and I don't want him to be. We want different things in life and we live on opposite sides of the country. There's an unspoken commitment though. I'm the only one he sees, and he's the only one I see. It's casual and low maintenance. But why does it feel so crushing that I haven't heard from him yet?

I text him yesterday and he said he'd be here.

He's just not here yet. That's what it is. I try to convince myself and then resort to sticking my nose into Autumn's business to take my mind off of it.

"I mean…," I tease her, "we are staying for an entire weekend. And since you came a day early, it could be a four-day-stand."

I can tell she must be at least half a bottle in by how loud she laughs and it only makes me want to catch up as we make our way to the room. I have an order to things though, before I can have more than this one glass. I don't just drop off my luggage in the room like Autumn does, I unpack everything. I put it in its place. I get bottles of water and my ear plugs and put them on the night stand too. I'm just a little OCD like that. It helps me feel settled.

"This one's for you," she hands over a keycard without acknowledging my comment, simply shaking her head in feigned dismay.

This is the same lodge as last year and it doesn't escape my knowledge when we get off the elevator that this is the same floor Nick was on last year. I spent an extra two days with him last time, lost in the sheets and taking off from work for the first time in months just to prolong saying goodbye.

I have to blow a stray piece of blonde out of my face and focus. This trip is not about him, no matter how much my libido may disagree.

Autumn's already plopped herself onto a bed. She knows the drill.

At first, when we started going to all of these events so frequently, she would stare at me like I was an alien with two heads whenever we bunked for a conference, but now, she lays back on her bed, kicks her feet up and gives me the itinerary while I do my thing. All the while, her bag lays on the floor, unzipped and spilling out everything she packed. Except her dresses, which are always hung up in the closet. She gets the right side, which she barely uses, and I get the left.

"I'm glad you're finally here. I was thinking I wasn't going to make it and by the time you got here I'd be dead asleep."

"I should have just gotten on the flight with you."

"Yes," she says pointedly as I unzip my bag. "Yes you should have." The way she says it makes me laugh. She is *always right* after all and her tone doesn't hide that fact.

"Hey," I finally get the courage to ask her although I turn my back to her, busying myself with my clothes, "did you happen to hear from Nick?"

"Mmm. Not yet." She answers and I let the frown stay in place as I put everything away. "Am I already boring you?" she asks with humor dripping on every word.

I turn to look over my shoulder, folding a pair of jeans to slip in the dresser drawer, "You know I love you."

We may be completely opposite in a lot of ways, but we're also a perfect match. Autumn and I started this marketing meet up company together and when we did I questioned if we really should. I didn't want to risk a decade long friendship over business. I'm so glad we took the risk though. Three years later and we're closer than ever and the business practically runs itself. We connect businesses with the firms they need to take their companies to the next level. I evaluate them, every nook and cranny and data point they have to offer to identify what they're lacking and how they can improve. Autumn does the socializing and connecting and most importantly, updating our clients and keeping them on track.

"So it kicks off tomorrow with a key note speech at noon, lunch served during. Then we have a workshop with the promotional team."

"You sound bored as all hell," I call out as I make my way to the bathroom to put my toiletries in their place. We've been through these conferences a dozen times this winter already. All the clients are new, but the talks are the same. So "bored" is a word that's rather accurate to describe how we'd feel if we had to sit in on the talks. This is the last one before the holidays then we have a decent break. I'm looking forward to PJs and downtime.

Autumn gets stuck attending the workshops this time around. Luckily, I'll be meeting with every client one on one, face to face, making sure we're on the same page and they're comfortable with the conclusion we've come to. Change can be unwanted, and even scary at times. But, like I tell each and every one of them, change is necessary. If you want to be at a level you've never been to before, you need to do something you've never done before.

"I don't come here for the lectures." Autumn stretches on the bed and adds with a yawn, "You don't either."

"Let me guess, is it for the lobby attendees and booze?"

She belts out a laugh and corrects me, "Again, I freaking wish." I'm still busy unpacking when she comments, "Speaking of getting some—"

"You're getting some?" Both of us have been single for nearly two years. My reason is easy; I'm only interested in what I have with Nick at the moment. I don't see a reason to stop or to want more. Although that's not something I shout from the rooftops.

Instead, I stick with something simple for an excuse as to why there's no ring on my finger: I'm a workaholic and my expectations are unreasonable. At least that's what my therapist said. And by therapist, I mean a bottle of Cabernet and a slurring best friend by the name of Autumn.

Even though she's well aware of the truth, after all, Nick is her brother. She's known since day one, a few months into working together, and she doesn't judge. One more reason I love her.

She finally answers my question regarding whether or not she's getting laid. "Unfortunately no, not since the Rivera Maya."

My brow lifts at the memory of sunshine and mojitos on the white-sandy beaches. "That was a good trip." Another trip I met up with Nick on. *Damn, I can't get him off my mind.*

"Mmm hmmm," Autumn hums and reaches into the mini bar, grabbing a bottle of water for herself before sitting cross legged on the end of the bed.

"I have no idea why you don't snag someone and settle down," I comment after plugging in my charger and then fishing out my phone from my bag to plug in while we're up here. I already have a dozen emails and four messages waiting for me. And wait they will continue to do. After the flight I had today, everything can wait until tomorrow morning. The conference doesn't start until noon and regardless of how late we stay out tonight; I'll be up at six. It's something about these events, maybe the excitement or the social interaction… whatever it is, I can never sleep. It doesn't matter how comfy the mattress is or how plush the pure white comforters are. Unless Nick happens to wear me out in bed. My thighs involuntarily clench at the thought. I check the messages just to be sure. None are from Nick and my heart drops a little.

Autumn holds up her finger, closing her eyes for a moment of silence so she can yawn again and oblige, and then dig into the bottom of my now nearly empty bag for the foldable steamer and set it on the floor of the closet, next to a set of sexy black heels, although they're simple the heels are so thin, they reek of sex appeal.

I make sure my heels are hot, my lingerie a class-A knockout and my dress, professional and nothing less. Simple and natural makeup, but a bold red lip. I love confidence and I wear it subtly, but to pack a punch. It may seem like an oxymoron, but it works for me. It keeps me lifted and motivated. So long as I have sexy panties and a pedicure, I'm convinced I can conquer the world.

It takes me a minute of digging at the bottom of my nearly empty bag for the extra charger for my laptop before I realize Autumn isn't talking anymore. Lifting my gaze, I see her fiddling on her phone.

"Hey, I thought you said something about 'getting some'?" I remind her.

She smiles brightly at me even though sleep is written all over her expression, holding up her phone and says simply, "Your star crossed lover is here."

CHAPTER 2

THE BAR IS SLIGHTLY DARKER THAN EVERYWHERE ELSE ON THE main level of the hotel. The lights are softer. So dim that the lit glass shelves lined with glass bottles behind the bar are really the main attraction. Although it's a Friday night, it's nearly midnight and most of the guests on this level are gathered around a stone fireplace, leaving the bar stools vacant and perfect for a private conversation. There's only a single couple seated at the bar and then there's me and my red dress.

My heart's been racing ever since I left Autumn in our hotel room to come down here. I don't remember being this eager before. I don't remember missing him as much as I am right now. "What'll it be?" the bartender asks me. Resting her palms on the bar, she leans forward to tell me when I purse my lips in indecision, "The cosmos here are pretty stellar." Her perfectly pluck brow raises as if to ask, *want one?*

"I'll have one of those then," I answer with a smile that's relatively genuine. All the nerves have me on edge. With a pat on the bar and a "coming right up," the bartender turns her back to me to make a pretty concoction of liquor in a tall skinny glass. I can't help it even though I'm irritated with my own impatience; I peek at the clock on the wall at the far end. It's only been ten minutes of waiting. It's still ten minutes too long for my taste.

With a tap on my phone, I bring up the text messages. *Meet you at the bar.* He texted it nearly fifteen minutes ago. Not even a half minute after Autumn telling me her brother was here, he texted me. And that's all he said: *Meet you at the bar.*

He gave the command and I obliged.

I don't remember being this needy ever before. But then again, I can't remember ever waiting on him. This time feels different. And I don't like it.

"Here you are," the bartender's voice is soft like the smile on her lips. Thanking her and then taking a sip, I pretend like I don't want to text him. I've never been *that* girl. Clingy, and left wanting. I've been busy all my life and for the last few years, Nicholas has been right there every step of the way, never making me feel like things weren't enough.

I just want him here. The second he's here, I know everything will be alright and this weird anxiousness will be gone.

"Did you wear red for me?" The seductive cadence and deep voice behind me eases everything in me in an instant. From my head to my toes, including those butterflies in the pit of my stomach. I don't have time to turn around, his strong arms wrap around my front, his shoulders cradling me as Nick kisses my neck. Right there, in that spot just beneath my ear that's so sensitive. His rough stubble tickles my neck as he leaves me. It leaves me hot and bothered, but so relaxed. So very at home. That's how it feels with him. He feels like home even though I never see him there. It's always hotels. Still, that doesn't change how I feel.

I reach up and behind me, my fingers trailing along his short hair until he brings his lips to meet mine. Pressing them lightly at first, until my lips mold to his. I part mine for him, and he nips slightly before deepening the kiss.

Even when he kisses me, the smile doesn't leave. It never falters. The electric tingle races through me, from head to toe. Until he breaks the kisses, leaving me breathless and trailing the tip of his nose against mine.

"So did you?" he asks, taking the seat next to me and I'm in such a haze, I don't remember why he's waiting for an answer. His handsome smirk widens into a grin when he sees the effect he has on me. "Wear the red dress for me?"

"Oh," the blush rises to my cheeks before I answer, "You know I did." I haven't an ounce of game in me. That's what Autumn says and she's right. I don't care to either. I'm not here for games.

"I love it," he comments and before I can let my smitten comeback get the better of me, the bartender's back.

"Hello, there. What'll it be?" she asks Nicholas and takes a glance at my glass, still nearly full as Nick looks at what's on tap.

He's going to get the lager. I know it. He knows it. But he takes his time, looking at each one before telling her, "A lager please."

"Short or…"

"Tall," he's quick to answer.

"Tough day?" I tease him as he slips off his jacket and gets comfortable, adjusting on the stool.

"Long," he answers and slips his hand over mine. The tips of his fingers toy with mine. "It's got a good ending though." He smirks, before lifting my hand to his lips, kissing my knuckles one at a time.

"Hasn't anyone told you, flattery will get you everywhere," I joke and he laughs. A deep rough sound that I love.

"Maybe once or twice," he answers and thanks the bartender as she places his beer in front of him.

He doesn't waste any time, taking a long swig although his left hand stays over mine. He doesn't look at me after and suddenly the air feels different again. That instinctive flip in my stomach goes off and I pull my hand away to readjust in my seat.

"You doing okay?" I ask him. My nerves get the better of me. I always trust my gut, I have all my life and it's never steered me wrong. If things feel off, it's because they are off.

He hesitates before letting out a small huff that's a humorless laugh and running his hand up the back of his neck.

"I might be moving soon," he tells me and wraps both of his hands around his beer.

Flip, skitter, halt. That's what my heart does.

"Oh yeah," I suck at keeping the nerves out of my voice. "Where to?" I ask him because it's the polite thing to do. It's the obvious question. Even though nerves dance along my heated skin.

"Out of state, the company is still nailing down the details," he answers me and I watch the cords in his neck tighten as he swallows.

"Oh, when will you know?" Anticipation and slight relief are there, but still, this is a serious conversation. And we don't have those. Not about us. If ever one of us needs something, we're there for each other, but those moments are few and far between. I don't recall a single conversation we've ever had about "us." Although I'm completely aware, that's exactly what this is.

"This week."

"Really?" My brow shoots up my face and I can't stop it. It gets a huff of laughter from Nick, who nods his head and takes another gulp of his beer. "Really," he answers. "What do you think about that?"

"About you no longer being available for our get togethers on a whim?" I clarify, merely to take up time so I can find the right answer.

"Yeah," his voice is low, coaxing. "Will you miss me?"

There's a pitter patter in my chest that lights up every nerve ending in me. "Of course I will," I answer honestly.

"Yeah," he agrees, "I don't know for sure yet." The thick air around us dissipates into a casualness that's familiar.

"Company decision?" I question and he nods.

"Yeah, something like that," he teases and absently runs his thumb along the dew of his beer glass.

"It's weighing on you?" I question, noting how he seems lost in the conflict of whether or not to move.

"It's a big decision," he says but the way he says it sounds as if it's not so unordinary.

"So if you moved… we wouldn't be able to meet up in hotels anymore. And have our dirty little secret rendezvous."

"Is that what this is? I'm your dirty little secret?" he toys with me and I gently smack his arm and then return to nursing my drink.

"Seriously though, is that why this feels different?" I almost ask, why it feels like all of this is a long goodbye, but I don't.

"Things just… they might change a little and I wasn't sure what you'd think about it," he tells me and a nervousness settles in my gut. Change. Sometimes when I use that word, my clients get this wide-eyed, defensive look. I can feel it coming over me.

"We don't need to talk about it," I'm quick to shut it down. "All I want tonight is a kiss. Is that too much for a girl to ask?" I don't want to talk about this right now. There are too many unknowns and what ifs and I am not ready to say goodbye when he's just sat down. I know that's where this is headed and I'm not ready. I'm not willing to agree to goodbye. Or to going back to being friends. That's exactly what this feels like.

"Mmm," Nick hums and then leans close to me, kissing me and silencing my inward complaints. The kiss isn't deep, but it's soothing and when he breaks it, I keep my eyes closed for just a moment longer, wanting to make sure I remember it forever.

I whisper with my eyes still closed, "God, I missed you."

CHAPTER 3

Nicholas

Her long blonde hair is a messy halo from her running her fingers through her locks. It only adds to the sex kitten look she has going on. I love that she did it for me, even more that she's not ashamed to admit it out loud.

If only I wasn't afraid of losing this, these moments of inhibition with this captivating woman, I'd tell her right now what's happening. I'd tell her everything's changed and lay it out for her to accept or to walk away.

"Your room?" she asks, her eyes half lidded as she bites down into her bottom lip.

"Damn right," I answer her beneath my breath, leaving cash on the bar and then helping her off her stool. Her small hand slips into mine and I lead her towards the elevators, listening to click of her heels and loving how she holds on to our clasped hands with her other, her shoulder brushing against mine as we walk, as if she needs to touch me, needs to have her body close to mine.

I get it. I more than get it. I love it. Which is why I'm not ready for change, but something had to give. I live for these moments with her, after tonight, it'll never be the same again.

"You smell like man," Olivia hums when the elevator dings and the doors slide open.

"Is that right?" I question, hitting the button for my floor and waiting for the doors to close as my cock hardens to an unbearable degree.

There's a hair of an opening, before they shut completely, and I lift her hands above her head, gripping her wrists and pushing her small body against the elevator wall with mine. It's quick, it's instinctual. A simmering want and desire rushes through me, when she gasps and I catch it, sealing my mouth over hers with a kiss.

"Nick," she moans in my mouth and I love it. She rocks her body against my length and my response is a deep groan of need that vibrates through my chest.

Nipping her bottom lip, I release her the second I feel the elevator slow. I only have a moment to adjust my cock in my pants and stare down at her breathless, sagging against the wall.

"Two more minutes," I tell her, hoping to ease the ache so obvious on her face. With my hand out, she takes it, righting herself and the doors open. No one's here to watch us, no one in the hall, but still, we're professional. Her clients could be on this floor after all, and she prefers discretion, apart from a kiss here and there.

I can't count the number of times I've slipped a key card into the door with Olivia behind me, caressing my arm and waiting patiently for the soft beep and gentle click of the door being opened. It's a heady rush each and every time. The anticipation, the desire that flows freely between us. From the first time, a drunken night with a goodnight kiss turned into more, to two weeks ago, it only gets better with Olivia.

She leaves me wanting more.

Pushing the door open, I motion for her to enter first, and whether she's tipsy from the wine or drunk on lust, Olivia slides past me, making sure her curves brush against me as she does.

Her hips sway and the simmer in my blood only gets hotter.

The door closes with a resounding click and I don't have to command her, she turns at the foot of the bed, facing me as she unzips her dress and lets it fall from the curve of her shoulders down to a puddle of fine fabric at her feet. She makes a move to take her heels off next and I stop her.

"No," I order, "keep them on tonight." My voice is deep and I let her hear every ounce of need I have for her. Her lips part just slightly, her breasts rising with the quick inhale in the quiet room, and I swear my cock leaks precum at the sight of her, turned on by the simple fact that I'll fuck her tonight in those sex kitten heels.

I could imagine her lying on the bed behind her, her legs in the air as I pound into her, then the slim heels dragging down my back as she screams my name. I could, but I don't, because her hazel eyes entrance me, reflecting the same concoction of need and want in the moonlit room. The thick curtains are open, but the sheer ones are closed, giving a breathtaking view.

The mountain range behind her, the bright moon that filters into the room against the plush white comforter. And in front of it all, a beautiful woman who wants me as badly as I want her, slowly but surely, unstrapping her bra and letting it fall to the floor.

With her fingers moving to her hips, I motion for her to stop and finally move, closing the distance between us in three long strides. Every step closer, the collar around my neck feels tighter, suffocating me for still being dressed.

She tilts her head for me to kiss her, but I don't. Her eyes are closed and it takes a moment before she opens them, staring up at me as I tower over her naked form, all but heels and thin satin panties. "Hands at your sides," I tell her and she listens. She loves the submission as much as I love the domination. She knows it all now, every command, every wish I have. "Fucking perfect," I mutter beneath my breath, letting her see my gaze roam down her body.

Trailing my thumb down her bottom lip, I let it fall to her collarbone, then lower, teasing her breasts one at a time. It's the only touch I give her for now. Her soft moan fills the room and her eyes close as her head falls back, lost in pleasure.

I take my time, still fully clothed, dragging my touch down her body to rid her of the red thong. She only touches me when I bend down, her hand on my shoulder, to step out of the underwear.

Tossing it carelessly beside us, I keep my gaze on her, and plant a kiss just beneath her navel, then lower, dragging the tip of my nose down further until I'm right where I want to be, my lips at her clit. I suckle gently and her fingertips brush my shoulders, but she's quick to correct herself.

"Nick," my name is a mix of a pant and a moan on her lips. I taste her, parting her lips and dipping two thick fingers inside her. She's already wet, already whimpering. I stroke her, curling my fingers to be sure to hit the sweet spot at her front wall.

"Please," she begs with true desperation as she sways, without anything to keep her steady but the heels she chose to wear tonight. Her arousal coats my fingers as I stroke more ruthlessly, pulling her pleasure from her. Her smell, her soft sounds and even the heat of her body being so close is addictive. She's a drug and I've been addicted for as long as I can remember.

I can barely take it, crouched down in front of her, hard with my own need and desperate to be inside her. Quickening my movements, I suck on her clit and the instant gasp is followed by her nails digging into my shoulders as she clenches around my fingers and screams out my name.

I withdraw in an instant, all too aware that she's already gone over the edge, finding her orgasm.

Smack! My hand lands hard on her ass in reprimand and she can't even jump, her balance is so disturbed from her pleasure that she falls into me. "Bad girl," I growl at her ear as I lift her by her ass, throwing her onto the bed behind her.

I don't waste the moment undressing. In an instant I'm between her legs, still clothed and nipping her neck. My right hand travels up her body, my left unzips my pants and pulls out my cock. I stroke it once, before slamming into her.

She screams out, her neck arching, her mouth the perfect "o" and I stay just like that, buried to the hilt for only a moment. Just one to let her adjust. That's when I finally kiss her, my tongue delving into her hot mouth and silencing her strangled screams of pleasure as I ravage her.

Pistoning my hips, gripping her own to keep her where I want her. Her heels thud as they hit the floor, one by one, unable to stay on as I fuck her ruthlessly.

She's so tight, so hot and so close to coming again already. Her second release is what pushes me to have mine.

I groan her name in the crook of her neck, feeling the warm air of her moans on my cheek as she cums with me. Pulsing around me as the waves of my own release pulse through me.

Both of us breathless, both of us sated, I slip out slowly watching her wince as I do. She rolls on her side, breathing heavily with her eyes closed.

I pull the covers around her before heading to the bathroom, finally stripping down and gathering a warm washcloth to take care of her.

It's silent until I climb in bed with her, everything taken care of so she can fall asleep. "Sleep well," I tell her, knowing she'll stay with me tonight

She doesn't though and I'm certain I can't either.

This could be our last time together. There's no way I could possibly sleep. Her fingers trail along the grooves in my chest, and when she brings them up higher I lean down to kiss her hand.

She hums in satisfaction, but she still doesn't sleep. I could bore her to sleep, talking about the merger that just went through and how the company is sky rocketing, the stocks booming. She'd listen to it all, with the same expression she gives me now, as if I'm her beloved Prince Charming.

"I don't want to sleep," she finally breaks the silence.

"What do you want for Christmas, Olivia?" I ask her, running my thumb down the curve of her neck and feeling the pull of my lips into a smirk when she shivers.

Naked and tired, Olivia stretches lazily and then sidles up closer to me under the sheets, "More of this," she answers and I have to keep my expression the same, unmoving, so she doesn't see the loss I feel deep inside. Her eyes are closed, but I don't want to risk her seeing.

"Nothing else?" I question, knowing she isn't going to get more of these meet ups. Not for a while at least with all of the changes coming.

Slowly peeking up at me, her hazel eyes a mix of wildfire and calming ocean shores, "Fine, all I want is a kiss." Her voice is soft and her hand on my chest even softer. Leaning down to kiss her, I let the kiss linger, waiting for her to hum in approval. She does and I knew she would. I love that sound. I love how easily she kisses me.

"I hate that I have to leave you tomorrow," she says it so easily, so used to it. She's alright with what we have. She would be fine with this for as long as I let it happen.

"Hopefully I'll see you soon," I answer her and her eyes open, staring at my chest rather than meeting my gaze.

"Do you know when that will be?" she questions.

I hate that I have to answer her the way I do, "No," I tell her.

I bet she thinks she's gotten away with hiding her disappointment, but I see it. "That's alright," she tells me, even though I know she feels that same ache in her chest I do at the thought of not having another night like this planned. She can't say goodbye so easily.

Her pointer traces my collarbone when she whispers what we've told each other every time for years now, "It's never goodbye. Only until next time."

CHAPTER 4

Olivia

"**W**HY DO I CHOOSE THE WALK OF SHAME?" Nick's first response to my groggy morning question is a rough chuckle that jostles the bed. "I can go get your things," he offers, "Or Autumn can bring them?"

I shake my head, brushing my cheek against his firm chest before resting my head back against him, "It's okay, I'll walk it with pride," I answer with a simper and lightheartedness.

The early morning sun is peeking in and I check the clock to find it's nearly eight. Last night filters in as my eyes adjust to morning and the easy rest in Nick's bed changes into the reality that I need to leave it and I may never share one with him again.

"You're really leaving?" I question but I didn't mean to. The disbelief simply slipped out.

He breathes in deep and his chest moves with it, so I remove myself from the cozy spot and sit up, covering myself with the sheets. As I do, the ache between my thighs intensifies. I'll feel him for days.

"Yeah, just one night this time. I have to get somethings settled," Nick doesn't look at me as he talks, instead he reaches for the bottle of water on the nightstand and hands it to me.

"Thanks," I tell him and my smile is weak. I drink down as many gulps as I can, trying to pause the unwanted thoughts filtering through my mind.

"You okay?"

"Huh?" I look up into Nick's steely blues to find them riddled with concern. "Fine," I lie. "I just have to get going."

With the excuse spilled, I gather the sheets, pushing them out of the way and search for my dress and underwear.

"You don't have to go. We can order in breakfast," he offers but there's no hope in his voice.

I was already a drink down last night, but still. How did I go to bed with him one last time, knowing that he was leaving? How did I think I could do it? Stay here with him and say goodbye?

I struggle with my strap and Nick climbs out of bed, still naked and in all his glory to help me.

"Olivia," his voice is gentle. "You don't have to run off," he whispers at my neck and then pulls my back into his chest.

"I'm not running off," I lie. "I just need a shower and to prepare."

I turn around, conscious of the fact that I haven't brushed my teeth. I usually use his toothbrush, but I also typically stay. This morning isn't typical. I can feel that in my bones.

"Never goodbye. Only until next time." He smiles when he says it and that's why I can only nod, not trusting myself to speak. With a wave of my hand, I leave him there, and put on a brave face when I open the door to my shared room with Autumn. I don't want her to know how much I'm breaking right now. Nothing is certain. He may not move. It may not be over. That thought is the only thing that keeps me glued together.

I wish next time was a given. For the first time since we started it, I'm all too aware that it's not a given. No matter how much I want to lie to myself.

The taxi ride is almost forty minutes long and it's excruciating. All I want is my pillow so I can bury my head in it and let all of these unwanted emotions out.

"I miss you already," the second the plane landed, I messaged Nick first. I haven't heard from him since we said goodbye at the resort and again, I find myself not used to the waiting. The lack of an answer from him. I check it again, and a good thirty minutes later, I have nothing. No answer from him.

I have loved every conference we've ever done, but not this one. This one is stained with loss. Undeniable and irrefutable loss. I glance at my phone again, to see no response from Nick. With tears pricking at the back of my eyes, I'm tempted to message Autumn. She's his sister and he's leaving me. Tension works its way into my gut and I shift on the leather backseats of the cab. They protest in response.

Is this really the end of it? It can't be. There's a sinking feeling in my chest and I need to talk to someone about it, but who? Autumn's the only one who knows, and what am I supposed to say to her? *Your brother is ignoring me?* We're grown adults and I knew what this was. I just wasn't prepared for this. We're never ready for goodbyes. At least I'm not. I thought I could avoid it with Nick, I thought I'd never have to say it. Checking my phone again and noting the lack of a message from him, I was apparently wrong. The conclusion I've come to is the worst of them all, because that's what my gut is telling me. *It's over.* He's moving on and that's all there is to it.

I keep thinking, it was too good to last. Wasn't it? It was so easy and natural. Everything always fell into place with Nick… I should have known better than to think it would last or become anything more. Fuck, it hurts. It's not supposed to hurt, when you keep yourself at a distance and make sure the relationship is casual. It's not supposed to hurt when it ends. But I'll be damned if that's not exactly what I'm feeling right now.

I check my phone and again, there's no response.

"Right up here," the taxi driver says absently and before I can answer, the words catch themselves at the back of my throat.

Oh my God, he's here.

My heart does that fluttering thing my stomach was doing only days ago. Sitting on the footsteps to my front porch, his large frame taking up the small threshold. I can't think straight, let alone breathe. He's right here. Waiting for me.

Nick must feel my eyes on him as the taxi slows in front of my townhouse because he looks right up at me. Those steely blues stealing my breath with their intensity.

My heart races, beating wildly at the sight of him.

"Mam?" the cab driver's voice alerts me that I need to pay and get on my way.

"Sorry, sorry," I answer breathlessly, frantically searching for cash so I can get out and go to the man I haven't been able to stop thinking about.

I don't have a chance to get my luggage, Nicholas gets it for me. Carrying it up to my porch steps and waiting there for me.

Anxiousness tingles its way through me and I barely hear the taxi drive off as I stand on the steps, looking up at him and whispering, "What are you doing here?" Praying and hoping he's here for more than a real goodbye.

CHAPTER 5

Nicholas

WHAT AM *I* DOING HERE?

"Right now, I'm trying to gather up the strength to ask you something," I answer her. I can barely swallow, barely breathe. Even though it's winter and the cold is blistering, making the tip of Olivia's nose a rosy red already, I'm burning hot.

"I have to know, do you want me, Olivia? Do you want more?" Her bottom lip falls open and her hazel eyes widen with surprise. I can't bare for her to answer me without telling her everything, without giving this the best shot I can give it.

"Because I want you. I want all of you. I love our stolen nights and I'll do everything I can to keep giving them to you, but I need more." A quick intake and a single step forward, closing the distance between us is all that pauses the confession I've been working over in my head all week. "I want to be with you, really be with you. Every day and always. Not just a secret rendezvous. I want it all. The picket fence, kids, I want it all… with you. And only you."

I don't know if I've said it all and I'm certain I've said most of it wrong. I'm nervous and I'm terrified. Terrified that she doesn't want this. It will destroy me if she says no. She's all I want and all I've wanted since I first laid eyes on her.

She still hasn't said anything, although she takes a hesitant step forward and I use that closeness to take her hands in mine, running soothing circles along her wrists with the rough pad of my thumb.

"Do you want me, Olivia? Because I'll move here, with you or get my own place, so we can be together like we should. If you don't, I understand, but I need to know."

The silence is awful. It rips at me from the inside as I wait for her to say something. Every deep breath she takes I prepare for her to tell me no.

"You asked me what I want for Christmas. At the hotel, you asked me and I lied to you," her voice is soft and riddled with emotion but I can't decipher it. I need an answer.

"I know. A kiss. You said all you wanted was a kiss." I can't bear it if she tells me that now. I'm not ready to say goodbye. I nearly backtrack, I nearly give in and tell her I'll go back to only hotel rooms and discreet rendezvous if that's what she wants.

"I lied. I lied to you," her voice cracks and it echoes the feeling in my heart. "I want so much more than a kiss. All I want for Christmas, is you."

Relief washes over me and it comes with a warmth I'm unfamiliar with. It's better than the heat between us when I first see her across the bar. It feels like home.

"I couldn't tell you because A, it's cheesy and B, I didn't think I could have you."

"Just say the word, and I'll move here. I'm ready to be with you, Olivia, I don't think I can fathom not being able to see you again."

"Same," she breathes the single word.

"That's a yes? You want this? You want me?"

"All of you." She nods, quickly and vigorously. Tears make her hazel eyes glassy. "I want all of you too."

Thank fuck.

I can't describe the relief, immediate and all consuming. With one arm scooping around the small of her back and the other spearing into her hair, I kiss her, the woman I love, with everything I have.

"I love you, Olivia," I tell her for the first time, solidifying what we have. What we've had all this time but neither of us was willing to risk bringing it to life.

"I love you too," she whispers against my lips, in the warm air between us. "You don't have to leave do you?"

"I took two weeks off to figure all this out. I want to figure it out with you. I told Autumn. She knows."

"She does?" her eyes are full of shock. It's comical really.

"You can't be mad; I swore her to secrecy." There's a smirk on my lips and before she can answer, I kiss her again. And again.

She nuzzles her nose against mine, before looking up through her thick lashes. "Two weeks to figure it all out?"

"Yeah, and if we need more time, I'll make it. I want us. More than anything, I know I need you."

"I figured it out. Move in with me and let's spend two weeks in bed." She says it so seriously, yet easily. As if it's so simple and I chuckle, planting a kiss on her forehead that makes her smile. She has the most beautiful smile.

"We can start with me helping take your luggage inside," I offer and she nods watching me while I gather her things and she opens the door. The moment it closes, she's on me, her arms wrapping around me with a fierceness. Dropping the bags to the floor, I hold her back.

"I thought… I thought we weren't going to get this," she whispers and before I can ask what she means, she kisses me, standing in my arms on her tip toes. "You make me happy and I don't want to be without you." She speaks so quietly, I barely hear her.

"Same," I tell her, brushing her hair back and waiting for her to finally look up at me.

"I've never been the girl for fairytales, but I want a happily ever after with you."

Resting my forehead against hers, all I can focus on is the warmth in my chest. Everything about this, about *her*, feels right.

"You can say it again," she tells me. "Tell me you love me again."

"I love you Olivia. I want to love you forever."

"I love you too."

JUST A LITTLE CRUSH

I had to convince myself it was just a little flirtation between us.

When I first met her at the bar, she was already taken.

She was my younger sister's friend from college who was moving to our small town after graduation. Smart and beautiful, with a smile that made me feel things I'd never felt before, I was hooked instantly. My pulse would race and I found myself eager to make her laugh, to have her brush against me, even if it was only friendly flirtation. Before I knew it, I turned into some schoolboy with puppy love just at the sight of her.

I thought: this feeling won't last. I shouldn't be thinking about settling down. She's just a passing fascination.

But she kept coming around and that desire never went away.

The timing was never right. We became too close, too good of friends to risk anything.

Neither of us ever crossed a line, and at some point, I started to believe it really was only a harmless little crush.

Until one night, I kissed her …

This is a cute and sexy friends-to-lovers romance. Enjoy!

CHAPTER 1

Every Sunday night during football season, a game blares from the corner of the bar. The TV mounted on the wall was updated last year, the pool table is even newer and although the back room and one side of the bar is taken by men with gray beards who have come here for decades, this half of The Peanut Bar and Grill is ours.

It's been ours for three years now, ever since I moved to this small town. The only thing missing is our names carved into the tabletop at our regular booth.

Same crew every Sunday, and on Wednesdays too for half-price nachos. A smile grows on my lips as the bar cheers, someone shouts in protest and Dani, the bartender, breaks out in a laugh. She and I are alike; neither one of us really cares about football, but this is a part of home.

Nick and Michelle, high school sweethearts who have been married for five years now, are cuddled up in the corner of the booth. They'll leave early, just like they have since she found out she's pregnant.

It wasn't even on the menu until Michelle told the owner she was craving them during her first trimester. He's her neighbor and said it's the least he could do.

I take another sip of my pale ale just as the happy couple makes the rounds to say goodbye, root beer float in hand.

Jackson and Nate mock protest over them leaving although every single one of us knew it was going to happen. The other five of us will be here till close most likely.

Nate and his girlfriend, my close friend Anne. The rest of us are the single bunch: Jackson, Cheryl, and me.

"Have twice as much fun for me," Michelle says and sighs sweetly as she gives me a hug, her belly nudging against mine. Her flowy cream blouse peeks out from her jean jacket that wouldn't close around her if she tried. It's not maternity, but it's darn cute.

"Where's your sweater?" Nick questions, cutting me off in a protective tone that's all too adorable just as she's snatching it from the seat with a smirk on her face. It's cute how he is with her, and just as cute how she toys with him.

His smirk matches hers once she gives him a peck on the lips.

I can't help but feel a pang of jealousy watching the two of them wave as they exit the bar. Hand in hand. Madly in love.

Another sip of my beer heats my cheeks as I peek at Jackson. Nick and Michelle had one side of the booth. Nate and Anne, the other. Then Cheryl and I took the outside seats while Jackson, Cheryl's older brother, sat at the barstool closest to the table.

That's been our setup for years.

Three years of sitting just feet away from a man I have a crush on, every single week. Ever since I moved to this small town.

"Another?" Dani calls out, catching my attention. Her dark eyes stare back at me and it's only then that I look down and realize my glass is nearly empty.

"Yeah," I answer and the tall brunette is already pouring me another. She works this side of the room. Her brother works the other. The Peanut Bar is a family place. Practically everything in this town is that way.

It's all close quarters and routines. Everyone knows everyone and also their business.

Which is why my fingers fiddle with my drink a moment too long before I nudge Jackson, opting to hand him the empty glass, which he easily exchanges for the full one Dani's holding out to him to pass to me.

My heart does a little pitter-patter every time he looks my way. His sharp blue eyes and charming smile aren't what gets me, although they don't hurt. There's something else about him. And when his fingers brush against mine, in that small moment of contact, a heat blazes through me.

For three years it's been like this. And every day that passes without acknowledging what he does to me, only makes it harder the next.

The bar cheers again as the screen shows a playback of the game. Cheryl's busy chatting with Nate and Anne. The couple behind us, neighbors of Cheryl, leans over the back of their booth to join the conversation.

I stare up at the screen, pretending I don't want to glance back at Jackson, pretending I don't wish he was sitting next to me and the whole damn town knew we were a thing.

Jackson's my friend, tall, dark and handsome … but *only* a friend.

The timing was simply never right for us to be anything more.

When I met him, the butterflies were there, the instant attraction undeniable … but I tried to deny it, because I had a boyfriend. It was a long-distance situation—I'd graduated college and left that town to come here, but I was determined to make it work. Cheryl, my friend from college who convinced me to move here, introduced me to her brother and it was damn hard to keep my impression of him to myself.

Jackson greeted me with a charming smile and a laugh that made me feel things it shouldn't have. After three years of this charade, Cheryl is well aware I have a crush on her brother.

I wasn't the first of her friends to feel puppy love for him. Apart from some teasing here and there, she's kept that information to herself and we remain the closest of friends.

Thank God. I love her like family, and I don't know what I would do without her. Without any of them really. She became the sister I never had while we were in college. As far as I'm concerned, this town and these people adopted me.

Which is why I'll never cross that line with Jackson.

Back then, when she first introduced us, I thought: he's not into me like that, and he's not going to be hanging out with us all the time anyway. So I need to get the idea of the two of us out of my head.

Only he did keep coming around, and those feelings kept growing. I didn't realize just how tight knit this town is.

Over the following months, I realized I couldn't deny what I felt. So I did the right thing, I ended the three-month relationship I had so I could confess to Jackson how I felt. But when I went to the bar, in that spot across from me, right where Jackson is sitting now, there was a cute little redhead by the name of Mallory attached to his hip. And she made him smile, so I couldn't hate her.

Back and forth for years, one of us was always taken. I'd convinced myself it was meant to be that way because as time went on, he became my rock for so many things. Just like Cheryl.

"You want a root beer float?" a masculine voice murmurs close to the shell of my ear. My body heats with a flush that I'm sure is visible. And that baritone cadence elicits an ache of desire between my thighs.

He knows exactly what he's doing. The cocky grin on his handsome face tells me so as he stands back upright, a hand on the back of the booth. He towers over me in blue jeans and a simple plaid button-down.

"We could get one with beer and ice cream?" Jackson offers, lifting his glass in mock cheers before taking a sip. The bar erupts as our team scores, yet the noise seems to fade and blur behind him. Even with the scent of beer in the air, I know exactly how he smells. It's like amber and woods, mixed with a hint of freshness.

Instead of saying anything at all that's on my mind, I answer as I should, in a teasing, nonserious manner. "You want beer with ice cream?" I shake my head gently, a crease between my furrowed brow as I add, "What is wrong with you?"

He lets out a laugh and motions for me to slide down the booth so he can sit next to me.

The leather is still warm from where Michelle was sitting as I scoot back. It's quiet back here, slightly more private but not really.

"So you don't want to split ice cream with me?" he questions, a touch of his Southern drawl coming through, along with feigned vulnerability in his puppy dog eyes.

Yes. Jackson knows exactly what he's doing when he flirts with me.

And I know what I'm doing when I flirt back. "If by 'split' you mean I get a whole three bites before you devour it, then sure." I shrug and pull a leg up onto the seat so I can wrap my arm around it. My black leggings and baggy gray knit sweater keep my appearance casual. Although I did spend time on my makeup, keeping it relatively natural but with a hint of pink. Heavy mascara and a braid down my left shoulder were the finishing touches.

His hand runs down the side of his chiseled, stubbled jaw as he chuckles. "I asked you last time we split a dessert if you wanted more," he protests.

Leaning closer he adds, "If I knew you were going to hold it against me, I wouldn't have touched your half." He's close enough now that I can feel his heat, I can smell him too and it's just like I knew it would be.

Before I can answer, a balled-up napkin hits Jackson square on his nose. "Get a room," a grinning Cheryl calls out from across the booth. Nate and Anne are laughing, and the couple behind them in the booth adjacent to ours is laughing too. Not at us, thankfully. They don't seem to notice and with a smile, Cheryl's already left the table. With a bit of a tipsy sway, she's headed to the bar before either Jackson or I can answer.

Thump, thump, my heart batters against my rib cage in protest, but this tension doesn't affect Jackson in the least. He's never bothered and I know it's because he doesn't feel what I feel.

He doesn't feel this pull between us like I do.

My throat's dry and I try to swallow down my nerves with a sip of the cool beer as Jackson leaves my side, the leather groaning as he goes.

CHAPTER 2

Jackson

"Y ou should just go for it, man," Nate comments, sidling up beside me at the bar as Dani puts in the order.

"And you should mind your own damn business," I joke back at him, pretending like Aubree doesn't get to me. Like I don't want to slide in next to her and press my lips against hers. I have to hold back a groan at the thought. I'm not a lightweight, but four lagers and apparently I'm feeling the effects.

"I think you two should just get together for a night. Just saying it might be good to finally clear that sexual tension."

My body reacts to the suggestion, but so does the last sober bit of me. "And ruin our friendship?"

Nate's smirk and lifted brow piss me off. "Don't act like it's not a possibility," I tell him lowly, leaning against the bar top, hoping he gets it. He's been joking about it for months since he caught me staring at her like some lovesick puppy dog. "If we did anything, you know damn well it would change everything between us."

Nate's dark eyes narrow as he seems to consider my dilemma. It's only ever been a joke. Nothing like the conversation we're having now and how I'm riddled with anxiousness.

"How would you feel if some guy came in and they started making out?" he asks and as he does, I set my glass down a little too hard on the bar top. It doesn't crack, but the sound is jarring enough that Dani turns from the tap, her brow raised.

I raise a hand in defense and say, "Didn't break it. Sorry."

"No harm, no foul," she answers with a grin.

"Come on, how would you feel," Nate presses, dropping his voice so no one can hear. Honestly, I'm not sure if they can or not in this crowd. I'm tipsy and the bar is loud, but in this small town everyone seems to hear everything even when it's whispered. "If some guy came in, hit on her and they hit it off." He gestures behind us. "If they were making out in that booth you were just sitting in beside her."

"She wouldn't do that." My head shakes and my entire body stiffens. I never knew jealousy until Aubree introduced me to her boyfriend years ago. I'm not a fan.

"If it happened, you wouldn't like that."

"I'd be happy that she's happy." I give him the lie and take refuge in my beer. It's crisp and cold still, even though it's the last of it.

"Bullshit," Nate says, not letting up.

Squaring my shoulders, I stare him down. "Let it go, man."

Every other reason gets caught in my throat:

If she was into me, I'd know by now.

If it was going to happen, it would have happened by now.

Nate shrugs, the jersey he's wearing pulling tighter on his shoulders. "Fine," he states casually, but then adds, "Don't come crying to me when some other guy is the one to get cozy with her 'cause you don't have the balls to kiss her first."

I'm paralyzed with a mix of emotions. I don't trust myself to answer. Nate seems to notice my lack of a response and glances over my way.

"Fuck, man, I'm sorry. Just ignore me. All right?"

Anger bristles along my shoulders as I turn to face the TV in the corner, although it also allows me to watch Aubree from the corner of my eye.

"I mean it, I'm sorry. I just … think you two would hit it off."

My tongue sweeps along my bottom lip as I watch Aubree finish her beer. Her cheeks are flushed, her hair's in a loose braid and a smile graces her face from whatever my sister just told her.

"I just can't risk changing some things, you know?" I say, finally answering Nate.

"They're going to change either way," he tells me in all seriousness and there's an ache in my chest. A familiar pull like the sense of loss. Loss of something I've never even had.

The moment Aubree scoots from the booth, her hand reaches out to me as she stabilizes herself, fixing her baggy sweater that swallows up her small frame. It's these little touches that get me.

How she knows she can rely on me. How she likes to even.

"You all good?" I ask her and she lets out a small laugh. That sound. It wriggles its way through me, warming me. Her hazel eyes slip to mine and she bites down slightly on her lower lip. "Just have to run to the ladies' room."

"You might want to walk, it's a bit crowded," I tease her. It's cheesy and the grin Nate has growing on his face tells me he heard it too.

Whatever, she still laughs.

Shaking her head, she brushes past me, and everything inside of me wants to wrap my arm around her waist, pull her in and ask her if she wants to come home with me.

It's a feeling I'm used to. And so is this chill that sweeps in the moment she walks away.

"Dani, she needs another," I call out to the bartender the moment Aubree's gone.

Dani's quick to place the beer down in front of me even though it's for Aubree.

"She didn't even ask who 'she' is," Nate comments.

Reaching over the tabletop, I snag an orange slice Dani forgot, and drop it into Aubree's glass. "Can't I be happy with this as it is?" I ask him genuinely.

Before he can answer, Aubree's right there, watching me place the beer at her seat.

"You looking out for me? Or just trying to get me drunk?" There's this small smile she gives me sometimes. It's there now as she lifts the beer to her lips and slips deeper into the booth to give me room to sit if I want to.

"Maybe a little of both," I joke, questioning if I should sit. If I should push it a little more tonight than I have before.

"Which one would you prefer?" I ask her, feeling this hot nervousness prick along every inch of my skin as she stares up at me.

She smirks back, all flirtatious and never breaking eye contact when she says, "Maybe a little of both?"

CHAPTER 3

Aubree

CHERYL LEANS IN CLOSE, A SMIRK CLEARLY WRITTEN ON HER face. "Just do it, Bree." She comes even closer to nudge me, her tipsiness making her sway as she adds, "You can't keep teasing him like this."

The grin on her face is as wide as it can be as her gaze lifts from me and moves to the topic of the conversation behind me.

My cheeks can't get any hotter.

"Your drink's empty." A deep yet flirtatious man's voice reaches us from down the bar. *Kill me now.* Cheryl and I grabbed barstools beside Nate and Jackson when the game went into overtime. Both of them have since moved. It's like musical chairs in this place.

It took a whole two minutes for the guys to my right to start chatting us up. They weren't paying attention to the game in the least.

"Let us buy you your next round. What are you ladies drinking?"

He raises his voice to speak over the sounds of the game on the bar's TVs. The crowd roars in the background. Whistles blow. I don't care much about the score, but the atmosphere is amped up. The end of the night is getting close.

Cheryl beams at me. "See? If you don't make your move, somebody else is going to step in. Those guys are hot."

"Those guys are hot because you're drunk," I joke, although I don't have much room to talk. I, too, am far from sober.

"No, they're genuinely hot." Cheryl sneaks a peek over her shoulder, her cheeks turning a bright pink as she takes them in.

The bar is emptying out. Quite a few people reached their limit by the fourth quarter and headed home, but Cheryl's having a good time. Nate and Anne made it through most of the fourth before they went home to make out with each other.

And Jackson …

Jackson is still here.

I can feel him in the bar. Maybe it's just because I'm drunk as well, but I am acutely aware he's still here, even with my back turned. He's behind me now at the booth I was sitting at only an hour or so ago.

I wonder if he's watching. If those guys come closer, he's going to see. The Peanut Bar isn't that big, and there aren't many people left. Nerves eat at me as I wonder if he even cares. All I can think about while these guys are flirting with me, is whether or not Jackson can see. What the hell is wrong with me?

With a short sigh, I push my beer away and look back at my good friend. Her teeth are sunken into her bottom lip as she glances their way again.

Cheryl's right. I should make a move, one way or the other. Three years is a long time to shove my feelings down. Three years is a long time not to go home with a man because of a little crush that's never going to go anywhere. I should either get up and confess to Jackson that my heart skips a beat every time I see him here, or I should let those guys buy us drinks.

The moment I suck in a breath and peek at Jackson, I turn right back around.

It's silly to be afraid of rejection like this, but I am. If he outright turned me down, it would hurt like hell. And then I could never show my face again at this bar. Never ever. This place is like a second home to me.

"Pale ale," I call to the guys down the bar. The one closest to me nods and I shrug, offering a smile. "That's what I'm having, anyway." He's cute. Handsome even, although the jersey makes him seem a little young. He's definitely in college, and old enough to be in a bar so I'm thinking twenty-two maybe.

"I'm tempted to ask him if he's going to be a dentist because his teeth are freaking perfect," I comment to Cheryl and she pats my arm a little too hard.

"Hell yes," she says, a little too loud. "Now we're going to have some fun.

Or at least you are." She gets up from her stool, the legs scraping against the wooden floor as if she's leaving me. The urge to grab her arm and cling to her has never been stronger.

"What?" The one word that spills out of my mouth sounds utterly pathetic and I don't even care. "You are not leaving me," I whisper in a hushed voice.

"I'm just going to the restroom. You get the first pick of the guys."

"Cheryl!" I reach for her sleeve, but she's already too far to pull her back.

The two guys don't miss a beat sliding down farther, like they're coming in for the kill.

"So, a pale ale?" the blond with the gorgeous smile questions and then motions for Dani. I don't miss how high her brow arches and that sly, comical smile she gives me.

"Mm-hm." I don't trust myself to speak, but I settle on some small talk.

"Hi, guys. Having a good night so far?"

"Depends," the blond one says. "Are you?"

My cheeks flare with heat. He's not subtle in the least but I play it casually. "I always have fun on Sunday nights."

The truth is, I'm always invested in being here on Sunday nights. Our crew has a good time together and it's my wind down time. My safe place. But I'd be lying if I said I wasn't here for Jackson too. My smile slips as I think of him yet again. I like being around him. I like having an excuse to look at him and listen to his jokes and just be in the same room. I've had to come to terms with making the most of it and enjoying my Sundays over the last three years. If it was truly painful to be here with him, that wouldn't be any fun.

The barstool scrapes as the blond hunk takes the stool next to mine, the one that used to be Cheryl's, and purses his lips. "You could have more fun, I bet." His tone is soothing, but I see through it all.

"Oh yeah? And how's that?" If I wasn't thinking of Jackson, I'd ask him if he wanted to cut to the chase.

As it is, even when I'm looking at this man who's obviously interested in me, all I see is the image of Jackson sitting here only hours ago.

My heart's beating faster, but I don't know if it's because I'm genuinely interested in this guy or because I'm nervous as hell about what's going to happen. If I click with some random man at the bar, what happens to my feelings about Jackson? Probably nothing. He doesn't have any for me, so we'd both move on with our lives like grown adults. All the while this guy talks, my thoughts scream in my head. I nod and comment when it seems appropriate. His friend hovers, more invested in the game now.

But damn if I don't want Jackson to be jealous. At least for him to notice that someone else has approached me. It sends a shiver down my spine to imagine his eyes on us, but I don't look to see if he's watching.

"What are you doing after this?" the blond hunk questions. My lips part but someone else speaks before I can.

"We're going to my place." Jackson's deep, masculine voice breaks into our conversation and heats my core.

My heart pounds and I let out a long breath. It's so damn hot in here. I hadn't noticed that before. I pull at my sweater, hoping to feel a little breeze.

Before I can say anything, shock and heat overwhelming me, Jackson's strong arm wraps around my lower waist. The thermostat must have fucking broken in this place.

Jackson's body curls around mine as he bends down and kisses the crook of my neck. Right there in that spot beneath my ear and I think I must have died. It's heaven, it's sinful. It's a fantasy come to life. "That's what she's doing after this." His chest is a deep rumble against my shoulder and I can barely look back at the man who just bought me a drink.

I don't even know how I'm sitting upright.

The brush of his lips fills me with butterflies. A fluttering mess of them. Gulping down the beer, I give myself a moment to steady. Jackson. Possessive of me in the bar just because a guy offered me a drink?

This might be my only shot to play along with him. I turn my face to his and kiss his cheek before I can overthink this. If he's going to cross this line for a joke or whatever Jackson's thinking … I'm going to cross it too.

My blond would-be hero throws his hands up with a smile when I glance back at him. "Didn't realize."

"Sorry, I should have said—" I'm not able to finish before Jackson cuts me off.

"No problem." His tone is familiar, yet harder, more dominating. He leaves no room for further conversation. And the other guys get the hint.

They back off, looking toward the hall leading to the restroom, leaving me staring up at him, his arm still wrapped around me. His hold is looser now, but it's still there.

"You drunk?" he questions, glancing down at me for only a moment.

Maybe more than a little tipsy. "Not so drunk that I don't know what I want." The words slip out before I can stop them and his brow raises in surprise.

I rip my gaze away and take another sip of beer, but it doesn't do anything to change the way I feel right now.

I've never been hornier in my life. I didn't come here with sex on my mind. I'm in leggings and a sweater. That should be enough of a clue that I didn't plan on doing anything but cuddling up with a hangover cure after this.

Jackson says something and I'm not quite sure what, but his hand leaves the bar and I'll be damned if I'm going to let him leave me like this.

"What was that?" I question, my voice sultry. I didn't mean for it to come out like that.

"Just cockblocking you," Jackson jokes. He picks up his drink from the bar behind me. That hammering in my chest intensifies. Is he … is he toying with me? 'Cause that kiss is still burning my neck.

"Oh yeah? What would you call this?" I say, then lean forward, hook my arm around his neck, and kiss him full on the mouth. My lips press against his and at first they're hard, but they mold to mine instantly.

He kisses me back with an intensity I didn't expect. He tastes like beer and hunger. He tastes better than I ever imagined he would. I kiss him deeper, wanting to remember it after tonight.

That's when it hits me. We're in the freaking bar still. Everyone is here. His sister. Our friends. I pull away with a slight panic.

Jackson smirks down at me. A gorgeous, handsome, and somewhat cocky smirk. It's a look that keeps me calm while everything else blurs around us.

I almost ask him if he wants to get out of here, but the words fall short. My heart stops with the fear that he'll reject me. Tell me it was all in fun, and it's not like that. I'm just a friend of his sister. I just wanted those guys to back off. That's what he'll say.

In my short moment of fear, Jackson pushes a stray lock of my hair back and leans in again for a gentle, yet demanding kiss.

This time, he flicks his tongue against my lips until I part them for him. Inwardly I sigh with relief. It's been three years of waiting, and honestly, I thought it would be a lifetime. I never thought Jackson would kiss me at all and especially not like this. He's tasting me like I tasted him. I swear, he wants me too.

He lets out a groan against my mouth. "You want to get out of here?"

CHAPTER 1

Jackson

There's no going back.

That's all I can think as my hands roam down her soft curves in the back of the car. Her lips haven't left mine and if I thought that this may not be the only chance I have with Aubree, I'd contain myself. I'd show a semblance of control, but as it stands, I have none.

There is nothing but desperation for her not to stop. To just let me kiss her.

Soft moans pour from her lips, subtle and just as desperate as my touch. The Uber slows to a stop and I barely look up, checking for a red light or a stop sign. Instead I see my front lawn.

I pull my lips from hers, but intertwine our fingers and keep her close. "Let's go," I tell her. Tomorrow is vaguely on my mind. The questions and concerns. Every time a thought pierces through the haze of lust, I shut it down by kissing her again.

As we climb out, Aubree kisses my neck in that tender spot above my shoulder and it only makes my dick harder. The simple act elicits a groan from me and the moment I close the car door, I lift Aubree into my arms.

With a gasp of surprise and delight, she wraps her legs around my hips. One of my arms supports her from under her ass, the other braces her back and keeps her close to me. Her lips find mine again and I swear to God I'm in heaven.

The scent of her hair around me, the feel of her warmth against me.

I want more. I need more.

It's dark inside when I unlock the door and kick it open. It's not as smooth of a transition as I'd like it to be, but I'm able to do it all while kissing her. Little nips of her bottom lip and the sweet heated gasps she gives me have me impossibly hard.

My front door bangs recklessly against the wall, and I don't give a fuck.

"Make sure it's locked," she whispers and I have to chuckle.

"Yes, ma'am," I comment as I set her down gently, for the first time letting her go. She flicks on the corner light of the living room. She's been here a thousand times before, but never just the two of us. With the click of the lock, I look over to see her standing in the middle of the living room, looking so out of place as she stares back at me. Her wide hazel eyes are filled with lust and desire.

As if knowing I've dreamed of this moment, she crosses her arms in front of her and slowly pulls the sweater over her head, letting it drop to the floor into a puddle of fabric beside her.

I can barely breathe, paralyzed by the sight of her stripping. The wooden floor creaks as I take a single step toward her. She sinks her teeth into her bottom lip, her cheeks flushed as she unhooks her bra, letting it fall to the floor. I take another step forward and another, so very aware of what's about to happen.

There's no going back.

Vulnerability shines in her hazel eyes as she looks back at me, but she doesn't stop. As her thumbs hook into the top of her leggings, I place my hands over hers and lower my lips to the shell of her ear to whisper, "Let me."

Her head falls back slightly as she murmurs her agreement. My lips travel down her body, leaving openmouthed kisses as I go. I take my time to pluck her hardened nipples and smile against her heated skin when she moans from the touch.

From what I do to her.

Groaning against her curves, I nip along her body as I lower myself to my knees. As I tug her leggings down, I pull her lace underwear along with it.

Her fingers spear through my hair the moment I peek up at her. She's bared to me and I lean forward, tasting her. Her eyes flutter as her head falls back and with that I take a languid lick and then another. Her arousal is sweet on my tongue.

Both of her hands brace against my shoulders as she struggles to stay upright when I suck her clit. I massage my tongue against her and my sweet Aubree digs her nails into my shoulders, sucks in a breath and then calls out my name.

My name.

My hands dig into her ass to keep her where I want her. Precum leaks from my cock as she writhes, the leggings still wrapped around her ankles, preventing her from moving much at all.

"Please," she begs me and I can't take it anymore.

In a swift motion I lift her up, stepping on the leggings to rip them from her and hustle to the sofa. I'm not as gentle as I'd like to be when I lay her down.

She gasps from the sudden change of pace.

My shirt comes over my head, and I kick my jeans off as quickly as possible. All the while the sofa protests under us.

"Spread your legs for me," I murmur and she obeys, her wide eyes staying on mine. Without wasting a second, I slam into her.

Her wet, welcoming heat takes me like she's meant to. Her lips part in a gorgeous O and she holds her breath as I push myself deeper, rocking slightly so my groin massages her clit.

"You're so fucking tight," I groan and then lower myself down to her, bracing a forearm beside her so I can kiss her.

It's only then that I move. Pulling nearly all the way out before pushing all the way back in. The head of my cock presses against her back wall and I can barely take it.

"Jackson." She moans my name, her arms wrapping around my back. Her head thrashes from side to side as I push myself in deeper and fuck her harder with each thrust.

There's a moment when her hands brush against my chest, with her chest rising and falling with each heavy breath, that our eyes meet. My heart hammers, my blood heats and I swear she almost says what I'm thinking.

Instead she kisses me, pressing her lips to mine as if she would die without it.

I go slow for a moment, wanting it back. Wanting that moment back and needing to know what she was going to say.

The three words are right there for me too, but I swallow them down and lower my chest to hers, holding her as I fuck her faster, but deeper still.

"Fuck!" she yelps and her pussy flutters around my cock. My thumb finds her clit and a cold sweat forms on my back as it all intensifies.

Her muffled cries of pleasure fill the room and I fucking love it. I've always wanted her, I've fantasized about it, but this? The sight of her getting off on my cock is better than I could have imagined.

"Jackson." She calls out my name again, this time with desperation as I hook my arm under her knee and pull it up so I can get even deeper.

"Don't worry," I say and kiss her neck. "You can take me." With that whispered, I piston my hips, fucking her deeply and roughly.

She comes again, screaming my name this time and I can't stop. I take her savagely. Without holding back a damn thing and I don't come until she reaches her third climax.

CHAPTER 5

Aubree

IT'S ALL SLOW AND FUZZY WHEN I FIRST WAKE UP, WHICH ISN'T uncommon for the morning after a Sunday night out. It all depends on how the game goes. If it's a close one, with lots of tension and shouting, I can still feel it in my muscles the day after. But something is off. I know it even before I'm aware I'm unfortunately hungover.

It's not the lingering effects of too many shots that's making me feel heavy and sated, though.

Since when did my blankets have this much weight to them?

It only takes one weak stretch to feel another person under the sheets. With wide eyes and a quick glance around Jackson's living room, all of last night tumbles into my memory.

Oh, no, no, no, no, no, no, no.

It comes back all at once, and the shock feels like a shot glass slamming down on the bar. Jackson. *I came home with Jackson last night.*

It's futile to pull the sheet up against my bare chest as I stare down at his naked form. How the hell did we both sleep on his couch?

I did more than *sleep* on this sofa.

The cushion groans slightly and I slow my movements as I attempt to slip out, still very much naked and groggy.

Every little moment flashes back and the conflicting emotions intensify. He kissed the side of my neck in front of the entire bar. He upped the ante in the game we played for years. Was he jealous of the guys who were hitting on me? Or … I don't know. All I know is that it became something else when I kissed him back.

I barely remember anything about the ride home. All I remember is his mouth on mine, the deep murmurs and lust-filled groans. And how warm his body felt against mine.

Last night was better than I ever imagined it would be. The morning after, though? Well, there's a reason I've never dreamed of this moment.

Bottom line: we crossed a big red line last night in front of everyone. That truth is a flashing bright light in my face as I tiptoe across the living room in search of my underwear.

Sex with your best friend's brother is a no-no. I can already see the look of shock on Cheryl's face. I can already imagine how awkward our group outings with friends will be.

Blood drains from my face and the regret slips in.

I never meant to take it this far.

My heart pounds as I stand paralyzed, clinging to Jackson's navy blue comforter which is pressed against my chest. His living room is neat and masculine in the pale early morning sun filtering through the blinds. Apart from our clothes from last night strewn across the carpeted floor.

Eventually, I take in Jackson's sleeping form. His firm—and bare—ass is fully on display, his arm hanging over the edge of the sofa. He's dead to the world and guiltily I lay the comforter across him. His face is turned toward the back of the sofa, and his other arm is tucked under his pillow in a way that shows off his muscular frame. Broad shoulders rise and fall with every deep breath. Just as I feel a touch of ease, he mumbles something I can barely hear and I freeze. A beat passes and then another.

All the while, the slight chill in the room skims across my nakedness.

Clothes. For the love of all things holy. Where are my clothes?

It doesn't take long to spot them, but each quiet moment comes with a hint of regret.

Why does Cheryl have to have the hottest brother in the history of the world? It's not fair. That's what I've told myself for so long now. It's not fair, because I can never be with him.

Except I have been with him. We were together last night. He wanted me to come home with him, and I said yes, and now …

Now I have to get out of here.

Part of me wants to touch his shoulder, wake him up, and give him a repeat performance. To fake it until we make it, so to speak.

A big part of me, actually. Most of me. I want to feel his body against mine again. He was powerful and confident over me in a way that no other man has been. At the same time, he was familiar. Safe. Jackson knows me really well, and for good reason. We've been friends for years.

Oh, Aubree, what have you done?

The reality, though, is that I have morning breath, bed head, a hangover and regrets a mile long, as well as a growing list of insecurities and uncertainties. So the only faking I'll be doing is faking that everything is okay until I am safely home and clinging to my own pillow.

I silently gather each garment like I've been trained by the CIA in extraction methods.

My purse dangles from one corner of the coffee table. The garments scattered around the room tell a definite story about what happened last night. Two people couldn't get enough of each other, and they couldn't even aim for the furniture when they took their clothes off.

Not that I need the clothes to tell me anything. I remember how amazing it felt to be in Jackson's arms. I remember how much I wanted him. Kissing him woke something up in me. Something that's been bubbling under the surface for way too long.

I step into my clothes quickly and quietly, then snatch my phone up from the ground. There's a text from Cheryl. It's from last night, about half an hour after I left the bar with Jackson.

> **Cheryl: You did it!! Good for you!! Which of the guys did you go home with?**

I text her back with trembling hands. My pulse races as I press send.

> **Aubree: Don't hate me. Jackson. I'm at Jackson's house. I spent the night here. I'm never going to be able to look him in the eye again.**

Never mind that I'll have to look Cheryl in the eye. She'll know I slept with her brother. She did egg me on, but it was a joke. It was all supposed to be harmless fun. My stomach does a nervous flip. I won't be able to stand it if he walks out here all hot and handsome and plays it off like a joke.

Like it didn't mean anything. With both hands running down my face, I wish I could just get in my car and drive away. My fingers fly across my phone ordering my escape car.

My heart pounds as I glance over my shoulder back at Jackson. I don't think I'd be able to play it cool if he sauntered out and pretended it meant nothing.

I can see things going both ways. Next Sunday could be stiff, with us walking on eggshells and all our friends wondering what's going on. Or it could be normal, with both of us pretending to be comfortable. Like it was just a part of the flirtatious game we play.

Or maybe …

Maybe we could be holding hands at the bar. Maybe Jackson could be there as my real boyfriend and not just a decoy for the men who wanted to buy me a drink.

The phone buzzes in my hand and I clutch it to my chest, listening hard for any sign he's waking up. One beat passes and then another of me staring at him like a weirdo.

Without any sign he's woken up, I check my phone.

Cheryl: It was just one night. No big deal. You guys got it out of your system ;)

Out of my system. I swallow thickly.

Reality crashes down around me. Not a soul knows about the crush. The genuine feelings I have for him. No one is going to understand and nothing is going to be all right.

What was I thinking? This isn't the start of a new relationship. This was a one-night stand. In fact, it was a mistake.

My throat tightens. That's exactly what Jackson will say. It was a mistake for the two of us to jump into bed together. Our friendship is too important to screw it up with emotions.

What a mess.

The only way to begin cleaning it up is to leave before he gets out of bed. As if on cue, my phone informs me the getaway car is approaching. It's a little cowardly, I know, to run away after a one-night stand. But if that's all it is, then it won't be anything new. That's what you do when things aren't serious. You go back to your life before they get serious.

I hesitate at the door, my stomach sinking. He might worry about me when he wakes up.

Maybe I should leave a note. I half turn back to the kitchen, but stop myself.

What would the note say?

I had a nice time last night—see you at football!!

Or …

We should talk about this soon so it's not awkward.

Or …

No hard feelings, whatever happens.

Each idea I have is worse than the last. *Shit.* It's better if I don't say anything. It's best if I don't look back. It's better if I chalk it up to a tipsy mistake and leave it in the past where it belongs.

The future with Jackson has to do with friendship. Because we're friends. Really good friends. And that's all we're going to be.

CHAPTER 6

Jackson

The thud of the front door is far too soft to be what woke me up. If I had to guess, I'd say it's the pounding in my head from a vicious hangover that did it.

With a foggy mind and a heavy body, I lift myself up before realizing what happened.

Aubree. Holy shit, did that really happen last night?

It only takes a moment of listening to the silence in this empty place before I hear a car door shut out front. *Fuck!*

I'm sober in seconds, jolting from the sofa and running toward the door although I don't get far. My foot bashes the coffee table and I seethe, sucking in a deep breath and wincing from the pain.

"Aubree!" I call out as if she could possibly hear me. By the time I get to the door, I realize I'm completely nude and can't open the door more than a few inches.

The bright morning light blinds me for a moment as I watch the four-door sedan head down the suburban street. Taking Aubree with it and leaving a sense of dread to creep in.

Shit, shit, shit. Running a hand through my hair, I search for a note or for anything at all.

Last night comes back in waves. The drinks, the kissing, fucking Nate texting his friends to flirt with Aubree. I know it was him, trying to prove a point and yeah, he was right.

Seeing her with them … I lean against the wall with my bare ass pressed against the cold surface and regret swarms me.

Last night, I crossed a line, but she crossed it with me. That's the only hope I have, so I hold on to it. Even though she snuck out. Even though there's no note.

I'm quick to find my boxers, putting them on and then searching for my phone in the pocket of the jeans I wore last night.

It's dead … great. Of course it is.

Letting out a sigh, I resign myself to coffee, an Advil and giving myself a moment while the charger brings it back to life.

As the coffee maker sputters and hisses, I remember how she kissed me. The passion and the desperation. A groan leaves me and my head falls back as my dick remembers last night too.

You can't fake that. She wants me. Or at least she did last night. And it was fucking incredible.

An asymmetric smile pulls my lips up as I add sugar and creamer to my cup and then stir it, the spoon tinking against the ceramic.

Suddenly, the hangover isn't so bad. My pinky toe that's stubbed? Not a big deal. The smile lingers until I check my phone, when it promptly vanishes.

Three texts wait for me, and not a single one from Aubree. My heart sinks further down with each.

> **Nick: I heard you left the bar with Aubree … what's going on there?**
>
> **Nate: So you guys do it?**

It's the last one that leaves me wishing Aubree hadn't run off this morning. It's from my sister: **FYI she's freaking out a little. You might want to let her know your friendship is still intact.**

The phone clatters to the counter as I run my hand down the back of my head, cursing myself for taking her home last night. I should have kissed her and told her I wanted to see her. I should have said one damn thought I've had for years about her rather than keeping it to myself.

My phone pings again and although I know it's not her, I wish it were. It's only my sister, asking if I even remember last night because the town is now being informed one text at a time.

Fuck, fuck, everyone knows and I have no idea what it means for us. Panic is something I'm not used to. Not at all when it comes to Aubree. But it's all that takes over until I shove it down.

I've wanted Aubree for so long and now I'm afraid I'm going to lose her … but I'll be damned if I let that happen.

CHAPTER 7

Aubree

A T LEAST I DON'T HAVE TO GO TO AN OFFICE BUILDING. THAT'S one small consolation as I stare at my phone wishing a message would pop up. None do, but I count my blessings on the Uber ride back to my apartment, which is on the second floor of a neat brick building with a hair salon on the ground floor and a couple more units up above. I don't mind the muffled sounds of the dryers and music coming through the floor. It's still quiet when I shut the door and lock it behind me with an exacerbated sigh. Not early enough for the first clients of the day.

Thank God I don't have a set schedule, because I desperately need a shower. There's no way I can sit at my desk and go to work while I'm wearing clothes that smell like Jackson.

Maybe it's pathetic, but I can admit it makes me a bit somber to take them off and drop them in the hamper.

I go through all the motions. Shampoo and soap and conditioner. I dry my hair and put on makeup.

Unsurprisingly, it doesn't help. With a hot cup of tea at my side, I take my seat at my computer with a long to-do list and a mind that's full of Jackson. And what we did last night. And how I left him sleeping on the sofa. And how I wish I were still with him. I should have pretended to be sleeping for as long as it took.

In my defense, I'm not good with hangovers.

Graphic design has nothing to do with the man I slept with last night. For fifteen whole minutes, I concentrate on my projects. A new logo for a company based in the city. A banner for an artist's website. The background for a set of wedding invitations.

None of them are exactly presentable … but I try.

All of it takes way longer than it should, because I can't focus.

The only thing that draws my attention is my phone. Every two minutes, I stare at it, willing it to ping and let me know Jackson texted me to tell me how much he wants a repeat of last night.

After about an hour, I find the tea cold and my thoughts turning on me.

I don't know what's worse. If Jackson texts or if he doesn't. If he ignores what happened last night, then I guess that's something to go on. If he texts and wants to talk …

Butterflies flutter deep in my stomach. It's hard to tell if they're the nervous kind or the excited kind.

Of course, there's always the third option, which is that he texts and says we should pretend it didn't happen and was a mistake.

I fly out of my seat so fast the office chair nearly hits the wall as it rolls backward and I put my phone on the kitchen counter, plugging it in to charge. After that, I buckle down for a solid hour of work. There's not a chance in hell I'm going to miss a deadline and get laid off because I let my crush tear up my heart.

It doesn't take long, though, for it to buzz from all the way across the apartment and I'm out of my seat before I can think twice. It's silly to run across my little apartment just for a notification that could be a text from anyone, but I do.

> **Jackson: You ran off this morning. I should have at least made you breakfast.**

Not even one emoji.

How am I supposed to answer this? How am I supposed to respond? I guess I'll have to play it off like I'm fine and absolutely not obsessed with the outcome of sleeping with my best friend's brother.

> **Aubree: Sorry—I just didn't want to be late for work!**

I sent the exclamation mark before I can think twice. Damn it, I should have changed that to a period.

The typing indicator dots appear on my screen and hover there for what seems like forever. He could say anything right now.

Option A: Let's forget about it. See you Sunday.

Option B: We shouldn't say anything about this. Keep it between us.

No, I correct my thinking, it's too late for that. Cheryl saw. She knows we left together. Everyone who was still at the bar knows. And even if they didn't, there's no way we're pretending it didn't happen.

Jackson: Let me buy you dinner tonight?

My heart's racing slows up slightly, hope in sight. I send a message back without thinking.

Aubree: You don't owe me food just because we had sex :)

I mean it as a joke, but no new dots come up on the screen.

Jackson doesn't say anything.

Not right away. And not in the next hour. Or the hour after that.

The afternoon crawls by. It's the slowest day I've ever lived through. I leave my phone in the kitchen and force myself to work on my projects. This is not a good productivity hack, but it does mean my list gets smaller and smaller as the minutes pass. I answer emails I should have responded to a month ago and put in a couple bids for new projects.

I even cold email a handful of companies I think would like my work that have been on my to-do list forever. Sending cold emails is basically a new record for me. I put it off as long as possible because I hate writing those emails—they seem salesy and weird. I know putting myself out there is a big part of my job, but I still don't like it. I'm supposed to bring in a certain number of clients so I have to. But cold emailing ahead of the deadline … I am … desperate for a distraction.

All this to avoid deciding what to do about Jackson's text.

Do I say something? Ask for clarification?

Send him a message talking up last night as a joke?

That probably wouldn't play very well. Or—I don't know, maybe it would. He's always been laid back and funny. We've never had this much pressure between us.

In the afternoon, I give up trying to work and check his socials. He hasn't unfriended me. Hasn't posted anything there, either.

"Oh, God, Aubree." I bury my face in my hands. He's probably working. It's Monday. Jackson works in finance and it's always busy, even when it's not the craziest part of tax season. He's busy, that's all it is. This isn't a disaster.

We've avoided disaster lots of times. When I first moved back to town,

I had a boyfriend. We were going to do the whole long-distance thing and stick it out together. It didn't last longer than three months. My feelings for him cooled once we weren't in the same town. And … my feelings for someone else were heating up.

Jackson.

I felt myself falling for him every Sunday at the football games. I waited for his calls and blushed when I got texts. When Cheryl and I would hang out with him, I tried to be the best, shiniest version of myself, all while I told myself I was being casual. The real me. At some point, those two people got mixed together. I got more comfortable with Jackson.

Too comfortable, to the point that I broke up with my boyfriend, intending to tell Jackson how I felt.

I was too late. He was already seeing someone else.

What's a girl to do? I told myself it was a crush. You don't bring up a crush to your best friend's brother when he's dating someone else. It was a reasonable crush too. Jackson had treated me well. He'd been kind to me instead of brushing me off as one of his sister's friends, and it would be hard for anyone not to feel something.

And he was sweet. And funny. And he liked flirting with me. But it wasn't … real.

Defeated, I sit back farther in my chair, pulling my legs up and letting the swivel rock me back and forth.

I still feel him all over me from last night. It doesn't matter that I've showered. Doesn't matter that I have fresh clothes and a day of work behind me. The imprints of his kisses are still on my skin. The places where our bodies met are still buzzing from the contact.

When I glance at the clock next, it's five fifteen.

I take my teacup to the sink and wash it. It's probably the most thorough bath the teacup has ever gotten in its life. Work's over. There are no new messages from Jackson on my phone. Nothing laughing off the text I sent him, or asking for a reply.

If he hasn't messaged by six, I'll text him and put myself out of my misery. I can't let this hang over my head all night. Or for the rest of my life. I can't go to the game next weekend feeling all twisted up inside, like I've ruined something.

I haven't, really. The way to think about this is as a nice, onetime thing.

We both enjoyed each other, and that's enough. It's a choice to make it awkward with him. I can choose to make it normal instead.

Right?

Although that doesn't explain why I feel this sense of loss inside my chest. This ache for something more.

A knock at the door makes me jump.

I can't deny that it causes a flood of feelings. Embarrassment, because I've been waiting for this knock. Fear, because what if it's not him? And hope—hope that it's Jackson standing on the other side. Who the hell else could it possibly be, though?

I place the teacup in the drying rack as gently as my nerves will allow me and head to the door with even strides so it doesn't sound like I'm running. *It might not be him, anyway.*

I get up on tiptoe to look through the peephole. My heart beats fast and feels skittish. I've never had a crush as strong as this one. Not even when I was a teenager and all my hormones were out of control. The guys in my high school had nothing on Jackson.

Jackson's in the hall outside my apartment, waiting patiently, a bag of Chinese food raised in his hand. "Hey," he calls out. "You hungry?"

CHAPTER 8

Jackson

I'm not hungry in the least. Even with the scent of Chinese food wafting from the coffee table. The TV plays some sitcom in the background but none of it means a thing.

Not when Aubree doesn't move for the food either. Not when she keeps stealing glances at me and blushing every time our eyes meet.

My nerves work their way through me as I stare at Aubree, needing to tell her exactly how I feel. It's now or never.

I told myself if there was even a hint that she didn't regret last night, that she wanted to be something more, I was going to do it.

And now's my chance.

It's so quiet, my dry swallow is audible. My cheeks burn with the heat of embarrassment when she stares down at her plate, speechless.

"I loved last night. I've had feelings for you for years." I can't stop now. She has to know. I leave my hand on the coffee table, palm up and she notices. Her gaze moves to it and then back up to mine.

"I didn't know I was that good in bed," she jokes and I laugh, a genuine chuckle to match hers. But I don't back down.

My anxiousness scatters. The relief of knowing she's not running at the thought is all I needed.

Before I can say anything, she scoots closer on the sofa, her warmth immediately evident. "You were pretty good in bed too, if I might add," she teases me, her long lashes fluttering.

My thumb rubs a soothing circle over her knuckles as I debate on the next step.

"Just tell me what to say." I practically beg her like the desperate man I am.

"What?"

"I will say whatever I need to … to get you to say you'll be mine right now," I tell her in all honesty. The subtle shock, the awe that follows, lets me know that she hears me. And that she knows I'm serious.

"I want to be with you. More than friends. I can't go back to being just friends."

"Jackson …" Her hand leaves mine and she tucks it into her lap.

That slight panic of losing her comes back.

"I'll be damned if I lose you, Aubree," I confess, not hiding my desperation. "This isn't some one-night fling. I don't want that."

She whispers the one fear I've had for years that kept me from kissing her, "What if it doesn't work?"

"What if it does?" My answer is immediate and her gaze falls to my lips, then darts back up to me. "I want you. If you want me too, just say yes."

A beat passes. And then another. Too many seconds go by, filling me with an anxiousness until she whispers, "Yes."

That's all I needed for relief to take over and to lean down and capture her lips with mine. I don't even realize what I'm doing until this gentle kiss is over and a soft moan of satisfaction falls from her lips. With her eyes still closed, I take her in and this moment between us.

"I mean it, Aubree," I tell her, then clear my throat and wait for her to peer back at me. My heart hammers but I don't hold back anymore. "I could see you walking down the aisle … I can see all of what I want in the future, happening with you."

Her chest rises with a slow, yet deep inhale at my admission.

"Jackson," she says, merely whispering my name, her longing gaze never leaving mine. With her small hand she fists the fabric of my shirt, taking what's hers as she pulls me down, devouring my lips with hers and letting her hunger take over.

Her soft body presses against mine and she climbs into my lap and all of last night comes back with a force. My cock is hard in an instant and I smile against her kiss as she pushes my shoulders back, easing me onto my back on her sofa.

As she sits up, straddling me and pulling her shirt over her head, I chuckle. "You are so damn good with your words, you know that?"

That sweet feminine laugh I know so well brightens up her face as she reaches behind her, unhooking her bra. It falls easily from her, revealing her supple breasts and rose petal nipples. I can't help the tortured groan that escapes me.

"Was that a word, Jackson?" she says, teasing me as she leans down, her palm resting beside my head. Her hair falls in front of her, obstructing my view. "I'm not sure I—"

In a swift motion, I grip her hips and flip her smart ass over so she's beneath me and I'm on top. Her gasp of surprise is accompanied by her legs wrapping around my hips.

I lean forward, pressing myself into her and rocking my hips.

"You teasing me, Aubree?" I murmur, letting the hint of a threat hang between us. "I think I could find a way to tease you back."

Her lips part with the sexiest fucking inhale I've ever heard in my life.

"Oh yeah," she says in a breathy voice. "I think I'd like that."

"Like?" I cock a brow.

"I think I'd love it if you teased me for the rest of my life, Jackson."

An asymmetric grin pulls at my lips. "Now that's the challenge I've been waiting for."

EPILOGUE

Aubree

One year later

THE CHEERS ERUPT FROM EVERY SOUL IN HERE, INCLUDING Michelle, who's got the baby in a carrier. The little one wears the cutest pair of baby earmuffs you've ever seen, which is a must for game nights at the bar. Technically she's too young to be allowed in, but this is a small town and even if she's not yet one, she can't miss this make-or-break game to see who's headed to the playoffs.

Just like old times, we're all here in our booth at The Peanut Bar. Nick and Michelle and baby. Nate and Anne. Cheryl and me.

The only one missing is Jackson.

Not *missing* missing. Just late. Late for the game that takes place at the same time every Sunday. My foot taps erratically wondering where the heck he is.

"He's going to miss the second quarter," I fret to Cheryl. I'm not exactly worried for him. He's a grown man and The Peanut Bar is in the same place as always. We even planned to come here separately, me with Cheryl and him with …

Well, nobody. Since we're together. A smile creeps up to my lips as I check my phone again. *Together*, together.

We've been together since the night with the Chinese food. The awkward Sunday football game never happened, because it was never awkward. We simply showed up and announced we were a thing and ordered everyone a shot to celebrate. I'll never forget Cheryl's scream and Anne's hug of unadulterated joy. *About time* was said a lot that night.

"The first quarter's not over yet." Cheryl pats my arm with a gleam in her eye. "Relax. Want another drink?"

"I've barely had any of this one." The IPA sloshes in my glass as I tilt it.

Because I don't want to have fun without him. Jackson's easygoing, but I take my time with him seriously. If I'm going to get buzzed at the bar, I want it to be with him standing next to me and ready to take me home.

Fine. I want everything to happen with him standing next to me. It's a huge victory to be with him, in my mind. He represents growing into myself as a woman and taking control of my own life. For once, I didn't shove down my feelings and pretend they were worthless. I acted on them, and now I have the best man I could imagine.

Our team kicks off the ball, and the players rush around the field, arranging and rearranging themselves for the next series. I like when we play defense. Cheryl thinks offense is more exciting, but I like standing up for what you've earned. Plus, there's a chance we catch an interception, which is the most thrilling thing that can happen in football.

The opposing team's quarterback lines up, catches the snap, and throws the ball.

One of our guys jumps into the air, his hands up high. Almost—almost—

He misses.

"Oh, man, that was close."

Nobody else in the bar reacts. I turn to Cheryl to see why not, but she's not looking at me.

She's looking at the man who just walked in through the front door of the bar.

Jackson.

He's not dressed for a football game. No well-worn jeans, no sweatshirt or jersey.

He's in a trim-cut suit that hugs his shoulders just right. A suit I've never seen him in. One that looks expensive as hell.

My mouth waters although my head is wondering if I've slipped and fallen. I could be dreaming right now and I wouldn't want a soul to wake me up. This is more than what he wears to the office. He's taken more care with his appearance, and everybody notices. How could you not? He's all dark hair and blue eyes and wearing a jacket that fits him like he was meant to be on the cover of a magazine.

"Hey, Dani," he calls out although his sharp gaze is pinned on me. "Can you turn the volume down a second?"

I barely glance to the left. The bartender smiles. The volume lowers on the TVs. To my shock, nobody protests. My heart flutters in my chest. *What's happening?*

Jackson strides over to me, eating up the distance too quickly for me to process that this is even real. He gives a wave to all our friends at the bar and everybody else who's come to watch the game. "I want all of you to hear this, okay?"

"What are you doing?" I whisper beneath my breath although he takes my hands in his.

With a nervous smile, he gets down on one knee.

Oh my God.

"Aubree, I've had a crush on you since the first day we met."

My mouth drops open. He did not. I had the crush on him.

Jackson laughs. "I know. I never told you, because I didn't want to scare you off. But now the whole town can hear, and I don't care. I want them all to know how much I love you. I want you to know how much I love you. I want to spend every Sunday with you for the rest of our lives. Will you marry me?"

"Yes," I squeak. I take his face in my hands. "Yes, of course I do."

"Do you want to see the ring first, maybe?"

Laughter fills the bar, and it's so warm and welcoming. That's the sound of my friends being happy for us. Our friends. We didn't have to give any of them up.

I can barely get out the words as I tell him, "I'd marry you without a ring."

Jackson shakes his head and pulls a ring box out of his pocket. He opens it with a flourish. From behind him, Cheryl gasps. "That's way bigger than you said it was!"

"What?" he answers, sheepish and proud and before he can respond, I pull him to his feet and kiss him. Fisting his shirt and desperate to seal the deal. A cheer goes up from all around us. This is what it means to have a good life. This is what it means to be happy. As soon as I'm done kissing Jackson, he slides the ring on my finger and steps out of the way.

"What are you—"

Cheryl throws herself at me, wrapping her arms around my neck. "Do you have any idea how hard that was to keep a secret?" She laughs. "Let me see, let me see." Cheryl takes my hand and looks down at the diamond sparkling on my finger. "It's perfect." Then she tugs her brother back into place at my side. "You're both perfect together. I'm going to give the best maid of honor speech."

"Who said you were going to be—" Jackson begins.

"Oh, stop," I say, cutting him off. Dani turns the game back up on the TVs. "She's going to be my maid of honor. And you're going to be my husband."

He gives me that charming smile that makes everything around us fade to nothing.

"I love you, Aubree."

"I love you too."

PRETEND YOU LOVE ME

W WINTERS AND AMELIA WILDE

All I have to do is pretend. When the lights go out and the chill of the cell creeps in, I know I must go along with everything he says.

His sharp gaze fades into the darkness, and nothing else matters but surviving this moment.

I'll do all he asks. I'll obey every command and submit on my knees. There's not an ounce of me that's willing to risk losing more than I already have.

All he desired was revenge, and now all he desires is me.

This mafia story is an explicit abduction romance with violence and dubious consent. It's short and provocative, with a jaw-dropping twist. The tale's decadent darkness allows us to escape into the fantasy. Please be mindful of these triggers prior to reading.

PROLOGUE

The front door creaks open ever so slowly and softly. The faint sound is immediately drowned out by the loud music, the laughter and the clink of chips falling onto the poker table in the back room. The space is filled with cigar smoke and brutal men whose faces hold genuine smiles as they gamble with stolen money. A half dozen of them are tucked away in the back of the modern home.

Seven men filter in through the front, dressed all in black, with leather gloves but no masks.

In that very front room there's a crib and next to it a lullaby sound machine on the fireplace mantel, meant to lull the infant into a sweet dream. Chubby little hands wrap around a rattle as wide eyes watch but can't see that far as the men take careful steps through the hall.

The floor groans in protest, but just like the front door, it's unheard. Not a single one of them expected anything more than drinking and betting during their monthly poker game.

The song's soothing refrain is punctuated by the staccato bang of guns cutting through the night. Feminine steps race down the stairs at the front of the home, rushing with the silent terror of a mother. Her screams are joined by shouting. Chaos only lasts a moment, one blur, one execution carried out seamlessly and planned for years.

The lullaby never stops as one of the assailants grabs the woman by her waist. The baby can't see how she struggles in the unknown man's arms to reach her child. She pleads and prays but can't do anything other than thrash in the arms of someone more prepared, and far stronger than she.

The sweet melody is at such odds with the silence that follows a bullet pinging on the tiled floor. Bodies lie around the poker table, blood seeping into the sides of tailored suits and what were once crisp white button-downs.

It's quiet, all but the cadence of a lullaby the infant has heard since before he was born. Footsteps aren't so careful anymore as the music suddenly halts and the men filter out. The woman is carried away, all the while fighting for her child.

One man approaches the crib, and two rough, callused hands wrap around the top railing. A bundled baby, wrapped tightly yet those little arms somehow escaped, looks up at dark eyes.

A gruff voice whispers something to the man who stares down at the child, and he only gives a nod in response. He's murdered more men than he's shaken hands with.

The man carefully picks up the child, bringing the one-month-old to his chest. "Hush now, little one."

Madelyn

My breathing hardly comes in as another scream tears through my throat. Tears prick my eyes, burning them as I slam my fists against the trunk.

I've been taken, I'm trapped and nothing is in my control anymore. A terror that threatens to consume me takes over.

"My baby!" I cry out again, pleading with men who ignore me. "Please!" I beg them.

They won't listen, though. Even as panic tenses all my body, and adrenaline pounds through my veins, I'm all too aware they won't listen to me.

I know what he wants. My racing heart slows.

A chill settles through me as I hear a knock on the steel roof above me. "You be quiet now, you don't want to wake the baby," a man says, his voice carrying through the metal enclosure of the trunk.

"Please," I whisper so lowly, I'm not certain a soul could hear.

The command comes out final yet tinged with sympathy, although I may be wrong. Perhaps I only imagine a semblance of mercy. "You listen to me, and everything will be all right."

Connor
Two days ago

My brother's footsteps crunch in the snow. Fletcher's silent, but I'm more than certain I know what he plans to say. A bitter wind whips by, my black tie waving in the breeze as I stare down at the carved stones in the ground. Two people who should have never been laid to rest will lie here for all eternity.

"What is it?" I barely manage to ask after I swallow the hard lump in my throat. It's all for them, for my wife and son I lost years ago, yet it feels like I've betrayed them.

"Is there anything I can do?" my brother questions behind me and it's so softly spoken, the harsh wind nearly drowns out the words.

Turning to face him, his hands are splayed across the front of his charcoal suit. Remorse wears itself on his face whenever we find ourselves here.

"It's been six years," I say, telling him a truth he already knows.

He only nods and then clears his throat as he takes the necessary steps to close the distance between us. He swallows so hard it's audible before he says, "Friday night, it's set."

With my brother in front of me and my past behind me, I'm all too aware that what I'm going to do next is cruel and unforgivable. He took my wife and child … this is a fair trade.

"Are you sure about this?" he asks.

I don't answer him; all I know is that I need this to happen. More than I need to live.

CHAPTER 1

THE TREMBLING IS CONSTANT AND I COULDN'T STOP IT IF I tried. Another shudder runs through me as the chill of the cell slips across my barely covered skin. My shoulders shake involuntarily as I bring my knees into my chest and stare at the vent where soft promises filter through of what awaits me. I can hear all the men, everything they're saying and how they're to leave me alone.

He said no one touches her.

Leave her there until he's ready.

They don't ask questions but they know I'm here, tucked away in the basement, huddled in a corner of my cell.

There's a soft drip from the spout in the cinder block wall behind me that's a relative constant and occasionally the heat kicks on, a loud click signaling its start but the warmth isn't for the cell, it's for upstairs.

The cotton nightgown I was wearing when I was taken is torn and thin, leaving me freezing, alone and waiting for the same person as the men upstairs: Connor Walsh.

Just thinking his name does horrid things to my heart. It skips and halts in place. The rough stubble of his jaw, the hard lines of his cheekbones and the depths of his dark copper gaze only add to the dominating air that surrounds him.

He's a damaged man with nothing left to lose. Men like him are dangerous. That's what my husband used to say. He knew that all too well and now he's dead.

Leaving my fate in the hands of a man hell-bent on revenge.

The unmistakable sound of a key turning in the lock from up the stairwell sends a pulse of shock and a new wave of terror through me. The first step on the narrow wooden stairs seems hesitant, as if whoever owns the movement is unsure of it. With my palms scraping against the grit littering the floor I attempt to scoot backward, as far away as I can get, but the stone wall at my back is unyielding.

Step by step, he takes his time.

His black jeans come into view first, followed by his black button-down with the sleeves rolled up to his forearms. The shirt is tight on his broad shoulders, and then those eyes … they pin me where I am.

Connor is a hardened man; I've known him nearly all my life. Or at least I've known the whispers of him. In this small run-down town with corruption on every corner, two feuding families ran things for decades. There was my husband's family, the mob formed by his father, and there were the Walshes.

Now there's only Connor Walsh.

His heavy footsteps stop outside the barred door of the cell. The room I'm confined to feels so much like a prison, for a moment I think of Connor as my warden.

The tension is thick between us and even though he's feet away, I'm enveloped by his heat.

The cords in his neck tighten as he swallows, his gaze roaming down my body, appraising every inch as it travels lower.

Too much time passes in near silence and fear takes over, begging me to plead with him. "My baby—"

"You'll do what I say." His tone is low and his words spoken with a cadence that's calm and eerie. It's one I've never heard from him. One that paralyzes me. "Did you hear me?" he questions and tilts his head, as if willing me to defy him.

Something I have no intention of doing.

"Anything. I'll do anything you tell me to," I say, the words leaving me in a rush.

"Good."

"My baby?" I'm barely able to get the words out. He's only a month old. My little one.

"He's fine." He has the decency to pull his eyes away from me as he speaks. "He's taken care of, and you'll be with him soon."

Hope rises along with an eagerness to get to my baby.

"Come here," Connor commands and I don't hesitate. Unsure of whether I should stand or crawl, I crawl, lifting the torn nightgown and balling the fabric in my fists. The floor isn't gentle on my knuckles but I don't care.

It's not until I get to the bars that he tells me, "You could have walked."

Embarrassment colors my cheeks and just as I look up at him to tell him I don't know what he wants, he reaches through the bars, and his strong fingers wrap around my throat.

Instinctively my hands reach up to his, and I instantly regret it.

He isn't tight with his grip, just firm, not so much that I feel the need to fight. Slowly, reluctantly, I lower my hands. All the while his amber gaze blazes and keeps me still.

"Stand," he tells me and I do as he wishes.

A chill filters through and my nipples harden; the thin gown does nothing to hide that fact. Staring down at the veins in his arms, I attempt to hide the shame of what comes over me.

"You know what I want from you, don't you?" he questions, his breath low and not hiding his desire.

I attempt to nod without looking up at him, but his grip tightens and my eyes flash to his.

"Yes," I answer in a whisper.

My heart pounds as heat floods through me with the way he looks at me. It's the same way he looked at me years ago, before the war, before the bloodshed, before he became the man he is today. Years ago when we were reckless and life hadn't taught us how harsh it could be.

His hand loosens just enough for his thumb to brush along my bottom lip, prompting me to open my mouth.

"Suck," he murmurs this time and I do as I'm told. The roughness of his skin begs me to scrape my teeth along it and I do. I suck the taste of him, I press my tongue against him and give him exactly what I know he wants.

It's only when my eyes close that he pulls away, leaving me standing there with the bars between us and a power imbalance that puts me at his mercy.

He reaches into his pocket for the key, and plays with it between his thumb and pointer, as if debating.

My pulse rampages but before I can beg for anything from this man, he tells me, "Your child needs you. Get him back to sleep, then you'll come to me. Understand?"

CHAPTER 2

Connor

VOICES COME THROUGH THE BACK DOOR AS I MOVE THROUGH the house. My brother and three of our men are outside, having a smoke. Their cigarettes are orange flares in the dark. The wood beneath my feet doesn't creak to announce my presence. They don't hear me getting closer to the door.

I pause to listen. At times their voices are muffled by the sound of the vengeful wind. In general, they're not paying attention. The men talk freely among themselves, not bothering to give the surrounding woods more than a cursory glance. It's not the woods they should be worried about. It's me.

After years of working for me, and knowing how close to the edge I've been, they should be more than aware of that fact.

Their lack of attention will play into my hands, but it frustrates me just the same. I haven't had the luxury of letting my guard down.

Most people have no guard at all, even the men who are supposed to. They can't keep their mouths shut. A man who can listen is always better off. That's what it takes to survive in the world today. You have to keep track of what's going on around you, even with people you claim to trust.

I don't trust anyone. Least of all the men outside. My brother is the only one who deserves my trust, and he's the only one who will get it. Everyone else is expendable. Everyone else can be replaced in a heartbeat. The vast majority of the world simply takes up space until someone has a better use for it.

I wouldn't have thought that when I was younger. I had softer ideas about the value of human life. Now, I don't give a fuck.

Except when it comes to my new captive and prize.

Madelyn.

Everything in me screams to go back to her. It's unsettling. I shut off my emotions six years ago. It was like flipping the switch to a circuit breaker. Every feeling apart from rage died out in an instant, and I haven't let any of the others come back. It would be impossible to focus with my mind occupied by sentiments and morals.

"What do you make of it?" Fletcher asks the men. They feel secure, out in the backyard. It's a mistake. The cover of darkness isn't a cover at all. Just because they've carried out the mission successfully doesn't mean it's any safer. Loyalty has been questioned recently. I deliberately chose the three newest men, fledgling additions.

If loyalty isn't given freely, I won't demand it. I'll simply cut their throats.

"She'll run the first chance she gets," answers the first one. I recognize the voice as belonging to Matthew. After a long drag of his cigarette he adds, "Had that look in her eyes. She's ready to bolt."

"Not if she cares for her child," my brother points out. I swallow thickly at the reminder of the little boy. Those emotions I thought long dead shove themselves to the surface and I clench my fist in response.

"You think he'll really keep her?" asks the second, Nathaniel. He lights a new cigarette and it casts orange light across his face. "Like he really wants to keep her as his … what? Sex slave?"

"It's sick," Matthew practically spits out. "More than a little."

"Is that the first hint you ever got that my brother's sick?" my brother asks in a light, joking manner, but there's a razor blade at the heart of his tone. I don't have to see him to know there's a smirk on his face. Right now he's seemingly charming and at ease, but it conceals a lethal side of him.

"You think I'm sick?" I say as I stride out into the backyard. They've been in the business too long to look truly surprised, but the first one frowns. He didn't want me to overhear him call me sick. It's a lapse. The third man has been silent and he remains still, his arms crossed as he leans against the brick of the house.

The other two exchange self-conscious glances, like they've been caught with their dicks out.

"She's in a cell, isn't she?" The question is followed by another drag from the first man's cigarette. "After all that screaming."

I'd rather stay cold, but emotions run hot. "She's doing what I told her to do."

He smirks. "How? Doesn't seem like she'll be very cooperative."

"That depends on who handles her. So it's a good thing you assholes won't be touching her."

He huffs a humorless laugh with his hands up. "I'm not the one who wants to. You spent too long in there. People are going to think you want her, and she's not like that."

"Not like what?"

The first man darts a glance at his buddy. This is risky territory, and he knows it. The mood is lightening but my face isn't.

"Worth it," he says. "What happens if she gets to you? What happens if she makes you even sicker than you already are?"

"I'll let you know if I feel ill when I'm done with her." I let a smile spread over my face. That's what he's watching. He doesn't see the quick reach for the gun at my belt. He's too busy laughing.

The safety's been off since we took her. I've been waiting for this moment. Waiting for one of them to step out of line.

Damn it, I wasn't supposed to care. None of the comments were going to get to me. I wasn't going to feel anything for her. Not at the house. Not in the cell. Nowhere.

Not until it was time.

The situation is already getting out of control, but my gun isn't.

I pull the trigger, sending a bullet through his head. Anger surges through my veins. There are things no one can ever know about Madelyn. There are things I'll have to keep buried deep until this is over.

A spatter of blood lands on my cheek as his body drops with a dull thud. I've been at this long enough to recognize the sound of a dead man hitting the ground.

I wait a beat.

Watch him.

No sign of movement comes from the body, except for the blood seeping out of the wound.

I swipe at the blood on my cheek with the back of my hand.

The other men are silent. Cigarettes burn at the tips of their fingers. Not a soul makes a move. The second guy was standing close enough that he has to be bloodied. Impossible to tell for sure with our dark clothes and the dark night. His face is frozen.

"Mind cleaning this up for me, brother?"

Fletcher doesn't appear disturbed in the least by the death of one of the members of our team. His mouth quirks. Not quite a smile. Not quite a frown. More like acceptance. Like he expected this. All of them should have expected this from me. I've been this person for six years now. I'm not going to change because Madelyn is in a cell.

"Not at all, boss."

I adjust my sleeves as my brother steps over to the body. He bends down and feels for a pulse. It's not necessary. The man's dead.

"Did anyone else have any comments about my future wife before I leave?"

I didn't intend to react to what they were saying, but my pounding heart didn't get the memo. *Sick.* I'll be damned. It was a simple bullshit comment that didn't mean anything. I felt it like a bullet through flesh.

The anger I've kept buried for the last six years is alive and well. It doesn't matter that I flipped the switch. It's all come back in an instant.

None of them has a damn thing to say. The only thing that surrounds us is silence and the threat of imminent death if they dare to say another word.

The third man taps the ash off his cigarette. He backs up half a step from the body, leaving room for my brother to roll the dead man onto his back.

"Get the wheelbarrow," my brother orders.

Everyone snaps into motion. They'll need to dig a hole at the edge of the woods, tip the body into it, and cover him back up. Not a single word is spoken in protest. Now that I've made my point, we shouldn't have any further conflict.

I've been patient. I've been meticulous. I've been planning.

Now that I have her, I'm going to use her to my advantage and use her for my pleasure.

If that makes me sick, so be it. It's time to enjoy the spoils of revenge.

CHAPTER 3

WITH HIS HAND ON MY SHOULDER AND HIS ROUGH HEATED skin against mine, he opens the bedroom door.

The baby is sleeping. Soundly and at a distance where I'll hear if he wakes.

This is the price I'll pay for the life I lead and the desires I've had for as long as I've known what it means to exist in this world.

A fire is already lit, surrounded by a stone mantel that reaches to the ceiling. The simplicity and masculinity of the room are undeniable. A gray textured wallpaper lines the back wall, while woodsy tones paired with blacks and grays add to the dominating atmosphere. The massive bed is a king and at the end of it is a tufted warm brown leather ottoman.

I've always seen Connor as a rugged man. Ruthless and foreboding. I never could have imagined his private room to have such warmth and elegance. The harsh lines and darkness certainly fit his persona, though.

With a heavy breath, I peek down at myself and my arms instinctively cover my chest. The torn cotton gown appears cheap and out of place in a space like this. My knees are dirty and although the room itself is warm and expensive, all I feel is cold and trapped.

"This needs to come off," Connor whispers behind me, his warm breath just beneath the shell of my ear. His light touch on my bare shoulders as he brushes down the straps of my nightgown causes me to shiver involuntarily. A line of goosebumps travels down my curves as the nightgown falls. It doesn't do so elegantly, as silk would have. As it catches at my wide hips,

Connor uses both hands to push the garment down and his thumbs hook my underwear, tugging it along with the fabric.

Completely bared, my nipples pebble and I struggle to inhale as I stare straight ahead at the roaring fire. The flames lick and hiss while Connor takes his time, barely touching me, but exposing me exactly how he wishes.

My body isn't what it used to be and as his hand splays against my stomach, my eyes close with worry, but his hum of satisfaction spreads a new sensation through me. He nips the lobe of my ear and a gasp is forced from me.

As my breathing picks up, his hand lowers and his chest hits my back.

His fingers slip down to my sensitive clit. He takes his time, toying with me until my body buckles forward. His forearm braces me against him and he tsks.

"You'll stay still as I play with you," he tells me, his tone holding a note of warning. His hardened length presses into my backside through his jeans. His hard body demands that I take it.

My hand, though, acts on its own accordingly, grabbing his wrist as his hand moves lower still to my slit.

His body stills and the air changes. I can barely breathe knowing what I've done. I've stopped him, I've deliberately disobeyed.

"I haven't—" I start to say but can barely speak. "Since the baby," I add, pushing out the excuse. I haven't touched myself or been touched.

My chest rises and falls chaotically, uncertain how he'll react.

All at once, he leaves me, and I only turn when the sound of the sheets and comforter being lifted is louder than my pulse racing in my ears.

In the near silent room, all I can think about is my now dead husband's cruelty. Random flashes greet me of every time my needs were denied. Memories drift into my mind of my brother and how he died needlessly. Every dark moment passes in the flick of a second. My throat closes and the strength I thought I had fades to nothing but a facade.

I watch the dark shadows play along Connor's body as he pulls his shirt over his head, dropping it to the floor to form a puddle of clothing. His hands move to his belt and it comes off nearly violently to the point where I'm tempted to take a step back. He drops it, though, and it lands with a heavy thud. His jeans are next, and in one swift motion his cock juts out.

In only a moment, the damaged man is completely bared to me and waiting.

"Get on the bed," Connor commands and my body moves immediately, instantly obeying. Everything in me is at war; every want, every need, every thought and memory.

The bed groans softly as I climb onto the center and lie down on the luxurious sheets. My head sinks into the pillow and my gaze finds the spinning fan.

He's deliberate as he crawls up the bed, but his touch still startles me and brings me back to the present when he asks, "Is there something on your mind?"

My answer is immediate and submissive. "What would you like to be on my mind?"

Sliding between my legs, he spreads my thighs and his hard body covers me. His warm skin presses against my chest and he caresses my curves. His mouth greets me, his lips molding to mine instantly as his tongue parts my seam.

It's been so long since I've been kissed like *this*. Heavily and wantonly. Since I've been moaned into by the mouth of a man. His tongue strokes against mine as his fingers press into the flesh of my hips and he keeps me pinned. It feels as if he's everywhere all at once.

Consuming me and demanding attention equally as much as desire.

When he breaks the kiss, I breathlessly stare back at him, transfixed by his copper gaze.

"You will think of nothing but this. Of how much you need me to take you."

The light of the fire displays the harshness of his collarbone and corded muscles as I part my lips to answer. I can't, though, because he's far too concerned with silencing me with another kiss.

It's demanding and brutal, but the gentle motion of his hand slipping between my thighs is very much at odds. He's focused on my clit until I writhe under him, unable to stay still as he told me I should.

Every nerve ending lights on fire, a bundle explodes in the pit of my stomach and I cry out my pleasure as an orgasm rocks through my body. It happens so quickly and so unexpectedly, smothering every thought and doubt along with it.

He's off of me the moment I've come, and it doesn't take me long to figure out why. From his nightstand he gathers a bottle, and I watch him stroke himself with lubrication before pouring more in his hands.

It's only then that his fingers slip lower once again, spreading the lube at my entrance.

On his knees between my thighs, he slips the head of his cock between my folds, toying with me before pressing in slightly. My breath hitches and my hand splays against his chest as if that could stop him. With his dark gaze focused on mine, he tells me in a murmur, "I will ruin you for everyone else, but I intend for you to enjoy every moment."

With that he presses in deeper, stretching me and making my lips form an O. The sensation stings for a moment until he's fully inside of me, pressing against my walls. Connor stills, allowing me time to adjust.

My blunt nails dig into his shoulders as I wrap my arms around him, the heels of my feet digging into his muscular ass, as if I could hold on. As if doing so will save me from the far too intense sensation.

As I stare above me wide eyed and attempting to breathe, he kisses and nips my neck, relaxing me slowly as he pulls out gently and presses back in.

His lips find mine again and I'm able to kiss him, to cling to him, grateful and relieved. My body heats with every small movement. Every rock of his hips causes him to brush against my clit and it isn't long before I tilt my hips, wanting him deeper.

The moment my body instinctively welcomes him, he smiles against my lips. "You're my good little whore, aren't you?"

At his question my eyes meet his and he slams inside of me, brutally.

My head falls back and a strangled moan leaves me.

"Your cunt was made for me to fuck," he tells me as his hips piston.

His body pins me and his left hand finds my neck. Fingers wrap tight around my throat as he pounds into me, relentlessly and bringing about an intense sensation I've never felt before.

The bed bows with every hard thrust.

"Come on my cock like you want to," he groans into the crook of my neck. My pebbled nipples brush against his chest and it's all too much. "Come for me, my good little whore."

I do it. Unashamedly, I come undone for him.

The moan of satisfaction only extends my pleasure.

The orgasm is still raging through me as he kisses me again, riding through my release and fucking me deeper and harder. "That's my good girl. You're so fucking perfect."

He doesn't finish like that. He turns me over onto my stomach, grabbing the base of my hair and tugging as he fucks me from behind, dragging out every orgasm and pausing before he reaches his own climax so he can take more time with me.

"I'm going to enjoy every inch of you. I'm going to make you completely mine."

CHAPTER 1

SHE'S TERRIFIED WITH THE MEN WATCHING.

At least that's how it looks from my perspective. Her previously timid glances have turned to wide-eyed stares. Her chest rises and falls rapidly. Are these real nerves or is she pretending? Or is she just feeling the effects of what we did together?

Fuck knows I am. She's perfect. I already knew she would be. But last night was fucking perfect.

When she's cleaned up, presentable as she can be given the circumstances, I bring her out to the kitchen. She barely slept. All she wears is my T-shirt and an oversized pair of pajama pants rolled up at her hips.

Her hair is combed through but her fragility and delicate features are entirely exposed. For a split second I question my pride given her fear. But she's fucking perfect and she's mine. All mine. Forever.

She is the only good to come from chaos and war. How could I not be obsessed with her?

With hesitant steps, I have to press against the small of her back to bring her to the kitchen. It's modern, much like the entire estate, with clean lines and granite and stone that touch nearly every surface. I imagine she'll change it. As far as I'm concerned, it's hers to do as she wishes and needs.

Her delicate hand forms a fist, balling up the fabric of my shirt as we enter the room. Her bare feet pad softly, almost silently, on the cold tiled floor.

The men have arranged themselves there around the table. None of them appear to have slept last night. There's always the risk of retribution. No one will be safe or secure for weeks, months, maybe even longer. Not until the last enemy is snuffed out.

My brother watches Madelyn and I get closer without so much as a glimmer of recognition in his eyes. Best for everyone that way. He's the only one who knows her. He's the only one who knows the whole story. And it'll stay that way.

"Madelyn, this is my brother." I bring her over to him first. She's shaking like a leaf as he holds his hand out for her to shake.

"Hello, Madelyn," he says easily with the charming air he's known for. Although he's kind, she's still hesitant and looks to me first before she takes his hand.

"Hi," she says. I can hardly hear the words as they make small talk.

Madelyn lets me introduce her to all the men. She's a good actress. She's known who these men are for years. Knows their faces.

And they know her. They know far too much.

I don't care for the way they look at her, gazing too long and appraising. My hand itches to clench a fist, to express my rage for their indecency. I don't. I have to pretend I don't feel the anger surging inside every time one of them looks down at her body instead of her face. I have to pretend that there's nothing behind this but revenge.

That she's my captive, that this was planned in the way they're aware. That we haven't used them and there weren't ulterior motives.

The sound of the baby crying drifts into the kitchen. It's soft. He has the calmest cry.

Madelyn reacts instantly, her body tensing up as she looks over her shoulder, toward the hallway to her child. She bites at her lip but doesn't take a step toward the sound.

"Go," I tell her.

She hesitates, those wide eyes peeking up at me.

"Are you going to make me repeat myself?" I question lowly with a hint of playfulness, although she doesn't let on that she registers it.

Her eyes meet mine, and I swear I can see real fear there. *Of them? Of me?* I have to admit I like the look of it in her eyes. If that makes me sick, then so be it.

I take her jaw between my thumb and forefinger and tug her lips toward mine. I have to pretend I don't enjoy it. That it's part of the job. But it feels damn good to have my fingers on her skin. Her pulse is right at the surface. Her heart is beating hard, and something else flashes into her eyes. Desire. She can't hide it from me, no matter how well she pretends with the other men.

It's a good thing I have practice in following the plan. I want to drag her back to my bedroom, but this little performance is important for what happens next. The men need to see us together. They need to see me controlling her and her submission. There can be no question about what's happening between me and Madelyn.

Revenge. Ownership.

Nothing else. There is only one truth now: she is mine.

"What did I tell you?"

Madelyn parts her lips. "That I'll do what you say."

I want to say that she needs to do more. That she needs to kiss me, right here, right now. Make me believe it. But that would end my ability to speak, and I have more to say. The baby cries out again. He sounds more desperate now. Hungry or lonely, it's hard to tell. I don't let on that I'm responding to the noise too. A man like me shouldn't ever want to comfort a crying child. Certainly not one that everyone believes is another man's child.

"What else?" I ask her. "What else did I tell you? There are only two things that matter. You will do what I say … and what else?"

"That I'm yours." *I'm yours* sounds sweet on her tongue. It doesn't matter that we're in a room full of killers. It doesn't matter that I'm the most dangerous one of all.

"Do you think what's mine hesitates in my own home?"

Madelyn shakes her head, pressing her face more firmly into my hand.

It's going to be hell to let go of her. I keep thinking I can make this easy. I've endured many difficult things over the years. Staying in control is my entire life. I even planned this operation from start to finish. Everything about it was my doing. This should have been the simple part—pretending she's just a captive who will marry me against her will.

"You're a mother. And you're my fuck toy. You'll marry me and love me in every way I crave." I say these words in a cruel, mocking tone that's meant to hurt her, but they're true. They're the only real thing about this situation. Madelyn will marry me. She'll stay my fuck toy. And she is a mother.

The baby cries again, and my fingers tighten in spite of all my control. It's a sound designed to attract attention, but I can't give in. I can't be the one to scoop the child from the crib and give it whatever comfort it needs. Not with the eyes of my men on me.

"Don't you love me?" I say in a taunting tone.

Madelyn flinches, and once again, I'm flooded with confusion. Is she flinching because she doesn't believe me or because she's afraid of reality? Now is not the time for that conversation, but damn, I wish it were.

"I love you," she says, her voice soft.

I pull her in for a brutal kiss.

This—this is the thing I can't stop. I meant for it to be quick, but once her mouth is against mine, I'm consumed with how sweet she is. She doesn't pull away from the harsh bite. Instead, she gives into it. She's obedient that way, but it only makes me want to keep her here with me.

It's a dangerous line we're walking.

Until we follow this situation to the end, everything will be as uncertain as it is now. Anything could happen. That's one thing this life has taught me. It's not over just because you want something to be done. It's over when the last threat is finally defeated.

We're not there yet. Not even close.

I pull away from her, and Madelyn stumbles. It takes all my willpower not to pull her into my arms and steady her. She catches herself before I have to and straightens slowly, her breath coming fast.

"Now go," I order.

The baby wails now, sustained cries. I can see the physical pull he has on her. Maybe it's similar to the pull she has on me.

Once Madelyn has her balance, she leaves quickly, not glancing back at any of us.

Not surprising. She doesn't want the other men to look at her. It was hard enough for her to be in the kitchen with all of them. Still, I would have felt some satisfaction if she'd looked back for me.

It doesn't matter. I'm the one who ordered her to go. That doesn't include hesitating to see if I'm watching. I made that clear enough when I spoke to her. I can still feel her warm flesh pressing against my fingers when she shook her head. It's unreal, how this woman gets under my skin. I almost wipe my palm against my pants just to get the sensation to go away. I can't let it influence me.

I can't bring myself to do it. The tingling where our bodies touched lingers on my hand.

I want to follow her more than anything. Instead, I imagine her entering the baby's room, her body relaxing as she sees her child again. She's a good mother, and she would soften. Murmur something to him as she came in so he'd know she was there.

I was right. The cries taper off. She must have him in her arms now, holding him close.

If we were different people, I'd be in there with her. I feel more regret about that than I should. Having feelings like this is almost overwhelming, given how hard I've worked to keep them suppressed over the years.

It doesn't matter. I won't let them interfere. Madelyn and I will get to the end of this, whether it goes as planned or blows up in our faces.

I turn back to the men gathered at the table. If they noticed anything different about the way I treated her, they don't give any sign of it. That's a relief.

"Time to move on," I tell them. "Any movement or word? Has anyone heard anything?"

CHAPTER 5

HE FILLS ME WITH EVERY THRUST. EACH MOTION IS FORCEFUL and brutal, yet it all brings nothing but pleasure. With a pillow under my hips, he fucks me deep and rough. A cold sweat breaks out along my skin. I'm sore, deliciously used and my entire being is exhausted and sated.

As he buries himself fully inside of me, his hand roughly plucks my nipples and his pubic hair grinds against my clit. He's an expert at playing me, at depriving me of pleasure until he's ready.

It's been that way for years now, and the memory of our first time against the brick wall of an alley flashes before my eyes as he tells me to come like the good little whore I am.

Just like he did then.

And I obey, dutifully coming undone for a man I've loved in secret for years.

As he loses himself to pleasure, the rhythmic pulses of his cock press against my walls and I swear I could come again just from the sensation.

He holds me, kisses me for a moment and then climbs off, leaving me waiting for a damp cloth to clean up. He's gentle as he does it. I've always been in awe of how this man can be so cruel and so hell-bent on murder and vengeance, yet in the dark of night, alone with me, he has a side to him no one else sees.

Although I suppose it's the same for me. I'm a duplicitous woman who married a man only to get back at him for my brother's murder.

The bed groans as he wipes between my thighs and the cuffs attached to the bedpost clink.

"Do you want to use these?" I ask, only because they've been there since I arrived and he hasn't once mentioned them.

"No, it's for if they come in," he states simply, even though dread consumes me.

No one can know I was a rat. No one can know we planned this for years. So much is in the hands of deceit. "You'll say I put them on you at night," he tells me, tossing the cloth into the laundry bin and then climbing back into bed, pulling the sheets and comforter over us.

I can only nod as words evade me. I don't know what all his men think or what they're telling one another. I don't know if I'm playing the part well enough.

My whispered words are laced with fear when I ask, "Do you think they'll find out?"

"My brother knows and no one else. No one can ever suspect you were a rat, even if I told you exactly what to do. They would never trust you."

"I know, but have they said anything?" I ask him as I turn onto my side, staring into the eyes of a man I fell in love with before I was even on his radar. Years ago, before my brother died and I vanished. Before he met a woman who gave him his first son.

Before tragedy. Before this life requested we pay our dues.

Back when all I wanted was him and I thought that would be easy.

"You're giving me that look again." Connor breaks up my thoughts with a gentle murmur, his fingers tipping my chin up and forcing me to look at him.

My handsome brutal protector peers down at me.

"I know I used you. I know you fell for me before I fell for you."

"I loved you so much, I was willing to marry the enemy." My heart aches knowing what I've done.

"You wanted vengeance too," he reminds me and I nod in agreement. I wanted to kill him, but Connor convinced me to destroy them all. Every last one of them from the inside out.

"When did you want me?"

"Always." His answer is easy and confident, without hesitation. "When did I fall in love with you, though? When did I … feel this possessiveness over you?"

"Was it when I got pregnant?" I ask him the question I've wondered for the last nearly year. Everything changed when I told Connor I was pregnant.

"Before that." He admits, "I couldn't stand the idea of him touching you." I remember the argument we had. Connor didn't want me to go back. But we were so close to having our plans realized, and I wanted vengeance more than I cared to protect myself.

"He could have found out the baby wasn't his."

"We were careful …" I start and all the thoughts and worries race through my mind. "If Nolan wasn't yours—"

"He's mine." His answer is final. "That is all that matters. No one will ever hurt him."

My throat closes, wanting nothing else than for my son to be safe. With the feud between families ended by bloodshed, he should be safe.

"I will do anything to keep him safe."

"What if they find out?" It is my only worry. The only thing that keeps me from sleeping peacefully now.

"Fletcher and I would kill them all before we let anything happen to you or our son."

The anxiousness doesn't leave me. "I just want it all to be over," I whisper, my gaze falling to his chest.

His hand wraps around mine and he brings my knuckles to his lips, planting a kiss there before telling me, "I asked too much of you." The remorse and regret are evident in his tone.

"What's done is done."

That's what we've said for years as we fell deeper into each other's arms and more and more consumed with plotting an execution to right the sins of the past.

I'm only grateful I'll no longer be sleeping with the enemy.

"You did everything I told you to. You are my good girl." He kisses my forehead and the pride and comfort that come with his praise nearly lull me to sleep.

"I love you. Not only for what you do for me, but because I know you. I know all of you."

His hand slips down my curves when he tells me he loves me too.

"You didn't answer my question, though … When did you fall for me?" I don't know why I need to know so badly. But I do.

"Around the time I told you we were pregnant?" I guess.

"I loved you before that … you know that."

"I know, I just—" I have to steady my breathing before I can get out this pain that radiates inside of me. "But when you … when you wanted to stop it all … when you wanted me to run away from him and be with you because I was pregnant … I was afraid to tell you because I knew you didn't feel for me what I felt for you but something seemed different that day."

He smiles weakly and stares at the spinning fan as he says, "I'll never forget that day."

Before I can press him again, wanting to know when, he tells me, "I fell for you when you came to me with a proposition. It was slow, not all at once. When you told me you knew how I felt." His words are choked and I remember that moment. When I met him at his wife and child's gravestones. My dead husband took from us a love that will always be missed. But Connor and I found each other and he won't take that away now.

He pulls me in close. "I fell in love with you when my soul realized I needed you to exist. I don't know how else to describe it. Without you, I didn't want to live."

Silence surrounds us as I realize the depth of our connection.

"It's our secret, though," he reminds me.

"I know."

His voice is reassuring when he tells me, "You'll do well playing the part, you have before."

"I'll pretend as long as you want, whatever you want. So long as you love me."

His grip on me tightens and he pulls me in as close as I could possibly be. He's my savior, though everyone else thinks he's my enemy. I can only hope I'm the same to him.

"Tell me you love me again," I whisper against his lips.

"I love you."

"I love you too."

A KISS TO KEEP

It started with a kiss. A single kiss that shook me to my core. A kiss to silence me, and a kiss to numb the pain.

I took his hand and in turn, he took me away. I thought when we ran away, we'd never have to look back.

I was wrong.

I think Sebastian knew, and so did I, that he'd be pulled back into this life one day. There was no way we could have gotten our happily ever after. Scars don't ever fully go away, and this sinful place is etched into our flesh.

I don't know how I'll ever forgive him for bringing me back here. Even when he kisses me the way he does… no kiss can take away this pain.

He's still my everything, but I don't know how we'll survive this.

A Kiss to Keep is an extension of Chloe and Sebastian's story, *A Kiss to Tell*. Although it can be read on its own, it's recommended you start with *A Kiss to Tell*.

PROLOGUE

Chloe

I REMEMBER THE HUM OF THE ENGINE. IT'S FUNNY HOW THAT'S WHAT stayed with me all this time. We took off in the shadows of the night, with what little bit we had that was worth taking with us and we drove away as fast as we could.

We didn't stop running, not for a long time, and I didn't have to ask him why.

No one leaves that place and gets away with it.

Crescent Hills is nothing but sin and misfortune. It's designed to keep every soul trapped there in a fog of devastation. I grew up surrounded by violence and agony. Living in fear and in anger. The constant turmoil kept me fighting, but I knew I would never be anything more than a name on its list of victims. That's the truly unfortunate part. I never wanted to call it home, but back then, I knew I'd never have another.

Until Sebastian.

He was always the only one for me, because he stained my lips with his and scarred my skin with his burning touch before I ever considered letting a boy touch me. Well, any boy other than him. No one else could have compared.

It all started with a kiss.

He followed me behind our high school. I didn't know it and I never would have guessed he felt even a fraction of what I'd felt for him. He had to have though, because that unfortunate day, I turned around after crying so hard and there he was. I was embarrassed to be inside with the other kids, so I hid outside, trying to suppress the shameful tears. The second I heard him, the second I turned around to see who'd followed me, Sebastian pushed my back against the brick wall and crushed his lips against mine.

Stunning me. Stealing my breath from me. Forcing me to think of him. Which was worlds better than being consumed with the tragedy that plagued me. That moment changed everything.

Because he kissed me, and I never forgot that kiss.

Because I took his hand and he led me away.

A sad smile plays at my lips as I rest my cheek against the cold glass. It was freezing cold when we ran away over a decade ago. We were barely more than kids then. Time's changed us so much. But it can't change everything.

It's fitting that it's bitter cold now that we're returning.

Now that we're going back into the nightmare.

"I never thought we'd go back," I whisper into the silent cabin of the car. The stereo works just fine, but I can't stomach the idea of music right now. I don't want to ruin any songs with this ominous day, knowing they'll be forever associated with this memory.

Bastian lays his hand on my thigh, and I merely glance at his touch, ignoring his warmth when he tells me, "I didn't either."

I think he just says what he thinks I want to hear.

I think he knew one day, he'd be drawn back to this life.

"I love you," he tells me in a rough voice, one that's been silent for hours. My sad smile lifts just slightly, and I lay my hand on top of his although I don't want to.

I love him, but I hate this place.

He says we're coming home.

But this was never my home.

I don't say "I love you" back. And Bastian doesn't react when I don't. That's what hurts the most. He knew what this would do to us.

And he did it anyway.

CHAPTER 1

Chloe

W E'VE BEEN DRIVING FOR DAYS NOW. THE SNOW'S BARELY slowed us down. The prolonged silence, however, makes every minute seem longer than it is.

The closer we get, the faster the snow falls though. And we're close now. I know we are. I recognize these streets, even the backroads that have no names.

The air has changed, and it makes my stomach churn harder every time I breathe in.

"So you had a good time then?" I ask Bastian, picking at some barely perceptible fuzz on my sweater. My heart ticks faintly in my chest, almost like it's afraid to really beat and pump life through me. Instead it's this timid movement, leaving me counting the seconds until things are right again.

Clearing his throat, he shrugs. The motion draws up his jacket, pulling it tighter around his shoulders as he turns the wheel and the car takes a left down a back alley.

It takes real effort not to close my eyes as we pass the bar. A bar I know so well and wish I didn't.

Everything is different, yet it's all painfully familiar.

The sign looks worn and old, but even when I was a child, it looked just the same. Ragged and decrepit. Time's aged it, but not enough to really change it.

"It was a good week," he finally answers me, and his answer pulls my gaze from the gutters full of dirty snow to his steely blue eyes. "I'm sorry

I had to go so quick and for so long. I missed you though," he adds with a warmth in his voice that travels straight to my veins.

He's my drug. A living, breathing drug. He's been gone a little over a week, leaving me all the way across the country to come back here. Now, I'm joining him, which is a nightmare come true for me.

"I missed you too," I admit although the words come out strangled still and I have to rip my eyes away to stare back out the window.

As if beat-up houses and barren streets were something I'd ever want to look at.

This particular road has stayed with me all my life. As the disquiet forces me to readjust in my seat, I ask Sebastian again, "Are you sure we should be here?"

Tick, tick, goes my heart, then a pause. My heart refuses to do anything at all, leaving a chill to travel down my arms as we pass Dixon Street, and Sebastian gives me a pointed look. We grew up on the same street, this street, but we've never lived in the same world.

I don't know how I fooled myself into thinking running away from here would change that.

"I know this is sudden…" He trails off and reaches his hand for mine, but I'm already crossing my arms so I pretend not to see it.

I swallow my response along with the regret from saying anything at all.

He can comfort me, but he's ignoring the flashing red light warning that this is exactly what we shouldn't be doing. I don't want comfort in that. He can keep it for himself.

"Never mind," I whisper and my warm breath fogs the window.

As the car moves over a speed bump and then a pothole in the old road, I jostle with it, passively letting the movement take me how it wants.

"How are you feeling?" Bastian's voice is low and apologetic, yet strong. He's always strong. Never faltering, never needing to lean on me.

It should be a blessing, but it feels like a curse.

"Second trimester is worlds better," I tell him and breathe in deep, feeling my shoulders stretch and rise before settling back down against the heated seat. "And I love this car," I comment.

"Smooth ride, huh?" he says just as we go over another pothole and I have to let out a small laugh at his dry humor and irony.

The second of ease between us is spoiled when we drive past our old high school, filled with haunted memories.

Mostly. The only two days I want to hold on to are the first day he kissed me and the day when we drove away years later. Every other day I spent here can rot in hell.

"It took me years to get over this place," I tell him, feeling the raw admission scratch up my throat with every word. Like I had to drag them out of me.

A second passes as the car slows to a stop under a red light.

"I know," Bastian says and this time when he lays his hand down for me to take, his eyes stare at me. His eyes pierce into me, begging me to feel what he feels. "I have to do this, Chlo."

I can't resist pulling down the seatbelt to lean over the center console so I can kiss his cheek. His rough stubble is short and it nearly scratches my lips as he tries to capture my own with his. But I avoid the kiss, settling on giving him a peck on the cheek.

Sebastian leans closer to me, ready to take one regardless, I know it.

With the groan of the leather seat protesting the movement of his broad shoulders, I prepare to give him a cheek and nothing more. I just can't kiss him; I can't give him that bit of me, not when he's hurting me the way he is.

He won't tell me why he *has* to be here. Why now? Why are we back?

Without a straight answer, things can't go back to being right between us. I won't allow it. He needs to know that. And all I know is that it has something to do with Carter Cross.

The red light turns to green as he sits up, and with it the car behind us beeps. Bastian's focus doesn't budge, not until I grip his hand. I thread my fingers between his and pull his hand to my lips, kissing the back of his hand as the car behind us beeps again.

Sebastian's frustration shows with his sharp, narrowed gaze aimed in the rearview mirror at the person behind us.

Always with a temper. What did I expect marrying the man everyone used to fear? He earned his reputation, and some bad habits die hard. The very thought makes me close my eyes with contempt. How could I think they'd died at all?

"Let's just go." I push out the rushed words as Bastian sits there, staring in his rearview and ready to pick a fight. "I want to lie down," I say, giving him the excuse and he buys it. His expression softens, but only slightly.

He doesn't ask and I don't tell.

I ask and he doesn't tell the whole truth.

We can't live like this, but we can suffer in silence until it kills us.

Well, mostly silence. The quiet hum of the engine keeps us company for a moment until he speaks.

"You can't hold back from me forever."

His words are heard, but not answered. Not for another two blocks.

"And you can't keep lying to me and keeping secrets," I finally counter, although my voice isn't as strong. It never comes out as strong as his, but it doesn't need to. My words are just as right as his are, and we both know it.

He's reticent again until we drive out of Crescent Hills, away from where our past lies restlessly. I don't understand why we didn't stop or where we're going.

He said we were going home. And Crescent Hills is the only home I've ever known, but we've driven out of it.

It's not until we pull into a long gravel driveway, nearly fifteen minutes away from the world I once knew, that I give him a questioning gaze laced with worry.

"I thought here would be better," he tells me and with his words, massive iron gates part, creating a large opening for us to enter.

They're beautiful and behind the gates is a grand estate, but it's far too much and there's no way in hell I want to live like that. In a massive house with more rooms than I would ever fill.

"We could never afford something like this." Anxiety consumes me, wondering what the hell he did, who he stole from, or if he sold his soul to the devil until he speaks.

"Not this one," he tells me when he catches my gaze. "That one's not ours." The relief is only slight.

"None of these are ours," I remind him. "Our apartment is on the other side of the country. I said I'd come for a week, but none of these are ours unless we decide together." I stress the last word, *together*, waiting for him to look me in the eyes. I can hear the gravel lift up under the tires just as easily as I can hear the pounding of my chest. Even if it still feels like a faint tick. That damn tick is loud.

"I know," he finally agrees with me, rounding the large white stone home and driving past it, down into a tree line for a slow minute and then another. The trees are a mix of burnt auburn and evergreen. And the evening light casts shadows and sprays of light on the gravel road and barren dirt path.

We have to drive deep into the winter forest before I see a much smaller house. I almost want to call it a cottage, but it's too contemporary. I have to lean forward in my seat to get a better look as he parks the car, although he keeps it running.

The word "motherfucker" nearly leaves me under my breath. If I could pick a dream house, it would be this one. It's set back deep under a canopy of mature trees, but with an opening for sunshine. There's a wraparound porch and so many windows with pale blue shutters.

"This isn't going to be like the last time, is it?" I ask him and he doesn't answer immediately. "You're not going to buy this house and wait for me to cave, are you?" I push him. Suddenly, that tick is becoming more of a slam with his ever-passing silence.

"Do you like it?" he asks me and I close my eyes, refusing to believe he did it again.

"You didn't," I whisper, praying he really didn't.

"I bought it," he tells me, letting the words slip out as if they don't matter. Just like the last time he decided to have a house built here.

"Motherfucker," I mutter, finally speaking the profanity aloud.

"I'll sell it if you don't love it, Chlo. We can up and leave and sell it no problem," he's quick to tell me, but that's not the point.

"You can't keep doing this shit!"

"Keep? It's only here, only about finding a place to stay," he argues back, letting his voice rise.

"Yes! Only here, the place I told you I never wanted to see again," I retort, and my voice cracks with outrage. "Do I have to remind you what happened to the last place? Good things don't happen here, and you should have taken that as an omen!"

The sky darkens at my words, the sun setting further into the trees, and I don't like it.

"This isn't okay," I tell him in the calmest voice I can manage. I focus on taking one deep breath and then another.

"Don't get worked up. I didn't mean to upset you."

"How could you have thought this wouldn't upset me?" I bite back. And then snidely add, "Oh, that's right, because you don't listen to me. Because I say words that don't mean anything."

"Don't do that." Sebastian's voice is low as he stares at me. His gaze is heated and so penetrating I can barely look at him, but I do. "Don't make it out like I don't care, Chloe. All I care about is you."

"Then why are we here?" I can't control the emotion in my voice.

The quiet forest seems to get darker with every minute we sit here arguing in the car.

"Because Carter needs me," he answers me in a tight voice.

Carter. His best friend. The one he left behind in order to run away with me.

I could never relate to that friendship. A friendship he calls family. Because I had no one to leave behind. Friend, family, or otherwise. I only ever had Sebastian.

"And that's his place?" I surmise. "The big one when we entered?" *Big one* doesn't quite do it justice.

"This is all his property, but the place we're going is deeper in the land. Private but safe and close. He lives there with his brothers," Bastian answers, all the tension leaving him. He knows I have a soft spot for Carter. What he doesn't know is how guilty I feel about everything that happened. But how could he, when he doesn't even know I'm very aware of what actually happened all those years ago?

"And what did he need you for?" I ask him, meeting his gaze. I can already see that he's going to lie. His tell is the way he narrows just his left eye, ever so slightly.

"You never tell me anything," I say before he can disrespect me with another lie.

"What you need to know is that you're safe here, and that I love you and I would do anything for you."

My first instinct is to correct him and tell him it's not about what I need to know, it's about telling me everything because I'm his partner. And those are the words sitting there on the tip of my tongue until I look in his eyes and see a hint of worry, and I let his statement digest.

Safe here. Are we in danger? My hand moves to my belly and the fear of loss is all too real. The last time we left this place, death remained behind.

The lingering memory of the nightmares and the fears creep into my mind. But I know what happened back then, and it can't be that. I pray it's not that.

I don't know if it's just being back here that causes chills to trail up my arms and down my spine, or if it's something else. I swallow my question, knowing Sebastian won't answer me anyway.

"Just come with me," Bastian asks, holding out his strong hand for me to take.

It doesn't mean I forgive him when I place my hand in his. And it doesn't mean we're okay when I follow him up the paved walkway to the gorgeous red walnut French doors.

All it means is that it's getting late, I'm tired, and I don't want to fight right now.

I fought all my life just to get by. I thought I was done fighting.

I thought wrong.

CHAPTER 2

Sebastian

"**I**S HE GOING TO BE A PROBLEM?"

I ask Carter the only question that's been eating away at me as we drove down here. The hate, the anger… the fear, it's all mixed into a deadly concoction that's been destroying my sanity for days. Ever since I left Chloe, all I could think is that this prick would go after her. That Romano would take her away from me.

Even though I knew she was safe, I couldn't sleep not having her right here by my side where she belongs. I don't know how we lived so long thinking we'd get away from it forever, but we can't. I'm not running away; I'm not going anywhere. "I'm going to fucking kill him."

"Romano's a dead man and he knows it," Carter answers, the early morning light filtering in from the large window behind his desk.

"While he's still breathing, he's a fucking problem," I respond and run my thumb along my jaw. "I thought about how we could do it on the way over to pick up Chloe and then that cop had to show up."

"Officer Walsh is a menace. He thinks he can question everyone and wait in parking lots for shit to go down and that he'll somehow be the hero? He doesn't know shit. Not about how things work around here, or about how deep these cuts go. All he's doing is delaying the inevitable."

"He has damn fine timing." I blow out the statement, sitting back farther in my seat and hating that this new cop had to come down here and force us all to wait for what's rightfully ours. Even though he's former FBI from New York, all we have to do is wait until he turns his back, just like they all do. He'll learn what it's like down here and how far a piece of paper and a badge will get him.

"Romano's not going to make a move or leave that gaudy piece of shit he calls home. Not unless he has a death wish."

Fuck, just hearing his name causes adrenaline to rush through my veins and I have to sit up straighter, gripping the arms of the leather chair as I struggle to stay still. "I hate doing nothing."

"You and me both," Carter answers.

"You didn't screw him over, though. He didn't send out a hit order on you," I tell him. Chloe is everything to me and I would do anything for her. Leaving the mafia behind and being marked was a risk I was willing to take for her. But I'm back now, and I'm not going anywhere. Not when so much is at risk. The fucker has to die. No one is coming after me or my family.

"I heard about his guys going to Chloe's when I didn't show up and he realized I'd left that morning after we got the hell out of here when we were kids," I say. The sickness burns up my throat and I have to swallow it down, along with the hate and the rage. "Romano didn't try to kill someone you love."

I take my words back when I remember what Jase, Carter's brother, told me last week. The little bit of information that changed the reluctant relationship the Cross brothers had with Romano. "I'm sorry. I heard about your brother." I'm not the only one Romano went after. I'm the only one to get away though.

Carter reacts more strongly than I thought he would. He's younger than me by only a few years. In a lot of ways, he was the younger brother that I never had. But back when we were just kids, he never liked to talk about his emotions. Never. He'd always preferred to just be alone.

"Romano will pay for what he did—to you, and to the rest of my family." His statement is strained. I don't miss that he says "the rest," which means he still sees me as his family too. Even though I haven't been at his side through all of this bullshit.

Some blood you're born with. Some blood you choose.

He leans back slightly and a grimace mars his face as he touches his chest. He's still healing.

"You all right?" I ask him and he nods, still taking a moment to process the pain. To process all of it.

"I miss him," Carter confesses after a minute and his eyes get glossy. He coughs it away, pretending to be nothing but cold on the outside. But with no one to fight in this cold war, you can only look inward.

"Aria's changed you," I comment, knowing it has to be her who's brought out this new side of him.

Carter grins at me, not denying it. He knows it's true.

"I'm sure Chloe's changed you too."

Chloe. Just hearing her name does something to me. My Chloe Rose. "You could say that."

Carter chuckles, a knowing grin growing on his face. "What'd she say about coming back?" he asks, the smile never wavering even though every trace of humor vanishes from me instantly.

I have to look away, feeling a hint of shame that she didn't want to come back. She fought me on coming back. "She doesn't know what it feels like being away and missing it, you know?" I finally settle on that truth. "She hates this place."

Carter's smile dims, but the corners of his lips kick up at the last comment. "Don't we all."

"She doesn't have anyone left here."

"You think she'll come around?"

"I fucking hope so." The temperature of my blood drops and I tap my foot restlessly against the leg of the chair as I watch the early morning sky turn darker with the gray clouds moving in. I stayed away for as long as I could. I needed to so I could keep her. The only worry that keeps me up now that I know she's safe is whether or not she'll stay with me. She was always meant to leave me, she's too damn good for me and for this life. But I'll be damned if I let anything happen to her, whether she stays with me or not, she'll be staying here, where it's safe and she's protected. We had to come back; I have to end Romano.

"Does she know? Does she know about what you did before you left?"

I hold his gaze, letting the memories of the life I used to live, the one I'm walking back into, play before us. The violence, the murders. It was an exchange I had to make, one I don't regret because it means Chloe's by my side.

"No." I answer him in a single word, spoken so firmly that it practically ricochets off the walls of the room. "She can't know."

Carter gives me a single nod of acknowledgment.

"And what about Marcus?" I ask Carter, quick to change the subject so I can get rid of this revolting churning in the pit of my gut. I know where I stand with Romano. One of us will kill the other, but he has everyone foaming at the mouth to end his life. I don't know where I stand with Marcus, though. No one ever knows where they stand with him until it's too late. "Is Marcus going to be a problem?"

Carter's eyes are assessing as he stands from his desk, turning around to look out of his window as the snow starts to fall. I know somewhere beyond those trees Chloe is in bed still, sleeping, safe and sound.

"Marcus is always a problem."

CHAPTER 3

"You hungry?" Bastian's voice startles me and I jump back from the opened suitcase of clothes I set on the sofa.

His rough chuckle at my expense makes me want to smack him, but his strong arms wrapping around me send a warmth through me, calming all those nervous feelings that wormed their way in. "Didn't mean to scare you," he says low and deep, pulling my back into his chest.

As I reach up behind me to wrap my arms around his neck, he kisses the crook of my neck right in the small gap my baggy sleepshirt allows him.

With my eyes closed and breathing in his woodsy scent, I remind him, "I'm still mad at you."

Last night we slept together, my legs tangled with his and my entire being happy to be by his side again. We avoided the argument for the time being … and then I woke up alone. It wasn't until I found his note on the nightstand that the hollowness in my chest went away. He was only going to see Carter while I slept.

I don't like this insecure feeling. The nerves are a permanent stitch in our relationship. Like one day I'll lose him. I'll wake up alone, and that's how it will be for the rest of my life.

I don't want another man to take his place. I only want Sebastian. His lies and hidden truths are what give me that feeling that it's all going to unravel though. Lies he's carried for years. Secrets he needs to let go of.

He rocks me gently, and that's how he gets me every time. He didn't use to give me this so easily, so freely. The touches, the kisses, the obvious need for me to feel loved.

And I didn't use to feel like I needed it. But I do. I need him. I need this. Just like I need the air to breathe.

"So food? Yes?" he asks again and I stand up a little straighter, nudging him away because he doesn't acknowledge the fact that there's this gaping hole between us. How can we fix what he refuses to admit is broken?

"I'm going to unpack this stuff first." My knee prods the suitcase and the insides of it jostle slightly as I get back to the unpacking I've been tending to. It's mostly clothes and bathroom essentials. "I assume you're having everything back home packed up and moved here without my knowledge?" I ask him, peeking over my shoulder just in time to see him cross his arms and lean against the wall.

My gaze drifts to the corded muscles that line his arms and I know he's doing that shit on purpose.

It's quiet and I hate that I think he's not going to answer me, when suddenly he does.

"It can wait until you tell me you want to stay." He readjusts and adds, "I know you like the apartment, I wouldn't do that to you."

"Are you thinking we could keep it? And have both places?" I ask him, noting his every moment as I fold a sweater I'd pulled out of the suitcase before he came in here.

"We have options," he answers and I huff out a sarcastic laugh.

Options. I have to stare at the plush cream sweater as I toss it onto the sofa and then retrieve the next piece of clothing from the suitcase. It's an old shirt of mine, but one of my favorites that reads *Carpe Diem*. I have never felt so much betrayal from a shirt before. Even this garment has taken Sebastian's side.

"With you writing, we can go anywhere, do anything. Remember how you told me that?" he reminds me.

"I didn't mean you could drag me along to wherever you wanted to go against my will," I answer him flatly.

"You said you'd go wherever I wanted to take you. Change your mind?" he says, and the tone of his voice changes. The way the words float in the air longer, needing more attention and wanting to be heard so much more than any other words… the way he says them makes me pause.

Tick. My heart's counting the seconds. That's what it's been doing. Savoring each one and recognizing that they matter.

"I came here, didn't I?" I ask him, leaving out the emotional damage threatening to spill into each syllable. I remember the way I felt when we were first together. Counting each day and waiting for the one where we inevitably said goodbye.

I don't want that. Ever.

It's quiet, too quiet. The kind of quiet that turns to nights filled with loneliness and heartache.

I focus on the room and change the subject as I ask, "You had someone decorate this place?" It's a bitch move to cower away from the argument because I'm afraid to lose him. I hate myself for it.

This is the exact reason he thinks he can keep secrets from me. He knows I don't want to fight. Not with him.

He stares at me hard for a moment, reading into every detail of my expression the way he always does. I wish he wouldn't.

"Yeah," he answers and his single word tests the tension between us.

It's still there, smoldering, but I don't add fuel to it. I don't want to fight with him, ever. Not when he's the only hero I've ever had. The only knight in shining armor I've ever wanted. Even if he's all dinged up and damaged but pretending he's not.

I can pretend too.

"I like it," I tell him as I toss the shirt onto the pile, folded nice and neat even though I'm debating on finally donating it now that it's taunted me. Taking in a slow breath and releasing it, I say, "I really like the whitewash on the furniture with the light woods. And the cream walls, it's very calm and relaxing." All the while I talk, I fold another sweater and toss it down, making my pile lean a little. "It needs some pops of color I think, but I really like it."

It looks like I could have plucked this house straight from the pages of a *Good Housekeeping* magazine. I attempted something like this at the apartment, but it wasn't quite right. It was just items I bought and put in the rooms, but they didn't fit the way I thought they would. "I think I may even love it."

"Is that right?" he asks me easily, and even his lips tick up into an asymmetric grin. My heart recognizes something powerful between us: I love to make him happy and make him smile … in turn, he wants that for me too.

It's still just ticking along though.

I don't know how long my smile will last here.

"Yes, that's right," I answer, avoiding the unknown and focusing on the here and now. On the fact that if I'm not ready to fight, I want to love him. It's only one or the other, with no happy medium. Because either way, we're together.

Knock, knock, knock. The three timid knocks save me from a strained breath.

Bastian makes a move to get the door and turns to walk out of the room, letting me return back to this new reality.

It is my reality and it's already better than I anticipated, but I can't shake the nervousness. "I'd like it better if you'd tell me the truth," I whisper lowly under my breath, knowing that's exactly why the ticks are being counted.

"Chlo," Bastian calls my name from the foyer, a gorgeous foyer with whitewashed floors and an iron lantern chandelier. I wasn't being complimentary for the sake of a truce; whoever decorated this place knew what they were doing.

My bare feet pad on the floor as I make my way to the front entrance, following the sound of a feminine laugh.

"I hope so," the woman says as I enter. That ticking turns to something else when I see her. Something like a war drum being beat with the handle of a machete.

I'm in shapeless pajamas and feeling the heaviness of the bags under my eyes and she's… put together and chic and beautiful. And a woman I don't know.

"I know she'll love it," Bastian tells her and then they both spot me in the threshold.

"Hi," the petite brunette says with a shy wave. She rocks on her heels as I look between her and Bastian, who's holding a tray of something covered in tinfoil.

"Chloe, this is Aria," Sebastian tells me and I look between the two of them again as I say hi. I have no clue who she is. The name Aria means nothing to me.

"I wanted to give you guys a housewarming gift. Food for Sebastian… because … well, because he's a man and I don't know what men like… and this for you," she says clearly, politely, matter-of-factly as she hands me a brown kraft gift bag with a white lace design and white tissue paper. Something tells me she's already been here, given that the bag matches the décor.

"It smells delicious," Bastian comments and then looks at me pointedly to inform me, "Lasagna."

"The guys all love it when I make pasta, so … I hope you like carbs," she says with another one of those laughs I heard before I walked in. A nervous kind of laugh which has me wondering what she has to be nervous about.

"The guys?" I prod.

"Carter and his brothers," she clarifies as I absently open the gift and mentally try to place her from back when we lived here, but I don't remember an Aria. A single sheet of tissue paper's already out before I realize she's intently watching me open the gift bag as she chews the inside of her cheek.

I don't have to pull out the rest of the tissue paper to see it's a frame I can easily remove from the bag.

With the empty bag cradled in my right, and the frame in my left hand, I turn it over to see a beautiful drawing of Sebastian and me. It's a sketch of a photo I remember from years ago when we first got together.

It's all done in a deep blue charcoal, but so finely sketched and on a thick cream canvas. The multiple shades of blue add dimension and capture the details perfectly. I'm awestruck for a moment at how thoughtful the gift is. And how breathtakingly beautiful it is.

We were only two kids really, barely out of high school and trying to find our way through the shit life we were born into.

Sebastian's holding me on his sofa, and I'm nestled in his lap with my knees pulled into my chest, looking at the camera while he's looking at me. I remember when Carter took this picture, only days before we ran away. Bastian asked him to. I remember it like it was yesterday.

"Do you like it?" she asks nervously, and her voice brings me back to the present.

"It's beautiful." I have to clear my throat as I set it down on the round beechwood table in the center of the room. "I love it," I admit honestly. "Thank you."

"Let me see," Bastian asks and even though I move to hand it to him, he stands behind me, both of his hands on my hips as he peers at it over my shoulder.

Watching his reaction, I see how his expression softens. I can tell he remembers too. Some memories here weren't the worst. Some of them are the best.

"Carter showed me the picture a couple of days ago when he was telling me about how him and Sebastian were so close growing up." Aria's voice grabs my attention. "He told me all about how you stole Sebastian's heart. It was such a sweet story," she says, and her voice is nearly singsongy.

I wonder which version of the tale she got, because I don't remember it being "sweet" exactly.

"You drew it?" Bastian asks, and my mouth drops open when she nods.

"You're so talented," I comment.

"I'm so happy you love it," she says cheerily, more at ease than she was a moment ago. "Carter thought you'd like it but … you know, he's a guy and I think he likes to make me feel like I'm good at drawing, so he'd say just about anything to make me smile."

"Is Carter your…?" I don't finish, not sure if Carter's married or dating. The least Sebastian could have done is told me that much.

"Oh," her eyes widen and her gaze moves from me to Sebastian, then back to me. "I'm with Carter. I'm his … fiancée," she tells me and when she says the last word, she smiles, a kind of sweet, innocent smile and then looks down at her hand. Her ring finger is barren. "No ring yet, it's been a little crazy recently."

"Let me take this to the kitchen. I've got to make a quick call and I'll be right back," Bastian says and without waiting for a response, he leaves the two of us. The kitchen is in the back of the house and I listen carefully as his footsteps disappear.

"Crazy, huh?" I prod, not wasting a moment to get details on what happened this past week while Sebastian was here and I wasn't.

"We found out we're expecting," she says and lifting her voice a little higher, immediately tells me, "Congratulations, by the way." She shakes her head and rolls her eyes. "I meant to say that first thing, but I swear my head isn't on right."

"First, thank you. And second, you can blame that on the baby now and for probably the next eighteen years or so I've heard."

My comment makes her laugh again, and any bit of jealousy I had vanishes knowing she's with Carter.

"Congratulations to you too," I tell her and prod again, my left hand resting on the table, "I haven't seen Carter in … gosh," I blow a strand of hair from my face, remembering him as a sixteen-year-old kid, "in years."

"Really?" she asks, seeming surprised. "Well, he has a lot of respect for you and for Sebastian. He speaks really highly of you two. And he seems really happy to have you two back."

Guilt is what makes my smile slip the way it does. I feel it falter and I can't stop it.

I know why we left, even though Sebastian doesn't know that I know.

I know what happened when we took off too. What happened to Carter specifically.

"He's a good guy," I tell her and try to ignore the regret. If I'd known everything he'd go through at only sixteen and have to face alone because his best friend left, I would have made Sebastian come back. It's ironic that I can admit that, yet coming back now, the thought never occurred to me.

"So, how far along are you?" I ask her, trying to hide everything I'm feeling, but she sees it just like Sebastian does, if her wary expression is anything to go by.

"Not far at all," she tells me and offers a small smile as she touches her lower stomach. "We only just found out."

With a nod, I acknowledge what she said, but new words fail me.

"You okay?" she asks with hesitancy.

"I just wish Sebastian would tell me why we're here," I blurt out the truth. "Why now?" I don't bother keeping my voice low as I spill the truth to a perfect stranger.

"It's funny how they keep things from us," she says a bit lower, a bit more serious than she's been, "as if we aren't going to find out." The small eye roll and shake of the head are meant to add humor, but I can see how she really feels in her eyes, in the way her smile struggles to stay where it is.

"Carter too, then?" I ask her, feeling the race in my pulse.

"He tried; I think he knows better now." The moment the words leave her, she bites down on her lower lip and peeks over her shoulder at the door, as if he could come in any second. For a moment I think she's worried he'd come here, worried he'd see her talking to me about him. But then she mutters, "He better know better now," in a tone not meant to be negotiated.

"He's an asshole sometimes," she tells me, playing with the nonexistent ring missing from her finger. "He's rough around the edges and difficult at times. But he loves me, and I told him I want to know what's going on. Even if he thinks I shouldn't know, not knowing makes it harder on me, you know? Which makes it harder on us."

She's saying every single thing that I could say right back to her.

"I told him, I'd let him know if I didn't want to hear." Again she looks over her shoulder, this time as if summoning him, but the man doesn't show himself. "And if I want to know something, he answers. And I do the same for him."

"Right." I nod in agreement.

Her last sentence is spoken with finality. "Being raw and open is scary as fuck, especially in this life, but it's the only way I know how to survive."

Those words, each and every one, settle into the very marrow of my bones. "I don't think I can stay here if Sebastian doesn't tell me what's going on," I confess to her. Bastian isn't anywhere to be seen or heard; I have no idea what he's doing, but he needs to hear those words. "I'm afraid he's going to choose this place over me, to be honest." There's the truth. The heart of the matter. He's wanted to come back since the day we left, and now he's done it, without my permission. If I say I don't want this, I am certain he's not going to choose me.

"Why would you say that? You're all he talks about."

"Because he's been waiting for me to leave him for years. He'd let me walk away if he thought it was the right thing to do by me."

"Do you want to walk away?" she asks.

"No," I say, and the answer is easy. "I don't even mind this place. It's not what I was thinking when I told him I'd never come back. This isn't Crescent Hills and I could be happy here. The only thing I really care about is that he's not telling me what's going on. And with the history of what happened before, I want to know. I don't want to go crazy worrying."

"I know that feeling," she mutters beneath her breath. "What did he tell you?" she asks me, and I shake my head along with giving her a shrug.

Swallowing and feeling my dry throat tighten, I answer, "He said he wanted to come home. He said Carter needed him." Every word feels drier and drier in the back of my throat. Like it's suffocating me to tell this woman and admit how little he tells me. "I know something's wrong," I confess to her.

She only nods her head in response, her eyes darting behind me, but when I look she finally speaks. "He's not there, I was just checking."

Feeling an oncoming chill from the draft of the front door, my right hand absently rubs my opposite forearm.

"Do you know why he came back now?" I ask her and again, she nods and answers, "Yes."

"Is it bad?" I question.

"The bad just passed, now it's just waiting for things to settle, I think. There are some loose ends, but they'll be tied up shortly."

A beat passes, and the ticking in my chest speeds up, feeling each second slip by me faster and faster.

"I'm sorry, I'm a little guilty. Carter asked Sebastian to come back because of things with me, I would think. Things were the worst..." She trails off as her bottom lip wobbles, but she catches it between her teeth and swallows her words.

"Are you okay?" I ask her, feeling for the first time that she's more like me than I could have ever known.

"I am. I am now," she adds.

"Do you want to talk about it?"

"Maybe one day, but I don't think today is a good time. I'm grateful Bastian came back. I'll tell you that much. And if you're worried, I wouldn't be. But I really think you two should talk." Her gaze again moves behind me, and this time I know he's there. She lets her gaze linger and the floor softly creaks behind me.

"We should," I answer and hear the floors protest once again, but still far behind me, maybe in the doorway. As if he's stopped there and doesn't dare to move any closer.

"Sorry to intrude… I just wanted to say 'hi.'" She gives me a small smile and an odd wave before tucking her hair behind her ear and turning to leave.

"Thank you so much for the gifts." My response is nothing but polite, even though inwardly I'm prepared for confrontation with the man standing behind me.

"If you ever want to hang out or just talk, I'm right there or happy to come over even."

"I'm going to take you up on that," I answer her and then watch her leave.

CHAPTER 4

Sebastian

"WHAT DID YOU TWO TALK ABOUT?" I ask her before Aria's even through the doorway. Anxiety spreads along my skin. I thought the two of them would hit it off. But the atmosphere in the foyer reminds me of a funeral home.

"About what's going on."

My pulse picks up. "And what is going on?" I ask her, swallowing thickly and refusing to believe Aria told her anything specific. Chloe's pregnant, for fuck's sake. She doesn't need the stress or the fear. The last thing she needs to do is worry. I've got her.

"I don't want to not address these things anymore. We need to talk about it." Her words echo off the walls of the foyer as the door closes and the biting chill of the bitter weather joins us.

"What things do we need to talk about?" I ask her, as if I don't know. There's so much shit she doesn't know. And if she learns the truth, how could I ever keep her?

The thought sends a prick down my neck that doesn't stop until it reaches the base of my spine.

The uneasy feeling stays where it is when she turns around, staring into my eyes and swallowing thickly. "I want to know everything."

The hell with that. "No."

Her baby blues widen, the shock apparent. Even I'm surprised by the way the single word sounded so harsh. "You don't need to know this shit." I give her the simple explanation, and a light sparks in her eyes.

"It's not about need, Bastian. It's about want," she grits out. "I love you and I'll never stop loving you, but I hate how you think I'm so delicate and easily broken." Her tone is severe and unrefined. "I deserve to know the truth."

"The truth about what?" I ask again, knowing the one truth I will never tell her. Never.

"Everything," she demands.

I was her savior. That's how she looked at me. Like I was one of the good guys, and it did something to me. It made me a better man. I will never let her take that back, because I don't know what will happen to me if she does.

My lips part, ready to give her a partial truth, enough to keep her at a distance. Something to satisfy her curiosity, but her bottom lip quivers and her arms cross, showing me her swollen stomach. She's only just started to show.

"Tell me why you needed to come back right now," she asks when I hesitate.

I question if Aria told her something I'll have a hard time explaining, or if she told her anything. Fuck, what was I thinking leaving the two of them alone? "Carter was in trouble," I start and she cuts me off.

"What kind of trouble?"

"The kind that wound up with a lot of people going to funerals this week," I answer her sharply and wait for her reaction. I get none. Nothing. The blunt answer doesn't faze her in the least.

"Why now?" she asks and when I feel a deep crease settling in my forehead, she elaborates. "Why didn't you come back before? It's obvious…" she hesitates, but doesn't hold back when she continues, "It's obvious he's been putting people in the ground for a while now… yes?"

I nod, and my heart hammers. The skin across my knuckles draws tight as I flex my hands into fists and then relax them, thinking about all the shit that's happened since we've been gone.

"He didn't need me, but this time, it was important to him that he did everything he could…" I almost tell her how it was the first time he was fighting for something that mattered, but I don't have to.

"Because of Aria?" she questions and again I nod.

It's silent for a moment and I watch as the tension in her shoulders lessens. The hope that she's been given just enough to drop it toys with me until she asks, "Did he need you to do what you used to do?"

I can barely nod in confirmation. Every muscle in my body is tight, waiting for her to run, to cower, to be afraid or angry or disgusted. I never liked the man I was without her, but it doesn't change the fact that's who I am. I can run away for years, but I'll always be a murderer. I don't want her to look at me that way. I don't even know if she knows the extent of what I've done, both years ago and just last week. And what I'm willing to continue to do.

"Did you want to hurt them?" she asks quietly.

I answer her with questions of my own. "Why would I want to do this? Why would I want to hurt people?"

Another question is all I get. "Why wouldn't you? That's what you did before, and living out there, away from all this… nothing made you happy. You moved from job to job and you hated them all."

"I was happy with you and bored with work… that's life."

"No," she responds sharply, "you lost your passion."

"I lost my family," I correct her, raising my voice and stressing the statement. I feel the harsh words linger between us. The room feels colder than it ever has before. Anger simmers, although not for her; anger at my past, anger at this shit life I was dealt.

"You are my family, we are family. But Carter was too."

She starts to speak, but her words turn to ghosts of thoughts as she stares back at me and starts to cry. "I wish we'd never left him behind," she croaks and I swallow my confession that I wish we'd never left at all.

"Come here," I say and hold her close, forcing her body to mold with mine. "I love you and I don't want to see you like this."

A shudder runs along her shoulders as she tries to calm herself down. Can't she see this is the exact reason I don't want to tell her these things? I don't want her to live with the pain. I can bear it for the both of us.

As if reading my mind and finding fault in my conviction, she whispers against my chest, "I don't want you to lie to me." Her hot breath sends goosebumps down my skin in a wave.

"I don't lie to you. I've never lied. I just keep some of this shit from you, so you don't have to deal with it." It's a half truth. It's always only a half truth.

"You don't think I know? Or that I wouldn't find out?" she questions as she lifts her gaze to me. Staring back at me are worry, sadness, and desperation even. And it stuns me.

"I know more than you think," she says in my silence.

"I would never bring you into danger," is all I can say, because it's the only truth that matters to me anymore.

"Is that why you came up here before me? Because it was too dangerous?"

I almost lie, I almost hide it from her so she doesn't have to know, but I can't. "Yes."

"Why not tell me?" she asks as if it's that simple. As if I could risk her knowing who I am at my core and leaving me.

"I don't want you to know. I want you to be happy and to trust that I'll take care of it. All of it."

"That's not fair. I don't want it to all lie on your shoulders. I want to help you. I want to be there for you."

He sounds desperate when he tells me, "You do help me, and you are there for me."

"How can I, when I don't know what you're going through?"

"I just want you to love me."

"You already know I do."

"Show me. Kiss me. Kiss me like you love me." I miss her kisses the most. When she's angry and she's holding back, I know she keeps them from me. And all I can think is that she must not need them like I do. She must not feel the same thing as I do when she lets me kiss her.

I can keep secrets so easily. But I can't keep her touch as easily. I need to feel it every day. She makes me feel like it's all worth fighting for.

"Kissing doesn't make it better," she says softly, but her gaze lingers on my lips and the fight in her cadence is weak at best.

"Fighting won't either," I answer her and that's when her eyes lift to mine.

"Are you sure about that?" The seductive tone doesn't go unnoticed, and neither does the challenge.

One large step is all it takes to dwarf her small frame under mine. She doesn't back away, she doesn't reach out to me, but her breathing quickens and her baby blues spark with a heat I've longed for.

"Kiss me, Chlo. Even if it doesn't make it better, it'll feel better, and that counts for something, doesn't it? Life is what we feel. That's what keeps us alive."

Leaning forward, she places one hand on my chest, barely touching me, hesitant and careful. She stands on her tiptoes next, taking her time to plant the smallest of kisses against my lips. Her soft, feminine touch may feel like nothing to her as she brushes her lips against mine, but to me it's everything, even if it's only miniscule to her.

I can feel the faint wetness she leaves behind as she pulls away, her eyes still open. I can even hear her heart running wild so close to mine, no matter if she's so restrained in front of me.

"There," she whispers and tries to move back, but I wrap my arm around her waist and pull her in closer to me, forcing her breasts against my chest, her hips pressed to my thigh, and a small yelp of surprise slips from her.

"Again," I command her, barely breathing. Moving my other hand to the small of her back, I keep her pinned to me. "Kiss me again." Although my voice is strong and the words are a demand, both of us can hear my desperation, so why hide it? "I'm fucking begging you, Chlo," I whisper the strangled truth.

It's only a single beat, a single moment before she crashes her lips against mine, hungrily, greedily, searching for the same thing I need.

The feeling of being loved. Of knowing it and wanting nothing more than it. I could tell her a million times and she could do the same for me, but it's only when we kiss like this, raw and with everything we have, that we can feel it burning in our blood.

Her nails dig into the back of my neck as she parts her lips and my tongue dives into her mouth, massaging hers with swift, powerful strokes.

Lifting her ass up with one hand, she wraps her legs around my waist and I don't waste a single moment bringing her back to the sofa, knocking off the suitcase and placing my wife down in its place. She heaves in a breath when I finally pull away from her.

"Bastian," she breathes my name, rather than the oxygen she needs. I barely get a glimpse of her as I rip my shirt off and I hate it. I hate that anything gets in the way of what we both need.

I'm savage as I rip her clothes from her, tearing down the front of her shirt and pulling her pants and panties down as if they're scorching her skin and she'd be scarred if I didn't remove them this instant.

Her panting, her soft moans, the way she lifts her hips to help me and then tears at the button on my jeans, it all fuels me to move faster, to eliminate everything that keeps us apart.

She stares up at me, watching as I kick off my jeans and then grip the top of the sofa as I move between her legs. "I love the way you kiss me." That's all she says.

Cupping her bare pussy, I find her wet and hot and wanting. Her lips form a perfect O, and her eyes go half lidded as I finger fuck her, bringing her closer to the edge but not letting her get off.

Her little whimper of protest makes me smile. Her pout, the way she wraps her leg around mine and then digs her heel into my ass… Fuck, everything about her makes me hard.

I wait for her eyes to find mine and hold her stare before telling her, "Don't stop kissing me."

She isn't given the chance to answer, because I thrust myself inside her to the hilt, making her scream out in pleasure before slamming my lips against hers.

Our lips crash and our moans mingle in each other's mouths as I thrust into her over and over again. Moving out slowly, ever so slowly to tease her and then pushing myself into her in one swift stroke. Each time her head begs to fall back, but she keeps her lips on mine, struggling to breathe, to move away from the intensity, to get closer and have more.

A cold sweat breaks out along every inch of my skin as I pick up my pace, ruthlessly fucking her and claiming her again and again until her tight cunt spasms around my length and I groan as I lose myself deep inside of her.

Even then, she doesn't stop kissing me. Her body trembles under me and her nails scratch down my back, but her lips stay on mine. The two of us never parting, my Chloe Rose never leaving me. And we unravel together.

She's still panting, still feeling the waves of aftershock when I pull out of her slowly and move quickly to get beneath her, laying her limp body on my chest to nestle beside her.

"I love you." She doesn't moan the words or whisper them, but they get lost in the air just the same.

I kiss her hair, her cheek, her shoulder until she brings her lips to mine and kisses me gently, but with undenied passion. And it's only when she breaks the kiss that I tell her, I love her too.

I always have and I always will.

I don't know that she'll ever know just how much. She is my everything. My only. My hand moves to her belly, to the life we made together. I would do anything for my family. I will do anything and everything to make sure they will never have to be afraid. Our child won't experience the same life we had.

I won't allow it.

"What do you want to know?" I ask her, feeling her bare skin pressed against mine. Her hair slips through my fingers and I wait for her to ask any question and I'll answer it. "I don't want to lose you or lose this ever again, Chlo. If you need to know something, ask me. I'll tell you. I'll tell you anything." I breathe in deep before confessing, "But you may not love me anymore when you hear the truth."

"Sebastian, you're crazier than I am if you think I could ever not love you. Right now I want to know where and when you're working. I don't like waking up alone."

While kissing her hair and running my fingers down her back, I answer her, "I can show you one place I may be a lot." She readjusts on the sofa, moving her small body so more of her is on top of me. I fucking love it. I love how she wants me and how she shows me that she does.

When she lifts her head, her brunette hair tumbles down her shoulder, exposing more of her and I lean forward to kiss that crook in her neck. "You love it when I kiss you here," I whisper against her skin and she gives me a small, feminine moan of feigned protest.

With her hand splayed on my chest, she straightens and I'm forced to pull back. "I want two things," she says, staring in my eyes.

"What two things?"

"Show me this one place. And tell me something you've done that you think will change things between us. Tell me the worst thing, Sebastian."

I can't; I won't. I won't willingly lose her like that.

Her baby blues are bathed in desperation when she tells me, "I want to show you what I think of that side of you. The side you like to pretend I can't see."

CHAPTER 5

"**A** club?" I say, and the humor of the word rests in its cadence. "Thought you were tired of clubs?" My brow arches as I look up at Bastian when he opens the doors to The Red Room for me. The second he does, the vibrations of the music hit me, and somehow the dim lighting feels even darker than the night behind us.

"It's different when I'm not working in it," he comments and I have to clarify. "So you're not working here?" There's a small sputter in my chest, afraid that he's holding back. Afraid that he's not going to hold up his end of the bargain. It doesn't matter if he does or doesn't; I'm ready to tell him what I know. And that I love him for it. I love my dark knight. He's always been my hero.

His lips quirk up as he splays his hand on my lower back and leads me to the long L-shaped bar in the far right of the room. "Not exactly." Although he's casual, there's a tightness in every small feature of his stance and the way he walks.

His answer is one he would have given me a week ago. Hell, even two days ago. He would have left it there, and I wouldn't have had the balls to push for more. I would have let the unsettling feeling push us farther apart.

Not tonight though, not as we brush by the crowded room, past high tables and men and women whose outfits range from both custom suits and short dresses, to tattered jeans and thin white tank tops. "I'm working with the Cross brothers, and Jase owns this place, so if he needs me here, I may be here, but I won't be the bouncer or bartender."

His eyes hold a brightness, even though they're dark and in them I see the reflection of the bottles that line the bar, and more, so much more.

Passion, desire, a challenge, and … purpose.

It's disconcerting in some ways as I take a seat at the bar, sitting down on the leather stool. I could never give him this. I don't want him to fight, but that's what dark knights are meant to do.

"You want anything to eat?" he asks me and I shake my head, telling him I just want a cranberry juice. He signals for the bartender easily, but I can tell he's on edge like I am. On edge that the wall of mistruths and hidden secrets is breaking down between us.

"Bastian," the bartender greets him and then turns to me. "You must be Chloe," he says without missing a beat. With his sleeves rolled up and his tattoos showing on his forearms, the man looks deadly, even if he's smiling at me. Italian. Dominating. And sexy as hell.

"Sebastian's told me all about you and the little addition," he says, and his eyes drift lower as he searches for the baby bump. "Congratulations," he tells me.

"Thank you," I respond but I don't even know his name, and I could cringe at that. I know so little. I don't know anyone here, but that's going to change. Sebastian's only been here a week longer than me, but it's obvious that he belongs here. That he's welcome here.

There's a small piece of me that wants to be welcome here too. For once in my life.

"Chloe, this is Seth," Bastian tells me and Seth smiles broad and wide.

"It's nice to finally meet you," he tells me and then someone calls for his attention, taking him away but not before Bastian orders his beer and my drink.

"He works with Jase."

"Well obviously, since this is his bar."

"No, I mean…" Sebastian trails off and runs his hand along the back of his head. "Seth likes being behind the bar when he's not working. But he works really close with Jase," he tells me and then pauses. Even the music pauses a beat, as if to let the words sink in.

"What does he do?" I ask, and Bastian reaches for his beer. I turn around to thank Seth, seeing my drink right next to my hand for the first time. I hadn't realized he set it there, but he's already moved on to someone else.

"He does a lot of things. Whatever needs to be done. Fixes situations that get out of hand."

"You like him?" I ask, letting my finger sit on the rim of the glass. It slides along the edge and I wonder if it makes a sound given that the edge is wet, but it doesn't matter. The club is so loud, the soft sound would drown in it. Bastian nods, not showing me any emotion on his face, but steadfastly observing my reaction.

"Is that what you do too?" I ask him, not sure if I really want to know, but I damn well know that I want him to know I'll still love him regardless.

"No." Bastian takes a drink and then tells me, "I'll be staying with Carter, going places with him to make sure things go down the way they're supposed to."

"Situations?" I ask and before he can even say "yeah" again, I ask, "Like what you used to do?" His tax returns said he was a butcher for Romano, but the scars on his knuckles say otherwise.

This time he only nods, his lips pressed in a tight line. "If it needs to be handled. Yes. I handle it."

"So you're the muscle," I comment and take a sip of the bittersweet drink. I appreciate having to be sober for this. It's surprising how it doesn't bother me. How it even excites me. That's what surprises me the most.

"I know it's not what you thought I'd be doing when we settled down." He starts to talk, and I don't bother to let his mind wander down that path.

"I never thought I could tame you, Sebastian Black. I never wanted to either."

"Tame?" he says and huffs a humorless laugh. He swallows thickly, staring at the ring of bubbles on the edge of his glass as he adds, "I just want you to know … who I am."

"I've always known who you are."

Shaking his head slightly, he stares blankly ahead. "I've hurt a lot of people," he tells me in a voice so cold and low, as if I still don't get it.

"You killed them. You didn't just hurt them; you killed them."

The club life seems to get louder, but it bleeds together when he looks at me with that intense icy gaze.

"I know what you did," I choke out, needing to finally tell him the truth. "When we left, I know what you had to do before we could leave. I heard you talking about it on the phone."

"What?" Disbelief lays in the breathy syllable. His stern gaze hardens; the depths of the man he is showing. And I love it. I love this side of him. Dare I say, I may even love this side of him more. Not because I love what he does, or the actions. But because he's willing to risk everything to fight for what he believes in. I don't know what Carter's gotten himself into, but back when we were only kids, Sebastian did something I know I never could. He made an injustice just.

"We hadn't been gone long, maybe a few weeks?" The words race from me, so willing and eager to finally be heard. "Something happened with Carter and you wanted to go back. I thought we were coming back here, but we didn't. They told you not to. You were talking to someone about the people who were murdered, about the list … about Marcus."

"Chlo." Bastian says my name like he's daring me to tell him it's a lie, but the words keep running from me, running away like we did all those years ago.

"And when you came back to the bedroom, I waited for you to tell me what had happened. I wanted to know if Carter was all right. And you didn't say a word." Tears blur my vision, but I don't cry. "You never told me anything, even though I knew you were hurting."

"All I needed was you and you didn't need to know," he tells me in a single breath, the impact of my confession hitting him and turning his jaw hard.

"Did you think I wouldn't love you anymore for it, Bastian? Did you think I would leave you?"

"Chloe," he says, my name strained like it hurts him to say it.

"You would have never told me, and I get why. I get it."

I don't wait for him to respond before I continue on.

"And what you did after. When someone came for us." I barely get the words out, because I know that night changed him. It was right after he got the call about Carter, so we'd been gone maybe three weeks, constantly moving from place to place, not stopping anywhere. "The night after you got that call, there was a knock on the door."

"Chloe, don't." Bastian's words are only a breath of a wish. A wish to not just keep me safe, but to make it so I don't even know about the danger. It's an impossible task and he needs to know that, even if that means he thinks he failed me.

"I was awake when you grabbed the gun. And I hate that I pretended to be asleep. I know that's what you wanted, you didn't want me to know."

"It was Romano. I knew he'd send someone."

"And I heard everything." I whisper the confession that tears down the wall of pretenses between us. "I heard you nearly beat him to death, I heard the message you told that prick to give to Romano…" I swallow my words about how I heard him in the bathroom, cleaning up the mess and trying to hold back his own emotions. There's more than anger and rage inside of him. The fear that he couldn't protect me was almost palpable. "I was there behind the door with your other gun, Bastian. I was ready to fight with you, but you've never wanted that."

"No, Chloe-"

I cut him off before he gets carried away, before he can focus on something other than the problem that's keeping a wedge between us. "I don't want to be in this world, Sebastian. I belong here nonetheless, and I don't want to fight. But I won't be left in the dark, and I don't want you to think that I shouldn't know the truth or that when the time comes, I wouldn't be able to be at your side. I know it's my fault to let you think I don't know what you do… but you need to talk to me. I need to know what's going on."

His head falls back and the air leaves him as I grip his hand and beg him to listen to me. "It's one thing to let my mind run wild and think these things. It's another for me to know it. But Sebastian, I know. I know *you*." He turns to look at me as my last word cracks. I whisper, "How could I not?"

"You were never supposed to find out," he finally speaks, looking away from me and staring straight ahead, failure clearly written in his gaze.

I have to stop and take a drink, calming myself down. I thought letting the words out would feel freeing, but that's not at all what this feels like. Instead it feels like the unraveling I've been terrified of all this time.

"Did you keep it a secret because you wanted to protect me? Or because you wanted me to think you wouldn't do something like that?"

"Both," he answers me sincerely, looking me in the eyes.

"Well you protected me, and I love you regardless."

My chest rises and falls quicker, and I can't shake this nervousness, not until he asks me with a rawness in his throat, "You know that I love you more than anything. That I would be anyone you need me to be?"

"You don't need to change who you are, but you need to tell me if that's why we're back."

"It doesn't have to do with that. Romano's still here, but not for long."

"Then why?" I ask him, even though I think I already know. "There was a note?" My assumption brings his icy blue stare to mine.

"From Marcus. He warned me that Carter needed me and that we needed him." His gaze drops to my belly and he squeezes my hand. "I would never let anything happen to you, Chlo, and I wouldn't have brought you here if I didn't think we needed to be."

"Marcus said we needed Carter?" I clarify, feeling a wave of anxiety run through me.

"If it was only about Carter, we never would have come here. You know it had to be about you."

His words sink in slowly. Even after so much time, there's still a mark on my husband, a mark on me in return. "Can you trust Marcus?" I ask him, focusing on the fact that we're here; we're safe. And that Bastian will never let anything happen to me or our child.

"No," he says, and the answer is simple. He leans forward, pulling me into him and giving me a comfort I didn't realize I needed this badly. "But he was right about Carter and he's the reason why Romano's men never came back. I should listen to his warning rather than regret not doing everything I can. If anything ever happened to you, or our little one, I wouldn't be able to survive, Chlo."

I have to keep my breath steady; I have to keep telling myself that we're safe now.

"No one is going to hurt us here. This place is changing. Carter and his brothers are taking it over. We can't let it stay what it was, Chlo; you know what happened to us, what it was like living here."

"I know," I whisper, hearing the pain etched in his words, but also the fight. To fight what's wrong in the lowest and most depraved ways. To use violence and force in a world that's nothing but merciless.

"It's not our fight anymore, but that doesn't mean we should stand back and do nothing."

"Leaving this place wasn't doing nothing," I tell him and remember the pain, the fear, the courage it took to leave everything behind. But even as they leave my lips, I doubt the truth of the words I've spoken, because they were said out of fear.

"I didn't say that it was. But now, I know we can do more. I can feel it, Chlo. I'm supposed to be here right now." Taking my hands into his, the rough pads of his thumbs rub soothing circles on the back of my knuckles. Staring deep into his eyes and knowing that I see him for who he is and he sees me just the same, knowing that settles the harsh memories that creep up at the reminder of what used to be.

"I just don't want you …." He pauses to lick his lower lip and exhale a heavy breath. "I don't want you to think I'm…" His words are lost in the air in between us. "That I'm-"

"All you will ever be, Bastian, is mine. You are mine. Just like I'm yours. I made my life knowing that's who I was, and who I wanted to be." It takes more than I realized to admit the words out loud. "I don't want to be anything else and as long as you are mine, that is exactly who you will be to me." Pulling my right hand from his grasp, I cup the side of his jaw in my palm and feel the rough stubble as my thumb runs along his chin. "You're okay with being mine still, aren't you?" I whisper the question. It's so soft, it's nearly drowned out by the sounds around us.

"You're too good for me, Chlo." His hand covers mine and I can see in the depths of his eyes he doesn't believe that something so simple is all I need.

"It's all I've ever needed," I speak without thinking, without processing anything at all. "I wasn't whole until I had you, and I don't want to be anything but yours. I don't care if you believe the truth or not, it's still true."

"It's the truth that worries me."

"The truth is you're a good man who does bad, bad things." As Bastian pulls my hand away from his jaw, I can hear him swallow. I can practically feel it myself—the hard, aching truth that I do think what he does is wrong. And I do. On some level. But there's so much wrong in this world, I can't be bothered to let it destroy what I value most of all. "And you're mine. The only truth I just said that matters at all, is the last one."

"You still love me?" he asks as if it's a real question.

Letting a playful smile show, I tease him, staring at his lips as I say, "I love the way you kiss me." For the first time in so long, my heartbeat slows when I look back up at Bastian; it pitter-patters, it dances, it's desperately finding a new beat. It's when his eyes glance at my own lips that I realize it's been trying to beat in tandem with his.

The kiss he plants on my lips, with his hands barely holding on to mine, is soft and sweet. Everything turns to white noise and I know for a fact, this moment will last forever. To me, to anyone who ever steps foot here. They will feel it. They must. Because the world moves around us differently, refusing to let this moment go on as if it's meant to blend in, or meant to be forgotten.

My eyes are still closed when he pulls away. With a deep breath in and then out, I finally open them.

"I love falling in love with you," I whisper and barely notice how the world moves again around us.

I swear a blush colors my husband's face. It looks good on him; for all his tough exterior, a hint of vulnerability looks damn good.

He reaches up for the beer on the bar, but doesn't let go of my left hand and I don't move my right from his lap.

With an asymmetric grin he asks me casually, "You weren't already in love with me?" He can try to hide it all he wants, but I know there's a hint of fear beneath his words. How could this man ever think I didn't love him?

"I've loved you every day since that kiss," I confess to him as he lifts up the beer. When my words hit his ears, he sets the glass back down onto the bar. Staring at it, and listening as I tell him, "I love you every day and in every moment, but falling in love is something you can do over and over again."

"I want to fall in love with you every chance I get," he tells me and his voice is deep and rough, laced with a sinful desire and something else. Something pure and good. The need to be loved and to feel worthy of being loved.

Even as I bite down on my bottom lip, I smile genuinely. Snaking my ankle behind his muscular leg, I lean into him and whisper, "Then let's do it every day."

He takes a swallow of his beer before kissing me again, teasing me and I love it. He tastes like wheat IPA and something dangerous, something too tempting to ever resist.

I don't lean back as I catch a glimpse of Carter from the corner of my eye. Sebastian follows my gaze and we both watch him enter a locked door, guarded by two men who open it for him.

"I haven't said hi to Carter yet," I admit and wonder what that will be like. He's changed. We all have.

"That's his brother Jase," Bastian corrects me and I huff out a breath. "They did all used to look alike," I muster up the excuse, but Bastian doesn't seem to care. He takes my hand and my attention with it.

"Just don't stop loving me."

"I'll always love you." I speak clearly, very aware of the moment and where we are. "But don't hide anything from me. I can't live like that again. And I don't want to keep anything from you like I kept that secret."

"I have a lot to tell you then." He exhales the words. "Are you sure you want to know this?" he asks again and I just barely nod, giving him my consent to bring me into this place.

"It's not an easy story to tell," he admits to me and I already know he's telling the truth. This world is cruel and unforgiving, just as lawless as it is tragic.

"I want to know."

"Then let's start with Carter's story. Just promise me you'll still love me after this?"

"You're crazy to think I could ever not love you, Bastian. Today, tomorrow, forever."

I stare into his eyes when I speak to him, making him feel the depths of my conviction. I love this man and all he is. All that matters is that he loves me the same and that we'll be together.

The End

Here's to love stories keeping our hearts beating.
If you haven't read A KISS TO TELL, Chloe and Sebastian's
story from the beginning, I highly recommend you read it now
and fall in love with every piece of them.

SEDUCTIVE

He's forbidden, dangerous, and everything that's bad for me. More than that, the life he leads is exactly why I'd been on the run.

The seductive and powerful air around him is what drew me in, the reminder of what could have and should have been years ago.

His dark gaze riddled with desire could always see through me. Deep down to the core of what I craved most. *To be his.*

And so I agreed. I came back. I chose him even when I knew I shouldn't.

If only it were so easy to forget the past. If only our mistakes didn't hold on to us, harder and more violently than we could hold on to each other.

Seductive is an extension of Addison and Daniel's story, *Possessive*. Although it can be read on its own, it's recommended you start with *Possessive*.

CHAPTER 1

Addison

I KNEW WHEN I CAME BACK HERE THAT I WAS MAKING A CHOICE. I was choosing Daniel over everything. Over the life I'd live without him and where I'd live it—far away from here and these memories. Men like him come with those kinds of complications.

Men like him are… There are many words I could use to describe him. The most fundamental statement, though, is so easily admitted and it's the very reason I chose him.

Men like him need to be loved or the damage will consume them. More than anything. In this cruel world he's cemented into, with a tragic past and ruthless tasks ahead, he needed to be loved. He still does…

My gaze lingers on what looks like carrots or sweet potatoes, some sort of orange mush in tiny little glass jars. The packs are stacked high on the shelf. The black and white silhouette of a smiling baby stares back at me and I have to push my cart forward, listening to the quiet squeaks of the turning wheels as I think about how I ended up here.

I was reckless, that's how.

Grocery shopping with Daniel wasn't one of the things I was considering when I returned to where I grew up. I was thinking of the drugs, the violence, his brothers, and how powerful they've become. It wasn't like this back then. Not at all. It wasn't this bad. Back then, I thought they'd grow out of it one day. At least that's what I'd hoped. I didn't think they'd eventually come to rule this merciless world.

It's all surreal. Every day since I've been back has brought a fear and tension that's seeping into my every waking moment.

He knows. That's why I'm here.

Shopping for milk and orange juice feels like a sham. Like for a moment, I can maybe pretend this past week didn't happen. As if the white noise from the man on the intercom can drown out the sounds of the last six months.

"Feel like you're playing house, now?" Daniel quips as I stop and watch him settle a jar of salsa, two bags of tortillas, and a case of something else into the half-full cart. His tone is optimistic.

"I didn't say 'playing house,'" I correct him and note how cold it feels along with how dull my heart beats.

I wish I could fix my face right now; I wish I could smile and pretend like it's all fine, like they all do, but it's not and I'm finding it difficult to hide it from him. Especially after what just happened. I could deal with it; I was dealing with it. But things change. And the past month changed everything.

He doesn't hide a damn thing from me anymore, so it'd be unfair to hide from him. But what's left for him to see isn't what I want to be there.

I'm still staring blankly at the case beneath the bags of chips when his muscular forearm cuts off my vision. His strong hand wraps over mine on the handle of the cart and his other grips my chin, lifting it up. I have to look away from his rolled-up sleeve and into his dark eyes. With his rough stubble in need of a shave, and his hair messy on top, he looks as rough as I feel. Rough looks damn sexy on Daniel Cross though. It always has; it's who he's meant to be.

"I know it's been hard," he says, and his voice is low and calm, his gaze soft and comforting.

"Hard?" I force a smile to my lips as the bottom one wobbles and he looks past me, dropping his grip on my chin. I'm quick to reach out and take his hand though. I just need to feel him. "I'm sorry," I tell him quickly. That's what I am: sorry, pathetic, weak. The list goes on. I knew what he had become. What *they* had become. And I still chose to come back. I did this. It was my fault. But a lie slips out instead. It's easier to deal with it if I lie to myself the way he lies to me. "I didn't know what I was coming back to and it's been..."

"Hard," he answers for me.

"Stressful," I correct him and the tension grows tenfold between us. I look up to my right when I notice motionless figures and feel their eyes on us. My own are pricking, distraught from what's happened and how much I'm losing.

I can hear the harsh swallow Daniel makes and I watch the cords in his neck tighten as he holds my hand in his. He lifts my hand to his lips and then kisses my knuckles. One by one.

"It'll be okay," he whispers against my skin, and all the warmth from those words travels through me, calming me. Making me feel lighter, as if I believe him wholeheartedly.

It doesn't change what happened.

Nothing can ever change what happened, but we have a choice about how we handle it. I'm starting to think I made the wrong one.

That's why I hold his hand longer than he holds mine. That's why I stand there watching him leave when he tells me he's getting the rest of what's on the list and says for me to just get the bread. I don't miss the depth in his eyes, the distance that lingers. Every day, he's farther away from me. He knows. He can feel it too. It's like the slow unraveling of thick twine. It's obvious and torturous to watch.

It wasn't this way when we were just teenagers. It wasn't like this at all.

The power he and his brothers now have comes with violence I've never seen before and a harshness that's required to survive. Shopping for fucking groceries is his way of showing me it's normal, it's okay, that life is more than that brutal side of the Cross brothers and what they do.

I can't look past the darkness though. It's never going to feel "okay." This sense of danger that lingers in my blood is always going to be there.

I have to find my place with it. That's not something he can help me with. I have tried. I thought I was there. I was wrong.

It's caused damage I can't take back. That's what hurts the most. I can't take this last month back.

"You all right?" A deep baritone voice from behind me startles me. With a quick intake of breath and my hand reaching up to my rapidly beating heart, I turn around to see a man standing there. He's older, maybe in his late forties. Kind eyes with gentle lines surrounding them meet mine.

It takes me a moment to realize when he arches his brow that he's waiting for my response.

With a few blinks to bring my mind back to the present and a shake of my head, I tell him, "Fine, sorry."

I push my cart forward thinking I'm blocking his path, but he doesn't have a cart and he doesn't seem to have any intention to move either. His boot-clad feet are firmly planted and my eyes move from them, up his dark-wash jeans and button-down white shirt to his questioning gaze.

"I'm fine." My voice is stern and carries a harshness I don't like to use with strangers when I repeat myself; this guy needs to stay the hell out of my business.

When he crosses his arms, I can tell he has some muscle to him. The cotton fabric tightens around his biceps, just as my hands do on the handle of the cart. There's an air to him that changes, a knowingness about him that sends a chill down my spine.

It's a look I recognize. It's a look I don't like. The type of look that makes me want to run.

"I don't think you are fine," he challenges and the bitterness of having this man judge me creeps into the snide response I'm ready to spit out at him. He continues, stopping my words and any breath I was daring to take. "I know he's a murderer. I know he killed your foster father. And it looks like you're having a difficult time dealing with things… just from my perspective, Miss Fawn."

That prick that has crawled slowly down my spine flows over my body in a single wave, nearly buckling my knees. I can feel the color drain from my face. Slowly, just like the twine fraying and unraveling. I don't know who this man is, but I know damn well I shouldn't be talking to him.

I have to concentrate on keeping my breathing steady—in and out— and focus on not reacting.

Murderer.

My foster father.

Daniel didn't kill him.

My eyes dart to the man and I try to hold his prying gaze.

My head wants to shake just slightly, it wants to deny what he's saying, but it can't. I can't react. I can't show him a damn thing.

Daniel didn't murder him though. That happened years ago. Before I ever even thought of leaving this place, before everything else happened. I want to speak the words, the need to defend Daniel pushing the words toward the tip of my tongue.

I bite down on the inside of my cheek instead, screaming in my head to stay silent. But silence brings questions. Not just mine but also this man's.

I've never questioned my foster father's death. It was a burglary. That's what the news said.

The Cross brothers are good at covering things up. I've heard and seen things though. Especially recently.

I know what Daniel's capable of and what he'll do out of anger. I know he loved me back then. What my foster father did… That's the second reason I stay bitterly quiet, even as the questions choke me. I hate even thinking of that man. I was only a child and he was a predator. I'd rather spit on his gravestone than mention his name.

The third reason I keep biting the inside of my cheek until I taste a tinge of blood is the most important. The man who stands silent in front of me knows more than I do. I may be the sorry excuse for a woman Daniel's chosen to be his wife, but I'm not stupid. I'm smart enough to know when to keep my mouth shut. So I do. I stand there, waiting to see if a threat comes.

Near silence reigns with only the steady hum of the coolers behind us as I stare back at him.

After a moment, his lips kick up into an asymmetric smile. "Did you not know?" he questions but doesn't wait for a response. "Maybe you didn't know then, but you know now." His eyes narrow as he nods, persuading me to believe him.

"Who are you?" It's the first question I imagine Daniel asking when I tell him what happened.

"Cody Walsh. Your boyfriend knows who I am."

"Fiancé," I correct him.

His forehead scrunches when he stares down at my hand, the one lacking a ring, and subconsciously, my thumb runs over my ring finger.

"Congratulations," he comments. His demeanor has completely changed with every passing minute that he scrutinizes me, trying to determine where my place is in this world.

Truth be told, I have no idea what he'll find; I'm still trying to figure that out myself.

"Addison Fawn … soon-to-be Addison Cross," he says but doesn't infuse any type of emotion into the statement. It's only matter-of-fact. "Any relation to Bethany Fawn?"

Confusion travels over my face as I try to recall a Bethany of any sort.

"Oh, you don't know that either? She's the woman Jase, your fiancé's brother, has been seeing." Again, I don't answer, and I try to keep from giving him any response in my expression. He only smirks as he walks past me, letting me know to tell Daniel he said hi.

"Will do," I manage to bite out without an ounce of resentment as I accept his challenge.

I didn't know Daniel's brother was seeing anyone. I sure as hell don't know a Bethany *Fawn*. Apparently, I don't know a lot of things.

What I do know is already destroying me.

CHAPTER 2

Daniel

A HINT OF LEMON IN THE WOOD POLISH INVADES MY LUNGS AS I breathe in deep, gripping the armrests of the wingback chair. I can't look at my brothers, neither of them. I'm breaking down. The farther away Addison is, the worse I crumble. If they look too closely, if I speak too loudly, they'll see every fucking crack.

Too bad I can't help myself during this bitch of a conversation.

"We have a soft truce." Carter's voice is calm, but he knows my reaction will be anything but.

"Fuck that," I say, letting the darkly spoken words fall without looking at either him or Jase. I stare past my brother and into the woods that line the property through the paned window behind him. The shades of green blur as my blood heats with anger.

"He stays out of our way and we give him details. That was the truce." Carter speaks in time with the tapping of the pen in his hand on the desk.

"Going up to Addison and scaring her isn't exactly staying out of our way."

"He scared her?" he questions me and I don't have time to push out the snide remark: *How the fuck else should she feel?*

"Maybe we pissed him off with the last deal? We didn't exactly keep our word," Jase says carefully, and I can feel him watching me, gauging my reaction with every syllable, but I use everything in me to stay still and not give them any more than I already have.

Leaning forward, my throat is dry as I speak clearly to both of them.

"He walked up to my soon-to-be wife. He tried to get to her, to get in her head." My back hits the chair as I force myself to stay seated and not turn over every piece of furniture in my brother's office. "He left like a coward before I could get my hands on him. I want his fucking head!" My pulse races as I lose control with the last sentence.

We own this town. We own the cops.

Cody Walsh is supposed to be easy. He's supposed to be predictable. All that went to shit last month. Just like everything else.

Carter ignores me, or at least he ignores my anger to instead direct his comments to Jase. "If Walsh is pissed about what we did, he'll get over it. We do what we have to." Facing me and hardening his voice, he asks me, "What exactly did he say to her?"

"That we killed that prick. That he knows I'm a murderer and he knows she's not okay."

"That's how he said it?"

Carter's constant questioning makes me inhale sharply as I straighten my shoulders and stare him down, not giving him a single word in response. Not trusting myself to speak.

"He still needs us." Carter speaks first.

"And we still need him," Jase reminds us all. It's his ass on the line. This is all his fault. His sloppy choices made us take the deal with Walsh.

Although Carter's talking to Jase, the statement is directed at me. "Until we find the footage he's blackmailing you with, his head stays on."

My blunt nails tap along the polished wood in a soothing rhythm, so at odds with what I feel. "And what am I supposed to do in the meantime? Let him scare her? Let him get to her?"

"No," both Jase and Carter say at the same time. My eyes dart between the two of them, judging their response for sincerity until I can nod.

With my thumb brushing against the fleshy tips of my fingers, I ask Carter, my older brother and the one I rely on in order to move forward every day in this shit of a mess we've gotten ourselves into with a dirty cop, "What can I do?" I feel weak asking them rather than acting. I hate this and I know they can feel the turmoil rolling off of me in waves as I close my eyes and try to loosen my tight throat. "I need something to give her. Something to make all this better." *There's nothing to make it better*, a voice hisses inside my head and I lean forward, burying my face in my hands. I grit out the words between my clenched teeth as I add, "I fucking hate this."

"For now, I'll remind Walsh that our women will be respected and they stay out of it—"

"She said…" I have to swallow the hard lump in my throat before continuing as I stare past him again at the ambers and emeralds of the trees. "She said he seemed concerned, then he was… gauging her. He's trying to flip her."

"Concerned?"

"She isn't handling the recent events well." I can barely get out the words. Each syllable claws the back of my throat before it's spoken. "He approached her, she said, because she didn't look like she was doing well."

The leather behind Carter groans and protests as he readjusts in his chair opposite the desk from me.

"If he thinks she's a weak spot, he's wrong," I tell him and there's more defensiveness in my cadence than I wanted. "She would never tell anyone anything."

"No one thinks she would."

"That's why he brought up the foster fuck? You think he was gauging her to see if it was true? To see if she knows anything?" Jase asks.

"That's what she thinks," I answer him. "If he's trying to get more dirt on us, we need to end this now. Finish him."

"He can't know for sure about her foster father, how many fucking years ago was it? And Addison would never give anything up."

"How did he know?" I question them. It happened a decade ago. No one ever knew. It was only us.

"Forensics, maybe evidence." Jase sounds suspicious but shakes his head at the thought and shrugs as he adds, "Maybe word on the street, but I don't see how."

"He's bluffing. He had a hunch and he's testing us to see if we'll play into his hands."

It's quiet as the information is digested. This balancing act is getting harder and harder. What was once planks of wood feels like a thin tightrope now.

Carter takes a deep inhale before speaking. "Let's make him feel comfortable. That's the only way we can use him until we're safe to get rid of him."

Make him feel comfortable… I'm seething inside. This isn't the way things used to be. It's complicated and every move we make only gets us deeper and deeper into bed with the devil.

"Did you tell Addison about her father—" Carter starts to ask, but stops and corrects himself. "Foster father?"

I simply nod before replying, "Last night when she told me."

I remember the way she couldn't look me in the eyes before I told her. The way she turned her back to me to go to the bathroom. The way her knuckles turned white as she stood there gripping the doorknob, not moving but not asking. She wanted to know, but she knows better than to ask. That's what we decided. I tell if she asks, but she never asks. She doesn't want to know. "I told her because I thought she'd want to know the truth."

"It's been years."

"A decade."

"She never even considered it was us back then." I repeat my thoughts, but out loud now. "No one did."

"What did she say?" Jase questions, concern clearly written on his face.

The vision returns to me of her eyes closing slowly, her chin dropping as she took in a shuddering breath. Her response came out as nothing but a whisper and then she closed the door to the bathroom, leaving me sitting there, watching the glass knob and wishing it had been my hand she was holding when I confessed.

"She said, 'thank you,'" I tell them.

"Do you think she gave anything away to Walsh?"

"No," I say and my answer is hard as I glare at Jase. He stares back, unmoving, but there's sympathy in his expression.

"He can't prove anything," Carter says between us, cutting through the thinly veiled tension.

"Since when do we let someone make us feel threatened?"

"Since he has evidence that will put me away for life," Jase answers me. "We tread carefully until Declan can find something on him and get rid of every shred of proof Walsh has."

"He's digging into everything he can so we'll work with him," Carter says, then clears his throat and sits back farther in his chair. "I'll send him a message, letting him know not to go near Addison and that his concern is unwarranted."

"A message?"

"It's the safe—"

Anger forces me to rise from my seat. "A fucking message?"

"Calm down."

"You aren't the one who lost a baby! I lost my child." The strength in my voice is all but forgotten as I voice it for the first time. They already know, but I haven't said it yet. I haven't had the audacity to breathe that truth to life. "Your wife is still pregnant. Mine isn't." Everything cracks. The air, my voice, my damn insides shatter to brittle shards.

They sit there in silence as I slowly retake my seat. *Just breathe. Calm down.* How can I do either when everything is falling apart?

Jase's firm hand squeezes my forearm as he tells me, "I know it's difficult on her; we need to keep her safe and protected."

"It was stress. That's what the doctor said. She lost the baby and this bullshit isn't stopping. It's getting worse."

All that surrounds me is silence. All that lingers inside of me is guilt. I don't know how to fix this, and I don't think anyone else knows either.

"She isn't supposed to know anything. That was our deal. But she sees how tense everyone is. She knows how much danger we've been in. She's witnessed shit firsthand… I don't think she can handle this. She wasn't supposed to know any details. That's what she wanted." The admission flows from me like a Catholic at church. Safe in the confessional, waiting to hear my penance, praying for it all to be okay. *Just tell me what to do to make it all right.*

"Maybe that's the problem," Carter suggests, and I lift my blurred gaze to his dark one.

"What?" At least my question is presentable.

"Maybe she should know," Jase says before Carter. "Maybe if she knew details, she'd feel like she has more control. Control is a damn good way to deal with stress. Even if it's only in details and not action."

I don't have time to answer; a knock at the door interrupts the conversation. It's a soft rap, quick but firm.

Before Carter can tell whoever it is to come in, the heavy door creaks open, bringing with it the light from the hall, and Addison's shadow spills into the room before she does. Her hand stays on the edge of the door when she asks, "Is it all right if I come in?"

My brothers don't answer for me, but I nod once.

The room's so quiet I can practically hear her swallow as she steps into it, not shutting the door for privacy. "I just remembered something. Something I didn't tell you." Our eyes lock as she wrings her fingers around one another. Her hair's still damp from the shower, making it look darker than her dirty-blonde should be. Her lack of sleep is just as evident. Still, she's beautiful.

She clears her throat, staring at the intricately woven rug beneath the desk and stopping a small distance from me in her bare feet.

Her small form clothed in loose pajamas is at odds with the three of us. She belongs here though. She is my counterpart in every way. I only wish I didn't hurt her like I do.

"He brought up my last name," she finally says clearly. Her admission makes a deep crease settle in my forehead.

"Fawn?" I question and that gets Jase's attention.

She nods, glancing between Jase and me. "He asked if I was related to Bethany." She speaks directly to Jase as if he'd have an answer, but he wears the same expression I do.

"I never really knew my family, so… I don't know." The insecurity in her tone is undeniable, as is her curiosity.

"You should ask her," Jase comments. "We can have dinner tomorrow night."

"That would be good for us," Carter agrees. "I'll ask Aria if she's up for cooking." All the while I stare at Addison, waiting for her to give me some sign that she's all right.

Anything. I need something from her.

"I'll ask her," Addison quickly speaks up, then adds, "I'd like to talk to her anyway." A weak smile lingers on her lips as my brothers nod in agreement. It's quiet for a moment and I can see the questions in her eyes.

"Anything else?" I prod.

"Were you talking about Walsh?"

My brothers stay quiet. They handle their relationships the way they want and I do the same. I seem to be the only one failing though. "Do you want in on the details?" I always ask. She knows when something's wrong, when I'm worried. When things have gone to shit. I'd never make her an accessory, but I'll give her what I can if she wants it.

"No," she answers, and her smile turns tight, forming a straight line before she drops her hands to her sides and says she'll head out to talk to Aria.

"How are you doing, Addie?" Jase asks her before she can leave.

"Better. I think I just needed a hot shower." Time passes with a click of the clock, a second that waits for what else is on her mind. A piece of me is dying to scream for her to speak up. To ask. The piece that wants to tell her everything. The other part of me, the bigger part, wants to shield her.

She leaves as quickly as she came, which is probably for the best.

The less she knows, the less stress she'll have. She doesn't need to worry about this shit. It's our mess. Not hers.

I need to fix this. I just don't know how.

CHAPTER 3

Addison

Cody Walsh. A million questions linger in my mind after looking up his name online all last night. More questions scream in my head when I think about what Daniel confessed. They killed a man years ago who deserved to be hurt. They killed him because of what he did to me. They *killed* him.

How many moments have gone by where I've mentioned my childhood in passing? Or lack thereof, rather. We talked about how I was in home after home. When we found out I was pregnant, it was all I could think about. All I could talk about.

I was worried I wouldn't know how to be a good mother, because I never had one. It opened the floodgates for all those memories. When I was young, I didn't even think I'd ever be able to get pregnant. Just the thought makes my stomach churn; it's because of what he did to me. The doctors said the scar tissue on my cervix could make it harder to open. I had problems and complications. All the aftermath of the man who was supposed to take care of me.

I brought it up maybe three or four times in the last two months when we found out I was pregnant. I couldn't *not* talk about it. No matter how much I hate to go back to those times in my life.

Daniel had so many opportunities to tell me, but he never did.

I never asked, but how would I have even known to question it? Fear has been replaced by something else. Something larger than it. A dying need to know.

"Hey." Aria's tone is already consoling when she greets me, ripping me from my thoughts as I place the heavy porcelain plates on the counter.

I didn't expect to feel this way toward her. There's a gap between us now, when only weeks ago, nothing separated us. Now I'm careful with what I say and how I say it. I'm careful I don't put this sadness on her. Just like she's careful with me now.

"How's it going?" she asks.

I can hear the emotions in her voice just as easily as the clank of the dishes. The sympathy, the guilt I know she feels because she's still pregnant when I'm not. She and Chloe, Sebastian's wife, are carrying so well. *Glowing* is the correct term. And then there's me, dull with a forced smile as I turn to her, leaning the small of my back against the granite counter.

"Hey, yourself," I answer her with enough pep in my voice to lighten the tension. I don't want anyone to feel sorry for me. It's life. It's death. It's whatever fate has in store. I don't want her to look at me and feel pity. I'd rather she look at me and see how happy I am for her.

That's one shining light in all this darkness.

"We're cooking for everyone tonight, if you're up for that?" I ask her.

"Family dinner tonight?" Aria eyes me curiously as one perfectly plucked eyebrow arches. She knows something's up, but she doesn't ask. She used to always ask.

"Does that mean something's going on?" Chloe asks as she enters, the faint sound of bags rustling carrying through the kitchen with her. Her husband is best friends with Carter and his right-hand man, but she doesn't live in the main house of the estate like the rest of us. She and Sebastian have a place deeper in the woods; it's still protected though. At first, I thought it was sweet for all of us to live so close. But the more I think about it, the fact that we need to be protected, the more it startles me.

I watch as she sets a large brown paper bag down on the table, her belly protruding, round and an obvious sign that she's in her second trimester.

Taking off her light jacket, she lays it across the chair and then smooths her flowing cream blouse down her front.

"Carter told Sebastian and he told me," Chloe says, answering the unspoken question. "I brought everything for cheesecake," she adds easily with a genuine smile. She doesn't look at me like I'm broken, but that's because she doesn't know me well. She doesn't see how off I am like Aria does. She can't tell that I'm damaged goods because she doesn't know what I was like before. It's comforting, really.

"So?" she questions. "Is something going on?"

"What do you mean?" I have no idea what she's referring to. "Something is always going on."

"Well, have you guys been doing family dinners where this is normal, or is this a way for the guys to keep us in line?"

"I never thought about it like that." The murmured words are accompanied by a deep line settling into my forehead as I consider it.

"If something's up, Bastian better tell me," Chloe comments as she unloads the contents of her bag on the table.

"No, nothing's up. It's a little tense right now. But no more than usual. The only thing eating at Carter is a cop who's getting to Jase. He caused a little stir yesterday."

"How do you know for sure?" I ask her.

"Carter keeps me updated. We have a little ritual. It calms him and keeps his head clear to talk things out."

"I can't imagine how that could be calming." I don't realize I've spoken until the words are out there and the room goes quiet.

Chloe's huff is amused when I look at her with wide eyes. "You'd be surprised how much a conversation is worth." Her gaze falls for just a moment, but I see it happen. The haze of a smile falls along with it. "How have you been?"

Aria's been popping grapes in her mouth, but she pauses when Chloe ventures into *that* territory. Her bump isn't so visible. Our babies would have been about a month apart.

It's hard to contain the deluge of emotions.

"You can say it sucks. Or that it hurts. Or that you're better or worse… You can tell me to shut my mouth too and mind my own damn business," she offers after rattling off a list of appropriate responses.

I feel like it's my fault. Like I should have known better. I say the words in my head, because I can't admit them. Not to Aria and Chloe. Not to Daniel. I don't even want to know that's how I feel. But I do.

"We should make dinner," I suggest in a whisper. "Just because I'm suffering a loss doesn't mean I can't be happy for all we have," I add and Chloe gives me a small smile that doesn't reach her eyes.

"The dinner for the non-worrying mob wives," Chloe jokes.

"We are not the mob." Aria hisses the admonishment before eating another grape. "It's been hectic and there's always something to worry about, but—"

I don't want the tears to fall, but I can't hide them. My face is hot and my breath comes in short pants. The next inhale is harsh, and with it, both women come to me. "I'm sorry," I say, and my words are strangled as I rush past them for a napkin on the table so I can stop it all.

"Don't say that. Don't be sorry for crying. I've always thought that was the silliest of things."

"It's good to cry." Aria's voice is so soothing. She is my rock in all of this. She's steady and we share so much in common. She grew up in this life though. She didn't run away from it all. "Sometimes crying—showing mourning, showing vulnerability—leads to the best things."

I respond with the one truth the last six months has taught me and say, "You can't be vulnerable in this world."

She counters my statement as I swipe the napkin under my eyes, drying them, calming my breathing and feeling foolish all over again.

"Of course you can," Aria corrects me. "We all are. Trying to hide that isn't going to fool anyone." She emphasizes, "We're all vulnerable."

All I have in response is a sniffle and then I rest my head on her shoulder. "I didn't mean to cry though; I don't want you to think seeing you guys makes me sad." I can barely get the statement out, because it's not entirely true. Still, I don't want them to think it.

We hide truths like that, don't we?

"So, weird thing," I blurt out, cutting off Chloe, who no doubt has something sweet to say, and instead I help her move all the items on the table to the counter as I speak. It's back to business, back to cooking for this non-worrying dinner. "Did you know Jase has a girlfriend?" I ask them and my tone is so much peppier than I feel. I heard once though, if you speak like you're happy, you'll start to feel like it.

"Carter told me a couple of days ago. She's funny but with a dry sense of humor and she's very blunt."

"Sounds delightful," Chloe jokes.

"She's also coming to dinner, I think."

Aria eyes me before grabbing a large bowl from the lower cabinet and I take that as my cue to unwrap Chloe's cream cheese.

Looks like the dessert will be done before the actual meal at this rate.

"Bastian also mentioned she's a nurse. Should be good to have one of those in the family."

"Family," Aria says and rolls her eyes.

"I didn't mean in a mob way."

"Her last name is Fawn," I comment to no one in particular and unwrap the next bar of cream cheese. "I wonder if she knows if we're related."

"Like biologically? Or from… Is your last name your mother's or did you get that from a…?" Aria stops mid-thought and it's then that I realize from the look on her face that she was going to say *foster family* but stopped herself because she thought it would hurt me to hear it. She stopped herself because she knows about the fresh wounds.

She knows because Carter told her.

Or maybe she's known since I came back. I wonder if Carter told her everything all the way back then.

"You know I still love you, right?" I question Aria and quickly add, "And that I'm happy for you, both of you?" I look between them both, hoping they know it's true. I may be held together by glue and tape and questioning my decisions, but I know I'm happy for them.

"I know," Aria answers with kind eyes. She repeats, "I know."

CHAPTER 4

Daniel

TYLER ALWAYS HID IT FROM HER. HE WAS GOOD AT IT THOUGH. Tyler's all I can think about as we sit down at the table. Three brothers and a friend. One brother late, as per usual. Another never coming to a family dinner again.

He didn't have this problem with Addison. He was good at hiding it. He hid so much from her; I just don't know how he could do it.

"The candles are a nice touch," Addison says and smiles warmly at Aria, who does a small curtsy and the three girls let out a peal of feminine laughter.

Addison's is short, genuine. But it disappears quickly. It's like the warm water of the ocean, splashing on the tips of your toes before retreating all too soon. I miss it already. I find myself staying still, wanting it to come back.

The day must've gone well for her. With a glass of wine in her hand and a beautiful flush in her cheeks, she's unwinding with the help of the alcohol.

"Just let me smell one more time," Aria says and inhales close to the large goblet at the same time Carter wraps his arm around her waist and pulls her into his lap. Another wave of giggling leaves the women and then is replaced by soft hums as the other two women are kissed and kiss back, falling into their seats for dinner.

Mine's already seated, and when I look to her, her lips are on the wine glass. So instead of kissing her, I place my hand over hers on her lap. My fingers slip into the spaces between hers, feeling her soft skin, her warmth. Before she places the glass back on the table, her fingers close around mine, bringing them closer together, and she doesn't let go. Not until the large bowl of antipasto salad is passed.

"Looks delicious, ladies." Sebastian's compliment is rewarded with a story from Aria about how she learned a new recipe for the main dish.

Lasagna, candlelight, and delicate dishes, the hum of chatter and constant smiles. Everything in the room is full of life, but that's not how I feel. It's not the reality I'm living in.

If Tyler were here though, he'd fit right in, and that would help Addison. He was good at hiding. He would have been good for her.

I wash the thought away with a single swig of the bourbon in front of me. I try to tell myself he's on my mind because of what happened recently. And not because I truly think Addison would be better off if he were still here.

It's not like before. Nothing is. I have to remind myself of that sometimes. The memories of what used to be, the reminder of Tyler and what life was like back then…it's an ebb and flow of past and present. We're better now. So long as we're together. I won't let anything change that.

Reaching up onto the table, Addison's grasp is small and comforting when she lays her hand on my wrist. It's a shock to my system to feel her touch in this moment.

"You okay?" Her question is soft and murmured so no one else can hear.

"Fine," I answer her because it's automatic. I don't tell her more because she doesn't ask. She doesn't let go like I expect her to though. She eats with her left hand, leaving her right on mine. And I leave my hand just where it is, needing to feel that warmth, needing to feel her to make all this regret go away.

So long as I have her, it's all okay. I just need to know I still have her.

Addison

He's supposed to be the strong one.

The man is supposed to be the rock. That's what the world leads you to believe, but I think it's bullshit. Why else would I feel more complete, more grounded when I'm trying to hold Daniel together?

Aria and Chloe put a Band-Aid over my pain. They make me forget temporarily, and that's worth something. They make me feel like it's normal to be down right now, and that's worth even more.

But holding on to Daniel, holding him together, that feels like purpose. It feels like belonging and worthiness. One small touch, and it's like the pieces have been soldered back together, making them stronger than they ever were before.

Even if it is just holding his hand and smiling with his family, *my* family.

"Where's Bethany?" Aria asks and my eyes dart to hers although she's slipping her fork into her mouth with her focus on Jase. I know she's asking for my benefit though.

"She couldn't come tonight, but she'll be here tomorrow. She's getting some things adjusted."

"Adjusted?"

"She went through a hard time."

His answer quiets the room for a moment until I speak up. "I'd like to meet her."

Daniel's hand shifts under mine until the back of it is to the table and his palm is against mine.

"I bet you would," Carter comments with the hint of a smile.

"You'll like her," Jase says after a quick drink from his tumbler. The ice clinks as he sets it down on the table. "I don't know anything about what Walsh said, but she may know. If not, you'll still find plenty to talk about."

"Walsh." I roll my eyes as I say his name and take a sip of wine as I feel everyone's eyes on me. The nervousness in the room creeps up a notch. The dark red is sweet, with a hint of lingering decadence. I bring my gaze to Carter's at the head of the table and tell him simply, "He doesn't like me much, I don't think."

"He doesn't like me much either." Jase's response comes with a huff of a laugh from Sebastian as he sits back into his chair with ease, resting an arm over Chloe's chair behind her shoulders.

"He has poor taste then," I offer Jase and that gets me a small laugh from Chloe and her husband. Daniel only observes and half of all my senses are focused on him, focused on me. Everyone's waiting to see if I'm going to break down again. I can feel it. They're waiting to see if I'm okay. And I'm not, I know I'm not. But isn't it okay if I'm not all right?

It sounds like a paradox, but I think it's more real than anything.

Carter takes a deep breath, then says, "He's not going anywhere soon, but he'll get on board. Or I'll take care of it." His darkly spoken words are overshadowed by Jase's.

"He will," Jase adds and then tells me he's sorry that I felt uncomfortable yesterday. That it never should have happened. He tells me he'd never let anything happen to me. None of them would.

They say we're family, and I know we are.

There's a pit in my gut though when Aria speaks. "Don't worry, Addie, we're in this together."

"Right," I say and nod in agreement, then thank God when I bring the glass up to finish the small pool of wine in it when she tells me, "Nothing bad can happen if we're in it together."

The glass hides my immediate reaction.

I don't know why she says it when she knows that's not true. Bad things happen regardless. Bad things have already happened.

When I set my glass down, I smile at her instead of saying just that. The words still exist though. I can feel them in the tense air. I think everyone can.

Until Chloe stands up abruptly and remembers the cheesecake. She's sweet enough to bring the rest of the bottle in for me too.

"I can't get tipsy with both of you out of commission," I tell her, not wanting to keep drinking in front of them.

"Please, have a glass for me," Aria requests with a yawn.

"I already did," I remind her. The wine was her idea, and not a bad one.

"Then have another one for me." Chloe's cheerful with her pleading eyes and faux pout as she holds out the bottle.

"Well, how can I say no to that?" I jokingly respond to cut the tension in the room more than anything else.

Another round, a plate of sweets, and the story of how Chloe and Sebastian came to be a couple turns the night around. That and the fact that Daniel pulls me into his embrace. My right side is pressed to his hard, toned body, and his stubble gently scratches my hair as he sets his chin on my head and then kisses my crown.

Maybe it works both ways. Back and forth. The rock thing. That makes it difficult, though, when both people are breaking apart.

CHAPTER 5

Her laugh is addictive. It's my drug. The way her cheeks flush, the way her back arches just slightly and her shoulders shake so gently—it all soothes something inside of me that I don't even know is broken until that sweet sound seeps into the crevices and calms the hurt that follows me every day.

That's how I knew I loved her.

The sad, pretty girl who was always around when we were kids smiled easily enough. It wasn't real though. It was a smile that wanted to be more. She wanted to laugh.

And everything inside of me wanted to hear it. I *needed* to hear it.

Just like I needed to hear it tonight. Everyone else's laugh turns to white noise, just like the clinking of the silverware on empty plates and the dull hum of Aria saying something to Carter. All I can hear is Addison's laugh. All I can watch is how her shoulders curl in, and instinctively, her hand finds my lap.

I'm quick to catch it with my own, to squeeze it gently. When she leans into me, humming a small good night to Chloe as she leaves, I kiss her hair and try to memorize everything about this moment.

It's perfect like this. This is how it should be all the time. She should laugh every day. She should smile and reach out to me while she catches her breath with the soft murmur of happiness lingering on her lips.

Every day.

It's easy to say we're broken. It's easy to feel the pain. To hold on to this though—the moments I feel what's really between us—to let ourselves feel it, that's the easiest thing I can do, and the hardest just the same.

"Night." Carter's voice is accompanied by a tight squeeze of my shoulder as they walk behind us.

Addison makes a move to clean up the dishes but Jase reaches for them first, clearing the table and collecting the few remaining dishes in one stack balanced in his left hand. "I got this," he says with a smirk and winks at her. "You cook, we clean."

"Thanks," she tells him and he tells us good night, exiting the room, leaving us to head to bed.

The sound of an empty room is the worst sound. I've spent too much of my life in quiet spaces.

"You had a good time tonight." I hold Addison's hand as we walk, not wanting to let her go just yet. There were good moments and bad ones too, but I don't mention the tense ones.

Carter or Jase…whoever it was who thought to have the dinner tonight, was right. We never had dinners growing up, not like this. Not after our mom died and everything happened. I could hardly stand to walk into the eat-in kitchen, let alone sit at the table with hope like I did tonight. "We should do it more often."

"Yeah. It was fun," she tells me as we walk down the quiet hall to our wing. The walls are decorated with her photographs. Moments she thought were worthy of capturing on film. Before we get to the bedroom, she stops, lifting her hand from my grasp to touch the edge of a carved black frame mounted against the walls, which are painted a pale dusty blue.

"This one's my favorite of the ones I took while we were away," she says softly.

Her fingertips trace over the glass and down the alley that led to the bar where she first saw me again after so many years had passed.

While we were away. Is that the way she thinks of it?

"I think I like the others better."

"What others?" she says and turns to me quickly, her hair swirling from her shoulder to tumble down her back. Her genuine curiosity makes her eyes widen slightly and it forces my lips to curve up.

"The ones of you in my bed," I answer her and then quickly nip her lower lip as lust just barely reaches her eyes. My blood simmers with desire for her and the need to touch her always.

"You're bad, Daniel Cross," she whispers playfully with passion in her voice as I open the door behind her while letting my lips caress the crook of her neck.

Her eyes are still closed when I pull back. She swallows with a gentle hum and lets her head fall back to rest against the molding that lines the bedroom door.

I find myself trapped in her words. *You're bad, Daniel Cross.*

She knew it all along. She can live with that. She can love me still, even knowing all the wretched things I've done. It's this world though, the world she fled and the world I dragged her back to, that's doing the harm.

I want so badly to blame it on that when I brush the loose strands of her hair off her collarbone with the backs of my fingers so I can kiss her there. I wish I could blame it all on this place. It's only when I stop touching her that she opens her eyes.

A hint of a smile plays at her lips when she finally looks back at me.

"Come to bed with me." I give her the command when we get into the bedroom. With the curtains parted, there's no need to turn on the light. It's dimly lit, but enough so that I can see her perfectly when my eyes adjust. I can see her standing in the doorway, slow to follow me and hesitant to do what I told her.

Hesitant to come to bed with me.

All she's thinking about is the sex. It's not because she's uncertain if it's safe; the doctor said it was last week. Our first time getting pregnant was an accident. She's questioning if we should try for a baby on purpose.

Whether or not we should try again. Whether we should use protection.

Whether she wants this like I do.

Whether she wants me still… I know that's a question that drifts into her mind when she looks at me like that.

That part of me that doesn't know it's broken until she heals me… it's screaming in pain right now.

"I think I just need to sleep. There's so much on my mind." Her excuse falters in the air as she heads to the dresser, taking off her earrings. I can hear them clink in the small ceramic trinket bowl.

"Tell me," I insist and then clear my throat, pretending like I haven't been devastated every night she's looked at me like that and made some kind of excuse. "Tell me what's on your mind."

"I haven't processed everything."

"You can talk it out with me." I ignore the thump in my chest as I speak. The battering of something hard against my rib cage aches with every small movement.

"Like you talk things out with me?" She turns from the dresser, tense and on the angry side. She seems to realize her quick temper before I can react, crossing her arms over her chest. "Sorry," she apologizes in a hushed murmur. When did it get to be like this? Where we can't talk. The start of a conversation turns into a fight, even if we know we need each other.

Tucking her hair behind her ear, she looks me in the eyes and says, "I know you would… if…"

I close the distance between us and make my way over to finish the thought for her and say, "If that's what you wanted."

"Right," she breathes, the tension leaving her, her arms falling to her side the moment I place my hand on her hip. "It's my fault," she tells me with a harsh swallow.

"Come here," I tell her and my words come out low and rough. There's an edge that's demanding, I know there is. It's a part of me that I'm trying to soften for her. It's still a part of me though.

Falling into my chest and pressing her body as close to mine as she can, she breathes so softly I almost don't hear the admission just under my chin, "I don't know what I want anymore." I tighten my hold on her, wishing I could go back to moments ago. When she was laughing and reaching for me. She confesses, "I'm scared."

It's the first time she's shown me this raw sincerity since we lost the baby.

"It's all right to be scared." With my arm wrapped around her lower back, I splay my hand against her shoulder and rock her slightly, just slightly. She pulls back a tiny bit, only to see me, her chest to mine. I watch as the moonlight filters in from the subtle movement of the curtains, reflecting in her gaze. There's so much vulnerability there. Even now. Even after all we've been through. How much more can she take?

"Kiss me." I give her the command and her posture relaxes, her composure softening the instant her eyes close, and she stands on her tiptoes to bring her lips closer to mine. I keep my eyes open. I watch as she reaches up with both hands, twining her fingers behind my neck as she pushes her lips against mine. She doesn't hesitate this time.

"I love you," she whispers against my lips, peeking up at me through her thick lashes. The curtains sway and bring with them a sudden gust of late-night air, carrying the faint smells of early spring with them.

"I love you too," I tell her, but it's not enough. They're only words that don't compare to what I feel inside.

I'm sorry I put her through all of this. I don't admit it though, because more than sorry, I'm selfish and I wouldn't change it. That's the most fucked-up part. I can't live without her. Even knowing how it breaks her.

"Get ready for bed," she tells me with a weak smile. The smile that's not a smile. The fake one she's always had.

I'm still fully clothed, shoes and all.

The wooden floor creaks in time with her deep inhale as she turns from me and I do as she wishes, letting her take the lead although I don't know how long she'll want it.

"Tell me something and I will," I barter with her.

"I feel lonely," she tells me with her back to me and I can only watch as she pulls the sheets back, sitting on the edge of the bed.

Lonely. Lonely like the quiet halls I hate. Even though I'm right here, it's still lonely. I know she's right.

"Lonely?" I repeat as I drop my watch to the dresser, letting it fall where it may with my gaze still pinned on Addison as she strips down slowly, leaving a puddle of clothes at the side of the bed. She does it every night. She has for the longest time. In the morning, she'll gather them and drop them in the basket. When she has energy; that's the excuse she gave me when I teased her about it before. The memory kicks my lips up into a small smirk, but it fades when I catch her profile in the dark room, the pale light showing me the lack of playfulness, the lack of happiness she's always held on to.

The months we've been back here have worn her down.

"There are moments when I'm okay but they're so fleeting. Recently," she adds quickly. "It's been a lot to take in."

"You don't like being back here, do you?" I question her and that gets her attention.

Turning to face me fully, she doesn't even bother to grab the sheets to cover herself as she answers me with shock clear in her cadence. "Of course I do." She swallows before adding, "I love your family. I've always loved them."

"Things are different now."

"We're all different," she comments without sparing a second between my statement and hers. Her gaze is bold, challenging even. "Just because things are different doesn't mean the pieces I love aren't the same."

I take my time pulling my undershirt over my head and dropping it to the dark wood floor. I strip down to nothing but my boxer briefs before climbing into bed. All the while she watches and waits.

Taking her hand in both of mine, the hand that still doesn't have a ring on it, I run my thumb across its barren finger and ask her, "Did you feel lonely before we lost the baby?"

"No," she answers me quickly and with a slight shake of her head. "It was after. Even with everyone around us… even with you, I just feel lonely sometimes. Like glimpses of loneliness. And I don't know what to do to shake it."

"You aren't alone, and this will pass."

"I know," she admits. "I know. It will pass, but I just don't know what to do in between. I don't know if I'm able to handle it all."

"Do you still want to marry me? You still want to stay here with me?"

"Yes," she answers quickly although she's just as hasty to look down at our hands. Like she spoke without thinking. Like there's a but.

"Then why no ring?" I ask her quietly and then clear my throat. "Why don't you want to wear it? I asked you to marry me weeks ago. You picked out the ring, but you don't wear it."

"Are you going to wear a ring?" she rebuts.

"An engagement ring?" She nods at the clarification. "Is that what you want? For me to wear a ring?"

Looking past me and out of the cracked window still bringing a gentle breeze, she admits, "No."

"You have to help me understand, Addison." The frustration in my voice is clear as I run a hand down my face and reposition on the bed as I pull my hands away. "It feels like…you aren't completely here with me any- more." Admitting the words makes my chest feel tighter, makes my hands feel colder and numb.

"I'm trying to be," she admits with a single harsh swallow.

"I get wanting to wait to try again," I say, and she tries to interrupt me but I stop her with a finger over her soft lips. "I understand that. It hurts, but I get it. I get that you feel lonely, because I do too. That's what happens when you lose someone. And we did. But I don't understand not wearing my ring. I can wait for you to come back to me and deal with this together; I just need to know that you will or what to do to help you. Losing the baby… I know it's because of everything else. I know it has to do with being here and that you don't love it."

"I never said that."

"You didn't have to."

"I just don't know my place."

"It's next to me. That's your place, with me." My words are rushed and full of frustration.

She starts to speak again, but she has to close her eyes and swallow thickly first, reaching out to me. A moment passes with an uncomfortable pang in my chest. The soft tips of her fingers run down my rough knuckles, tracing scars before she kisses them.

"I want you to wear the ring I got you." She nods once but she still doesn't speak, and she doesn't take her gaze off my knuckles. "I know it's harder, being around my family when the last time you saw them you weren't with me." My words make her still. Every piece of her is frozen as I speak the truth she doesn't say out loud. That's why she's not wearing the ring. It has to be because of that. We came back to the place where she didn't belong to me.

"You're mine now. You're going to find your place and I'll figure out how to help you. We're going to get married. We're going to have a baby one day."

The mention of a baby breaks her composure and I hold her tighter when her face crumples. Kissing her hair, I breathe the words, "I love you and you love me; there's no reason the world shouldn't know that. There's nothing to hide."

"It's not about hiding, it's…it's just everything is…" She trails off as she struggles to voice another word and attempts to move away from me, but I put my hand over hers.

"Just tell me," I say.

"It's never going to just be us. Our past…even right now. It's more than just us and I am struggling."

"Because of Tyler—"

She cuts me off before I can say more. "No. Your other brothers. Your life. *This* life." Breathing in deeper, heavier, she focuses on keeping her breathing steady as she looks me in the eyes to state, "You come with a lot of baggage, Daniel Cross. Some of it, I carry too."

"If this isn't what you want, you shouldn't have come back." I can't describe the way my blood chills and everything hardens. My jaw, my stiff back, the thump in my chest that quiets to a dull ache.

"I know, it's all my fault." The hurt in her voice reflects in her gaze.

"Stop saying that. We're in this together. None of this is your fault."

She looks like she'll say something, but all she does is nod slightly, refusing to open up and tell me what's going on in that beautiful head of hers.

"Don't keep it from me."

"I'm struggling to handle it; I need help."

"Tell me how."

"I just can't wear your ring," she confesses weakly.

"What part of not wearing my ring is supposed to help you?"

"Are you so dense, Daniel?" The contempt is unexpected. "You gave it to me after I found out. You gave me a ring because I was pregnant. That's the only reason. And we never should have gotten pregnant. It was an accident. I wasn't ready. It's my fault!"

"Addison—"

"I'm doing my best and I'm highly aware that it's not good enough. I couldn't even carry our baby," she says, and the last two words are a strangled mess between the shuddering sob she holds back.

"Don't say that… You are more than enough." I stress my words, grasping both of her hands in mine firmly and holding her gaze with mine to steady her. "Not a damn thing is your fault. Nothing but keeping all of this from me and letting it tear us apart. You have to talk to me."

"You have to talk to me too." She whimpers the plea as her watery eyes look up to mine.

"I can do that." I'm quick to acquiesce to her request. "I can talk to you, but you have to tell me if it's too much."

"It's all too much," she admits, "but I still want it. I still want you."

The relief that blooms inside of me is instant. It's everything I needed.

"One thing at a time." I wait for her to nod at my words, to know she's listening. "You are more than good enough. You're too good for me, but I'm keeping you anyway."

"Daniel—"

"No." I don't let her interrupt me. "You got to tell me, now it's my turn to tell you."

"Okay," she whispers, her grip getting tighter as she waits.

"You are with me and I am with you. We can't let each other be lonely. I'm right here," I whisper against the shell of her ear and then plant a gentle kiss against the tender skin beneath her ear. "We're going to be okay. You're going to find your place…so long as it's right next to me. We have to talk. We can't hold it in." I'm careful with my next suggestion. "You don't know your place, because you don't know what's going on. I want to tell you. I want you to know."

"The stress…" The words leave her sounding more like a helpless question than a statement.

"I think it will help, not hurt to know. It's the not knowing that's stressful."

She doesn't respond even though I give her time to.

"Do you think you'd be all right with that? Instead of you asking, I just tell and if it's too much, you tell me to stop and I will."

"Will that help you?" she questions me. The hope in her voice is there, but it's surprising that it comes with this particular question.

I almost tell her I'm fine. I'm so close to saying just that. Which would defeat the purpose of all of this. "Yes. It fucking kills me that I can't tell you what's eating at me."

"Okay then. New rules. You tell me everything unless I say stop." Fear and hope swirl in her glossy gaze.

"The loss is something we have to go through together and maybe we'll have moments where we feel alone, because we were wishing those moments were with the little life we never got to hold. But if you can try to remember I'm here, I hope it will help."

She swallows her words rather than responding. I keep going though. I'll take the lead and she'll follow. She has to. I don't know how this can work otherwise.

"I gave you the ring because I love you. The only reason I didn't give it to you sooner was because I wasn't sure you'd say yes. I thought I had a little anchor knowing you were pregnant. It wasn't an obligation because you were pregnant. It wasn't that, Addison. Don't think that."

She searches my expression, maybe in an attempt to determine if I'm sincere or not. It's what I deserve. Years ago, I kept everything from her, for a very long time. Our relationship started with lies, and it's carried on with secrets. She'll learn to trust me though. She has to. I won't give her any reason not to.

"I want you to wear my ring. I want you to come to bed with me, be with me again, even if you want to be safe and wait to try again. I need you, Addison."

It feels like I've emptied everything out. Leaving me hollow and waiting with nothing but the hope that she'll know this is all I've got. It's everything, every bit of me, and I don't know if it's enough but I'm damn sure going to try.

"I need you too," she finally whispers in the warm air between us, making it feel even hotter than it already is. I'm still on edge, waiting and needing more of her.

"Tell me we're going to be all right. That you're going to be all right." It's a command.

"I'm going to try," she answers, and I know it's because she wants to be honest and that she doesn't actually believe it. She doesn't know deep in her bones that it'll work. It never has before.

"You're going to succeed. You are meant to be with me, Addison. There's no way this ends otherwise. I need you and I need my family." I suck in a breath, ready to tell her if we have to, we'll leave. We did it before; we can do it again. It'll kill me, but for her, I'd do it.

"I need them too," she says, quick to cut me off. "I want this to work. Not just us; we work, and I love you, but this place. I just…I don't know."

"You don't know, that's exactly it. You don't know anything and that's the problem. I'll fix it. We'll fix this."

"I don't know that I can handle it," she confesses with a quivering bottom lip. "I've never felt so insignificant and weak." As she speaks, her voice goes dry and cracks at the words.

"I've put you through hell, and you survived."

"They've gone through worse. Aria—"

"Don't compare your story to hers; it doesn't change your pain." She's unraveling in front of me. Six months of being here and I've never seen her like this. How did I let it get this bad? "Get on the bed. In the center."

"Daniel—"

"The bed. Get in the middle, now." I emphasize my words and slowly pull away from her, keeping my gaze pinned to hers. "You can handle it, Addison. You can take everything."

Her shoulders drop heavily as she swallows, and her chest rises faster with every breath as she stares back at me. Not moving.

"I need you, Addison, and you need me. That's why we're off, why everything feels wrong. Get on the bed."

I've never had to repeat myself. She's always listened before, and staring at her now, not knowing what she'll do, I can't breathe. I can't lose her.

"On the bed, Addison. Don't make me tell you again."

Addison

I've loved this man since before I knew what love was.

I've craved him, adored him, fucking worshipped him.

But never like this. An intense heat ignites inside of me, a spark hotter and brighter than the sun dances on every nerve ending in my body.

I'm paralyzed, needing to feel him take me, own me, and devour me exactly how he wants.

I need it more than he'll ever know.

Slowly, I obey, although I don't know how. Every movement is gentle and meticulous. My hands reach the center first and immediately my fingers dig into the mattress.

It's so slow. Time moves so slowly. A part of me knows it's because I'm trying to remember this moment. Remember it all and hold on to it forever. I need it in the good times and the bad. In the horrible moments, I need this. What we have right now. I wish I could just stay here forever. Being his and him being so completely mine.

Bared to him, I wait and watch. His cock is hard and ready as he strokes himself in front of me, pacing, debating what he wants me to do, what he needs from me.

All the while, those sparks tingle up and down my body in waves of want.

Instead of climbing on the bed, pinning me down, and ravaging me, he asks me, "Why do I love you?"

His words are hoarse and at first I hear him wrong. I hear, "Why do you love me?" but I catch myself before the answer can leave me.

"I don't know," I answer him.

Instead of answering me, he tells me to spread my legs wide so he can see me.

"Fuck, I can see how wet you are from here," he breathes out deep with frustration as my fingertips run along the length of my pussy and then rub my swollen clit so he can see. A shiver of desire runs down my body from my shoulders to the tips of my toes. It's cold compared to the heat that burns between my thighs for him to enter me.

"Why do I love you?"

I close my eyes, pushing my head back into the mattress, and move my hand away, hating that I don't know what to tell him.

I don't know why people fall in love. I know why I love him though; I want to answer him that. *Ask me something I know.*

"Eyes on me. Don't you dare close your eyes." His steps are hard as he rounds the bed, getting close enough to backhand the inside of my thigh as punishment. The sting is fierce, but the touch is so needed, all I feel is a spike of desire shoot through me.

My breath is stolen from his admonishment, seething through my teeth and desperate.

"Put your fingers back on that pretty cunt of yours and look me in the eyes when you tell me you don't know why I love you." There's no hurt in his eyes, no pain in his voice, even though I feel it, deep down inside of me. Past everything physical, I feel it.

Tears prick at the back of my eyes as I let my fingers touch my warmth. His gaze parts from mine, only to watch me.

I have to give him something, so I tell him what I know. I tell him why I love him, praying he loves me the same.

"You know I've wanted you for as long as we've known each other. You know I'd risk it all to be with you."

My fingers slip just inside my entrance as I start to say the next reason, and a soft moan spills from my lips in its place.

"Fuck," he mutters. The word is a groan on Daniel's lips and hearing it makes my body heat.

"Touch me please," I beg him, but he shakes his head.

"Why else?" he asks huskily, the need showing through his intended words.

"You know that I would die without you. Whatever makes a person a person—I'd die if you weren't here anymore."

"I don't want you to ever say that again. Don't you ever talk about that. You're not allowed to die."

A short laugh that's not humorous at all bubbles from my lips. I feel crazy, on the verge of tears, feeling the pain of a great loss at the very thought that he might die. "That's my fear. It kills me, Daniel. You can't die."

"Well, for you then, I'll do my best not to," he tells me as the bed dips with his weight while he climbs over my body.

Pinning my wrists above my head, he nearly kisses my lips, but he moves to suck the arousal off my fingertips before our lips touch. The light, warm feeling is a stark contrast to his hard cock pressed into my thigh.

I try to writhe under him, but he keeps me still as he takes his time. The second he braces his forearm beside my head and positions himself, I suck in a deep breath and stare into his dark eyes.

He enters me slowly, torturously so. Taking his time to stretch me. The gentle sting elicits an instant heated wave that forces my back to arch. He doesn't stop, he just pushes in deeper and stays there, pressing against my walls and forcing my lips to form a perfect O.

Still inside of me, he tells me, "Because I want to grow old with you. I want everything you want, whatever it is, because it'll make you happy. I want my family to love you and protect you, in case something ever happens to me.

"You don't want those things unless you love that person. I love you more than I love myself, Addison. I need you to know that."

I only know I'm crying because he bends down to kiss the tears.

When his lips finally brush against mine, I steal them, kissing him hard and with the passion I have for him, for what's between us.

With his left hand still pinning my wrists down, he ravages me, a savage taking of what's his. I scream my pleasure into his mouth, letting the strangled moans take over when my climax hits me with a force I've never felt before.

It's all consuming. It's everything I've wanted and needed and the only thing I'll ever crave for as long as I live. Because it's him.

CHAPTER 6

Addison

"It's a pretty ring." The timid voice carries across the large kitchen. "Blue under it; that's unique. Is it a blue diamond?"

I didn't even hear her walk in. As I stirred the sugar into my coffee, watching the white swirl of steam, I was focused on the ache between my thighs and the memory of Daniel kissing me all over last night.

He only left me to get the ring from my nightstand and to put it on my finger. If this ring ever comes off my hand, it'll be because someone took it from my grave.

"It is. It reminds me of forget-me-nots," I answer her. "That's why we went with this one."

"You picked out your ring together?"

"I know it's not traditional—"

"What is anymore?" she says and shrugs. "If you haven't guessed, I'm Bethany." The smile she gives me reaches her eyes.

I laugh, short and with a single breath. It's genuine. "I guessed as much," I answer her with a smile.

It's only us in the kitchen and as she pulls out one of the tall chairs at the island, the sound carries through the open space.

"First, I want to say hi. Second, I want to say I'm sorry. Jase told me… about the baby."

My little piece of heaven splinters, but only slightly as I take my seat.

"Thank you," I answer her.

Holding on to my mug of coffee, I pull it up to my lips to keep me from saying more. The warmth billows into my face as I take a long sip, praying for composure.

I don't want to break down. Especially not in front of her, someone I don't know. This…Bethany Fawn. I don't know that I'll ever be okay with losing our baby. Especially if we never get pregnant again, if we never have a little one to hold. I don't see how it's possible. I don't think there's anything wrong with that either.

"I heard you got a ring too," I say as I lift a brow and when her gaze catches mine, I make a note of staring down at her ring finger. She pulls her hand into her chest with a blush rising to her cheeks.

"It was a shock, to be honest," she answers but the content note in her voice and the smile on her face remain the same. "We're quite different… Jase and I," she adds when I look questioningly at her.

"Yes, they are…different. That's a word for it." We could write a book about the Cross brothers and how *different* they are. There's a time and place for that conversation though. "So Jase told me your last name is Fawn?"

"It is."

"Mother or father?" I ask her and then shake my head as I let out a sigh at my ridiculousness. "This isn't an inquisition. I'm just… I'm very curious."

"It's fine," she responds and then she leans forward on the chair to rest on the counter. Her thin cream sweater is pushed up to her elbows. Paired with her dark blue jeans, it's a simple look, but something about this woman screams that she's anything but simple.

"My father's last name, but he didn't stick around after I was born."

"My father's last name as well," I tell her and feel a chill sweep over my skin.

"You're a couple years younger than me, right?" she questions me and I nod. Daniel told me what he knew of Bethany.

"A little over a year younger."

"What's your father's first name?" I ask her as my gaze sweeps over her facial features. She doesn't look like me, nothing but her lips. My father's lips.

"Jeremy," she answers, and I tell her the middle name, "Nathanial. Jeremy Nathanial Fawn."

"This is weird." Bethany pushes out the same thought I have.

"I think your dad left your mom because my mom was pregnant with me." The years make sense. "That's why you didn't grow up with him." Not that I grew up with him either. He left my mother and my mother left me.

"So he knocked up my mom and had my sister. Married her and they had me. Then he left us when I was a baby, because your mother was pregnant with you?" Bethany fills in the blanks.

"He got around, as if I needed another reason to hate the thought of him."

"My mother had substance abuse issues; I always thought that was why he left us," Bethany muses. "He was good at leaving," she comments with a crease in her forehead, as though a bad memory is creating a groove right there. "That's what my mother used to say." She doesn't try to hide the bitterness as she turns her back to me, leaving her seat so she can go to a cabinet to get herself a mug. I note that she already knows where they're kept and where everything else in the room is too.

"If it makes you feel any better, he didn't stay long and what I knew of my mother and the men she was with, it's probably best you grew up without him." With another sip of coffee, the room's quiet except for the muffled hiss of the coffee machine. I don't comment that I was a child when I knew them. Either of them.

"Yet we both received his last name," Bethany says as she leans against the cabinet and then offers me a half smile curved with sarcasm before lifting her mug and telling me cheers. "Lucky us."

"If we hadn't, we never would have known."

"We're sisters. Same father, different mother."

"Right." I nod in understanding. Curiosity nags at the back of my mind, but I can't bring myself to ask her any questions. That part of my life is long behind me. I wish it would stay in the past. I don't want to think about my father or how many other children he had.

"Do you have any other siblings?" she asks me and I shake my head no as I reply, "All I had growing up was a rotating address until I met…" I pause and wave my hand in the air. My throat's dry but I shake it off. I'm stronger because of what I went through. But that doesn't mean I want to relive it with this woman. Biological sister or not. My curiosity can wait until I'm better prepared and in a more stable state. Everything is chaos now and it doesn't look like she's going anywhere anyway.

"The Cross brothers," she answers for me. "So you knew them before all this? Back when things weren't so…"

"Yeah, but I left. I left before a lot of things happened. I left when things got bad. What a wonderful mother I'll be." All of our past history hits me at once and the same thoughts I had before, the ones that tell me I don't deserve Daniel, I don't deserve a happily ever after, and I don't deserve to be a mother come back. Weaker than before, they're only whispers and not screams. Nonetheless, they're back.

"Don't say that. You were young and you didn't know. You'll be a great mother. I hardly know you, but I know that. We'll be better than our parents."

"How can you know?"

"One, because you're already thinking about it. Already wanting more for your children. And two, because we're loved. Love does… Love changes a person.

"The best thing you can do for a child is to love them. You can ask anyone that. It's the thing they need most. If you love Daniel and he loves you, you're already off to a better start than our parents."

"God knows one thing these men do is love hard," I comment, agreeing with her and hoping she's right. "Even with all the shit they're in."

"They do," she agrees with me, casually reaching in the fridge for creamer. As if this is only a mundane conversation and not the turning point in my life that I feel it is in my bones.

"So you're going to try again?" she asks me.

I want to tell her I'm scared. Scared to try, scared to lose. Scared I won't be good enough. But I save those sentiments for Daniel. If I tell anyone, it should be him.

So I answer simply, "Yes." I want a baby with him. A life. I want to grow old with him and be surrounded by a loving family. To love and be loved. "We're going to try again."

CHAPTER 7

Daniel

"**I** JUST NEED TO KNOW." A RAW HINT OF EMOTION MAKES Carter's voice tight. He clears his throat as he leans back in the chair. "I would understand; I just need to be prepared and we can work something out." His voice is clearer, firmer, but he still can't look me in the eyes.

"I'm not leaving. There's nothing else for me. I can't leave."

"But Addison—" he argues, already having it in his head that we need to leave.

"She doesn't want to leave either." It's quiet for a moment, then Carter finally looks at me, letting the statement sink in. "We're staying and we'll be all right."

The ticking of the clock in his office is ever present. It fills the silence until he nods in agreement.

"A lot happened," he comments.

"It will settle down. It'll slow down."

A knock at the office door accompanies his hum of agreement.

"It will," he tells me before calling out, "Come in" to whoever it is at the door.

Addison.

"Am I interrupting?" Her question is softly spoken, but it carries through the room clearly as she stands there, not in the room, but not out of it either.

"Not at all," Carter answers. His shoulders are straighter, his expression firmer. He really thought we were going to leave. He has the look of a man who'd already accepted loss.

"I was hoping to talk to both of you…" She trails off as her gaze drops to the floor nervously before peeking back up at us. "I had a thought."

A prick of uncertainty creeps along my spine as she slowly walks into the room and stops at the chair next to mine. With her grip on the back of it, she chooses not to sit as she tells us, "I want to pay a visit to Officer Walsh."

"The hell you are." My answer is immediate. And also ignored. Addison's stare is unmoving and directed at Carter.

He doesn't answer, neither of them looking at me.

"The fuck you are," I say to emphasize my position. "There's no reason for you to be anywhere near him."

"Other than the fact that I'm with you. That my place is beside you…so yeah, there is."

Carter's still quiet and the ticking of the clock is louder, just like the rush of my blood is in my ears.

"Daniel," she says, and Addison's tone is gentle.

"No. You shouldn't be concerned with this."

"I don't want to be mixed up in this, but I don't want to be afraid of this man. I don't want him to think he can get to me."

"Are you sure you want to do that? You getting involved is more…" Carter talks to her, again, ignoring me.

The irritation grows as the two of them discuss this as though it's a casual conversation.

"Stress? No. I think the stress comes from not knowing. I need to know. And if I can do something, I need to do it."

"I don't want you to—"

"To go to a police station? Where you have plenty of men in your back pocket?" Addison cuts me off and slight desperation seeps into her cadence. "I…" She pauses and swallows thickly. "I want you to think about it. Think about what I should be doing and what it would do for me." She puts her hand over mine to tell me, "I want to do this. I want to show that man who I am and that I'm with you. With all of you," she amends, giving Carter a nod.

"Just think about it." She leaves me there, my foot subconsciously tapping against the leg of the chair. The second the office door closes, I admonish my brother, "You couldn't back me up with that one?" The sarcasm is thick and unforgiving.

"You weren't lying, were you? She does want to stay."

For the first time in a long time, my brother smiles.

"If she wants to stay, then, Daniel, for the love of God, let her. Let her do what she needs to do."

CHAPTER 8

Addison

"**T**WO SETS OF EYES ARE ON HIS OFFICE IN CASE HE SHUTS THE door."

"I know," I answer Daniel.

"If we lose sight for even a moment, I'm coming in."

"I know," I repeat and even though I'm attempting to sound agitated, I'm anything but. "You're cute when you're worried."

His short huff is humorless, coming deep from his chest as we sit in the car.

"In and out, Addison," he tells me, leaning over the console to give me a peck on the cheek. I don't kiss him back, because I'm waiting, and sure enough, he asks again.

"You sure you want to do this?"

The way he asks it melts everything inside of me. I don't answer him with words; instead I put a hand on either side of his handsome face, feeling his stubble beneath my palms, and press a gentle kiss to his lips. His dark eyes are open and staring down at me when I pull away.

"I'll be right back," I murmur.

"And I'll be right here."

As I shut the door to the car, I hear him say he's starting the clock. I have five minutes. That's what he gave me and I'm just fine with that.

If I'm going to be here with Daniel, as his wife and as a part of his family, I'm going to make sure everyone knows exactly where I stand.

Even with that confidence, my heart hammers as I walk through the dark glass doors to the station. Officer Walsh's office is upstairs on the second floor. The elevator is empty, which doesn't ease my nerves at all. I have to shake out my clammy hands and give myself a pep talk.

I'm merely planning to apologize for being caught off guard. To thank Officer Walsh for asking if I was all right and to let him know that I'm more than all right and not to question where I stand with the Cross brothers again.

Daniel and his brothers told me where Walsh's office is. It's the back-right corner office. I'm glad I know where it is and that when I finally get close, his door is open and he's right in view. Alone, unsuspecting. Just like I was when he approached me.

It's hard to give him the benefit of the doubt. That he's only a cop looking out for a woman who's mixed up with men like the Cross brothers.

I try to keep it in mind as I raise my fist to the open door and knock gently.

Words were nearly spoken as he lifts his head, but when Cody Walsh sees me, they're silenced and instead he's slow to tap the papers in his hands on the desk. "Miss Fawn."

"Officer Walsh." I speak his name pleasantly. Forgetting the pounding of adrenaline in my blood and noting that he's only a man. Nothing more than human.

"I thought I'd see you again," he comments. "Please come in."

It's quiet for a moment as I try to get ahold of my bearings.

He speaks first, easing the tension. "You'll have to forgive my first impression. I don't know what to make of the relationships they have. Your fiancé and his brothers."

"Relationships?" I question, raising a brow and deciding to make light of it. "If Daniel has more than one of me…well, no wonder he's so stressed."

The short chuckle eases the officer slightly as he leans back in his chair, but his guard is still up. Something tells me it always is.

"Have a seat," he offers, and I shake my head, telling him I was just stopping by for a quick moment.

"I'm not the bad guy, you know?" he tells me, catching me off guard.

"I didn't say you were."

"You didn't have to," he responds solemnly. "I'm still getting a read on them and you didn't seem like you were all right," he explains although he doesn't have to.

"He's not a bad guy either." And I defend Daniel, although I don't have to.

"I didn't say he was."

It's quiet for a moment and I debate saying what's on my mind. I nearly don't but I decide I may never have another chance, so I should take it.

"You shouldn't have mentioned my past. The foster…situation. Without it, you would have seemed like less of a bad guy."

"Without it, I wouldn't have known whether or not you knew."

I hum in agreement, nodding although I don't take my eyes off of his.

"What do I owe this visit to?" he asks when I go quiet, taking him in and trying to see where he falls. It changes with every passing minute. "Did you have a message for me?" he questions.

"As if I'd do their dirty work? No, I don't have a message. I'm not privy to those conversations, Mr. Walsh. As you know, I appear to be the last to know most things around here." Lying comes easier than I thought it would. In fact, I kind of like it. There's a devilish spark that riddles its way through me as he asks me, "And you're okay with that?"

I'm not okay with it. But that's one thing that's changing. Daniel's right. I need to know. I was always meant to be a part of this. I *need* this.

Reaching into my purse, I pull out a Tupperware of fresh-baked cookies.

"For you," I say while offering the small container. "I made a larger batch, but not all of them survived."

He rises out of his seat but stops short of taking them for only a moment before accepting the gift. "Snickerdoodles?"

I shrug and say, "Cinnamon makes people happy."

"You made me cookies?"

"I was having a bad day; I was short with you and I apologize."

"I apologize as well; I sometimes forget that not every conversation is an interrogation."

Looking at the clock on the wall above his head, I see five minutes has already passed. Half of me is surprised Daniel isn't here, waiting behind me. The other half is relieved he's given me this. I can handle this, and I want him to know it.

Patting the lid of the Tupperware, I offer him a smile and say, "I hope you like them. And I hope you know where I stand now."

His statement keeps me from turning and leaving like I'd planned. "I'm just wondering what you see in him." Officer Walsh doesn't look at me with curiosity; it's simply matter-of-fact. "From what I read, you had a hard upbringing, you fell into step with a group of brothers who took care of your problems, but then you took off. You'd gotten away, you made a new life, and then you came back… Why? Why come back to this?"

"To them, you mean." It's not a question that comes from me so easily, it's a correction. "You obviously don't know them well…yet," I add. "If you knew them, you'd know why."

His chair groans as he heaves back. It gives with the pressure of his back pushing against it and then he clicks his tongue. He seems to debate his words and then he jokes, of all things, lightening the tension, "It's because he's good-looking, isn't it?"

I let a small laugh leave me before I playfully respond, "He's handsome. He has a really charming smile…but you should hear him laugh."

My heart does a funny thing at the memory of it from just the other night.

The officer's rough chuckle doesn't compare in the least. He's a handsome man, on the right side of the law, with power and a strength that any woman would find attractive. But he's not my damaged hero. He's not a part of my family.

He's a pawn in their game and I'm content in doing my part.

"Are you sure you know what you're doing?" he asks me just as I turn my back to him, and my smile nearly falters. Nearly, but I hold it in place.

Turning back around and leaning forward, I have to lower my voice and whisper as though what I'm telling him is a secret. "I'm absolutely certain."

I leave without another word, but before the door closes to his office, I hear him say, "I really hope you are."

The ghost of a smile on my lips doesn't leave; it stays right where it is even though I feel a chill down my spine. It grows colder with every step. Among the clatter of keyboards, phones ringing, and the white noise of the officers and secretaries talking, I hear the click of heels clearly. They're in time with the beat of my heart.

It's not until I'm outside of the double-doored station and a gust of wind blows my hair over my shoulders, tickling up my neck, that the chill leaves me. With a deep breath, I search for the car, finding it quickly, with Daniel leaning against it.

He is my home. He is my person. Beside him is where I belong, and I'll do whatever it takes to stay there. Every sacrifice it demands, I'll make.

ABOUT W WIN-TERS

Thank you so much for reading my romances. I'm just a stay at home mom and avid reader turned author and I couldn't be happier.

I hope you love my books as much as I do!

More by Willow Winters
www.WillowWintersWrites.com/books